Falling for him will be the end of her innocence — but could it be the beginning of a life-long love affair?

VIRGIN
WEDDED BY A BILLIONAIRE

Three timeless novels from three of your favourite authors

Also available:

MISTRESS:
TAKEN BY THE TYCOON

Three ruthless heroes, three powerful passions

VIRGIN

WEDDED BY A BILLIONAIRE

Anne Mather

Carole Mortimer

Trish Morey

M&B™ and M&B™ with the Rose Device
are trademarks of the publisher.
Harlequin Mills & Boon Limited, Eton House,
18-24 Paradise Road, Richmond, Surrey TW9 1SR

VIRGIN: WEDDED BY A BILLIONAIRE
© Harlequin Books S.A. 2010

The Virgin's Seduction © Anne Mather 2005
The Innocent Virgin © Carole Mortimer 2006
A Virgin for the Taking © Trish Morey 2006

ISBN: 978 0 263 88027 4

010-0110

Harlequin Mills & Boon policy is to use papers that are
natural, renewable and recyclable products and made from
wood grown in sustainable forests. The logging and
manufacturing processes conform to the legal environmental
regulations of the country of origin.

Printed and bound in Spain
by Litografia Rosés S.A., Barcelona

THE VIRGIN'S
SEDUCTION

Anne Mather

Anne Mather says: "I've always wanted to write – which is not to say I've always wanted to be a professional writer. On the contrary, for years I wrote only for my own pleasure and it wasn't until my husband suggested that I ought to send one of my stories to a publisher that we put several publishers' names into a hat and pulled one out. The rest, as they say, in history. And now, more than one hundred and fifty books later, I'm literally – excuse the pun – staggered by what happened. My e-mail address is: mystic-am@msn.com and I'd be happy to hear from any of my readers."

CHAPTER ONE

ELLIE came to find her as Eve was shovelling manure out of Storm's stall. The work should have been done that morning, but Mick hadn't turned in today and Eve had offered to help out.

Nevertheless, Eve felt a little self-conscious when the old lady raised her handkerchief to her nose before saying, 'Come outside. I want to talk to you.'

Eve didn't argue. You didn't argue with her grandmother, and the old lady's cane tap-tapped its way back along the aisle between the row of empty stalls. Meanwhile, Eve jammed the fork she was using into her wheelbarrow and, after checking to see that she had no dirt on her hands, followed Ellie out into the crisp evening air.

It was November, and the scent of woodsmoke banished the smell of the stables. Already there was a tracing of frost on the trees in the copse, and the lights that surrounded the stable yard had a sparkling brilliance.

'Cassie's coming tomorrow.'

The old lady waited only long enough for Eve to emerge from the doorway before making her blunt announcement, and her granddaughter's stomach tightened. But she knew better than to show any obvious reaction, and with a shrug of her thin shoulders she said, 'Don't you mean Cassandra?'

'No, I mean Cassie,' retorted the old lady shortly, wrapping the woollen pashmina she was wearing over her tweed jacket tighter about her ample form. 'I christened my daughter Cassie, not Cassandra. If she wants to call herself by that damn fool name, I don't have to follow suit.'

Eve acknowledged this with a wry arching of her dark brows, but she thought it was significant that Ellie was wearing the wrap Cassie had given her several years ago. Was this a sign that she'd forgiven her daughter at last? That the rapidly approaching demands of old age had reminded her that her time was slipping away?

'How long is she coming for?' asked Eve casually, aware that, whatever Ellie said, this was not going to be an easy time for any of them. She and Cassandra could never be friends, and it might be easier all round if she simply moved into a hotel for a couple of weeks.

'She didn't say.' Ellie's tone was grumpy. 'As usual, I'm supposed to accommodate myself to her needs. Oh, and by the way, she's bringing some man with her. I don't know who he is, but knowing Cassie he's probably someone who can help her with her career.'

'Oh, well…' Eve tried to sound philosophical. 'If she's bringing a boyfriend I doubt if she'll be staying long. He must have commitments; a business, maybe.' She tugged her lower lip between her teeth. 'What do you want me to do?'

Ellie's eyes, which were extraordinarily like her granddaughter's, narrowed in surprise. 'Why should I want you to do anything?' She gave a shiver as the wind, which had a decidedly northerly bite to it, whistled across the stable yard. 'I just thought I ought to—to—'

'Warn me?'

'To *tell* you,' she insisted tersely. 'If I could put her off, I would.'

'No, you wouldn't.' Eve's tone was dry. She wasn't taken in by her grandmother's last remark. 'You're really delighted she's coming to see you, even if she is using this place as her own private hotel. As usual.'

'Eve—'

'Look, I understand where you're coming from, Ellie. I do. So—would you like me to find somewhere else to stay while she's here? I'm sure Harry—'

'We'll leave the Reverend Murray's name out of this.' The old lady looked scandalised at her suggestion. 'You can't stay with him. It wouldn't be seemly. In any case, this is your home. I don't want you to move out.'

'Okay.'

Eve was dismissive, but the old lady wasn't finished. 'This is Northumberland,' she said, with a quaver to her voice. 'Not north London. You're not living in some smelly squat now.'

That was a low blow, but it was a sign that her grandmother wasn't as blasé about Cassie's visit as she pretended. Ellie seldom if ever mentioned where Eve had been living when Ellie had arrived to rescue her, and she could see from the old lady's expression that she already regretted speaking so bluntly. But Ellie must remember that the last time Cassie was here she and Eve had barely said a word to one another.

As if needing some reassurance, she added, 'Are you saying you don't want to be here while Cassie's staying?' All the ambivalence she was feeling about the visit showed in her lined, anxious face. 'Because if you are—'

'I just thought it might be easier all round if I left you to it,' Eve muttered unwillingly. She didn't want to hurt the woman who was her closest relative and her friend.

'Well, it isn't,' declared her grandmother, pushing the hand that wasn't holding her cane into her pocket for warmth. 'So we'll say no more about Henry Murray. And it's too cold to stand here gossiping, anyway. We'll talk about this again later. Over supper, perhaps.'

But they wouldn't, Eve knew. Her grandmother had spoken, and in her own way she was just as selfish as Cassie. Oh, she would never have abandoned her child at birth, or ignored its existence for the first fifteen years of its life. But she liked her own way, and Eve rarely felt strongly enough about anything to argue with her.

'You'll be in soon, won't you?' Ellie asked now, and Eve nodded.

'As soon as I've got Storm back in his stall,' she promised.

'Good.'

Her grandmother looked as if she would have liked to say something more, but thought better of it. With a farewell lift of her cane, she trudged away towards the lights of the house.

The hired Aston Martin ate up the miles between London and the north of England. Jake liked motorway driving, mostly because the journey—this journey—would be over that much quicker. He hadn't wanted to come, and the sooner this trip was over the better he'd like it.

'Shall we stop and have some lunch?'

Cassandra was being determinedly cheerful, but for once he didn't respond to her lively chatter. This was wrong, he thought. He shouldn't be here. Bringing him to meet her mother smacked of a relationship they simply didn't have.

Oh, they'd been spending time together, off and on, for the past six months, but it wasn't serious. Well, in his case it wasn't, anyway. He had no intention of marrying again. Or of setting up home with someone like Cassandra, he conceded ruefully. He liked her company now and then, but he knew that living with her would drive him up the wall.

'Did you hear what I said, darling?'

Cassandra was determined to have an answer, and Jake turned his head to give her a fleeting look. 'I heard,' he said. 'But there's nowhere to eat around here.'

'There's a service area coming up,' protested his companion. 'There, you see: it's only another five miles.'

'I'm not in the mood for soggy fries and burgers,' Jake told her drily. He glanced at the thin gold watch circling his wrist. 'It's only a quarter of one. We should be there in less than an hour.'

'I doubt it.'

Cassandra was sulky, and once again Jake permitted himself a glance in her direction. 'You did say it was only a couple hundred miles,' he reminded her. 'As I see it, we've covered at least three-quarters of the journey already.'

Cassandra gave a careless shrug. 'I may have underestimated a little.'

Jake's fingers tightened on the wheel. 'Did you?'

'Well, yes.' Cassandra turned towards him now, all eager for his forgiveness. 'But I knew you'd never agree if I told you it was over three hundred miles from London.'

Her fingers slipped over the sleeve of his sweater, seeking the point where the fine black wool gave way to lean, darkly tanned flesh. The tips of her fingers feathered over the dark hairs that escaped the cuff of his sweater, but he didn't respond to the intimacy of her touch. Three hundred miles, he was thinking. That meant they had at least a couple of hours to go. It also meant they would have to stop somewhere for Cassandra to toy with a salad and sip a skinny latte. Although she rarely ate a proper meal, she insisted on drinking numerous cups of coffee every chance she got.

'You do forgive me, don't you, darling?' She had nestled closer now and, in spite of the obstacle the centre console presented, she laid her head on his shoulder. 'So—can we stop soon? I'm dying for the loo.'

Faced with that request, Jake knew he didn't have any option, and although he didn't say anything he indicated left and pulled off the motorway into the service area she'd pointed out. It was busy. Even in November, people were always going somewhere, and Jake had to park at the far side of the ground. He just hoped the car would still be there when they came back.

'This is fun, isn't it?' Cassandra said, after they had served themselves and occupied a table for two by the window. As usual, she'd helped herself to a salad, carefully avoiding all the mayonnaise-covered options and sticking to lettuce, tomato and peppers. She sipped at the bottled water she'd had to choose when no skinny latte was available. 'It gives us a bit more time on our own.'

'We could have spent time alone if we'd stayed in town,' Jake reminded her flatly. He parted the two slices of his sandwich to discover the almost transparent piece of ham covering the bread. When would the British learn that a ham sandwich needed a proper filling? he wondered gloomily, as a wave of nostalgia for his homeland swept over him. What he wouldn't give to be back in the Caribbean right now.

'I know,' Cassandra said, reaching across the table to cover his hand with hers. Long scarlet nails dug into the skin of his wrist. 'But we'll have some fun, I promise.'

Jake doubted that. From what Cassandra had told him, her mother was already well into her seventies. Cassandra had been a late baby, she'd explained, and her brother,

her only sibling, was at least fifteen years older than she was.

Jake wasn't absolutely sure how old Cassandra was. In her late thirties, he imagined, which made her half a dozen years older than he was, though that had never been a problem. Besides, in television or theatre age was always a moot point. Actresses were as old as they appeared, and some of them got *ingénue* roles well into their forties.

'So, tell me about Watersmeet,' he said, trying to be positive. 'Who lives there besides your mother? You said it's quite a large property. I imagine she has people who work for her, doesn't she?'

'Oh...' Cassandra drew her full lips together. 'Well, there's Mrs Blackwood. She's Mummy's housekeeper. And old Bill Trivett. He looks after the garden and grounds. We used to have several stable hands when Mummy bred horses, but now all the animals have been sold, so I imagine they're not needed any more.'

Jake frowned. 'Don't you know?'

Cassandra's pale, delicate features took on a little colour. 'It—it has been some time since I've been home,' she said defensively. Then, seeing his expression, she hurried on, 'I have been busy, darling. And, as you're finding out, Northumberland is not the easiest place to get to.'

'There are planes,' Jake commented, taking a bite out of his sandwich, relieved to find that at least the bread was fresh.

'Air fares are expensive,' insisted Cassandra, not altogether truthfully. 'And I wouldn't like to scrounge from my mother.'

'If you say so.'

Jake wasn't prepared to argue with her, particularly about something that wasn't his problem. If she chose to neglect her mother, that was her affair.

'Doesn't Mrs Wilkes have a companion?' he asked now, his mind running on the old lady's apparent isolation, and once again he saw the colour come and go in Cassandra's face.

'Well, there's Eve,' she said reluctantly, without elaborating. 'And my mother's surname is Robertson, not Wilkes.'

'Really?'

Jake regarded her enquiringly, and with evident unwillingness she was obliged to explain. 'I changed my name when I moved to London,' she said tersely. 'Lots of actors do the same.'

'Mmm.' Jake accepted this. But then, because he was intrigued by her apparent reticence, he added, 'And what about Eve? Is she some elderly contemporary of your mother's?' Faint amusement touched the corners of his thin mouth. 'Doesn't she approve of you, or what?'

'Heavens, no!' Cassandra spoke irritably now, and he wondered what he'd said to arouse this reaction. 'Eve is— a distant relative, that's all. Mummy brought her to live with her—oh, perhaps ten years ago.'

'As a companion?'

'Partly.' Cassandra huffed. 'She actually works as an infant teacher at the village school.'

Jake made no response to this, but he absorbed both what she'd told him and what she hadn't. It seemed from his observations that Cassandra resented this woman's presence in her home. Perhaps she was jealous of the relationship she had with Cassandra's mother. Possibly the woman was younger, too, though that was less certain. Whatever, Jake would welcome her existence. At least there would be someone else to dilute the ambivalence of his own situation.

They reached the village of Falconbridge in the late

afternoon. The traffic on the Newcastle by-pass had been horrendous, due to an accident between a car and a wagon. Luckily it appeared that no one had been hurt, but it had reduced the carriageway to one lane in their direction.

The last few miles of the journey had been through the rolling countryside of Redesdale, with the Cheviot Hills in the distance turning a dusky purple in the fading light. Despite his misgivings about the trip, Jake had to admit the place had a certain mystery about it, and he could quite believe Roman legions still stalked these hills after dark.

A latent interest in his surroundings was sparked, and he felt a twinge of impatience when Cassandra shivered and hugged herself as if she was cold. 'This place,' she muttered. 'I can't imagine why anyone would want to stay here. Give me bright lights and civilised living every time.'

'I think it's beautiful,' said Jake, slowing to negotiate one of the blind summits that were a frequent hazard of the road. 'I know a lot of people who live in London who would love to leave the rat race and come here. Only not everyone has the luxury of such an escape.'

Cassandra cast him a disbelieving look. 'You're not trying to tell me that you'd prefer to live here instead of San Felipe?'

'No.' Jake was honest. Much as he liked to travel, there was nowhere quite as appealing as his island home. 'But I was talking about London,' he reminded her. 'You have to admit, there are too many people in too small a space.'

'Well, I like it.' Cassandra wasn't persuaded. 'When you work in the media, as I do, you need to be at the heart of things.'

'Yeah.'

Jake conceded the point, but in the six months since he'd known her Cassandra had only had one acting role that he knew of. And then it had only been an advertisement for some new face cream, though she'd told him that advertising work certainly helped to pay the bills.

They approached the village over an old stone structure spanning a rushing stream. The original Falcon Bridge, he concluded, glad they hadn't encountered another vehicle on its narrow pass. Beyond, a row of grey stone cottages edged the village street, lights glinting from windows, smoke curling from chimneys into the crisp evening air.

'My mother's house is on the outskirts of the village,' Cassandra said, realising she would have to give him directions. 'Just follow the road through and you'll see it. It's set back, behind some trees.'

'Set back' was something of an understatement, Jake found. Turning between stone gateposts, they drove over a quarter of a mile before reaching the house itself. Banks of glossy rhododendrons reared at one side of the drive, while tall poplars, bare and skeletal in the half-light, lined the other.

Watersmeet looked solid and substantial. Like the cottages in the village, it was built of stone, with three floors and gables at every corner. There were tall windows on the ground floor, flanking a centre doorway, uncurtained at present and spilling golden light onto the gravelled forecourt.

'Well, we're here,' said Cassandra unnecessarily, making no attempt to get out of the car. She gathered the sides of her fake fur jacket, wrapping it closely about her. 'I wonder if they know we're here?'

'There's one way to find out,' remarked Jake, pushing open his door and swinging his long legs over the sill. He instantly felt the cold, and reached into the back to rescue his leather jacket. Then, pushing his arms into the sleeves, he got to his feet.

The front door opened as he buttoned the jacket, and a woman appeared, silhouetted by the glowing light from the hall behind her. She was tall and slim, that much he could see, with what appeared to be a rope of dark hair hanging over one shoulder.

Obviously not Cassandra's mother, he realised, even as he heard Cassandra utter an impatient oath. The distant relative? he wondered. Surely she wasn't old enough to be the housekeeper Cassandra had mentioned?

The protesting sound as the car door was thrust back on its hinges distracted him. Turning his head, he saw Cassandra pulling herself to her feet and, unlike the other woman's, her face was clearly visible.

'Eve,' she said, unknowingly answering his question, her thin smile and tightly controlled features an indication that he hadn't been mistaken about her hostility towards this woman. 'Where's my mother? I thought she'd have come to meet us.'

The girl—for he could see now that she was little more—came down the three shallow steps towards them. And as she moved into the light cast by the uncurtained windows Jake saw her pale olive-skinned features were much like his own. He guessed her eyes would be dark, too, though he couldn't see them. She barely looked at him, however, her whole attention focussed on Cassandra, but he saw she had a warm, exotic kind of beauty, and he wondered why she was content to apparently spend her days looking after an old woman, distant relative or not.

Her mouth compressed for a moment before she spoke. Was it his imagination or was she as unenthusiastic to see Cassandra as she was to see her? 'I'm afraid Ellie's in bed,' she said, without offering a greeting. 'She had a fall

yesterday evening and Dr McGuire thinks she might have
broken one of the bones in her ankle.'

'Might have?' Cassandra fastened onto the words.
'Why is there any doubt about it? Shouldn't she have had
her ankle X-rayed or something?'

'She should,' agreed Eve, and Jake noticed that she
didn't let Cassandra's agitation get to her. 'But she wanted
to be here when you arrived, and if she'd had to go to
the hospital in Newcastle…' She shrugged. 'I've arranged
for an ambulance to take her in tomorrow—'

'An ambulance!' Cassandra snorted. 'Why couldn't you
take her?'

Eve's face was a cool mask. 'I have a job to do,' she
replied flatly. And now she looked at Jake fully for the
first time. 'Would you—both—like to come in?'

CHAPTER TWO

AN HOUR later, Eve was able to escape to her room to change for supper.

She'd spent the time between the guests' arrival and now escorting Cassie to see her mother, showing Jacob Romero to his room—Ellie had been adamant that Cassie shouldn't sleep with her lover under *her* roof—and arranging with Mrs Blackwood for refreshments to be provided in the library.

Eve, herself, had done her best to keep out of Cassie's way after she'd delivered her to her mother. Out of Jacob Romero's way, too, with his deepset eyes and dark, attractive features. She didn't know what she'd expected Cassie's escort to be like. She only knew she couldn't call him her *boy*friend. There was nothing remotely boyish about Jacob Romero, and from the moment she'd seen him standing beside his car in the courtyard she'd felt a curious sense of foreboding that she couldn't quite place.

She supposed she'd been expecting someone older. Cassie was forty-six, after all. But Romero was obviously much younger. Tall—he was easily six feet and more—with a well-muscled chest and a flat stomach tapering to narrow hips, he looked strong and virile. An impression increased by his hair, which was cut very close to his head.

He looked—dangerous, she thought. Dangerously attractive, at least. And sexy—a description that in his case wasn't exaggerated. It was easy to understand what Cassie

17

saw in him. What troubled Eve most was that she could see it, too.

She pulled a face at her reflection in the mirror of her dressing table. Then, shedding her shirt and jeans onto the floor, she went to take her shower. She was being fanciful, she thought. Ten years ago, feeling a man's eyes upon her wouldn't have bothered her so much. But she'd been harder then, wary and streetwise. In the years since she'd come to live with her grandmother she'd become softer. She'd let down the guard she'd had since she was old enough to understand.

Drying her hair later, she mentally ran through the contents of her wardrobe. Nothing very exciting there, she acknowledged. Skirts and blouses or sweaters for school; jeans and sweaters for home. For the rare occasions when she went out her grandmother had bought her a little black velvet dress, with long sleeves, a scoop neckline, and a skirt that skimmed her kneecaps. But this was not that kind of occasion, and she had no intention of attracting Cassie's curiosity by wearing something totally unsuitable for the evening meal.

She was tempted to leave her hair loose, something she often did in the evenings after she'd washed it. But once again she decided against drawing attention to herself. She plaited the glossy black strands into the usual single braid, securing it with a narrow band of elasticated ribbon.

After far too much deliberation, she put on a V-necked top made of elasticised cotton. Bands of ivory ribbon hid the shaping both around her arms and above and below her breasts, contrasting with the rest of the garment, whose jade-green colour complemented her pale skin.

She almost took it off again when she saw how well it suited her. She'd bought the top on one of her infrequent trips to Newcastle, and had pushed it away in a drawer because she'd thought it was unsuitable for school. Now, looking at it again, she saw she'd been right. It was more in keeping with the teenage girl her grandmother had found subsisting in a draughty squat.

But it was too late to be having second thoughts now. Besides, she doubted she'd be eating with her grand-mother's guests. She had no intention of leaving the old lady to eat alone, or of playing gooseberry to Cassie's *tête-à-tête*.

Zipping on a pair of black cords, she paused only long enough to stroke her lids with a dark brown shadow and run a peachy gloss over her mouth. Then, slipping her feet into heelless mules, she left her room before she could change her mind.

Watersmeet was a fairly large house, but over the years Eve had got used to it, and now she hardly noticed its high-ceilinged rooms and wide corridors. Some years before she'd come to live here central heating had been in-stalled, but the boiler struggled to keep the place at an ambient temperature. Consequently, at this time of year, fires were lit in all the downstairs rooms that were used.

Eve went first to the kitchen, to see how Mrs Blackwood was coping. The elderly housekeeper wasn't used to having guests, but very little fazed her. At present, she was rolling curls of homemade cream cheese in slices of ham, and an avocado dressing waited to be served in tiny ramekins to accompany each plate.

'Her Ladyship won't eat any of the dressing,' Mrs Blackwood explained, when Eve commented on the ar-rangement. The woman meant Cassie, she knew. Her grandmother didn't watch the calories these days. 'Just hope she approves of the sea bass,' she continued. 'I asked Mr Goddard to deliver it specially. I know how fussy she is about eating meat.'

Eve smiled. 'I'm sure it will be a delicious meal,' she said warmly. 'What have we got for dessert?'

'Bread and butter pudding and ice cream,' said Mrs Blackwood at once. 'I know it's fattening, but it is Mrs Robertson's favourite. I thought she deserved something really nice, after having that fall and all.'

'Mmm.' Eve nodded appreciatively. Mrs Blackwood's bread and butter pudding, which she made with brioche and peaches, was famous in the village. She usually contributed individual puddings whenever the church had a coffee morning, and it always sold out at summer bakes and Christmas fairs.

'You think your grandmother will approve, then?'

'I think she'll be delighted,' Eve assured her. 'Which reminds me, I'd better go and see how she is. I hope nothing's been said to upset her.'

'I shouldn't worry.' Mrs Blackwood looked up from her task as she made for the door. 'Your grandmother's a tough old bird, Eve. She's had to be, if you get my meaning. I'm not saying she doesn't love her daughter. Of course she does. But she's known her too long to be upset by anything Cassie says.'

'I hope you're right.'

Eve let herself out of the door and headed for the stairs. The large entrance hall of the building struck her as chilly, after the cosy warmth of the kitchen, and she wondered if she ought to fetch a sweater while she was upstairs. But then, as she put her foot on the bottom stair, she realised someone was coming down. Looking up, she saw Jacob Romero descending towards her, and that thought went out of her head.

He'd changed his clothes, too, she noticed, though she quickly dropped her gaze and stood back to let him pass before starting up. Evidently Cassie had warned him that they didn't dress formally for supper, but his fine wool camel-coloured sweater and black moleskin pants would have looked good in any company.

She supposed it was because they were expensive. Everything about him breathed money, which was par for the course as far as Cassie was concerned. Not that his dark good looks wouldn't have played a part. Eve had seen from the way the other woman looked at him that she very much coveted his body as well.

She'd expected him to perhaps offer a smile and go on, but he didn't. Instead, he stopped beside her, and she was instantly aware of his height. A tall girl herself she found she was usually on eye-level terms with the men she met, but Jacob Romero was several inches above her.

He was also much closer than she could have wished, and she had to steel herself not to step back from him. Was there a trace of cruel humour in the dark eyes? Was he as aware as she was of the effect he had upon her?

'I just wanted to thank you for having me here,' he said, the faint trace of some accent evident in his husky voice. Was he an American? If so, the intonation was very soft. Whatever, it only added to the sensual appeal of the man, and Eve couldn't prevent a shiver of apprehension from sliding down her spine.

'It's not my house,' she said quickly, aware that her tone had been much sharper than his. But, dammit, he disconcerted her, and she was pretty sure he knew it.

'You live here,' he murmured simply. 'Cassandra says you teach in the village. Is that an interesting occupation?'

'It's a job,' Eve responded, putting a hand firmly on the banister, making it fairly clear that as far as she was concerned the conversation was over.

He didn't take the hint. 'So—do you like living here?' he asked. 'It seems very—remote.'

'Far from civilisation, you mean?' she countered, aware that she was being unnecessarily blunt, but unable to help herself. He probably thought she was graceless as well as ignorant, she reflected. It wasn't his fault that Cassie was such a bitch.

'I meant it can't be easy having only an elderly lady as a companion,' he amended drily. Then, with a glint of humour tugging at his thin mouth, he added, 'Who am I kidding? You obviously don't want us here.'

'I never said that.' Eve was appalled that she'd betrayed her feelings so candidly. 'Naturally, Cassie's always welcome. This is her home.'

'Yeah, right.' He grinned at her discomfort, white teeth contrasting sharply with the dark tan of his skin. 'But it's not my home. I know.'

'That's not what I meant.' Eve had been staring at him, but now she dropped her gaze. 'You're deliberately misunderstanding me,' she said, concentrating her gaze some way below the shadow of beard already showing on his jawline. But the tight-fitting pants were just as disturbing to her present frame of mind, the velvet-soft fabric clinging lovingly to every line and angle of the bulge between his legs.

Dear God!

'I'm trying not to,' he said then, and his husky drawl scraped like raw silk across her sensitised flesh. He was much too close, much too male, and it was an effort to remember where she'd been going before this encounter.

'I—I have to go,' she declared hurriedly, attempting to move past him. 'Um—Mrs Robertson will be wondering where I am.'

'The old lady?' As her breasts came up against the arm he'd put out to stop her, she recoiled in panic. But all he said was, 'She's not in her room. Cassandra said she insisted on coming downstairs to eat with us.'

Eve gathered her wits about her. The knowledge that Cassie had persuaded her mother to leave her bed, when she really needed her rest, just to join her and her paramour for supper was bad enough. But what had just happened had added a tension she really didn't need.

Yet what *had* happened? she chided herself. It had obviously meant less than nothing to him. And was she so afraid of male attention that having her boobs accidentally crushed against his arm turned into a major event?

Once, she wouldn't have considered it. Once, she would have fought off any attempt to get close to her, and any man who'd tried would have been nursing an aching groin for his trouble.

She was getting soft, she thought, aware that he was watching her with a strangely speculative look on his dark face. But, dammit, her nipples were still taut and tingling, and the unexpected contact with his body had caused a disturbing explosion of heat inside her.

Shaking her head, as if the simple action would clear her confusion, she said stiffly, 'Where is she? My—Mrs Robertson, I mean.'

'*Your* Mrs Robertson is in the library,' Jacob Romero told her consideringly, and she guessed her slip of the tongue had not gone unnoticed. His brows drew together above his straight, almost aquiline nose. 'Are you all right?'

Eve did step back then. This had gone far enough. 'Why wouldn't I be?' she exclaimed, managing to sound surprised at the question. She smoothed her palms, which were unusually damp, down the seams of her cords. 'If you'll excuse me, I'll go and see if she needs anything.'

If she'd thought to escape him, she was disappointed.

He accompanied her across the circular Persian carpet that occupied a prominent position in the centre of the floor. Double doors opposite opened into the library, which had been her grandfather's study while he was alive, but now served as both estate office and sitting room.

It was a cosy room, the books lining the walls scenting the air with the smell of old leather. A fire was burning in the large grate and Eve's grandmother was seated in her armchair beside it. A footstool supported her injured ankle, and although Eve thought she looked tired, she was defiantly holding a glass of red wine in her hand.

Cassie was there, too, occupying the chair opposite. In thin silk trousers and a matching sapphire-blue tunic, she looked blonde and elegant. Someone had dragged her grandfather's old captain's chair over from behind the desk in the corner, and it was pulled strategically close to Cassie's; obviously with Jacob Romero in mind, thought Eve cynically. Which meant she was obliged to sit on the ladder-backed dining chair that Mr Trivett used when he came to discuss estate matters.

'Help yourself to some wine, my dear,' Ellie suggested when Eve made to sit down, but Jacob Romero intervened. 'I'll get it for you,' he said, indicating the chair beside Cassie. 'And sit here. My bones are more liberally covered than yours.'

Eve doubted that. There wasn't an ounce of spare flesh on his body. And although she wanted to demur, it would have seemed uncharitable to do so. 'Thanks,' she said, and ignoring the irritation she could feel emanating from the woman beside her, she turned to Ellie. 'How are you feeling?'

'I'm feeling much better this evening,' Ellie declared, despite the fact that her usually ruddy cheeks were pale.

'Don't look so disapproving, Eve. I didn't struggle down the stairs on my own. Mr Romero carried me.'

Eve only just stopped herself from giving him an admiring look. Her grandmother was no lightweight, and he had to be fit if he'd carried the old lady down from her room.

'Um—that was good of—of you,' she murmured lamely, accepting the glass of wine he'd brought her, but she was aware that Cassie was now preening herself in his reflected glory.

'Jake's immensely strong,' she said, her smile towards him warm and intimate. Her tongue circled her upper lip in a deliberately sensual gesture as he seated himself beside Ellie. 'I suppose it's because he gets plenty of exercise.'

The *double entendre* was unmistakable, but the object of her insinuation didn't respond in kind. 'My family owns a charter company in San Felipe,' he offered smoothly, leaning forward, his arms along his thighs. His thumbs circled the glass he'd brought for himself. 'I've been hauling masts and rigging sails since I was a kid, so lifting a lightweight like you, Mrs Robertson, was no problem.'

Ellie looked pleased. 'San Felipe?' she murmured, echoing the name as Eve absorbed the fact that he wasn't an American after all. 'Is that in Spain?'

'It's an island in the Caribbean, ma'am,' he said, and Eve had an immediate image of white sands, blue seas and palm trees. No wonder he was so darkly tanned. She guessed he must be brown all over.

Now, where had that come from?

'Jake's family own the island, Mummy,' Cassie put in smugly. 'His father's retired, of course, and Jake runs the company himself.'

'How nice.' Eve was pleased to see her grandmother wasn't overawed by this intimation of unlimited wealth. 'So what are you doing in England, Mr Romero? I'd have thought this was the time of year when most people visit the Caribbean.'

'It is, of course.' He sounded regretful. 'However, I'm obliged to spend at least part of the year in Europe.'

'Jake has business interests all over the world.' Cassie was evidently determined to impress her mother. 'We met last year at the Paris Boat Show—didn't we, darling?'

'I wouldn't have thought sailing boats would interest you, Cassie,' remarked Ellie drily. 'You were always sea-sick whenever your father and I took you out on the water.'

'That was years ago—' began Cassie snappishly, but before she could say any more Romero explained.

'Cassandra was one of the hostesses at the show,' he said, smiling at her hostile expression. 'She was very good at it, too.'

'It was just a fill-in between parts,' protested Cassie resentfully. 'I don't usually do that sort of thing.'

'Don't you?' Her mother seemed to perceive that she suddenly had the upper hand. 'Remind me, Cassie: what was the last part you played?'

Eve now found herself in the unlikely position of feeling sorry for her and, with unexpected compassion she said, 'You had a role in the remake of *Pride and Prejudice*, didn't you, Cassie? I think you played one of the Bennett sisters.'

'You *know* I didn't play one of the Bennett sisters,' hissed Cassie, giving Eve a filthy look, but her mother only smiled.

'Mrs Bennett, perhaps?' she suggested, enjoying the

moment. 'You'd be unlikely to be cast as an *ingénue*, if that's the term they use these days.'

'So, did you and Mr Romero spend much time in Paris, Cassie?' Eve asked quickly, realising her grandmother wasn't about to back off, and this time Cassie seemed grateful for her intervention.

'Just a few days,' she said. 'But Jake promised to look me up the next time he was in London,' she added, giving him a forgiving look. 'And that was six months ago, wasn't it, darling?'

'Something like that.' Eve noticed that Romero didn't respond to Cassie's frequent endearments. But she was taken aback when he turned to her. 'And my name's Jake. Or Jacob, if you prefer.'

'Yes.' Aware that all eyes were on her now, Eve was forced to be polite. 'Yes, right.' Then, dragging her gaze away from his disturbing face, she managed to smile at her grandmother. 'Um—I'll go and see how Mrs Blackwood is getting on. Is there anything I can get you?'

'Yes, you can get me another drink,' said Cassie at once, holding out her glass as Eve got to her feet. 'I'll have whisky, if there is any.' She glanced at her mother. 'Your choice of wine isn't to my taste.'

'Nor are your manners to mine, Cassie,' retorted Ellie, and Eve wished now that she hadn't offered to go and see how the housekeeper was coping. There was an ominous atmosphere building in the room, and she dreaded what her grandmother might say next.

'I'm not a child, Mother.' Everyone must have noticed that the honeyed 'Mummy' had given way to the chillier term. 'And I don't like red wine, as it happens. But you knew that.'

'I'd forgotten,' declared her mother blandly. 'Your visits here are so infrequent, Cassie. I can't be expected to remember everything.'

Cassie's lips tightened, and Eve guessed she was biting her tongue. She must know better than anyone that it would be unwise to antagonise her mother when there was a guest in the house. Particularly when that guest was someone she wanted to impress.

In the hope of avoiding any further argument, Eve set Cassie's empty glass on the tray. Then, keeping her back to the room, she managed to sneak the whisky bottle off the tray and into the cupboard below. Swinging round on her heels, she said, somewhat breathlessly, 'I'm sorry. There doesn't appear to be any whisky here, Cassie. I expect there's a new bottle in the kitchen. Why don't you come and get it?'

The face Cassie turned to her was hardly friendly. Eve was sure the words, *Why don't you get it?* were hovering on her lips. But politeness—or common sense—won out, and with a muttered, 'Excuse me,' to Romero, she pushed herself to her feet and flounced across the room to join Eve at the door.

She waited until the door was firmly closed behind them and they'd put the width of the hall between them and the library before speaking again. But when she did, her words were hard and accusatory.

'What do you think you're playing at?' she demanded. 'I saw the bottle of whisky on the tray when Mrs Blackwood was pouring us all a glass of the poor excuse for claret my mother insists on serving. Don't think I didn't see you spirit it away into the cabinet. I'd be surprised if anybody missed it.'

Eve's lips twisted. 'I should have known that nothing I did would please you,' she said flatly. 'And here I was thinking I was saving your sorry ass!'

'What do you mean?'

'Are you for real?' Eve stared at her. 'Don't you realise your mother is just waiting for a chance to explode this myth you've created about yourself? You're a fool if you think she's forgotten—anything.'

'With your connivance, no doubt.'

Eve shrugged. 'If you want to think that, I can't stop you.'

'Well, what else am I supposed to think?' Cassie balled one fist and pressed it into the palm of her other hand. Then, less aggressively, she said, 'She wouldn't say anything.' A beat. 'Would she?'

'If you persist in baiting her, I don't know what she might say,' replied Eve honestly.

'But she's baiting me!' Cassie made a sound of frustration. 'Am I expected to take whatever she wants to give without defending myself at all?'

Eve moved towards the passage leading to the kitchen. 'I can't answer that. I suppose it rather depends on how much you want your—guest—to know about you.'

Cassie's mouth tightened. 'Are you threatening me?'

'No!' The look Eve cast over her shoulder was incredulous. 'Why should I threaten you? I don't care what you do, do I? How you conduct your life means nothing to me.'

Cassie scoffed. 'Little Miss Prim,' she said contemptuously. 'I wonder if my mother has any idea of the kind of life you were living before she arrived like a fairy godmother to whisk you away.'

'She knows,' said Eve, and without waiting to see if Cassie was going to follow her she pushed open the door into the reassuring light and warmth of the kitchen.

'Does she?' Cassie came after her, evidently deciding that if she couldn't torment her mother, she would torment

Eve instead. 'Well, don't talk to me as if you're Goody Two Shoes! We both know you'd do anything to get a man like Jake to support you.'

Eve gasped. She was used to Cassie speaking as if Mrs Blackwood was just a cipher, but this time she'd gone too far. 'You're wrong,' she snapped. 'I've never prostituted myself to get any man, Cassie. And unless you're prepared for me to expose all your dirty washing, I suggest you back off!'

CHAPTER THREE

IT WAS still dark—and cold—when Jake got out of bed. The heating hadn't kicked in yet, and he padded across to the windows to look out on a grey world, with only the silvery trace of a rime frost to soften the outline of the trees in the paddock.

He'd slept alone, much to Cassandra's annoyance. He knew one of the reasons she'd invited him here was because she wanted their relationship to advance to another stage. But he wasn't interested in that, and the fact that her mother had arranged for them to have separate bedrooms showed that she didn't approve of them conducting any illicit dealings under her roof.

She'd even phoned him on his mobile, evidently deciding it was too cold to brave the chilly corridors of the house when she couldn't be sure how he'd respond. Cassandra didn't like taking no for an answer.

A flicker of light in the yard below caught his attention. His room overlooked the back of the house, and as he watched he saw a figure detach itself from the building and head off towards the cluster of barns and outbuildings that were just visible in the gloom.

Eve.

Her tall, slim figure was unmistakable. Dressed in jeans and a bulky sweater, the thick braid of dark hair swinging over her shoulder, she moved with an unconscious grace that stirred an unwilling awareness inside him. Which was crazy. She wasn't beautiful in the way Cassandra was beautiful. Her features were too irregular, her mouth too wide, her nose too long. Yet she possessed an almost exotic allure that pointed to a Latin ancestry, and there was a wealth of knowledge in her smoky grey eyes. He'd found himself wanting to bring a smile to those full, sultry lips, to feel her warmth enveloping him instead of that argumentative old woman she worked for.

He hadn't succeeded. Not yet, at least. For some reason she'd taken an instant dislike to him, and try as he might he couldn't get her to relax. She'd been forced to be polite to him during the rather tense supper Cassandra and her mother had created, but he'd been conscious of her disapproval all through the meal.

He pulled a wry face. He would have to do better, he thought, without really understanding why he should want to. Nevertheless, he turned swiftly from the window and went into the adjoining bathroom. Leaving his shower until later, he had a quick wash, cleaned his teeth, and ran his damp hands over his hair. That would have to do for now, he decided, and with a grimace at his reflection he returned to the bedroom.

Pulling on his oldest pair of jeans, he shivered a little as the cold fabric encased his warm skin. Then, grabbing the cashmere sweater he'd worn the night before, he thrust his arms into the sleeves and jerked it over his head.

He left his room a couple of minutes later. He'd hooked his leather jacket over one shoulder, and his trainers made little sound as he strode along the upper landing. Downstairs, he hesitated in the chilly hallway, not absolutely sure which way to go. But then he remembered the direction Eve had been coming from the night before and, taking a chance, he headed along the corridor that he hoped might lead to the back of the house.

He was right. Or at least partly so. When he opened the door at the end of the corridor, he found himself in the kitchen. The housekeeper, who had just been about to take a tray of freshly baked rolls from the oven, looked round in surprise, and Jake guessed he was the last person she'd expected to see.

'Mr Romero!' she exclaimed, pausing uncertainly. But then, realising she had to complete her task, she hurriedly set the tray of rolls on the scrubbed pine table and closed the oven door. 'Can I help you?'

Jake gave her a rueful grin. He hadn't expected to encounter anyone else either. 'I—er—I was going to take a walk,' he said a little lamely. 'I wanted to get out back of the house.'

'Ah.' Mrs Blackwood pushed the rolls a little further onto the table. 'Well, you can come through here, Mr Romero.' She gestured towards another door. 'That leads to the bootroom. You'll see another door through there that leads outside.' She paused. 'But are you sure you want to go out so early? It's very cold.'

Jake could believe it. He was glad he'd brought his jacket with him. 'I'll be okay,' he assured her. He nodded at the rolls. 'New bread! I can't wait for breakfast.'

'You can take one with you, if you like,' offered Mrs Blackwood shyly, and, although Jake was impatient to get going, he couldn't refuse her.

'Great,' he said, selecting one with a golden crust. Then, after taking a bite, almost burning his mouth in the process, he grinned again and made for the door.

Outside, he discovered that she hadn't been joking. It wasn't just cold, it was freezing, and ramming the rapidly cooling roll between his teeth, he swiftly shouldered into his jacket. Then, after fastening the buttons, he removed the roll again and set off in the direction he'd seen Eve heading.

It didn't take long to reach the stable yard. Low buildings occupied two sides of a cobbled courtyard, with the black bulk of a barn dominating the other. And it was from the barn that he could see light emanating. It filtered out, a golden finger penetrating the half open door. If he'd been further way he wouldn't have seen it, the light swiftly swallowed by the lowering shadows.

He doubted she'd be pleased to see him, but he crossed the yard anyway, still munching on the crusty roll as he rounded the door.

Eve was in the process of forking clean straw onto a handcart. She'd pushed the sleeves of her chunky sweater up to her elbows, and as she bent towards the bales stored against the wall of the barn the back of her jeans exposed a delectable wedge of skin at her waist. But she didn't seem to feel the cold. Obviously what she was doing was keeping her warm, but he couldn't help wincing when she jabbed the fork particularly viciously into the stack.

'Ouch,' he said softly, and had the doubtful satisfaction of seeing her reaction. He'd startled her, there was no doubt about that, and a becoming wave of colour invaded her pale cheeks.

She straightened automatically. 'What are you doing here?' she demanded, and once again he could hear the barely suppressed impatience in her voice.

'I thought I'd take a look around,' he replied easily, finishing the roll and dusting the crumbs from his hands. 'What are you doing? I thought Cassandra said her mother had sold all the horses.'

'All but one,' said Eve shortly. And then, because she resented his impression that he could ask her anything he liked and she'd meekly answer him, she countered, 'Where's Cassie?'

Jake shrugged, propping his shoulder against the wall of the barn and putting most of his weight on one leg. 'In bed, I guess,' he responded, unbuttoning his jacket and warming his fingertips beneath his arms.

Eve's fingers tightened round the shaft of the fork. She couldn't help noticing that by opening his jacket he'd exposed the fact that his tight-fitting jeans were worn in all the most intimate places. The fabric clung lovingly to his shape, soft and textured, and she wondered why a man who apparently had an unlimited income would want to wear something so old.

She'd hardly been aware of how she was appraising him until her eyes returned to his face and encountered his. He'd been watching her, and in an effort to show that he hadn't fazed her she muttered, 'Don't you know?'

Jake's eyes narrowed. 'Don't I know what?' he queried innocently, and her momentary spurt of defiance faltered.

'Don't you know where—where Cassie is?' she said, lifting her shoulders in a dismissive gesture. 'I'd have thought you would.'

'What you mean is, you thought we'd be sleeping together, right?' he suggested mildly, evidently enjoying her confusion. 'Well, I hate to disappoint you, but I slept alone.' His eyes darkened. 'Very well, as it happens.' Which wasn't entirely true.

'Oh.' Eve swallowed. 'Well—good.' She turned back to her task and attacked the straw with renewed vigour. 'I have to get on.'

He straightened. 'Let me help you.'

Eve's lips parted and she stared at him with disbelieving eyes. 'I—don't think so.'

'Why not?'

'Because you—' She moistened her lips before continuing awkwardly, 'This is a dirty job.'

'So?'

'So—I'm sure you don't want to get all hot and sweaty.'

'I get hot and sweaty all the time,' he told her drily. And then, because he could see what she was thinking, he added, 'I meant working on boats, of course.'

'I know that.' Eve's face felt as if it would never be cool again.

'Okay.' His grin said he didn't believe her. 'I just didn't want you to get the wrong impression.'

Eve pursed her lips. 'I think that's exactly what you did want me to do,' she muttered, barely audibly. She sighed. 'Look, why don't you go for a walk and let me finish this?'

'Because I want to see this horse you're doing all this work for,' replied Jake, taking off his jacket and flinging it over a rusting oil drum. He came towards her and took the fork from her unresisting fingers. 'See, that wasn't so difficult, was it?'

Eve took a deep breath and stepped somewhat reluctantly aside. 'Cassie's not going to like it,' she warned, and Jake turned to give her a knowing look.

'Do you care?' he said, beginning to fork straw onto the cart with surprising energy. 'You know, I'm gonna enjoy this. I've been sitting on my butt for far too long.'

Eve thought about voicing another protest, but then what he'd said distracted her. 'I thought you were used to manual labour.'

'I am.' Jake loaded the fork and tossed its contents onto the growing pile on the cart. 'But for the past six weeks I've been trailing around Europe checking on orders, arranging contracts, and generally pushing a pen for most of the day.'

Eve hesitated. She badly wanted to know if Cassie had

been with him, though why that should be of any interest to her she couldn't say.

'Don't you have an assistant who could handle the grunt work for you?' she asked, and Jake straightened, flexing his back muscles as he gave her a narrow-eyed stare.

'Why don't you ask right out whether Cassandra accompanied me?' he said, massaging his spine with a grateful hand. 'That's what you mean, isn't it? Has Cassandra's mother given you the job of finding out what my intentions are?'

'No!' Eve was indignant. 'And whether or not Cassie went with you is nothing to do with me.'

'Okay.' His hand moved from the small of his back to rub the flat muscles of his stomach, and Eve's breath hitched when he accidentally pulled up the front of his sweater and a cloud of night-dark hair spilled into the gap. The pull of an attraction that was as unwelcome as it was primitive swept over her, and she had turned hurriedly away when he said, 'Well, for your information, then, Cassandra stayed in London.'

'Whatever.' Eve didn't look back. Squaring her shoulders, she said, 'In any case, that's enough straw. If you want to see Storm, it's this way.'

She slipped out of the door and Jake pulled on his jacket, feeling vaguely irritated that she was treating him so offhandedly. What had he said—or done, come to that—to warrant the cold shoulder she was presently giving him? No, scrub that, he amended shortly. She'd been giving him the cold shoulder ever since he'd got here, and he didn't like it.

Deciding that if she wanted the handcart, she could fetch it herself, he buttoned his jacket and followed her outside. The skies were lighter now, but it was just as cold, and he pushed his hands into his jacket pockets as he trudged across the cobbled yard in her wake.

The stables were amazingly warm. Considering only one animal was in residence, he'd expected it to be only marginally less frigid than the barn, but it wasn't. Unless the company had something to do with it, he thought caustically. Obviously Eve preferred the horse to him.

Storm was stabled at the end of the row. He'd evidently heard them coming and was neighing a welcome as they reached his stall. A solid-looking chestnut, the animal had a distinctive flash of white between his eyes. Intelligent eyes, too, Jake noticed, as it nuzzled Eve's pockets for sugar or some other treat.

Eve pulled out a small apple and let Storm take it from her hand. He crunched away happily, showing surprisingly good teeth for his age. In Jake's opinion he wasn't a young animal, but he looked strong and well-muscled.

'How old is he?' Jake asked, when Eve said nothing, and she gave him a scornful look.

'He's a she,' she said, unlatching the gate and attaching a halter. 'Storm Dancer. And she's twenty-eight. My— Mrs Robertson used to breed from her when she was younger.'

Jake stepped back to allow her to bring the horse out, and Storm took the opportunity to nip his ear. She didn't bite him. She was amazingly gentle, actually, and he saw Eve watching her with some surprise.

'She seems to like me, anyway,' he said, finding a reluctant humour in the situation. 'Sorry.'

'I imagine females usually do,' retorted Eve hotly, and then turned scarlet when she realised what she'd said.

'You don't,' remarked Jake drily, following her and Storm Dancer along the row of empty stalls, but Eve didn't look back.

'I neither like nor dislike you, Mr Romero,' she said, the words drifting back over her shoulder, but Jake could tell she wasn't half as indifferent as she was trying to sound.

'I'm pleased to hear it,' he said, as they emerged into the morning air again. He held her gaze when she darted a glance towards him. 'That gives me some hope.'

Eve swallowed. 'Hope—for what?'

'That you might come to like me.' He glanced about him, allowing her to return to her task. 'Where are we going now?'

'*I'm* going to take Storm into the paddock,' she told him, concentrating on controlling the mare to avoid another visual confrontation. 'I think you ought to go back to the house. Cassie will be wondering where you are.'

He glanced at his watch. 'At ten after seven in the morning?' He grimaced. 'I doubt it.'

Eve tugged on the halter, causing Storm Dancer to toss her head in protest. 'You'd know, of course.'

'Because I've slept with her?' suggested Jake flatly, and once again he saw that he'd disconcerted her.

But he also saw the way she tried to disguise it. 'Well, you have, haven't you?' she demanded fiercely, and instead of feeling angry he knew an almost irresistible urge to take her face between his cold palms and kiss her.

Her mouth looked soft and vulnerable, despite her desperate bid for control, and he wondered how she would taste. He already knew what she smelled like. She probably hadn't showered before coming to attend to the mare, and the clean scent of her woman's body was overlaid with the faintest trace of perspiration. He found it an incredible turn-on, incredibly sexy, but it wasn't a good feeling. Dammit, he'd come here with one woman and now he was lusting after another. What kind of an animal was he when he got a hard-on just being with Eve? What the hell was the matter with him?

The fact that he hadn't wanted to come here was some comfort, but Cassandra would spit blood if she even suspected he was attracted to her mother's companion. She'd been trying for more than six months to get him to commit to a relationship, and it was only because he'd had the excuse of business meetings in various parts of Europe that he'd been able to avoid any serious entanglement.

He liked her well enough. She was good company when she wasn't continually trying to get into his pants. And he'd been glad of her company at many of the parties and social gatherings he'd been invited to while he was in London. But this… This didn't bear thinking about, and, abandoning any idea of helping Eve to clean out the mare's stall and spread the fresh straw, he jammed his hands deep into the back pockets of his jeans.

'Does it matter?' he asked dispassionately. Then, deliberately emptying his face of any expression, he added, 'But I guess I'd better go and let her know I haven't forgotten about her.'

As if that was likely, thought Eve painfully as he strode out of the stable yard. She had the feeling that, however he felt about her, Cassie would make sure she was not easy to forget.

She wished she hadn't taunted him now. Although she knew she was asking for trouble, something about Jake Romero got under her skin. And, despite her determination not to let him get to her, she'd enjoyed their verbal baiting. Enjoyed being with him, she thought, tugging rather viciously at Storm's halter again.

And how sick was that?

CHAPTER FOUR

JAKE went up to his room, showered, and changed into navy chinos and a long-sleeved purple polo shirt. He was downstairs again, having breakfast in the morning room, when Cassandra finally made her appearance.

Of Eve there was no sign, but as it was already after nine o'clock he guessed she'd probably left for work. Mrs Robertson was still in her room, of course, resting her ankle. Which was a shame, he reflected, because he would have welcomed the chance to avoid a *tête-à-tête* with her daughter.

Cassandra trailed into the room, still wearing her dressing gown. A red silk kimono that she'd told him some admirer had brought her from Hong Kong, Jake doubted it was warm enough for Watersmeet in November. But he knew she liked the garment. She thought it flattered her fair colouring. And, as she didn't appear to be wearing anything under it, Jake guessed where this was going.

'Darling,' she exclaimed petulantly, 'where have you been? I came to your room earlier but you weren't there, and I was worried. Now, here you are, scarfing down bacon and eggs as if you didn't have a care in the world.'

'I don't.' Jake had got up at her entrance, but now he subsided into his seat again. He didn't usually eat a big breakfast, but Mrs Blackwood seemed to think he needed fattening up, and he hadn't the heart to refuse her. 'This is good.'

'It's also very bad for your arteries,' said Cassandra irritably. 'So—where were you?'

'When?'

Jake was being deliberately obtuse, but Cassandra was like a dog with a bone. 'Earlier on. When I came to your room,' she said, running the cord of her robe through her fingers. 'And don't tell me you were in the shower, because I looked.'

Jake finished the last morsel of sausage and put his knife and fork aside. 'I went out,' he said, relieved at having avoided another confrontation about their sleeping arrangements. Then, in the hope of diverting her, 'Why don't you get dressed and go and see how your mother is this morning?'

'Do I care?' Cassandra was bitter. 'She obviously doesn't give a damn about me. Did you hear her making fun of me—of my acting career last night? Just because I had more sense than to be satisfied with life in this provincial backwater, she takes every opportunity to make me feel small.'

Jake shrugged. He couldn't deny that Mrs Robertson had been provoking. But he didn't know the family history, so it was difficult for him to have an opinion. Eve was the one he felt sorry for—caught in the middle of two women who seemed determined to rub one another up the wrong way. Yet Eve had defended Cassandra to her employer, despite the way she'd spoken about her this morning.

'Anyway, it's early yet.' Clearly Cassandra had other matters on her mind. Coming round the table to where he was sitting, she loosened the kimono. It fell open, revealing that his initial suspicions had been right. 'Why don't we go back upstairs?'

Jake pushed back his chair and got to his feet. Then he grasped the two sides of the kimono in his hands. But, although he knew she expected him to pull her closer, he jerked the two sides together instead. 'Go take a cold shower, Cassandra,' he told her flatly. 'I want to go out and see something of the countryside around here. If you want to come with me, say so. I'll give you forty minutes to get dressed.'

He suspected she swore then, but he couldn't be sure of it. Whatever, she wrapped the kimono about her and marched towards the door. 'I'll need at least an hour,' she said, glancing back at him. 'Do you think you can entertain yourself for that long?'

It was not a good day. Fridays usually were, but today Eve found it almost impossible to concentrate on her work. The children knew it, and consequently played her up more than usual, and she was forced to use her strictest voice to bring order to the class.

The day didn't get any better when she was summoned to a staff meeting when lessons were over for the day. They never had staff meetings on Friday afternoons. Most of the teachers who were employed at the small primary school were eager to get home to their families at the end of the working week. But the head teacher's face was grave when she joined them in the staff room, and Eve had the uneasy premonition that whatever they were about to hear was not going to be good.

She was right. It appeared that Mrs Portman had heard, just that afternoon, that Falconbridge was to be merged with a larger school at East Ridsdale. The local education authority had decided that their school had simply not enough pupils to warrant the expense of keeping it open, and although every effort would be made to find the teachers new posts, by the end of next term Falconbridge Primary would be closed.

There was a stunned silence after Mrs Portman had finished speaking. The women who worked at Falconbridge—and they were exclusively female—considered themselves almost family, and the idea of being split up and sent to different schools was almost as bad for them as it was going to be for the children.

'But can they do this?' asked Jennie Salter worriedly. Jennie was a mother herself, and her children were still young enough to come to school with her. 'I thought I read somewhere that parents were fighting these closures.'

'Well, they are,' agreed Mrs Portman ruefully. 'But I doubt if the parents whose children attend this school will be prepared to fight our education authority—particularly if it means their council tax is going to go up. There simply aren't enough of them to make a difference.'

'So the school closes at Easter,' said Eve, her heart sinking at the thought of having to look for another job.

'Officially,' agreed Mrs Portman. 'But naturally I don't expect you all to wait until then to look for other posts. Besides, as soon as the news gets out parents will start looking for alternative schools. Not all of them will want their children to travel to East Ridsdale every day—not when there's a private school in the vicinity.'

'That's okay if you can afford it,' muttered Jennie gloomily, and Eve put a comforting hand on her shoulder.

'It's months away yet,' she said, trying to be optimistic. 'You never know—you may get a job at Ridsdale and then you could continue taking the children to school yourself.'

'Fat chance!'

Jennie refused to look on the bright side, and Eve couldn't really blame her. It was hard enough to find work in this area as it was, without a dozen other people doing the same.

In consequence, she was in a rather downhearted frame

of mind when she walked home later that afternoon, and she was in no mood to respond favourably when the Aston Martin swept through the gates ahead of her. Romero was at the wheel, of course, and Cassie was sitting proudly beside him, lifting a languid hand—almost as if she was royalty and Eve was just a paid retainer.

She wasn't jealous, Eve assured herself fiercely. She'd never had anything from Cassie in the past and she didn't want anything now. But just occasionally she wished the woman would acknowledge her responsibilities.

The squeal of brakes brought her out of her reverie. The Aston Martin had stopped and was now reversing back towards her. Oh, God, they were going to offer her a lift, she realised sickly. And she could guess whose idea that was.

A window was lowered and Romero looked out. 'Get in,' he said. 'We'll give you a ride up to the house.'

'That's not necessary,' said Eve stiffly, and Cassandra gave a protracted yawn.

'I told you she'd say no,' she declared in a bored tone. 'Come on, darling. Close the window, can't you? I'm getting cold.'

Jake's jaw compressed. Having spent most of the day humouring Cassandra, he wasn't in the mood to listen to her griping now. But, dammit, Eve wasn't making it easy for him either, and he was tempted to make some excuse and hightail it back to London before he did something he would surely regret.

Eve looked cold, he thought. Her exotic features were unnaturally pale in the light of the lamps that lit the driveway, and, although she was wearing a navy duffel, the coat didn't look substantial enough to keep her warm. He forced himself to suppress the irritation he felt at her evident unwillingness to allow him to help her, and, ignoring

Cassandra's protests, he thrust open his door and got out of the car.

'It's a good half-mile walk to the house,' he said, aware that Eve had taken an involuntary step backwards when he approached her.

Her dark brows arched. 'So?'

'So it's cold, and you look tired.'

'Gee, thanks.'

'You know what I mean.' His eyes darkened impatiently. 'I guess it's been a long day at the chalkface.'

Had it ever? Eve pressed her lips together, wondering why she was so reluctant to get into the car. It wasn't just because of Cassie, though she knew the other woman was watching her with coldly narrowed eyes. She just knew she wouldn't be doing herself any favours by allowing this man to get close to her.

'I need a walk,' she said at last, meeting his challenging gaze with more defiance than honesty. 'You go ahead.' She licked her dry lips. 'But—thanks, anyway.'

'I wish I thought you meant that,' he muttered, but short of picking her up and bundling her into the car, there was nothing he could do.

Then he remembered something, and, opening the car door again, he leant into the back and extracted the long black woollen scarf he'd bought at one of the mill shops they'd visited. He'd been glad of its warmth when he'd climbed the hill to the ruined Roman fort at Housesteads—Cassandra staying in the car, nursing the headache she'd complained about ever since they'd left the house—but he didn't need it now.

'Here,' he said, going back to where Eve was waiting and thrusting the scarf at her. 'Do yourself a favour and wear it.' And when she didn't say anything he added, 'We'll see you later, right?'

Eve nodded, but she waited until the Aston Martin's taillights were some distance away before unfolding the scarf and winding it about her neck. He was right. She did feel cold. But it was an inner cold as much as an outer one. Even so, the scarf was luxuriously thick and soft. Unfortunately, it also had his scent on it, an equally luxurious mix of expensive shaving lotion and clean male heat. But, despite her earlier misgivings, she buried her nose in its warmth and, after repositioning her backpack, thrust her gloved hands into her pockets and marched up the drive towards the lights of the house.

Thankfully her grandmother was alone in the library when Eve went to find her. Mrs Blackwood had volunteered the information that Mrs Robertson had insisted on phoning the hospital in Newcastle and cancelling the ambulance Eve had arranged.

'She said her ankle was feeling much better this morning,' went on the housekeeper ruefully. 'Then the next thing I know she's downstairs, pulling photograph albums out of the cupboard. When I asked her what she was doing, she said she was trying to remember what Miss Cassie looked like at your age.'

Eve stifled a groan. 'Did—did she say why?'

'No.' Mrs Blackwood shook her head. 'I expect she was just feeling sentimental, that's all. What with Miss Cassie being here and all. But she oughtn't to be doing so much at her age. I told her that.'

'No.'

Eve had acknowledged that fact, but now, when she let herself into the library and found her grandmother staring idly into space, apprehension stirred again. The old lady had something on her mind, and Eve hoped it was nothing to do with her.

'Hi,' she said, her own problems fading into insignificance when faced with a greater threat. 'I hear you refused to go and have your ankle X-rayed, after all. So how are you feeling now?'

Mrs Robertson blinked, and then stared at her grand-daughter as if she was seeing her for the first time. 'I'm all right,' she said. And then, more gently, 'Have you just got home, my dear?'

'A few minutes ago,' agreed Eve, without mentioning the fact that she'd already been up to her room and put the scarf Jake Romero had loaned her into her wardrobe. She would have to give it back, but maybe not immediately. 'Um—Mrs Blackwood says you've been downstairs all day. If you insist on ignoring the doctor's advice, you should at least rest.'

'Because I didn't have that handsome young man to help me?' queried the old lady tartly. 'I managed.' She picked up the walking stick beside her chair and waved it meaningfully. 'I'm not helpless, you know.'

'All the same...'

'All the same, nothing.' Mrs Robertson sounded weary now. 'Stop grumbling at me, Eve.' She paused. 'Did I hear a car earlier?'

Which meant Cassie hadn't bothered to check on her mother, thought Eve unhappily. Didn't she care about her at all? Or, more importantly, didn't she realise she was playing with fire? For some reason, maybe because she was getting old, Mrs Robertson didn't seem to care what she said, and the previous evening's unpleasantness could be just the tip of the iceberg.

'Oh, I expect it was Mr Romero's car,' she said, striving for a bright smile. 'It—passed me on the drive.'

'So Cassie's back?'

'I imagine so.' Eve didn't want to get into a discussion

about her own encounter with them. She glanced about her. 'Have you had tea?'

'I didn't want any,' replied the old lady moodily, pushing the box at her feet out of the way and stretching her injured ankle. 'Where is she now?'

'Cassie?'

'Who else?'

Eve sighed. 'I expect she's gone upstairs to take off her coat,' she murmured awkwardly. 'She'll be down in a minute.' At least she hoped so. And without the disturbing company of her guest, if she had any sense.

'And has he gone upstairs, too?' asked Mrs Robertson evenly, although Eve knew she must know the answer to that as well as she did.

'Mr Romero?'

'Stop being obtuse, Eve. You know exactly who I'm talking about.' She paused, eyeing her granddaughter with shrewd grey eyes. 'What do you think of him?'

Eve swallowed, giving herself time to think. 'I—he seems—all right.'

'All right? What kind of an answer is that?' Her grandmother clicked her tongue. 'Don't you think he's too young for Cassie? She is forty-seven, you know.'

'Forty-six,' corrected Eve, before she could stop herself, and the old lady gave her a beetling look.

'Stop splitting hairs. Is she too old for him or what?'

Eve caught her breath. 'I—lots of women marry younger men.' She sought for an example. 'Look at Joan Collins!'

'Cassie is no Joan Collins,' retorted Mrs Robertson scathingly. 'And I don't believe I mentioned marriage. Why would he marry her when he can get what he wants without even buying her a ring?'

Eve felt her stomach tighten at the images her grandmother was unknowingly creating, and hurried into speech. 'So long as they're happy together,' she mumbled, wishing this conversation had never started. 'Um—would you like me to put these boxes away?'

'You know what's in them, of course?' The old lady arched an enquiring brow. 'I've shown you them before. Photographs. Some of them loose, some in albums. Your grandfather was very keen on photography. He said pictures are an incontrovertible record of the past. I thought I might show some of them to Mr Romero.'

'No!' Eve was horrified. 'You can't, Ellie. That would be malicious, and you know it!'

'Why?' Her grandmother was defiant. 'What's malicious about a few photographs? He might be interested to see pictures of what Cassie was like when she was a young girl.'

'You can't do that.' Bending, Eve gathered a couple of the boxes into her arms and carried them across the room to stow them in the bottom of the cupboard where they were usually kept. Then, straightening, she said, 'Anyway, I have something to tell you.'

'About Cassie? Or Mr Romero?'

'Neither,' said Eve tersely, hoping the sudden colour in her cheeks would be put down to her exertions. She gathered up another couple of boxes and stowed them as she spoke. 'According to Mrs Portman, the school is due to close next Easter.'

'No.' Her grandmother was shocked, and Eve hoped it would serve to distract her from thoughts of embarrassing her daughter. 'Why?'

'Oh, it's all part of the government's plans to make schools more efficient,' said Eve, stowing the last box with some relief. 'We've known for some time that Falconbridge is attracting fewer and fewer pupils, and those we have are to be transferred to East Ridsdale, which is bigger and more economically viable.'

'Since when has education needed to be "economically viable"?' The old lady made a frustrated sound. 'We're dealing with children here, not robots.'

'I know.' Eve came to stand beside her grandmother's chair. 'Looks like I'll be needing another job.'

'Just when you'd settled down,' exclaimed the old lady bitterly. Then, with a look of anxiety in her eyes, 'You won't move away, will you?'

Eve squeezed her grandmother's shoulder. 'As if,' she said softly. 'No, you're stuck with me now. This is my home.'

'You're a good girl.' Mrs Robertson reached up to cover her hand with her own. 'A better granddaughter to me than either Cassie or I deserve.'

'That's not true,' protested Eve, not wanting to get into Cassie's shortcomings again, but before the old lady could reply the phone rang.

There was an extension in the library and Eve went to answer it, not without some relief. Saved by the bell, she thought, picking up the receiver. 'Hello? Watersmeet Hall.'

'Could I speak to Miss Wilkes, please?'

'Miss Wilkes?' The woman's voice was unfamiliar, and for a moment Eve's mind felt blank. But then she remembered that Wilkes was the name Cassie used professionally. 'Oh, yes,' she said, making a quelling gesture to her grandmother. 'I'll get her for you.'

'Who is it?' the old lady asked as Eve made for the door, and she paused to whisper that it was some woman wanting to speak to Miss Wilkes. 'Cassie!' Her grandmother made no attempt to lower her voice. 'What does she want Cassie for?'

Eve shook her head helplessly, but she didn't have time to answer her now. Going out into the hall, she considered merely shouting Cassie's name up the stairs. But it was a big house, and it would be just like Cassie to pretend she hadn't heard her even if she had.

Instead, she ran up the stairs and hurried down the corridor to Cassie's room. A knock aroused no response, and with some trepidation she tried the door. Cassie could be in the bathroom and not have heard her, she reasoned defensively, but in any event the room and its adjoining bathroom were empty.

Sighing, she closed the door again, aware that there was only one place Cassie could be. In Jake Romero's room. And approaching that was an entirely different matter.

Even so, it had to be done, and, taking a deep breath, she walked back along the corridor to the room Mrs Blackwood had assigned to their other visitor. She knew it was on her grandmother's orders that the two rooms were some distance from one another, but, as both Cassie and her lover were young and agile enough to cover the distance without any problem, it was obviously a wasted effort.

Her first knock elicited a shrill protest, and her heart sank at the prospect of what she would find when the door was opened. But, to her surprise, it was jerked open almost immediately and Jake Romero confronted her—still fully clothed, she noticed a little breathlessly.

'Um—there's a call—for Miss Wilkes,' she stammered, feeling stupid—particularly when Cassie appeared behind him, draping a possessive hand over his shoulder. The older woman's sweater had been discarded, and her shirt was partly unbuttoned, revealing a tantalising amount of cleavage.

'A call? For me?' Cassie's brows drew together in some confusion. 'Are you sure?'

'You're the only Miss Wilkes here,' replied Eve shortly, recovering some composure. She started towards the stairs again, adding over her shoulder, 'You can take it in the hall, if you want some privacy. Your mother's in the library.'

'Privacy? In the hall?' Cassie snorted, forced to remove her arm from Jake's shoulder and button her shirt again with obviously irritated fingers. 'I mean, can you believe it?' she asked, turning to him for support. 'A house of this size and no phone upstairs. It's ludicrous!'

'I'm sure your mother doesn't find it a problem,' Jake retorted drily, aware that Eve's reaction to finding them together irritated him quite a bit, too. 'Go ahead. I need to take a shower anyway.'

'Oh, but we were—'

'You were about to go back to your own room,' said Jake flatly. He waited until she was outside, and then closed the door behind her with rather more force than was necessary.

CHAPTER FIVE

JAKE took the precaution of locking his door before going to take a shower. He didn't trust Cassandra not to come back after she'd taken her call, and the last thing he needed right now was for her to try and break the rules her mother had so subtly engineered. He didn't know why, exactly. It wasn't as if he couldn't say no. And since leaving London their relationship had definitely faltered, and he no longer had any desire to prolong it.

Perhaps it was seeing the way she treated her family, he mused, tipping his head to allow the hot water to rain down upon his shoulders. Cassandra certainly gave her mother little consideration, and if there was an argument that said the old woman deserved it, he was unaware of it.

As for Eve... Well, her situation was strangely ambiguous. She evidently worked for her living, and helped out around the estate when she could, yet there was an odd connection between her and the old lady that he couldn't quite put his finger on. There was affection there, and a gentle understanding. The kind of relationship, in fact, that he would have expected Cassandra to have with her mother.

But she didn't.

Had Eve caused the rift between them as he'd suspected on the journey here? She didn't appear to be devious in any way, but who was he to judge? He hardly knew the girl. But he did know, from experience, that appearances could be very different than they seemed.

Not least his own reaction to her, he admitted dourly, lifting his face to the spray. If she'd told him to his face, she couldn't have made her dislike of him any clearer. So why did he have this persistent need to show her he wasn't the bastard she apparently thought he was? Why, when she consistently provoked him, was he aware of her in a way that heated his blood and disrupted his sleep?

Crazy! Disgusted with himself, and with where his thoughts were leading, Jake swiftly soaped his chest and abdomen, suppressing a groan when he saw he was already half aroused. Dammit, what was wrong with him? Since when had he acquired this insane desire for a woman who had no interest in him?

He was drying himself when he thought he heard someone knocking at his bedroom door, but he ignored it. If it was Cassandra, he would be doing her no favours by opening the door. And if it wasn't...?

But he didn't go there. There was no chance that Eve would come to his door a second time. She'd made her opinion of what she'd found earlier clear enough, and, if he was honest, he would admit that that was what had initiated the soul-searching he'd indulged in during his shower. He resented it; resented her attitude. And he decided there and then that he'd had it with trying to humour her.

He dressed in narrow-legged woollen pants and a burgundy silk shirt. It was cold, but he'd found that Cassandra's mother tended to overheat the main apartments of the house. And, although it was chilly in the hall, and as he descended the staircase, he guessed the library would be almost uncomfortably hot.

He hesitated outside, not sure whether he ought to knock and announce his presence. But there was no light visible under the door, and he assumed he was the first to arrive. Without ceremony, he turned the handle and opened the door, and surprised a startled Eve sitting cross-legged beside the log fire burning in the huge hearth.

She sprang to her feet at once, reaching for the nearest lamp and flooding the room with light as he closed the door behind him. And Jake realised that any preconceived notions he'd had about her were just so much hot air. He couldn't ignore her; didn't want to ignore her. He'd been a fool to think he could.

She was wearing the same black cords she'd been wearing the evening before, but now they were teamed with a V-necked black sweater whose lace-trimmed neckline and bloused waist only hinted at the pert breasts he knew were beneath. Lamplight gave those smoky grey eyes an opacity he longed to penetrate, but perhaps penetration—of any kind—was not something he ought to be thinking about right now.

Nevertheless, just looking at her, at her pale exotic features and night-dark hair, he was arrested by the instinctive urge to know what it would be like to bury his hard swollen flesh in her softness…

Enough!

He almost growled the word aloud as she gazed at him across the back of the armchair she'd been using as a backrest, tugging a scarf of some kind from her neck. Evidently she'd been cold, even sitting in front of the fire, he thought, hoping he wouldn't regret not wearing a sweater. But then she held the woollen item out to him and he realised what it was.

His scarf!

'I tried to return this earlier,' she said, stepping forward to push it into his hands. She tossed the heavy braid of her hair over her shoulder. 'You didn't hear me.'

Once again he had to suppress the expletive that came

so readily to his tongue. If he'd known, he thought. If he'd only known it was Eve who had been knocking at his door...

But it was just as well he hadn't. 'I was probably in the shower,' he said, and saw the way her lips twisted at his words. She didn't believe him, he realised indignantly. She obviously thought he and Cassandra had resumed where they'd left off.

He wanted to tell her she was wrong, that it was because he hadn't wanted another argument with Cassandra that he hadn't opened his door. But he didn't. Instead, he moved towards her, dropping the scarf onto the desk as he did so, saying, 'How is Mrs Robertson this evening?' As if talking about someone else could cool his resentment. Dammit, she had no right to judge him. If he and Cassandra had chosen to make out on the front lawn of the house it would have been nothing to do with her, for God's sake. He glanced about him. 'I thought she'd be here.'

'No.' Eve didn't know what to do with her hands now that she didn't have the scarf to occupy them, and after an awkward moment she pushed them into her pockets. 'I expect she'll be down later.'

'Would she like me to—?'

'Carry her downstairs?' Eve interrupted him. 'No, I don't think that will be necessary.'

'Do you make all her decisions for her?'

His dark eyes were far too intent, and Eve moved a little uncomfortably under their regard. 'Of course not,' she said tersely. Then, moving purposefully forward, 'If you'll excuse me, I'll go and see if she—'

'And if I won't?'

Eve caught her breath. 'If you won't what?'

'If I won't excuse you,' he said softly. Then, his eyes

darkening, 'Come on, Eve, would it hurt you to keep me company for a few minutes? It's not as if I'm threatening to jump your bones.'

'You couldn't,' she asserted, hoping like hell that he wouldn't put her to the test, and his lips thinned.

'Don't be too sure,' he murmured drily, but Eve thought she could see reluctant amusement lurking at the corner of his mouth. 'You might do well to humour me.'

Eve shook her head. 'Why should you want me to?'

'Oh…' He considered for a moment. 'Perhaps I just want to know more about you. No harm in that, is there?'

Eve shivered in spite of the fire at her back. 'Cass— Cassandra will be down soon. She—she can tell you all you need to know.'

'I doubt that.' He gestured towards the chair behind her. 'Why don't you sit down and tell me yourself?'

'Perhaps I don't want to.'

'I'd gathered that.' His brows drew together. 'I wonder why?'

Eve expelled a nervous breath, but short of pushing him out of the way she was trapped. In more ways than one. With a sound she hoped he identified as frustration she stepped back and subsided into the chair he'd indicated with obvious ill grace. Then, when he made no attempt to seat himself opposite, but stood over her like some dark predator, she forced herself to look up at him. 'Well?'

Jake was intrigued in spite of her evident irritation. She was so aloof, so defensive, almost, and his earlier interest deepened into an attraction that had little to do with sex. Well, not a lot, he conceded honestly, aware that he was still sexually aroused by her cool, remote allure and, yes—why not?—her obvious reluctance to let him get close to her.

Why he should want to was not something he chose to

go into right now, and, realising he couldn't conduct a conversation from this angle—however advantageous it might be—he stepped across the hearth and took the chair opposite.

'So?' he said, when she made no attempt to speak to him. 'Tell me about yourself. Have you always lived in the north of England?'

Her shoulders seemed to sag at this question. But, 'No,' she responded shortly, leaving him with no choice but to ask another.

'Your parents lived in another part of the country?'

'I don't have any parents,' she replied. 'Is that all?'

'No, it's not all,' he exclaimed, annoyed in spite of his determination not to let her rile him. This was her way of avoiding any further conversation, and he wasn't going to let her get away with it. 'Everyone has parents, Eve. Or do you still believe babies are found under a gooseberry bush?'

Faint colour tinted the olive skin of her throat at this, and although he could defend his actions to himself, her sudden vulnerability wrenched his gut. 'I know where babies come from, Mr Romero,' she declared stiffly. 'Though maybe not as well as you do, I'll admit.'

Jake caught his breath. 'What the hell is that supposed to mean?'

Eve looked a little nervous now, and he suspected she'd spoken without considering the possible consequences. But she had no choice but to go on. 'I—don't have children, Mr Romero,' she said primly. 'Perhaps you do.'

He was fairly sure that that wasn't what she'd meant when she'd made that earlier observation, but he didn't contradict her. 'No,' he told her, his eyes enjoying her confusion. 'I don't have any children. None that I know of, anyway.'

If anything, her colour deepened, but she wasn't about to back down. 'Not everyone cares one way or the other,' she said, surprisingly, though her gaze flickered away from his as she did so. 'In any case, for your information, I never knew my parents. My biological parents, that is.'

Jake frowned. 'You were adopted?'

Eve sighed. 'Of what possible interest is this to you?'

'Take my word: I'm interested.'

She was silent for a long moment, but then she lifted her head and looked him in the eyes. 'For a time,' she agreed. 'I ran away when I was twelve years old.'

Twelve? He couldn't conceive of it. At twelve she'd have been—what? A girl with pigtails in her hair? A rebellious pre-teen who didn't know when she was well off?

'I didn't get away with it, of course,' she went on. Her gaze was riveted on her hands, which were twisted together in her lap now, and he wondered if she was aware of what she was saying. 'I was found and sent back. Twice, actually. But I only ran away again, until the authorities decided it would be easier to let Social Services take the strain.'

Jake shook his head. 'But you were so young.'

'I was old enough.' Her lips pressed together, as if to silence any further confidences. Then, with a gesture of dismissal, she added, 'It all happened a long time ago. I'd forgotten about it.'

But she hadn't. He could tell. And he badly wanted to ask her how it was that she was living in the north-east of England now, with an old lady who didn't seem like anyone's idea of a social worker.

Then he remembered something Cassandra had told him. 'You're related to the Robertsons, aren't you?' he said impulsively, and was then taken aback when her face, which had been filled with becoming colour, paled to an almost luminous opalescence.

'Who told you that?' she demanded tensely, and Jake shrugged.

'Cassandra.' He was wary. 'Isn't it true?'

Any answer she might have made was prevented by the sudden opening of the door. Immediately the main light was switched on, further illuminating their erstwhile intimacy, and Cassandra stood in the doorway, regarding them with a look of unconcealed fury on her face.

She was wearing a filmy cocktail dress this evening, which clung to her shapely figure, and although it had obviously been made by an expert hand, it was totally unsuitable for a family supper at home. She had evidently decided to use any means at her disposal to get him to change his mind, thought Jake wryly, despising himself for his arrogance. And he wasn't entirely surprised to discover her seductive efforts left him totally unmoved.

'What's going on?' Cassandra demanded, staring at each of them in turn, and Eve felt as if they'd been caught out in some illicit assignation. Which was ridiculous. They'd only been talking, for heaven's sake. Though she was fairly sure she looked as guilty as hell.

Jake got to his feet without concern. 'Well, let me see,' he said drily. 'Eve returned the scarf I lent her this afternoon, and I asked her how Mrs Robertson was this evening. I offered to carry your mother downstairs again, but Eve thought that wouldn't be necessary. Then we spoke about—'

'I don't want to hear all your conversation,' snapped Cassandra shortly, and Jake arched enquiring brows.

'No?' he said blandly. 'But I thought that was what you did want. You asked what was going on.'

Cassandra glared at him. 'And you knew exactly what

I meant,' she retorted, making no attempt to mince her words. Then, as if realising they had an audience, she sucked in a frustrated breath before continuing, 'How long have you been keeping Eve company?'

Jake shrugged. 'Does it matter?'

Cassandra pursed her lips. 'You didn't think to let me know you were going downstairs?'

'I'm sorry.' There was an edge to Jake's voice now that even Eve could hear. 'I didn't realise I had to post my whereabouts. I gather you've been looking for me. That is why you're so—put out—isn't it?'

Cassandra's teeth ground together, but short of accusing him of conspiracy, there was little she could say in her own defence. 'I thought—I thought you might have wanted to know who rang,' she said at last, turning to close the door, exposing the fact that the gown had virtually no back to speak of. Then, turning again, she posed against the dark panels. 'You usually do.'

He could have argued with her. He could have said that the only occasion he'd wanted to know who rang was when she'd answered the phone in his hotel in London. But it wasn't worth the pleasure it would give her to put him on the defensive.

Nevertheless, he saw how her words had affected Eve. He wasn't surprised, therefore, when she got to her feet and said she would go and see if Mrs Blackwood needed any help.

When they were alone, Cassandra covered the space between them with flattering haste. 'Thank goodness she's gone,' she exclaimed, her tone much warmer now than it had been before. She rested her hand on the unbuttoned neckline of his shirt, her fingers touching his naked skin. 'You'll never guess what's happened.'

Jake lifted his hand and used the pretext of taking her

hand in his to remove it from his chest. 'So tell me,' he said lightly. He glanced across the room. 'But shall we have a drink first?'

Cassandra sighed. 'You don't understand. This is important.'

'Okay.' Jake released her hand and stepped back to hook a hip over the corner of the desk. He folded his arms. 'Go on.'

Cassandra moistened her lips. 'I've been offered a part in *Evermore*.' Her eyes were alight with excitement. 'Isn't that amazing?'

'And *Evermore* would be?'

'Oh, Jake! You must have heard of *Evermore*! It's one of the most successful soaps on television at the moment.'

Jake refrained from pointing out that, as an infrequent visitor to these shores, he seldom found time to watch the news on television, let alone a soap opera, however successful it might be.

But he couldn't steal her thunder, so instead he said, 'Way to go, girl! You must be excited.'

'I am.' Cassandra wrapped her arms about herself with evident satisfaction. 'So's Amy.' Jake knew Amy Lassiter was her agent. 'That was her on the phone, of course. I attended the auditions weeks ago, and I'd given up hope of hearing anything positive, but apparently the—er—the actress they initially chose has pulled out, so—'

'They chose you.'

'Yes.'

'And is it a big part?'

'Well, it's only for three episodes to begin with,' explained Cassandra equably. 'That's how they do these things. They introduce a new character, and if he or she goes down well with the viewing public, they expand the role.'

'Ah.' Jake nodded. 'So I imagine you'll be wanting to get back to London as soon as possible?'

Which would and wouldn't suit him. But it wasn't his call.

'Amy's asked me to go back tomorrow,' admitted Cassandra, biting her lip. 'There are so many things to arrange—contracts to sign, script conferences to attend, rehearsals and so on.' She shook her head. 'I can't believe it.'

'You're going to be very busy,' agreed Jake, aware that any feeling of relief he had at being let off the hook was tempered by the knowledge that he was unlikely to see Eve again. But then the door crashed open and Cassandra's mother, leaning heavily on her cane, came unceremoniously into the room.

'Sorry about that,' she said. 'Lost my balance as I reached for the handle.' She pulled a wry face at Jake. 'So—what was that you were saying about being busy?'

Jake had to smile at Cassandra's expression. She'd been put in the same position as she'd put Eve in earlier. 'Your daughter's landed a part in something called *Evermore*,' he told her smoothly. 'Here, let me help you to your chair.'

Mrs Robertson took his arm with evident relief, and their progress across the room was necessarily slow. But, after she'd subsided into the chair, she regarded her daughter with shrewd, if faded blue eyes, and said, '*Evermore*, eh? Well, well, who'd have thought it?'

'Not you, apparently,' declared Cassandra shortly. She seemed undecided what to do next, and finally settled on taking the chair opposite her mother. 'Aren't you going to congratulate me? This is exactly the sort of part I've been waiting for.'

Her mother moved her shoulders in a dismissive gesture. 'I suppose this means we'll be seeing even less of you in future.'

'Do you care?' Cassandra was bitter.

'Some of us might,' retorted her mother drily. 'But if it's what you want...'

'It is.'

'Then there's nothing more to be said. I wish you luck with it. Goodness knows, you've been out of work long enough.'

'I've been resting,' snapped Cassandra angrily. 'Honestly, Mother, I'm an actress, not a—a schoolteacher, for God's sake!'

Jake stifled a groan. He guessed it had been unwise of her to bring Eve's occupation into the argument, and he wasn't surprised when Mrs Robertson took exception to it. 'Eve has brains, Cassie,' she said scornfully. 'Which is something no one could ever accuse you of.'

'How dare you?'

'What? You think learning a few lines and repeating them parrot fashion in front of a camera requires intelligence?'

'I think you know nothing about it.'

'I think I wouldn't want to.'

'Can I get anyone a drink?' Jake knew he had to put a stop to this before they both said something they'd regret. 'Mrs Robertson? Some wine, perhaps? Cassandra?'

His words caused a pregnant silence that was almost as hostile in its way as what had gone before. But after a few moments Cassandra's mother seemed to remember her manners, and in clipped tones she said, 'Yes, a glass of wine would be very nice. Thank you, Mr Romero.'

'No problem.' Jake blew out a relieved breath. 'Cassandra?'

'Scotch. With ice, if there is any,' she said, barely

glancing in his direction, and Jake moved towards the tray of drinks with real enthusiasm.

He gave the women theirs, and then poured a stiff Scotch for himself. The single malt was smooth and sleek, and he welcomed the heat it brought to his stomach. It helped to banish the memory of the unpleasantness he'd just witnessed. He stifled another moan when Mrs Robertson spoke again. What now?

'I suppose you'll be leaving in the morning, Cassie?' she said, and despite the coolness of her voice Jake was sure she was trying to be polite.

Cassandra didn't immediately respond, and he hoped she wasn't about to rekindle the argument. But eventually she said, civilly enough, 'Yes. I have to be back in London tomorrow.'

'Ah.' The old lady absorbed this with unexpected interest. 'So you'll be fairly tied up for the next few days? What with rehearsals and such?'

Cassandra was regarding her mother warily now, and Jake didn't altogether blame her. 'I expect so, yes.'

'Hmm.' The old lady was thoughtful. 'Well, as you pointed out earlier, I know nothing about these matters, Cassie, but I'd have thought that in the circumstances you're going to have little time to entertain Mr Romero.'

Cassandra's jaw dropped, but she quickly recovered herself. Then, her gaze moving from her mother to Jake and back again, she said tensely, 'Why should that matter to you?'

'Oh…' Mrs Robertson shrugged. 'Well, it's just that I wouldn't like Mr Romero to feel he's not welcome to stay on here if he'd like to.'

Cassandra gasped. 'You can't be serious!'

'Why not? I understand he's quite interested in the area, and unless he has some pressing business of his own in

London there's no reason why he shouldn't stay and finish
his holiday.'

'No!' Cassandra was on her feet now. 'I don't— Of
course Jake is coming back to London with me.'

Her mother arched a provocative brow. 'Isn't it up to
Mr Romero to make that decision for himself?'

'He can't. We—we drove up in his car.'

'He can always take you to Newcastle Airport. I believe
there are frequent flights to London, and from your point
of view it would be quicker.'

'You old witch!' Cassandra was trembling with fury.
'You think that by asking Jake to stay you'll ruin whatever happiness I have in accepting this part!'

'And your happiness is always the most important
thing, isn't it?' demanded her mother coldly. 'It doesn't
matter who you hurt, who suffers because of your—your
selfishness, so long as you're *happy*! It doesn't even occur
to you that Jacob might prefer to stay here. What are you
afraid of, Cassie? That Eve might steal him from under
your very nose?'

Jake didn't know what Cassandra might have done then
if he hadn't stepped between them. She looked mad
enough to scratch the old lady's eyes out, and, however
much her mother might deserve it, he couldn't let that
happen.

'Look, it's a moot point, anyway,' he said flatly. 'I can't
stay on—much as I appreciate your invitation,' he added
politely. 'Thanks, but I do have to get back to London
myself.' He managed a rueful smile. 'Sorry.'

CHAPTER SIX

THE FOLLOWING MORNING, however, it soon became apparent that Jake wasn't fit to go anywhere.

Eve encountered him on the first-floor landing as she was about to go downstairs for breakfast, and one look at his grey face and streaming eyes was enough for her to advise him to go back to bed.

'I think you've got flu,' she said, not altogether easy in the position of surrogate doctor. 'How do you feel? You look—dreadful.'

'Gee, thanks.' Despite the humour in his tone, his voice was thick with congestion. 'But I'll be okay.' He paused before adding, 'Cassandra has to get back to town today.'

Eve knew that. Although it hadn't been mentioned during supper, her grandmother had confided Cassie's news to her when Eve had helped her up to bed.

'And do you think you're well enough to drive over three hundred miles?' she found herself asking, even though it was really nothing to do with her. Indeed, she would feel happier when he and Cassie had gone. But he was shivering violently, in spite of the several layers of sweaters he was wearing, and she went on doggedly, 'I could always drive Cassie to the airport. She can easily get a flight to London. It only takes a little over an hour.'

Jake pulled a wry face. Remembering Cassandra's reaction when her mother had made a similar suggestion the night before, he doubted she'd agree. But the truth was, he did feel bloody rotten. He could think of nothing more appealing at this moment than crawling back into his bed.

'Let's ask her, shall we?' he said, wondering how he could be sweating when he felt so cold. Perhaps it had something to do with the fact that Eve was looking at him without any animosity at last. But he wasn't going to go there. He was in enough trouble as it was.

'Let's not,' said Eve suddenly, apparently taking the initiative. 'You go back to bed and I'll speak to Cassie myself. I'm sure she'll understand.'

'Yeah, right.' Jake raked damp fingers through his hair. 'I wouldn't hold your breath.'

Eve pressed her lips together for a moment. Then she shook her head. 'Go back to bed, Mr Romero. I don't think you're in any state to argue.'

Leaving him to do as she'd asked, or not, Eve hurried down the stairs to the kitchen. 'Mr Romero won't be leaving this morning after all,' she told a surprised Mrs Blackwood. 'He appears to have flu. Do we have any hot water bottles? He can't seem to stop shivering.'

'I think you'll find a couple in the cupboard there,' directed the housekeeper, checking the bacon she had sizzling under the grill. 'So, will Miss Cassie be staying on, too?'

'I doubt it,' said Eve, filling the kettle and switching it on. 'I told you what Mrs Robertson said about Cassie landing this part in a television series, didn't I? I don't think she'll risk losing that.'

'But if Mr Romero's ill…'

'Well, we'll see,' said Eve, wondering if she was being too cynical. After all, from the way she behaved Cassie obviously cared about him. But roles like this were few and far between—even if it might mean leaving Jake to the care of virtual strangers.

And she still had to persuade Cassie that taking a plane back to London was the best option, Eve reminded herself. It was going to be no easy task, she knew. Of course Cassie might refuse to go, and confound them all. And from Eve's point of view that could be the safest option of all.

Leaving Mrs Blackwood to fill the hot water bottles and take them up to Jake's room, Eve ran upstairs again to find Cassie. She hadn't been in the dining room, and unless she'd made an early-morning call on Jake—which Eve didn't even want to think about—she was probably still in her room, packing.

When she knocked, however, she didn't get quite the response she'd expected. 'Come on in, darling,' drawled Cassie, evidently mistaking her for Jake. 'I knew you couldn't wait until we got back to town.'

It was too embarrassing to open the door after that, and Eve waited outside, hoping Cassie would realise her mistake. But when the door opened the woman was standing there in nothing but a silk kimono, and that was barely fastened across her naked form.

Her reaction was predictably explosive. 'What are you doing here?' Cassie demanded. 'If you've come to try and persuade me to apologise to that old bitch, forget it! She's seen the last of me this time. I won't be coming here again.'

'Unless you're broke,' said Eve drily. She had heard Cassie say much the same thing before. 'In any case, I haven't come to speak to you about your mother.' She paused, and then went on forcefully, 'Mr Romero's ill. He won't be able to drive you back to London today.'

Cassie's mouth dropped open. 'Jake?' she said disbelievingly. Then, with hardly more sympathy, 'What's wrong with him?'

'I think he has flu,' said Eve, noticing the way Cassie's

eyes narrowed at her words. 'He has— He looks—' She strove for a suitable word. 'Sick.'

'Are you sure this isn't some clever ploy of my mother's to keep him here?' Cassie was sceptical.

'Why should Ellie want to do that?' Eve was confused.

'Didn't she tell you she suggested he should stay on here for a few more days?'

'No.' Eve frowned. 'No, she didn't.'

'Well, she did.' Cassie was truculent. 'I wouldn't put it past her to have spiked his drink or something. Anything to put one over on me.'

Eve sighed. 'You can't spike someone's drink with flu,' she said impatiently.

'How do you know he's ill anyway?' exclaimed Cassie suddenly. 'Have you been knocking at his door again?'

'No, I haven't.' Eve was indignant. 'I met him on the landing as I was going down for breakfast. His eyes were all red and streaming, and he could hardly speak. Go and see him if you don't believe me.'

'Oh, I can't do that.' Cassie recoiled as she spoke, as if Eve was going to grab her and drag her forcibly along the corridor. She shook her head. 'I daren't risk it. I mean, I can't afford to get ill now, can I? What with getting this part and everything. If I were to get flu goodness knows what they'd do. They might even give the part to someone else.'

'I doubt that,' said Eve flatly. 'And people can't help getting ill. I'm sure they're insured against things like this.'

'Well, I wouldn't want to take the chance,' said Cassie firmly. 'I'm sorry, of course I am, but if Jake is ill then I think I'm going to have to find some other way to get back to London.'

Eve was appalled. 'Without seeing him?'

Cassie shrugged. 'He'll understand,' she said carelessly. 'I'll phone him on his mobile when I get back to town.' Then, with a lightning change of mood, 'You'll take me to the airport, won't you, darling? Mummy said there are regular flights to London from Newcastle.'

'Don't—don't call me darling,' said Eve harshly. But she couldn't argue with her. She'd already told Romero that she'd take Cassie to the airport if she was willing to go. 'You'd better ring and find out when you can get a flight.'

'Oh, God!' Cassie's expression changed again. 'A flight!' She gnawed on her lower lip. 'How much do you think that will be?'

Eve shook her head. 'About a hundred, I suppose,' she said tightly, not really wanting to continue this conversation. But she didn't have much choice.

'A hundred pounds!' Cassie gasped. 'My God, I don't have a hundred pounds, and my credit cards are maxed out.'

Eve half turned away. 'Not my problem,' she said, just wanting to get away from her, but Cassie wouldn't let her go.

'Couldn't you lend me the money, sweetie?' she asked wheedlingly, stepping out onto the landing. 'I'd pay you back. As soon as I get paid. You know I'm good for it.'

'Do I?' Eve was sardonic. 'How many times have I heard you tell Ellie the same?'

'Forget Ellie,' said Cassie irritably. 'This is between you and me, Eve. Come on. Don't you owe me?'

Eve could hardly speak. 'You—you dare to ask me that?' she choked, but Cassie just looked bored.

'Haven't you got over it yet?' she protested. 'You've got a cushy number here, haven't you? You wouldn't have had that if it wasn't for me.'

'I'm here in spite of you,' Eve told her bitterly. But even as she said the words she knew she was wasting her time. There was no point in expecting Cassie to understand. She'd never cared about anyone but herself, and she wasn't going to change now. 'All right,' she said at last. 'I'll lend you the money for the fare and I'll take you to Newcastle Airport. But only because I don't want you bumming off Ellie again.'

'You're a pal.'

Cassie would have closed the door then, but Eve put out a hand to stop her. 'You'll have to get an afternoon flight,' she said. 'I've promised to help Mr Trivett this morning, but I'll be free this afternoon.'

'Lunchtime, then,' said Cassie resignedly. 'Try not to be late.'

There was to be an autumn fair in the church hall the next week, and Eve had promised Harry that she would go to the rectory on Sunday evening and help him sort everything out. The fair was in aid of the St Mary's restoration fund, the church where Harry was minister, and in the ordinary way Eve would have enjoyed the visit.

She and Harry had become good friends in recent months—ever since he'd taken up the appointment, actually—and she knew he was hoping their friendship might deepen into something warmer.

Eve wasn't so sure. She wasn't convinced she wanted to have that kind of relationship with anybody. Ever. And it didn't help matters to know that this evening she would have preferred to stay at Watersmeet—just in case she was needed.

Not that she would be, she supposed, as she walked to the rectory after evening service. So far Jake Romero hadn't left his bed, and since delivering Cassie to the airport the day before her involvement in his recovery had been negligible. Mrs Blackwood had supplied him with tissues and aspirin and plenty of fluids, and according to her he'd slept most of the day.

'The man's exhausted,' she'd remarked the previous evening, setting a dish of steak and kidney pie on the table. 'And sleep's the best medicine of all, as my old mother used to say. You'll see—he'll be right as rain in a couple of days.'

Eve didn't doubt it. Romero was a powerful man. He wouldn't like being laid low by a simple virus. Besides, he'd told Ellie that he wanted to be back in London by the end of the week.

Her grandmother had spent most of the previous day in bed, too. Despite the feisty way she'd spoken to her daughter, having Cassie there had tired her, and Eve was glad she was being sensible for once. She had joined her granddaughter for supper that evening, but Eve suspected she was glad Eve was going out. It gave her an excuse to have another early night.

Harry Murray opened the door himself when she reached the rectory. A tall, angular man, with long, lean limbs and a receding hairline, he nevertheless had the kind of genteel good-looking features that invited confidences. Despite his age—he was only thirty-two—he was a popular figure around the village, and the congregation at his church had increased considerably since he took over.

'Hi,' he said warmly, stepping back to allow her into the hall of the building. 'You look rosy. Is it cold?'

Eve grinned. 'I'm not sure whether that's a compliment or not,' she said, shedding her duffel into his waiting arms. 'But, yes, it is cold. According to the forecast, it could snow later.'

Harry's expression grew anxious. 'I hope not,' he said,

hanging her coat on the Victorian hatstand and leading the way into his study. 'It would certainly limit the numbers coming to the fair. People are more inclined to stay at home in bad weather.'

'Well, the forecasters have been wrong before,' said Eve cheerfully, unwinding her scarf and looking round the large room with incredulous eyes. 'My Go— Goodness! You've certainly collected a lot of stuff.'

'Haven't I?' Harry looked pleased. 'That's why I'm so grateful to you for coming to help me.'

'I'm sure you know there are any number of volunteers waiting for an invitation to help you,' declared Eve drily. 'Not least all the ladies.' She pulled a face. 'You're considered the local heartthrob, you know.'

Harry flushed. 'You're embarrassing me,' he said, but she noticed he didn't deny it. 'Anyway, would you like me to get Mrs Watson to bring us some refreshments first?'

'Oh, no.' Eve shook her head. 'I've just had supper,'' she added, running a rueful hand over her stomach. 'Let's do some work first, and then we can think about refreshments.'

He agreed, and for the next hour they were absorbed in sorting out clothes and bric-a-brac and all the many magazines and books that the parishioners had donated. Eve enjoyed looking through the books. There was always something interesting to find, and she had to be firm with herself and not give in to the urge to browse.

Eventually Harry got to his feet and brushed his dusty fingers against his worn cords. 'I think that will do for tonight,' he said, looking round at all the boxes they'd dealt with. 'Yes, I'm sure I can manage the rest of it myself.'

Eve, who had been stowing tins of fruit and vegetables

into a cardboard box, looked up at him enquiringly. 'If you're sure.'

'I am.' Harry put out his hand and helped her to her feet. 'I don't want to spend the whole evening working.'

'Okay.' Eve extricated her hand and looked down at her own dusty fingers. 'But if you don't mind I'd like to wash off this dust first.'

'Of course.' Harry went to open the door for her. 'You know where the bathroom is. I'll ask Mrs Watson to bring us some—what? Tea or coffee?'

'You choose.'

'Tea it is, then,' he said apologetically. 'I'm afraid I'm not a coffee-lover.'

The word 'lover' sounded incongruous on his lips, despite its innocent application, and Eve was uneasily reminded of Jake Romero. That was what her grandmother had said he was: Cassie's lover. Eve shivered as she hurried along the hall to the downstairs bathroom. It was not a description she cared for—in any sense of the word.

She took her time, washing her hands thoroughly and brushing wisps of dark hair from her smooth temple. She needed time to compose herself, to put Jake Romero out of her mind. But it wasn't easy.

It annoyed her that this should be so, but she acknowledged that he had got under her skin on more than one occasion. The truth was, she'd never known anyone quite like him before, and she told herself she wouldn't have been human if she hadn't found him attractive.

Though only physically, she assured herself. Nevertheless, it wasn't pleasant to feel that he had some kind of hold on her thoughts. She didn't need the kind of complication he presented, and she wished he'd just gone back to London with Cassie—then she could have forgotten all about him.

Pressing her lips together, she regarded her tense reflection with impatient eyes. What was she doing, wasting her time worrying about Romero? After all, aside from the obvious barrier his relationship with Cassie created, what man was going to look at her dark skin and hair when he was used to Cassie's porcelain-skinned, blonde-haired beauty?

Folding the handtowel back onto its rail with taut, controlled movements, Eve turned to the door. Harry would be wondering what she was doing, and she could just imagine his reaction if she told him she was wondering what it would be like to have an affair with a man like Jake Romero. Dear God, he would think she was mad. And who could blame him? She thought she was a little mad herself.

Mrs Watson, his housekeeper, had already brought a tray of tea and biscuits, and when Eve returned to the study Harry was pacing agitatedly about the floor.

He stopped when he saw her, however, and his eyes took on an expression of concern. 'Are you all right?'

'Of course.' Eve did her best to control her colour. 'I told you I wanted to wash my hands.'

'You've been almost fifteen minutes,' exclaimed Harry, gesturing her towards one of the squashy armchairs that were set beside a low occasional table. 'Sit down. The tea's going to be cold.'

'I'm sorry.' Despite the fact that she'd expected such a reaction, Eve found herself irritated now. 'I didn't realise you were timing me.'

Harry clicked his tongue. 'I wasn't timing you,' he said unhappily. 'I was just—'

'Impatient for your tea. I know,' said Eve, managing a faint smile. 'Well, I'm here now. Do you want me to pour?'

'If you would.' Relieved, Harry took the chair beside her and stretched his long legs out towards the fire smouldering in the grate. 'You'll have to forgive me. I tend to be rather possessive where you're concerned.'

'Possessive?' Eve echoed the word rather uneasily. She didn't want Harry to feel possessive of her. They didn't have that kind of a relationship. Not yet, at any rate.

'Yes, possessive.' Harry put down the cup of tea she'd just handed him and leant towards her. 'Eve, don't you think it's about time we put our association on a more— formal footing?'

'Oh, Harry—'

'No. Hear me out.' Harry was determined to continue. 'You must know how I feel about you. I've made it plain enough. And—well—when I hear that you've got some strange man living in your house, I can't deny I get jealous.'

'Jealous?' Eve was appalled. She wouldn't have attributed such feelings to Harry. He'd always seemed so placid, so easygoing. And as for making his feelings plain... Well, the only physical contact they'd had was a fairly chaste kiss when they said goodbye.

'Do you blame me?' he demanded now. 'I've been expecting you to mention him all evening, but you haven't.'

'But—Mr Romero was Cassie's guest, not mine,' protested Eve, amazed that he should feel he had the right to question her like this.

'Yet Mrs Robertson's daughter has gone back to London, hasn't she?' Harry persisted, and Eve expelled an indignant breath.

'Yes,' she agreed tersely. 'Mr Romero has only stayed on because he's not well.' She endeavoured to calm herself. 'May I have a biscuit?'

'Of course—of course.'

Harry immediately reached for the plate, but in his haste he succeeded only in spilling its contents onto the floor. Red-faced, he bent to rescue the scattered biscuits, just as Eve did the same, and they banged heads.

'Oh, dear!' Harry was contrite. 'I'm such a clumsy oaf!' He caught her shoulders, forcing her to look at him. 'Did I hurt you?'

'Not much.' Eve tried to make light of it, but she was intensely conscious of the weight of Harry's hands upon her shoulders, and the quickness of his breathing as he stared into her eyes.

She knew she should have anticipated that he might try to kiss her, but she hadn't. She glimpsed his intentions only seconds before he bent towards her, and although she turned her head, he still managed to press his wet lips to the corner of her mouth.

'Oh, Eve,' he said, when she recoiled with a muffled squeak of protest, and, misinterpreting her reaction, he buried his hot face against her neck. 'You must know I wouldn't hurt you for the world.'

Eve couldn't get away quickly enough. His heavy hands and coarse breathing reminded her all too vividly of another man's sordid attempts to touch her. Scrambling backwards off her chair, she managed to put the width of the occasional table between them before saying unevenly, 'I have to go.'

'Eve!' Harry got to his feet, his face flushed now with a mixture of excitement and embarrassment. 'You can't leave yet.' He glanced down at the table. 'You haven't drunk your tea.'

'I don't want any more.' Eve realised she had to say something to normalise the situation, or run the risk of Harry suspecting there was something wrong with her. There was, of course, but that was nobody's business but her own. 'I've just remembered: I promised Mrs Robertson I'd be back by nine o'clock, and it's almost that now.'

Harry frowned. 'You didn't say anything about this before.'

'I forgot.' Eve managed to offer an apologetic smile. 'What a memory, eh?'

Harry still looked doubtful. 'This isn't because I kissed you, is it?' he asked.

'No—'

'Because if it is, I want you to know that my intentions are strictly honourable.'

'Oh, Harry!' Eve pressed her lips together with a genuine feeling of remorse. 'I—I didn't expect this, that's all.'

Harry shook his head in obvious bemusement. 'But I thought we were friends—'

'We *are* friends.'

'—that we understood one another—one another's feelings.' He paused. 'Don't you care about me at all?'

Eve sighed. She had hoped to avoid this conversation. Feeling her way, she said, 'I've just told you. I consider you a friend. A dear friend,' she appended, when her words failed to produce any lightening of his expression. 'But—well, it's too soon to—to consider anything else.'

'Too soon?' Harry sounded bitter. 'We've known one another for almost a year, Eve.'

'I know.' She was uncomfortable now, and she desperately wanted to end this awful post-mortem of something that should never have happened. 'I'm sorry, Harry, but I'm just not ready to—to think of you in that way.'

'It's this man, isn't it?' he exclaimed, with a sudden change of attitude. 'This—what was it you called him?— Romeo or something?'

'It's Mr Romero.'

'Romero?' Harry repeated the word scornfully. 'What kind of name is that?'

'He comes from an island in the Caribbean, and it's a Spanish name, actually,' said Eve, resenting his implication. 'And you couldn't be more wrong.'

'Oh, I'm not wrong.' Harry was unpleasant. 'A man like that is just the kind of man *you'd* be attracted to. Is he sexy, Eve? Does he make your pulses race? I should have known it wouldn't take much for someone with your background to be seduced.'

Eve's lips parted in dismay and she clapped a hand to her mouth to silence the cry of protest that sprang to her lips. That Harry, of all people, should say something like that, she thought sickly. My God, did he also know she had Hispanic blood?

CHAPTER SEVEN

HARRY realised his mistake at once—realised that he had said something completely unforgivable—and his face crumpled. His cry of anguish was still ringing in her ears as she wrenched open the door of the rectory and ran for home.

But Eve never faltered. Snatching her coat from the stand, she rushed out into the cold night air, not stopping to put it on until she was far enough from the scene of her humiliation for it not to matter. Then, shouldering her way into the duffel's reassuring folds, she wrapped the sides closely about her.

But she was still trembling, and she wondered if she'd ever feel warm again. That Harry, of all people, should show such prejudice made her feel sick, and she couldn't believe he actually thought she might be holding him off because of Jake Romero. What did he truly think she was?

The question didn't bear examination. Shaking her head, she reached the foot of her grandmother's drive more through good luck than management. In the first few minutes after leaving the rectory she'd hardly been aware of where she was going, and she realised it was a measure of the security the old lady offered her that had brought her unerringly back to Watersmeet.

She was chilled to the bone when she reached the house and, letting herself into the hall, she headed straight for the library. With a bit more luck Mrs Blackwood might have left a decent fire going in there, and she couldn't wait to toast her freezing toes in front of its warmth.

She'd expected the room to be in darkness apart from the firelight. As her grandmother hadn't got up for supper, and Jake Romero was still confined to his bed, she was surprised when she opened the door and found a lamp burning. To her dismay, she found their remaining house guest stretched out in her grandmother's armchair, a discarded magazine resting across his flat stomach. He had obviously been reading, but now he appeared to be gazing into the flames.

He had heard her come in, of course. The room was so quiet you could have heard a pin drop, and the magazine fell heedlessly to the floor as he got to his feet.

'Eve,' he said, his voice still a little hoarse, but not as congested as it had been a couple of days before. 'I'm sorry. I didn't hear a car.'

'I walked,' said Eve flatly, and although the idea of warming herself in front of the fire had lost its appeal, she felt too cold to leave the door open.

'You walked?' Jake was surprised. 'I thought Mrs Blackwood said that the Reverend Murray would be bringing you home.'

Eve didn't know what concern he thought it was of his, but she managed a swift shake of her head. 'I preferred to walk,' she said again. And then, because it was expected, 'How are you?'

Jake shrugged. 'I'll survive.'

Eve frowned. 'Does Ellie know you're up?'

'Ellie? Oh, you mean Mrs Robertson.' He shook his head. 'I doubt it.'

'Then—'

'I'm sorry, but I was going stir-crazy in that room,' he said ruefully. 'Mrs Blackwood told me you'd be out for the evening, so I flung on some clothes and came down here.'

Eve was sure he hadn't 'flung on' the chunky cream cashmere turtleneck, or the soft navy drawstring pants that clung to his hips and moulded the strong muscles of his thighs. As usual, he looked powerfully male, and sexy as hell—another first for her, she thought bitterly.

'Did you have a pleasant evening?'

His question had caught her unawares. He could tell that. Watching her, huddled back against the door as she was, he guessed he was the last person she'd wanted to see tonight. No change there then, he acknowledged drily, yet he had the distinct impression that she was pale beneath the hectic colour the cold had painted on her cheeks. And her eyes were wide and unnaturally bright. Almost as if she was on the verge of tears.

Dammit, what had happened? What had that old clergyman said to her? If he'd made a pass at her, if he'd touched her, he'd—

Yeah, right. Jake arrested his fertile imagination at that point. This was nothing to do with him. Even if the old man had raped her—which was taking his suspicions to unbelievable lengths—what could *he* do about it? She wasn't his responsibility, and he doubted she'd welcome any interference he might make in her affairs.

'Um—Mrs Blackwood said you were spending the evening sorting donations for some fair that's to be held at the church, is that right?' he persisted, when she didn't answer him, and Eve expelled a tremulous breath.

'The autumn fair,' she agreed in a low voice.

Jake nodded. 'Well, you look cold,' he said, when she didn't elaborate. 'Come and sit down. It's much warmer by the fire.'

'Oh, I—I might just go up to bed,' she said, declining his invitation. 'I am rather tired.' She turned towards the door. 'G—goodnight.'

Despite the urgent voice inside him that was warning him not to get involved, Jake couldn't let her go like this. Moving with more speed than he'd have believed himself capable of in his present condition, he strode across the room before she could get the door fully open, and slammed his palm against the dark panels.

The door thudded shut again, trapping her inside, and she turned to look at him with wide—fearful?—eyes. 'What—what do you think you're doing?' she got out, her voice betraying the panic she was feeling. 'If you touch me—'

'I'm not going to touch you!' he exclaimed, annoyed to find himself in the position of having to offer a defence. 'I'm concerned about you. Correct me if I'm wrong, but I think something's happened to upset you. Did someone lay his hands on you? Is that why you're jumping like a cat just because I stopped you from opening the door?'

Eve turned, but she did so without putting any space between her and the wooden panels behind her. She was obviously making every effort to keep as far away from him as possible, and, despite dismissing his worst fears earlier, he was now firmly convinced that—what was it Mrs Blackwood had called him? Reverend Murray?—Murray had assaulted her in some way.

'No—no one's upset me except you,' she said, but he could hear the tremor in her voice. 'I wanted to leave and you stopped me. What am I supposed to think?'

Jake blew out an aggravated breath. 'Well, you've nothing to fear from me,' he said shortly, straightening up and putting a significant distance between them. 'I merely wanted to help.'

'To help?' There was a note of hysteria in her voice now. 'You can't help me.' She swallowed. 'Nobody can.'

It was a strange response, but Jake didn't have the energy to pursue it right now. 'If you say so,' he said wearily, and she tilted her chin.

'May I go?'

'Well, I won't stop you again.'

'Good.'

There was defiance in her tone, and, wrapping her coat closer about herself, she turned towards the door.

But she didn't open it. Instead, despite taking hold of the handle, she remained motionless for several tense seconds, apparently staring at the wall. Then, to his amazement, she slumped against the door, sliding down until she was huddled at his feet.

Jake moved then. Although he still couldn't be sure she'd welcome his assistance, he had to do something. Dropping down onto his haunches, he put out his hand and tried to turn her to face him.

She resisted at first, flinching away as if he'd attempted to assault her, and his anger towards Murray escalated to even greater heights. He was sure now that the man was responsible for her distress, and he wanted to wring his scrawny neck.

Eventually he succeeded in drawing her away from the door, and when he saw the tears streaming down her face he couldn't stifle a savage oath. 'I'll kill that bastard,' he muttered, hauling her into his arms, and although there was still some resistance, ultimately she subsided against him with a shaky sigh of defeat.

She was trembling, he could feel it. And she felt so cold, despite the heavy overcoat she had clutched about her. Her wet face was pressed against his sweater, and as she breathed soft strands of silky dark hair brushed his chin.

Almost involuntarily, it seemed, he turned his mouth against her hair, tasting its lemony essence, inhaling its fragrance deep into his lungs. His hand was at the nape of her neck, and the temptation to tip her face up to his and taste her mouth, too, was almost overwhelming.

He scowled. Was he no better than Murray? he asked himself disgustedly. He wasn't thinking of her feelings any more. He was just thinking about himself. Just because the knowledge that she was cradled between his spread thighs was giving him a hard-on of painful proportions was no excuse for this depravity. He was only in the house because Cassandra had invited him, for God's sake, and he could just imagine her reaction if she could see him now.

He needed to get Eve to the fire, he reminded himself grimly. Not just because she was physically cold, but because she seemed chilled both inside and out. She needed heat, and brandy, not necessarily in that order. And he could do with a shot of Scotch himself.

In the ordinary way, lifting her slim, athletic form would have been easy for him. She was at least forty pounds lighter than the old lady, and infinitely less cumbersome. But his arms shook as he lifted her off the floor, and he cursed the fact that two days in bed had left him as weak as a baby.

Still, in spite of her opposition, he managed to carry her across the room and deposit her in the armchair he'd been occupying when she came in. Then, trusting her not to try and run out on him again, he walked across to the drinks cabinet on slightly uncertain legs.

Eve watched him from beneath lowered lids, scrubbing her cheeks with a tissue she'd found in her pocket. She didn't want to consider what a pathetic fool she'd made of herself, and, no matter how understanding Romero had been, she'd allowed him to get way too close to her. After what had happened with Harry she ought to have had more sense.

But she hadn't known how she was going to react when he'd guessed that Harry had upset her. His immediate anger with the other man, his instinctive belief that whatever had happened wasn't her fault, had broken down the guard she'd kept around her emotions all these years. She couldn't remember the last time she'd cried like that, and although she could make excuses for it, it still didn't alter the fact that Jake had exposed a vulnerability she'd tried so hard to erase.

He came back with two of her grandmother's crystal tumblers and held one out to her. 'It's only Scotch, I'm afraid,' he said, his hand not entirely steady. 'I couldn't find any brandy.'

Eve was compelled to take the glass from him, though she hated even the smell of whisky. She guessed lifting her had robbed him of what little strength he'd had left, and she couldn't turn him down.

'Thanks.'

He nodded, bringing his own glass to his lips and taking a steady gulp. 'God, I need this.'

Eve glanced up at him. 'I'm not sure that drinking whisky is wise in your present condition,' she said, dipping her finger into her glass and tasting the raw spirit. She grimaced, only just managing to hold back a moan of distaste. It was no better in small doses. 'You're supposed to be recuperating.'

Jake looked down at her with a laconic gaze. 'Yeah, well, this stuff will do me more good than all the hot cocoa in the world,' he replied drily. 'You, too. Drink it up.'

'Me?' Eve shuddered. 'I can't drink this. It tastes horrible!'

'Pretend it's medicine,' advised Jake, not taking no for an answer. 'It'll warm you up.'

'I am warm now.'

Eve proved it by pushing the duffel off her shoulders, and for a moment he was transfixed by the pure curve of her nape rising above the round neck of her tee shirt. The shirt was long-sleeved, and a dusty pink in colour, and blended well with the tight jeans whose waistband dipped below her navel. But he hardly noticed what she was wearing. Once again he'd been treated to a glimpse of her delectably smooth bare skin, and the arousal he'd felt earlier manifested itself again with record speed.

Thankfully she was too busy pulling her tee shirt down over her midriff to notice the sudden bulge in his pants, and, putting his empty glass aside, he took her glass from her and swallowed its contents in one gulp. Then, squatting down beside her to hide his embarrassment, he said, 'Are you going to tell me what happened?'

She seemed startled by his question. Perhaps she'd hoped the Scotch would divert him—or her amateur attempt to focus his attention on his health. Either way, it hadn't worked. If he managed to put thoughts of her naked out of his mind, he was instantly reminded of her dipping a finger into her glass. God, did she have any idea how provocative that action was? Somehow he doubted it, yet there was an odd look of wary perception in her eyes.

'What happened when?' she countered now, and Jake guessed she was still hoping to avoid a confrontation. She grimaced. 'I must have got really chilled. I don't usually fall apart like that.'

'Eve!' Ignoring her immediate withdrawal, he put out his hand and captured her chin between his thumb and forefinger. 'Your falling apart, as you put it, had nothing to do with the cold and everything to do with the Reverend Murray. Just tell me what the old fool did, for God's sake. Did he hurt you?'

Eve tried to jerk her chin away from his hand, and when that didn't work she adopted a disdainful stare. 'Harry isn't old,' was all she said, in a scornful voice. 'He's probably younger than you are.'

Jake let her go then, surging to his feet in angry disbelief. What the hell was she saying? That while he'd been picturing her at the mercy of some perverted old lecher, she'd actually spent the evening with a man who might conceivably have expected a different response to his advances?

'So what really happed?' he demanded, looking down at her coldly, unable to hide the resentment in his gaze. 'A lovers' fight? A disagreement? Or has he dumped you for someone else?'

Eve winced as if he'd struck her, and all the earlier empathy he'd felt on her behalf came flooding back with renewed strength. Dammit, he hadn't been mistaken. Something had happened, something bad, and he'd only made it worse with his crass accusations.

'Eve—' he began, but she was already getting to her feet, gathering her coat against her, looking anywhere but at him. God, he thought, how could he have been so stupid? It would have taken more than a quarrel with her boyfriend to destroy the cool self-possession she always exhibited towards him.

'Eve, I'm sorry,' he started again, but she wasn't listening, moving past him with her eye on the door and the evident intention of putting as much space between them as possible.

He expelled a harsh breath. He couldn't let her go like this. He had to make her see that he'd felt betrayed when she'd told him that Murray was a young man, that his amateurish attempt at chivalry had been blunted by the realisation that she was—might be—involved with some-one.

The ramifications of that statement were too compli-cated to consider now. Nor did he choose to remember that Eve's affairs—her well-being—had nothing to do with him. Or what he was admitting by feeling as he did. He just knew that if he allowed her to walk out of this room without accepting his apology he'd never forgive himself.

Gritting his teeth against the anticipation of failure, he reached out and snagged a corner of her coat sleeve as she brushed past him. 'Wait!'

She yanked at the sleeve, and when she couldn't get him to release it, she simply dropped the coat on the floor and stumbled over it. Swearing, he stepped over the coat and managed to catch her wrist instead. 'Eve, please,' he said imploringly, forcing her to a standstill. 'You've got to give me a chance to explain.'

'What's to explain?' He could only marvel at the strength of will that forced her to lift her head and meet his gaze. 'I assume you think it's all right for a man to maul a woman he's supposed to have some respect for?'

'No!' Jake was appalled. 'Is that what he did?' He sought for a suitable way to describe it that didn't involve mentioning sex while he entertained methods of revenge all over again. 'I guess he—took advantage of you, right?'

Eve looked as if she didn't want to answer him. But then she blurted out painfully, 'He kissed me!'

She knew what he would think as soon as she said it. After all, what was a simple kiss between friends? How could she explain the outrage she'd felt when Harry had grabbed her and pressed his wet lips against hers without sounding paranoid? Jake knew nothing of her history. And she certainly had no intention of telling him now.

'He kissed you?' he echoed, and although he was trying to keep the incredulity out of his voice she knew it was there, just beneath the surface.

'Yes, he kissed me,' she said, trying to stare him out and not succeeding. 'I suppose you think that makes me some kind of a screwball, getting het-up over something so—so unimportant.'

Jake's eyes narrowed. 'But it wasn't unimportant to you,' he said, with more shrewdness than she'd given him credit for. 'Was it?'

Eve put up a nervous hand and tugged on a strand of hair that had escaped from her braid. 'It wasn't the kiss,' she admitted at last. 'It was what came after.' She didn't want to go on, but he had been kind and he deserved some kind of an explanation. 'He— Because I objected, he accused me of preferring someone else.'

Jake stared at her warily. Dammit, he'd been imagining she had few friends, holed up here with an argumentative old woman, but now it appeared that not only did she have an admirer, she apparently had more than one. It shouldn't, but it irritated the hell out of him.

'I see,' he said at last, and, realising he still had her wrist in a death grip, relaxed his hold. 'And do you? Prefer someone else?'

Eve's face flamed. 'No.'

'So you just—what? Don't like men in general?'

'No!' Eve snatched her wrist out of his grasp and rubbed it vigorously, as if to remove any trace of his scent from her skin. 'I just don't like being—touched.'

'I can see that.' Jake's voice was harsh to his ears, and he wondered if it was the unaccustomed amount of Scotch he'd consumed in a short time that was constricting his vocal cords. 'So, is this how you reacted when Murray touched you? Because I have to say it's damn demeaning to have someone behave as if you had some lethal infection.'

'I didn't.' Despite her efforts to maintain a semblance of composure, the accusation caught her on the raw. 'You don't understand.'

'So make me.'

'I can't.'

'Or won't.'

She shook her head. 'Why should you care about me?'

'Damned if I know, but I do.'

The atmosphere was suddenly electric. Jake didn't know if he was imagining it, or whether some chemical reaction had been activated by his words. Whatever—and with a lack of restraint he deplored later—he moved until there was barely an inch of space between them. Then, looking down into her startled face, he said thickly, 'Touch me. I promise I won't bite.'

Eve shook her head, but she didn't move away. 'This is crazy.'

'Agreed.' His eyes travelled lower, to the tantalising glimpse of olive skin exposed again above her navel. 'But just do it, eh?' He grimaced. 'To save my feelings if nothing else.'

Eve's breath came out in a rush. 'I don't believe anything I've done has hurt your feelings,' she said, the tip of her tongue appearing to moisten her lower lip. 'But if it has, I'm sorry.'

'Prove it.'

'How?'

How indeed? Jake hoped he wasn't being too ambitions in thinking he could cure something that had obviously been some years in the making. He had no real experience of phobias or psychological problems. He just sensed that whatever major hang-ups she had, they weren't going to go away by simply ignoring them.

'Come closer,' he said, hoping he wasn't being too optimistic in thinking he could control the situation.

Just standing close to her like this, inhaling the womanly scents of her body, was amazingly erotic. Images of the hot, steamy sex they could have shared if the circumstances had been different were enough to make him dizzy. And it was becoming increasingly hard to remember exactly who she was and why he was here.

'I think I should leave now,' she said abruptly, and Jake wondered if she'd read his mind. 'Thank you for—for listening to me. And you're right. I probably overreacted. In his defence, I have to say that Harry's never done anything to upset me before.'

To hell with Harry! Jake only just stopped himself from saying it out loud. He'd be happy if he never heard the man's name again.

'I don't recall saying you'd overreacted,' he said instead, his hands balling into fists at his sides. 'And I don't know what the bastard said, because you won't tell me me.'

'It wasn't important,' she insisted, taking a significant step back from him. Jake's hands rose almost automatically to prevent her from moving away.

'It was important enough to make you cry,' he reminded her savagely, and before he could prevent it his hands had settled on the bared skin at her waist.

He didn't know who was the most shocked—herself or him. He hadn't intended to touch her; dammit, she'd just spent the last fifteen minutes explaining that she didn't like to be touched. But as soon as his fingers met skin that was soft and warm and unbelievably smooth, any doubts he'd had about the sanity of what he was about to do went out of the window.

'Don't,' she said, the word torn from her lips, and he thought how pointless the protest was. In her agitation to avoid him her chest was heaving, and the hard peaks of her breasts were clearly visible beneath her tee shirt. She was irresistible, he thought. Irresistible and available. And, abandoning any attempt at playing the hero, he bent his head and covered her lips with his.

She tasted like heaven. That was his first thought. Her mouth was hot and deliciously vulnerable. Her breathing was uneven, short gasps that he inhaled deep into his lungs. She didn't touch him, even though he must have caught her off balance, but he couldn't ignore the fact that her breasts were crushed against his chest and her thighs were moving restlessly against his.

It wasn't the reaction he'd anticipated. He had to admit he'd expected her to fight him all the way. But, apart from feeling a little stiff, she acquiesced to his hungry kiss without obvious resistance. And he came to what he later realised was an arrogant conclusion that it wasn't being touched that bugged her, it was being touched by the wrong man.

The idea was exhilarating—the possibilities endless. Growing bolder, he slipped his tongue between her teeth and deepened the kiss. But his head swam with sudden dizziness as he explored her mouth, and he realised at once how weak he still was. He was swaying on his feet now, and he thanked God she hadn't tried to fight him off. If she had, he wouldn't have stood a chance.

His humiliation came swiftly and devastatingly. When he thought about it later he knew he should have guessed that nothing was ever that easy. Eve hadn't been acquiescent; she'd just been biding her time. The moment he showed his vulnerability, she was ready to strike.

He was shaking, his legs trembling with the effort of supporting his weight. He lifted his head, blinking in an effort to focus his swimming senses, and Eve immediately tried to take her revenge.

And she would have succeeded, too, if he hadn't chosen that moment to drag himself away from her. Bending forward, he was struggling to get his breath at the same moment that she brought her knee up between his legs. As it was, the crippling blow merely brushed its objective, but it was enough to send him staggering back against the desk.

He groaned, he remembered later, more because of his heaving lungs than her success. Nevertheless, she seemed to think she'd achieved what she'd wanted, and, snatching up her coat, she wrenched open the door and ran out of the room.

CHAPTER EIGHT

LIGHT filtering through a crack in the curtains got Eve out of bed. Dear God, she wondered, what time was it? It was usually still dark when she woke up.

Fumbling for her watch, she stumbled across to the windows and drew the curtain aside. Brilliant sunlight spilled into the room and a glance at her watch showed her that it was almost ten o'clock.

Ten o'clock! She was horrified. She'd overslept. Or rather, she hadn't. Remembering that she hadn't fallen asleep until well into the early hours, it was no wonder that she'd slept in.

Still, that didn't alter the fact that this was a working day—and, bearing in mind that Falconbridge Primary was due to close, she was hardly doing herself any favours by missing lessons. What kind of a report was that to put in her reference?

Downstairs, after a swift shower, Eve told the startled housekeeper that she wouldn't have time for breakfast. 'Oh, but Mr Romero said to let you sleep on,' Mrs Blackwood protested, and Eve felt an uneasy pang. What else had 'Mr Romero' told her? she wondered. And, in God's name, how was she supposed to face him after what had happened the night before?

'Where—where is Mr Romero?' she asked faintly, hoping she wouldn't have to see him before she left for school. Maybe almost twenty-four hours would be enough to blunt the memory of what she'd done.

What *she'd* done?

'Er—don't you know?' Mrs Blackwood was speaking again, and Eve tried to concentrate. 'I thought you must have said your goodbyes last evening. He left—' she glanced at the kitchen clock '—it must have been about half-past eight.'

'He left?' Eve was confused. 'What—you mean he's gone out?'

'He's gone back to London,' Mrs Blackwood informed her regretfully. 'I said I didn't think he was well enough to drive all that way, but he insisted he had to go. He must have had a call or something. On his mobile phone, you know. Maybe it was from Miss Cassie. Whatever—it was none of my business.'

'No.' Eve felt a sudden wave of depression sweep over her. 'Well, I'd better go and tell Ellie he's gone.'

'Oh, she knows,' said Mrs Blackwood airily. 'Mr Romero had a word with her before he left.' She pulled a face. 'Madam didn't approve, any more than I did, but what could she do? He was determined to go.'

Eve's shoulders sagged. 'I see.'

'Are you all right?' The housekeeper was looking at her anxiously now. 'You're very pale. Are you sure you're not coming down with the same complaint Mr Romero had?'

'You mean flu?' Eve could hear the irony in her voice. 'No, I'm all right. Just tired, that's all.'

'Well, you look after yourself,' advised Mrs Blackwood severely. 'And going without breakfast is a silly thing to do in the circumstances.'

'I'll get a coffee at school,' Eve assured her, hoping she wouldn't be too late for morning break. 'See you later.'

Despite the sunshine, it was still cold, and Eve walked briskly down the drive. She could have used her grandmother's Wolseley, but the old car was so cumbersome to handle that she usually preferred to walk. Besides, her mind was busy with other things, and she wouldn't have trusted herself behind the wheel of such a lethal weapon.

Depressingly, it didn't help to know that by leaving Romero had removed any embarrassment she might have felt at seeing him again. Despite what she'd thought earlier, deep inside she'd wanted to speak to him, to assure herself that she hadn't caused him any permanent damage by her reckless actions. Silly, perhaps, after the way he'd behaved, but she feared her punishment had been out of all proportion to his offence.

She caught her breath suddenly. Yet how could she feel that way? Compared to Jake Romero's, Harry's behaviour seemed almost innocent—his desire to prove his love for her the complete opposite of the other man's intentions.

So why did she care if she'd hurt him? If she'd really been revolted when Jake touched her, it shouldn't matter that she was never going to see him again.

But, unfortunately, it wasn't that simple. In her heart of hearts she knew that for the first time in her life she'd felt feelings stir inside her that she'd hardly known existed. And the truth was, if he hadn't shown how weak he was, how easy it would be for her to hurt him, she actually might have given in.

But to what? After all these years of keeping men at arm's length, did she really know? Oh, she knew about sex, about what a man wanted and how far he was prepared to go to get it, but even she could see that what had happened the night before had been nothing like that.

She really knew nothing about consensual sex, about consensual relationships—the kind Cassie had with her many conquests, for example. The kind she'd had—was still having—with Jake Romero.

Eve shivered. If nothing else, that should convince her that she'd made the right decision. Whatever Romero had wanted, it was not something she could supply, and she ought to be glad that he'd left before she did something she'd regret.

All the same, that didn't stop her from thinking about him during the endless day that followed.

Mrs Portman was unexpectedly understanding when Eve explained, truthfully, that she'd slept badly and that that was why she was late. But Eve could have wished that she'd ranted and raved and given her something else to worry about instead of what might have been.

The memory of how she'd felt when Jake kissed her followed her into her sleep for that night and many nights to come. And no matter how rational she could be in daylight hours, her subconscious persisted in relieving the sensuous brush of his aroused body against hers and the consuming hunger of his mouth.

Jake went home for Christmas. Alone.

Since his return to London at the end of November he'd succeeded in avoiding any intimate meetings with Cassandra. And, although she expressed her irritation in frequent phone calls, usually late at night after she'd finished at the television studios, thankfully the producers of the tri-weekly soap were pleased with her, and that had mollified her complaints.

For his part, Jake had no sensible explanation for his sudden aversion to her company. Oh, sure, he hadn't liked the way she treated her mother, but he'd never before considered familial loyalties a prerequisite in a girlfriend. His abortive first marriage had taught him that families could be both a blessing and a curse, and since then he'd avoided all attempts to introduce that kind of complication to a relationship.

So why had he agreed to go to Northumberland with Cassandra? A less cynical observer than himself might contend that the visit had been preordained, that it was the only way he could have met Eve, but he wasn't prepared to accept that theory. For God's sake, the girl had hated him on sight, and after the way she'd reacted to his lovemaking there was no earthly reason why he should want to see her again.

But he did.

Which was one of the reasons why he went back to San Felipe for Christmas. Not the main reason, he assured himself. That had to do with still feeling hungover from his dose of flu and needing some well-deserved sunshine after too many weeks spent in Europe in winter.

Even so, he hadn't intended to go. The British Boat Show was held at the beginning of January, and it would have been far more sensible to wait until it was over before returning home. As it was, he condemned himself to two long-haul flights in less than two weeks, and aroused Cassandra's fury for not thinking about her at all.

Not that her feelings had been high on his agenda of things to consider when he'd been planning his trip. On the contrary, his thoughts had been filled with images of another young woman, spending the holiday season in a cold and inhospitable climate with only two elderly women for company.

And Harry Murray, he reminded himself savagely. After the way he'd behaved, she'd probably revised her opinion of the sainted vicar of St Mary's.

He arrived back from his short holiday to find a handful of messages from Cassandra waiting for him at his hotel. Evidently she'd been calling him for the past three days.

He stuffed the slips the receptionist gave him into his pocket, deciding he'd read them when he wasn't depressed and jet-lagged. Right now, all he wanted was a shower, a stiff drink and his bed, in that order, and anything Cassandra had to say could surely wait until the following morning.

Despite the fact that it was only the middle of the morning, Jake took a shower, drew his curtains, poured himself a half-tumbler of Scotch from the bottle the Room Service waiter had left on the table, and tumbled into bed.

He fell asleep immediately for once, and he wasn't best pleased when less than an hour later the phone beside his bed shrilled its strident tone.

'Dammit!' he muttered, trying to reach the receiver without lifting his head from the pillow. But all he succeeded in doing was knocking it to the floor, and, swearing again, he hauled himself up and down. 'Yeah?' he said, when he got the handset to his ear. 'This had better be good.'

'Jake? Darling? Is that you?'

Cassandra! Jake scowled and flung himself back on his pillows. He might have known. He should have told the receptionist to hold all calls until the following day. As it was, short of lying to her, he could hardly deny he was there.

'Cassandra,' he said, hoping she would hear the censure in his voice. 'I was going to ring you later.' Liar! 'When I got up.'

'Oh.' She seemed nonplussed for a moment. 'You're in bed? But it's eleven-thirty in the morning.'

'It's only five-thirty in San Felipe,' he said, holding onto his temper with an effort. 'I just got back.'

'Oh, yes. I know. The receptionist at the hotel told me you were expected back today.'

'Really?' Jake would have a word with the receptionist concerned when he had the chance.

'Yes, really.' Cassandra didn't seem to notice the edge in his tone. 'I suppose she felt sorry for me. I've been trying to reach you for days. I thought you said you'd be back on the second?'

'It's only the fifth,' said Jake tersely. 'I got a later flight.'

'Yes.' Cassandra hesitated a moment. 'So—you're in bed at this minute?'

'I think I just said so.'

'Well, would you like me to come round, then? I could give you a massage. Did I tell you? One of the girls in the soap is really into shiatsu, and she's been teaching me all the moves. She says I have great potential—'

'Cassandra.' Jake interrupted her. 'Why did you ring? I can't believe you woke me up to tell me how good you are at some freakin' Japanese massage crap! For God's sake, you left enough messages. I thought there must have been a minor disaster, or something. Instead of which—'

'Mummy's had a stroke,' Cassandra broke in before he could finish, and suddenly every nerve in Jake's body was on high alert. 'It happened on Christmas Eve—can you believe it? I would have told you sooner, but you were away and your mobile was switched off.'

Deliberately, thought Jake grimly. But he was stunned at the news. He could hardly believe that the feisty old lady had suffered a serious attack. She'd seemed so tough, so indomitable. And Eve... How must Eve be feeling? He'd sensed she had real affection for her employer.

'How is she?' he demanded, fully awake now, swinging his bare feet to the floor. 'I assume you've seen her?'

There was silence for a long moment, and Jake was on

the verge of telling her to get a move on when she said, 'Actually, I haven't.'

'You haven't seen her?'

'No,' said Cassandra hurriedly. 'I would have made the trip, you know I would, but she'll be all right. It's not left her paralysed or anything. Eve said she had a bit of, you know, numbness to begin with, but that soon wore off. And it hasn't stopped her from talking—'

Jake blew out a breath. 'I can't believe you haven't been to see her,' he said, aghast. 'Dammit, Cassandra, strokes can be fatal.'

'I know that.' She was defensive now.

'And you didn't think you had a duty to go and see how she was for yourself?' Jake was appalled. 'Cassandra, people need their family around them at a time like this.'

'I know.' Cassandra was sulky. 'But she's got Eve, hasn't she?'

'Eve!' Jake snorted. 'Yeah, that's another story. You didn't think she might appreciate a bit of support, too?'

'Eve doesn't need my support.'

'You mean she's never been offered it.'

Cassandra gasped. 'What do you mean by that? What's she been telling you?'

'Eve hasn't told me anything,' retorted Jake shortly, aware that he had his own faults where Eve was concerned. 'I just think it's a lot to expect of a girl barely out of her teens. Particularly someone whose relationship to your mother is tenuous, to say the least.'

'Oh!' Was that relief in Cassandra's voice? 'Well, you could be right.' She paused. 'But she's not as young as you think, you know. She's twenty-five.'

'She's still a girl,' said Jake flatly. Then, deciding he was in danger of arousing her suspicions again, he said, 'Is Mrs Robertson in Newcastle Hospital?'

'Oh, she's not in hospital,' exclaimed Cassandra at once, as if that somehow exonerated her of much of the blame. 'She's at home.'

'At Watersmeet?'

'Where else?'

'So who's looking after her?'

Cassandra expelled a resentful sigh. 'Well—Eve and Mrs Blackwood, I expect. Eve has been on holiday since it happened.'

'From school, you mean?'

'Of course. You didn't think she'd gone dashing off to some exotic destination as you did?'

'I went home,' Jake reminded her. 'And why shouldn't Eve go on holiday if she wants to? She's entitled to a break, just like anybody else.'

'Not when Mummy's ill,' protested Cassandra brusquely, and then seemed to realise she'd condemned herself out of her own mouth. 'Oh—well, she wouldn't anyway. Eve doesn't do things like that.'

'No.' Jake conceded the point. He had the feeling there were a lot of things Eve didn't do, and he badly wanted to know why.

'Anyway—' Cassandra seemed to think it would be all right to change the subject now '—when am I going to see you?'

You're kidding, right?

For one awful moment Jake thought he'd said the words out loud, but it soon became obvious from Cassandra's anticipation that he hadn't. 'I—' He sought for an answer. 'Let me get back to you on that. Right now I've just got back from San Felipe and I'm pretty tied up.'

'Oh.' Cassandra's response was predictably terse. 'So you don't want to hear my news, then?'

Jake stifled a sigh. 'I thought I just did.'

'No.' Cassandra sniffed. 'I mean *my* news. About my part in *Evermore*.' She paused, evidently waiting for him to respond, and when he didn't she went on resentfully, 'Honestly, I thought you'd be pleased to hear that the preliminary showings—you know, to the press and the executives and so on—have all been positive, and I've been offered a three-month extension of my contract.'

'Great.' Jake wondered how she could consider that more important than her mother's health. 'So you'll be working in London for the foreseeable future?'

'Yes. Marvellous, isn't it? Whenever you're in town, I'll be available.'

I'll just bet you will, thought Jake sourly, not really understanding why her callous attitude should matter so much to him. Okay, so he'd really liked her mother, but so what? He couldn't make himself responsible for Cassandra's shortcomings.

No, the truth was, it was Eve he was concerned about. Eve—who'd been expected to bear the whole weight of the old lady's illness. And it was because of Eve that he was considering how soon he could ditch his schedule and take a flight up to Northumberland.

CHAPTER NINE

IT WAS late when Jake reached Watersmeet. He'd managed to get an afternoon flight, but what with it being an hour late, and the complications of renting a hire car, it was after six when he reached Falconbridge.

There were lights, as before, in the downstairs windows of the house, though this time the curtains were drawn. The arrival of his Ford, which had been all that was on offer, had apparently gone unnoticed, and Jake got out and locked the car before approaching the door.

Once again it was bitterly cold, but this time he was prepared for it. He'd bought himself a cashmere overcoat at Heathrow before boarding the plane, and although he hadn't bothered to fasten it, it was still incredibly warm.

A strange man opened the door to his knock, and Jake gazed at him with wary eyes. Who the hell was this? It couldn't be the Reverend Murray, could it? Had the bastard wheedled his way back into Eve's good graces while Mrs Robertson had been ill? He hoped to God he wasn't here because the old lady had taken a turn for the worse.

'Yes? Can I help you?'

There was such confidence in the man's tone that Jake revised his opinion. Besides, Eve had said Murray was a young man, whereas this guy had to be fifty if he was a day. The doctor, perhaps?

'Er—my name's Romero.' Dammit, this was awkward. He hadn't prepared for this eventuality. 'I'm a friend of—' He could hardly say *the family* so he compromised. 'Of Mrs Robertson's daughter.'

'Yeah? Cass.' The man didn't sound impressed. 'Well, she's not here.'

'I know that—'

'Who is it, Adam?'

Jake heard Eve's voice before he saw her, and he was amazed at the sudden clenching he felt in his gut at the sound. God, he was actually apprehensive of seeing her again, apprehensive of how she'd react when she saw him.

The man—Adam?—half turned at her approach, and because her attention was on him Jake had a moment to absorb her appearance before she noticed him.

She looked tired, he thought at once, the smoky eyes rimmed with dark circles. It was obvious that she hadn't been sleeping well; worried about the old lady, no doubt, unlike Cassandra. Even her hair wasn't neatly plaited, as it had been before. Instead, it was drawn back with a simple ribbon that allowed strands of silky dark hair to stray over the shoulders of the baggy beige cardigan she was wearing.

It made her look younger, he thought, feeling the pull of an attraction that was as insistent as it was out of place. Unlike the cardigan, which had to be a cast-off of the old lady's. It successfully covered her from shoulder to hip, its bulky folds hiding the womanly shape he knew was beneath.

'Jake—Mr Romero!' She'd seen him now, and her eyes had widened in disbelief. 'What are you doing here? Is—?' She looked beyond him. 'Is Cassie with you?'

'No—'

It wasn't the welcome he could have wished for, but it wasn't unexpected. However, before he could explain, the other man intervened. 'You know him?' he asked in some surprise. 'I was just telling him Cassie's not here.'

'I knew that.' Jake had a struggle to keep the edge out

of his voice, but he had no intention of letting this guy screw up his reasons for being here. 'May I come in?'

Eve glanced at the man beside her and then stepped back. 'I expect so,' she said, though there was little enthusiasm in her voice. 'I gather you're on your own. Did Cassie send you?'

'No, she—didn't,' he said, biting back a choice epithet with an effort. He stepped over the threshold, ignoring Adam's grudging stare, and breathed a sigh of relief when the door closed behind him. 'So—how is the old lady?'

Eve looked surprised. 'You know she's been ill?'

Jake sighed. 'Obviously.'

'So Cassie *did* send you?'

'No!'

'But she knows you're here?'

Jake shook his head. 'No to that, too.'

'Then how did you—?'

'I've spoken to Cassandra,' Jake put in levelly. 'That's all.'

Eve looked as if she was having some trouble in taking this in, and Adam seemed to decide that he deserved to know what was going on.

'Who is this chap, Eve?' he asked, giving Jake a suspicious look. 'I thought he said he was a friend of Cassie's?'

'He is.'

Eve couldn't blame him for being confused. She was having a struggle dealing with Jake's arrival herself, and it was difficult to be objective when just seeing him again had thrown all her carefully won indifference into chaos.

He looked so good, she thought, unconsciously pressing a hand to the suddenly hollow place beneath her ribs. In a long camel-coloured overcoat, open over black jeans and a matching sweater, and low-heeled black boots on his feet, he looked even better than she remembered, and she desperately wanted to tell him how glad she was to see him.

But of course she couldn't do that. Apart from the fact that Adam was standing watching him, with a look of wary speculation on his face, Jake was still Cassie's property, not hers.

'So if he's Cassie's—friend—' Jake didn't miss the deliberate emphasis Adam laid on that word '—and he says he knew Cass wasn't here, why the hell has he come?'

'You could start by asking me,' Jake observed pleasantly, even though he itched to make his own contribution to the aggression in the atmosphere. Forcing himself to concentrate on Eve instead, he said, 'How is Mrs Robertson. You didn't say.'

'My mother's fairly fit, considering,' Adam answered for her, and the relief he felt at discovering that Adam wasn't some unknown admirer but Cassandra's brother made Jake feel ridiculously euphoric. 'What's it to you?'

'Adam, you don't understand—'

'I stayed here for a few days last November,' Jake informed him smoothly, overriding Eve's protest. 'With your sister, as it happens. I got to know your mother then. I liked her, and when Cassandra said—'

'Who?'

'Cassandra.' Jake was patient. He'd already realised that her family never used her formal name. 'When she told me her mother had had a stroke, I was concerned.'

'Unlike Cassie,' said Adam tersely. 'That's her real name, by the way. Cassandra's just an affectation she uses when she's acting.'

'Adam—'

Once again Eve tried to intervene, but Adam wasn't having any. 'I still don't get it,' he persisted, glancing sideways at her. 'Is there something going on here that I should know about?'

'No!' Eve's denial was heartfelt, and Jake, who had had no intention of discussing his actions with Adam, guessed that a less arrogant man than himself would have taken that as his cue to get out of there. But he didn't. Giving him a covert look from beneath her lashes, she added, 'Look, why don't we all go into the library? It'll be warmer in there, and we can at least offer Mr Romero a drink, Adam.'

Adam shrugged his bulky shoulders. In appearance he was a lot more like his mother than his sister was, and it was obvious he resented the intrusion of a man he considered little more than Cassandra's—Cassie's—latest admirer. But he didn't argue, which impressed Jake. Evidently Eve's opinion carried more weight in this household than he'd imagined.

And it *was* infinitely warmer in the library. Looking about him, Jake was amazed at how much he remembered of this room, at how familiar it was. And memorable, he thought ruefully. He'd been standing right there when he'd done the unforgivable and kissed Eve. Poor fool that he was, he'd thought he could comfort her. That as soon as he laid his hands on her she'd realise what she'd been missing all along. Yeah, right.

Instead of that she'd stamped on his manhood and his self-respect, and he'd only just got away with saving his dignity.

'Would you like Scotch?'

Eve had moved to the drinks cabinet and was looking at him, and Jake gave her what he hoped was an encouraging smile. 'Great,' he said. Then, remembering he was driving, 'Just a small one, please. Over ice, if you have it.'

Adam snorted. He'd made his way across to the hearth and was now standing warming his back in front of the blazing fire. 'Waste of good whisky, if you ask me,' he muttered. 'Who ruins a good drop of Scotch with ice?'

'I do,' said Jake, determined not to let the other man rile him. 'Do you live in the village, Mr Robertson?'

'No.' Adam's bushy brows drew together above a bulbous nose as he spoke. 'I've got a farm further up the valley. Didn't Cass tell you?'

In actual fact, Cassandra—Cass—had told him very little about her family. Which had suited him very well. But after introducing him to her mother, she might have mentioned that she had a brother in the area, too.

'Did you drive up from London today?'

Eve was speaking, evidently realising that Adam was bent on being objectionable and trying to keep the peace.

'No. I took a flight to Newcastle,' Jake answered easily. 'I rented a car at the airport.'

'To come here?' said Adam unpleasantly. 'How sweet.'

Jake wondered if the man had a death wish. Right now he was having a hard time keeping his temper with the evidence of Eve's exhaustion there in front of his eyes. Did this guy have any conception that she appeared to be bearing the whole burden of the old lady's illness? What contribution had *he* made, apart from behaving like the ignorant lout he was?

'Ellie will be pleased to see you,' said Eve hurriedly, once again trying to lighten the mood. 'She's been virtually confined to her room since her illness. She'll be delighted to see a fresh face.'

'And such a pretty face,' said Adam sarcastically, clearly under the impression that Jake wouldn't—or couldn't—retaliate.

But this time Jake had had enough. 'Have you got a

problem with me being here?' he demanded, ignoring Eve's automatic attempt to come between them. 'Stay out of this,' he advised her, keeping his attention focussed on the other man. 'Well? Have you?'

Adam blustered. 'That's not the point.'

'Then what is?' Jake was intimidating in this mood, and Eve realised her uncle had definitely underestimated him. 'As I understand it, you don't own this house. So you don't have any say over who comes or goes, right?'

Adam was clearly agitated, but he stood his ground. 'Well, *she* doesn't,' he snorted, gesturing towards Eve. 'It's not her house, either.'

Which was a perfectly pointless thing to say, in Jake's opinion. Dammit, he knew it wasn't Eve's house. She only worked here. Despite what Cassandra had said about her being a distant relative, she was obviously treated more like a housemaid than a member of the family.

'He knows that, Adam,' Eve protested, putting a glass into Jake's hand now, as if that would prevent him from shoving his fist in the other man's fleshy face. 'For goodness' sake, what's wrong with you? Mr Romero's a guest, not an intruder. And, whether you like it or not, Ellie likes him.'

Adam grunted. 'If you say so.'

'I do say so.' Eve gave him a glass, too. 'Now, drink your drink and stop behaving like an idiot.'

'Who are you calling an idiot?' Adam was indignant, but Jake was amazed to see a reluctant smile tugging at the corners of his mouth. He gave a Jake a grudging look and then added gruffly, 'Sorry. But Cass's admirers usually rub me up the wrong way.'

Jake was taken aback. He'd never expected the man to apologise, and he supposed he should feel grateful to Eve for rescuing the situation. But he didn't. He was put out now, and he badly wanted to take his frustration out on someone.

Speaking between his teeth, he said, 'I guess this has been a rough time for both of you. Eve certainly looks as if she's borne the brunt of it.'

'Jake!'

Eve used his name without thinking, but he barely had time to register his approval before Adam said, 'I've got a farm to run, Mr Romero. A hundred and fifty acres and two hundred head of cattle that need milking twice a day. Doesn't leave me much time for anything else.'

'Then perhaps you ought to have thought of employing an agency nurse to look after your mother?' retorted Jake, swallowing half his Scotch in one gulp. 'Eve's not a servant, you know.'

'I know that.' Adam's voice rose an octave, but then he seemed to think better of tangling with the younger man. 'Anyway, what's it to you? Eve's big enough to make her own complaints if she wants to.'

'For goodness' sake!' It was Eve who spoke. 'Will you two stop behaving as if I wasn't here? I was quite happy to look after Ellie, Mr Romero. And Adam would have hired a nurse if I'd asked him to. As it is, he's going to take her to recuperate at the farm for a couple of weeks, so I can have a rest. Okay?'

Jake's jaw compressed. 'Is that true?'

'What? That Ellie's going to the farm for a couple of weeks?' Eve sighed. 'Yes, it is, as it happens. Adam's wife used to be a nurse, so she's quite capable of looking after her. Satisfied?'

He blew out a breath. 'I guess so.'

'Good.'

Eve sipped at the diet cola she'd poured for herself and hoped her words had defused the situation. Her earlier excitement at seeing Jake again had been dissipated by the atmosphere he and Adam had created, but that was probably just as well. Nevertheless, she was left with the uneasy awareness that she had let her feelings blind her to the real dangers here. She didn't honestly know why Jake had come. She could only take his words about her grandmother at face value. But she knew that whatever he said, whatever he wanted of her, she couldn't allow a momentary madness to develop into something even more destructive.

'Look, I'm going up to say goodbye to my mother before I leave,' Adam said suddenly, crossing the room to deposit his empty glass on the tray. He turned to Jake. 'Why don't you come up and see her? As Eve says, she'll probably be glad to have someone different to talk to.'

Jake only hesitated a moment. Despite the fact that he'd been waiting for Adam to leave so that he could speak to Eve alone, he couldn't ignore the olive branch the other man was extending.

'Thanks,' he said stiffly. 'I'd like that.'

When they'd gone, Eve breathed a sigh of relief. For a moment there she'd thought Jake was going to refuse— and how could she have explained that to her uncle? As it was, she just hoped their armistice would last as long as it took to visit Ellie and convince her that Jake's only reason for coming here had been to assure himself that she'd suffered no ill effects from the attack.

And it was probably true, Eve thought, gathering the dirty glasses onto a tray and carrying it to the door. After all, it was hardly flattering to know that the main thing he'd noticed about her was how tired she looked. As compared to Cassie, she assumed, her lips tightening with sudden pain. So what was new?

Jake hadn't come down when she returned to the li-

brary, and, unwilling to sit there waiting for him, Eve
decided to go out to the stables. She knew Storm Dancer
would already be safe in her stall. Mick, the man Mr
Trivett employed to do all the odd jobs around the estate,
would have seen to that. But she always gained a certain
amount of comfort from the mare's company, and hope-
fully Jake would get the message and leave before she got
back.

Storm Dancer was munching happily from her feed bag
when Eve rested her folded arms along the rails of her
stall. The mare looked up, but she didn't come to greet
her, and Eve guessed that even the promise of an apple
wouldn't distract her from her food.

'Your loss, old girl,' Eve said, and with a rueful smile
she glanced behind her. There was a neat stack of straw
bales piled against the wall opposite, and she pulled a
couple down to make a seat.

Watching the mare was almost as soothing to her ruffled nerves as grooming her would be, and, propping her
elbows on her knees, Eve cupped her chin in her hands.

She guessed she must have been sitting there for fifteen
minutes when she became aware that she was no longer
alone. Jake was leaning with folded arms against the
empty stall next to Storm Dancer's. His booted feet were
crossed at the ankle and there was a disturbingly intent
look on his lean, dark face.

The fact that he'd entered the stables without her hearing him caused her no small measure of unease. Her
thoughts had obviously been miles away, and anyone
could have come into the isolated building and surprised
her.

'Hi,' he said, when she looked up and saw him, and a
quiver of awareness stirred in her belly. But when she
would have got to her feet, he waved her back. 'Stay

where you are,' he said, straightening from the rail and coming towards her. 'I'll join you. This is as good a place as any to talk.'

Eve shifted a little uncertainly. 'I ought to be getting back.'

'Why?'

Why indeed?

'I'm cold,' she said, the facile excuse the first that occurred to her. 'I've been sitting here too long.'

'Don't I know it?' Jake seated himself on the bale beside her and took off his coat, draping its soft folds about her shoulders. It was still warm from his body, still smelled of his distinctive scent. The beautiful garment trailed carelessly on the stable floor, but he didn't seem to notice. 'I've been waiting for you to come back.'

Eve shivered, but not with the cold. 'How did you know where I was?'

'Mrs Blackwood said I'd probably find you here,' he replied, his breath warm against her cheek. 'She gave me strict instructions on how to find you.' His eyes dropped to her mouth. 'I didn't like to tell her I already knew.'

Eve's breathing quickened. 'I thought you'd leave as soon as you'd spoken to Ellie. After the way Adam treated you, I'd have expected you'd want to get as far from here as possible.'

'You wish?' he murmured, his voice low and vaguely suggestive, awakening all those unfamiliar feelings inside her again. 'Is that why you've been sitting out here? Because you were hoping to avoid seeing me again.'

Yes!

'No.' Eve thought she sounded at least half convincing. 'Why should you think that?'

His mouth compressed. 'You know why.' He paused.

'I suppose I should apologise. I had no right to try and kiss you.'

Eve's throat felt tight with suppressed emotion. 'I shouldn't have reacted as I did,' she said. Then, with a nervous sideways glance, 'Did I hurt you?'

His mouth twitched. 'If I said you did, what would you do about it? Kiss it better?'

Eve's face flamed, but when she would have got to her feet Jake's hand on her knee prevented her. 'I'm sorry,' he said ruefully. 'I shouldn't have said that. Will you forgive me?'

He could feel her knee trembling beneath his hand, and he cursed himself for a fool. He'd already guessed that at some time some man had hurt her badly, and if he wanted to see her again he had to stop crowding her.

'Look,' he said, resisting the urge to slide his hand further up her thigh, 'can't we put the past behind us and start again?'

Eve's lips parted. 'There's nothing to start again, Mr Romero!' she exclaimed, and Jake thought he could willingly drown in the limpid beauty of her eyes. 'I think you're getting me mixed up with Cassandra.'

'No, I'm not.' Jake disliked the sound of that woman's name on her lips. 'I've thought of little else but you ever since I left here.'

Eve tensed. 'You're joking, right?'

'It's the truth.'

'Oh, right.' She was sceptical. 'So I'm supposed to believe that all the time you were making love to Cassandra you were really thinking of me? How sick is that?'

'I haven't had sex with Cassandra,' he snapped, resenting her sarcasm. He made an impatient gesture. 'What kind of a creep do you think I am?'

'I don't have an opinion, Mr Romero,' she replied

primly, irritating him anew with her refusal to use his given name. 'I hardly know you.'

'We could remedy that.' Despite his intention to move slowly, Jake allowed his fingers to stroke the inner curve of her knee. A nerve jumped against his hand and he felt the immediate quiver of apprehension that rippled over her at his touch. 'I want to.'

'Well, I don't,' said Eve, but her mouth was dry and she knew it wasn't quite the truth. His nearness was having a totally unprecedented effect on her senses, and although she wanted to dislodge his hand from her knee, curiosity—and an undeniable temptation—kept her from doing it.

'Don't you?' He leant closer and she felt his tongue stroke her ear. 'Are you sure about that?'

'Jake!' His name was a cry of protest, but when she turned her head to avoid his tongue she found his face only inches from hers.

And something shifted deep inside her—something that kept her staring at him when she knew she shouldn't be doing this, shouldn't be as close as this to any man, and particularly not this man.

His eyes were dark, and dilated to such an extent that she could hardly see any whiteness at all. And, although she was sure he must have shaved that morning, already there was a shadow of stubble on his jawline.

He had such a beautiful face, she thought, which was a crazy thought to have about someone who was so essentially male. But his was a hard beauty, his eyes deep, his mouth thin yet so sinfully sensual that any woman would be entranced.

A fine tremor ran though her which must have communicated itself to him, because he lifted his hand and allowed his knuckles to graze her cheek.

The tremor became an earthquake, and Eve felt her resistance ebbing as the shaking in her shoulders spread to the rest of her body. Her breathing was shallow, yet she could hear her heart pounding in her ears. She was transfixed. Yet how could that be when inside she felt as if a series of electrical explosions was tearing her apart?

His thumb moved to brush roughly across her lips and her tongue went instinctively to meet it. He tasted as good as he looked, she thought, and, as if sensing her submission, he pressed harder, causing her lips to part. And, God forgive her, she curled her tongue around him and sucked his thumb into her mouth.

She heard the catch of his breathing, the quickening of the pulse that beat against her tongue. He was watching her with a heavy-lidded intensity that even she knew was different than before, and the feelings inside her expanded to consume every part of her being.

She needed to touch him, and her hands rose almost jerkily to grasp the soft fabric of his sweater, as if by holding on to him she could control this madness inside. Beneath the wool, the heat of his skin rose to meet her clutching fingers, and she desperately wanted to burrow beneath his sweater and press herself against the hard flesh of his body.

'God, I want you,' he said, his voice hoarse and unsteady, and Eve could only gaze up at him, unconsciously inviting him to go on.

His hand settled at the back of her neck, under the soft mane of her hair, his touch warm and heavy, angling her head to his. His kiss when it came was different, too, hard and deliberate, taking as well as giving, as if he was afraid she was going to run out on him again before it was over.

But she didn't. She couldn't. The fire of that kiss had

burned away any resistance, igniting a path clear down to her groin so that her legs fell helplessly apart.

She didn't realise that Storm Dancer had finished feeding and was now standing watching them with soft, uncritical eyes. She was barely conscious of anything but Jake's needs, Jake's heat, the hungry pressure of his tongue forcing its way into her mouth.

He kissed her many times, over and over, until she was weak and clinging to him. He urged her back against the straw bales behind her and her breasts ached with the pressure he was putting on them, but she didn't care. He'd wedged one thigh between hers, so that there was no way she could avoid feeling his arousal. His shaft throbbed against her leg and she shuddered with the awareness of how big he was, how hard and male and virile—and dangerously out of control.

'Do you have any idea how long I've wanted to do this?' he demanded thickly, releasing her mouth only to nip her earlobe, to bite the yielding flesh of her throat. 'I knew you'd be beautiful and you are.'

'I'm—not —beautiful,' she protested unsteadily, but he wasn't listening to her. He'd parted the heavy cardigan to expose the thin vest that was all she was wearing underneath. He seemed entranced by the swollen globes of her breasts and, pushing the vest aside, his cold hands sought and released the catch of her bra.

Eve's head swam when her breasts spilled into his hands. His thumbs had found the sensitised peaks that had surged against his palms, and she ached now with needs of her own. There was a tingling in her stomach and a throbbing wetness between her legs that she'd definitely never felt before. She felt alive and desirable, and, clutching his face with both hands, she brought his mouth back to hers.

'Easy, baby,' he murmured against her lips, and Eve trembled. How could she take it easy when it was all so new, so exciting, so different from anything she'd ever experienced before? His tongue was making sensuous forays into her mouth, aping what he wanted to do to her body, and for the first time she faced the possibility of a man's lovemaking without fear or disgust.

'We've got all night,' he whispered, easing her back until she was practically lying on the bales, his hand sliding down to cup her mound through the tight cotton of her jeans. 'No one's going to interrupt us.''

No one, mused Eve dizzily. No one—not even Cassie. Cassie…

Eve's throat constricted. The thought was a chilling one. It reminded her of who Jake was, how she had met him. Dear God, what was she thinking, allowing this to happen? Was she so bemused by her own discovered sexuality that she was prepared to make love to a man who, by his own admission, was still seeing the other woman? A man who, by every law of decency, was forbidden to her?

He had bent his head and was about to take one engorged nipple into his mouth when Eve uttered a strangled denial. 'No,' she said, a very real panic giving her voice the edge of hysteria. 'No. No, you can't. You don't understand.' Wriggling out from under him, she hurriedly pulled the folds of her cardigan together and faced him with wide, agonised eyes. 'We can't do this. I can't do this. It wouldn't be right.'

Jake stared at her. Despite the fact that he was very obviously aroused, and his expression mirrored the frustration he was feeling, his voice was unnaturally quiet when he said, 'This is about Cassandra, isn't it? You think that because Cassandra introduced us—'

'No. No, it's not that.'

Eve moved her head frantically from side to side, but Jake's patience wasn't infinite. 'What, then?' he asked, his voice hardening a little. 'I've told you I'm not interested in Cassandra. Okay, so I know she's a relative of yours, but that can't be helped. She'll get over it.'

'No! No, she won't.'

The panic was rising in Eve's voice now, and Jake seemed to realise there was more than simple anxiety about a distant cousin going on here. 'What, then?' he said again, controlling his temper with an obvious effort. 'Why do we need to concern ourselves with what she thinks? She's not your keeper, is she?'

'She's my mother,' said Eve, her chest heaving with emotion. 'Now do you see why I can't have anything more to do with you? She's my *mother*!'

CHAPTER TEN

JAKE drove back to London in the foulest of moods. He left without seeing Eve again, driving through the night, arriving back at his hotel in the early hours of the morning.

He knew he'd have some kind of penalty to pay for bringing the rental car back to London, but financial concerns weren't of much interest to him in his present state of mind. He was angry—and gutted. He couldn't believe he'd been crazy enough to fall for Cassandra's *daughter*. Cassandra's daughter, for God's sake! No wonder there was no love lost between the two of them.

Or between Cassandra and her mother, he appended, remembering the conversation he'd had with the old lady before he left. For pity's sake, what kind of monster had he been dealing with? What kind of woman abandoned her kid without even telling her own mother that she'd had a child?

He'd got the story from the old lady, of course. Eve hadn't told him anything. After delivering her bombshell, she hadn't hung around to answer any questions. Even though he'd insisted that she couldn't say something like that without making some form of explanation, she'd refused to offer any excuses for her behaviour.

Like why she hadn't told him she was Cassandra's daughter before now. Oh, he wasn't a fool. Not a complete one, he hoped. It was obvious Cassandra had never acknowledged her daughter, and for some reason Eve was prepared to go along with that; to the extent that she'd let him think she was only there through Mrs Robertson's good graces.

Mrs Robertson! Jake ground his teeth together. Dammit, the woman Eve called Ellie was her *grandmother*! Whose idea had it been to hide their relationship? Surely not the old lady's? Without her intervention, Eve—

But he refused to think about that now. Not when there was nothing he could do about it. But as soon as it was light he intended to go and see Cassandra, and have her version of the story. There was no way he could put this to bed without hearing the truth from her.

The words he'd used mocked him. How the hell was he going to 'put this to bed', whatever Cassandra said? His feelings for Eve weren't going to go away that easily, if at all. No matter how often he reminded himself that she'd deceived him just as much as her mother had, he couldn't get her out of his mind.

He wanted her. No. More than that. He wanted to be with her. He wanted to take her in his arms and finish what they'd started a few hours ago—in the stables, of all places. And the knowledge that she'd spurned him was tearing him apart.

Yet he mustn't forget she was Cassandra's daughter. And how could any daughter of that woman ever be anything but trouble? If he had any sense he'd be grateful he'd found out in time, before he'd done something irrevocable. Like making love to her, for example. He had the feeling that if he'd ever possessed her body, if he'd ever found his release with her, there would have been no way for him to escape his demons.

He felt raw, he thought bitterly. Raw and frustrated. Desperate to make someone else suffer as he was suffering now. It was a new experience for him, and one he had no intention of allowing to happen again.

It was still barely three o'clock in the morning, and despite the adrenalin in his system that had enabled him to drive almost three hundred miles without even a break he was exhausted. He had to remember he'd hardly slept the night before, and although the time change between here and San Felipe had given him a little breathing space, his own limitations were catching up with him.

He needed to rest, and, stripping off his clothes, he crawled into bed without even taking a shower. He wanted nothing to refresh him, nothing to get his mind working again. But although he closed his eyes he remained wide awake.

The image of Eve's face as he'd last seen her drifted between him and the nirvana he sought. He could still taste her on his tongue, still smell her womanly fragrance on his hands, still feel her hands reaching for him, her mouth opening for his hungry invasion...

God! He groaned, rolling over and burying his hot face in the pillow. No matter who she was, no matter how she'd treated him, he still wanted her. The hard-on he had just wasn't going to go away, and he knew if he was ever going to get any sleep he would have to do something about it himself.

It didn't work. Not immediately, anyway. He just felt cold, and disgusted with himself for letting it happen. But eventually sleep overwhelmed him, and when he opened his eyes again it was daylight.

He ordered coffee and toast from Room Service, and then took a shower in the time it took for his breakfast to be delivered.

With several doses of caffeine and a couple of slices of toast filling the empty space inside him, he felt a little better. After dressing, he went downstairs and arranged with the concierge for the Ford to be delivered to wherever the rental company wanted, and then left the hotel.

It was still only a little after nine o'clock, and he'd expected Cassandra would be at the studios. However, after ringing her number and ascertaining she was still at her apartment, he summoned a taxi and gave the man her address.

He hadn't spoken to her. He'd hung up as soon as he'd heard her voice. He wanted to see her face when he confronted her with her duplicity; he wanted to be there when she tried to explain why she'd sold her own daughter to strangers as soon as she was born.

Cassandra lived in Notting Hill. She occupied half the top floor of a converted Victorian terrace house, and although Jake had never been into the place, he'd delivered her home a couple of times so he knew where it was.

His initial ring on the bell that served her apartment elicited no response. But, as luck would have it, one of the other tenants emerged as he was standing there, and he managed to save the door from closing and slip inside.

Postboxes in the hall gave him the number of her apartment, and Jake climbed swiftly to the second floor. He hoped she hadn't gone out in the time it had taken him to get here. Traffic in London was always hectic, whatever the time of day, and this morning was no exception.

Cassandra opened the door at his third ring. She'd obviously just got out of bed, and Jake recognised the familiar red kimono she'd wrapped about her naked body. He knew she'd be able to tell from his expression that this wasn't a social call, but he was surprised when she glanced guiltily over her shoulder before edging the door almost closed again.

'Jake!' she exclaimed in a low voice. 'What are you doing here?'

Almost the same words her daughter had used the evening before, thought Jake cynically. Well, it served him right for not warning her he was coming. Particularly as it seemed she wasn't alone.

'We need to talk,' he said flatly. 'Can I come in?'

Once again there was that nervous peep over her shoulder. 'We can't talk now,' she said, looking back at him. 'Darling, I didn't get to bed until after two, and I'm beat. There was a party at the studios, you see, and—'

'I'm not interested in where you've been or who you've been with,' said Jake, pressing one hand against the panels and propelling the door open. 'We're going to talk, Cassandra—or should I say *Cassie*? That is what your daughter calls you, isn't it?'

Cassandra's mouth fell open, and for a moment she did nothing to stop his advance into the apartment. But then she seemed to come to her senses and made a futile attempt to obstruct him. 'You can't come in here now,' she said. 'I—I'm not alone.'

'Do I look like I care?' Jake moved her aside with the minimum amount of effort and glanced round what was probably the main room of the apartment. Running from the front to the back of the building, it appeared to be half-kitchen, half-living-cum-dining-area. And, typical of Cassandra, it was grossly untidy, with articles of clothing and magazines strewn haphazardly across the floor.

'You have no right to force your way in here,' she exclaimed, bending to pick up what looked like a man's shirt and stuffing it behind one of the cushions on the sofa. 'This isn't funny, Jake. I don't barge into your hotel suite without an invitation, and you should do the same.'

'Oh, I've been invited here many times,' said Jake carelessly. 'So let's pretend I'm just taking you up on it.'

'Let's not.' Cassandra cast another nervous glance towards what could only be the door into her bedroom. 'I don't want you here.'

'Too bad, because you've got me.' Flinging himself onto the sofa, he linked his hands behind his head and crossed his feet at the ankles. 'Now, isn't this cosy?'

Cassandra seethed. 'What do you want, Jake?'

'Ah, that's better.' He was complacent. 'So, why don't you sit down and I'll tell you?'

She took a deep breath. 'I don't want to sit down.' Another glance at the bedroom. 'I don't have time to sit. I have to be at the studios in an hour.'

'That should be enough time.' Jake regarded her through his dark lashes. 'So, tell me about your daughter.'

Cassandra swallowed. 'I don't have a daughter.'

'Liar.'

Cassandra scowled at him. 'I don't know where you've got this preposterous story from, but—'

'Try your daughter.'

'Eve *told* you?'

Jake's expression hardened. 'Did I say her name was Eve?' he queried coldly, and Cassandra turned away to fuss with a pair of stockings that were draped over the arm of a chair.

'Well, who else could have told you such a ridiculous story?' she demanded, purposefully avoiding his eyes as she spoke.

'How about your mother?'

'My mother?' Cassandra did turn then. 'Oh, Jake, you know what that old witch thinks of me. How can you believe anything she says?'

Jake's gaze was intent. 'So it's not true?'

'No.' But her eyes shifted past him as she spoke. 'No, of course it's not true. Good heavens, Eve's—what?

Twenty-five? I'd have had to be an adolescent when I had her.'

'Your mother says you're forty-six,' said Jake bluntly. 'Quite old enough to have a twenty-five-year-old daughter.'

Cassandra gasped. 'I'm not forty-six!'

'No?'

'No.'

Jake sat up then, spreading his legs and resting his forearms along his thighs. 'So the birth certificate your mother showed me is a forgery?'

Cassandra stared at him. 'What birth certificate? How can you have seen a birth certificate?' She paused. 'Are you telling me you've been to Watersmeet? Without asking me?'

'I didn't know I needed your permission to visit a sick old lady,' said Jake harshly, pressing his hands down on his knees and getting to his feet. 'So? Is it a forgery?'

Cassandra hesitated. 'Whose—whose birth certificate have you seen?'

Jake shook his head. 'Well, not yours,' he said scathingly. 'But perhaps you could explain how a—let me see—how a thirteen-year-old girl, such as yourself, was pretending to be a twenty-year-old living and working in London at the time Eve was born?'

Cassandra's shoulders sagged. 'I don't see that it's anything to do with you,' she said bitterly. 'I think you'd better go.'

'Oh, not yet.' Jake's eyes were hard. 'I want to hear the story from your lips. I want to know how you could abandon your daughter to the care of people you knew virtually nothing about?'

'I didn't abandon her,' said Cassandra defensively, clearly deciding there was no point in continuing to lie.

'The Fultons were very good to me, actually. If it hadn't been for them I'd have been out on the street.'

'But you didn't know them. Not really,' said Jake harshly. 'You'd met them in a pub, for God's sake!'

'Yes, well…' Cassandra struggled for words. 'I could have had an abortion, you know.'

'But they persuaded you not to?'

'I was upset. They said they'd help me.'

Jake's contempt was palpable. 'Where was the baby's father?'

'Oh, he didn't want to know,' said Cassandra at once, wrapping the kimono closer about her. 'After—after I discovered I was pregnant, I never saw him again.'

Jake looked sceptical. 'Did you ever tell him you were having a baby?'

'Of course.' Cassandra huffed. 'As I say, he didn't want to know.'

'According to the enquiries your mother made after she discovered she had a granddaughter, you told the registrar you didn't know who the child's father was.'

Cassandra's face blazed with colour. 'What else could I do? I had to say something.'

'Why didn't you tell your mother you were pregnant?'

'You're joking!' Cassandra stared at him. 'Can you imagine what would have happened if I had?'

'She says she would have been quite happy for you to come home and have the baby.'

'Oh, right.' Cassandra was contemptuous. 'I'd spent half my life wanting to get out of Falconbridge. Do you really think I'd have given up everything I'd worked for the past four years to go back there because I'd been stupid enough to get myself pregnant? No, thanks.'

'You didn't even tell your mother about the baby!'

'No.' Cassandra nodded. 'How could I? She'd have insisted on me keeping it.'

'And would that have been so bad?'

'Are you kidding? We're not talking about the way things are today, Jake. Twenty-five years ago single mothers had a pretty tough time, socially and financially.'

'So you sold your baby?'

'I—I didn't exactly sell her.'

'No? What would you call it?'

'After Eve was born, the Fultons came to the poky bedsit where I was living and suggested that they could look after her. They'd been trying for years to have a baby of their own, but it just wasn't happening. They said they'd give her a good home and—and give me a certain sum of money, if I agreed to let them keep her.'

'So you sold her?'

'If you insist on being pedantic, all right. I sold her.'

'To a man who tried to abuse her when she was twelve years old.'

Cassandra sniffed. 'We only have Eve's word for that.'

'She ran away. Three times. She told me that.'

'So?' Cassandra turned away. 'Lots of kids run away from home.'

'The authorities must have believed her eventually. She was put into care, wasn't she?'

'She was uncontrollable.'

Jake wanted to hurt her, badly, but he kept his temper with an effort. 'Whatever—she spent the next three years with Social Services.'

'Until she ran away again, with some boy she'd taken up with,' Cassandra put in spitefully. 'When my mother found them they were living in a squat in Islington.'

'So your mother said,' said Jake, amazed that his voice

sounded so unthreatening. 'I'm interested to know how the old lady came to find out she had a granddaughter.'

'Didn't she tell you that, too?'

'Oh, yes, she told me. I'd just like to hear your take on it. As I understand it, you weren't averse to returning home when you thought you were dying.'

'That's a cruel thing to say.' Cassandra cast another apprehensive glance towards the bedroom door, almost as if she was more afraid of her visitor finding out that she'd once been diagnosed with a potentially terminal kidney disease than the fact that she'd sold her baby. 'I—I needed help.'

'Yeah, you needed help all right.' Jake spoke contemptuously. 'You needed a transplant. And because you were afraid your mother's kidney might not be good enough you had to tell her that you'd once given birth to a child, but that you didn't know where that child was, right?'

'Why ask me? You seem to know all the answers.'

'Yeah.' Jake felt sick. There was no remorse in Cassandra's tone at all. 'But your mother's kidney *was* good enough, wasn't it? You must have been kicking yourself when you found out you'd made your confession for nothing.' He made a helpless gesture. 'I don't know how you live with yourself.'

Cassandra's lips tightened. 'So? What are you going to do about it?'

'What am *I* going to do about it?'

'That's what I said.' Cassandra's face mirrored the uncertainty she was feeling. 'You're not going to tell anyone else, are you?'

'Who else?' Jake was scornful. 'Who would be interested?'

Cassandra shrugged, but she still looked wary. 'Nobody, I suppose.'

'Oh, I get it.' Jake had caught on. 'You're afraid I might give this to the tabloid press, aren't you? Well, don't worry, Cassandra. I won't tell anyone your dirty little secret. You're not the only person who's involved here.'

Cassandra stared at him. Then she uttered a scornful sound. 'Of course. I should have known. It wasn't concern for my mother that took you up to Northumberland, was it? It was Eve. My sainted daughter.' She gave a harsh laugh. 'My God, you're no better than me.'

'Oh, I am. Believe me, I am.' Jake couldn't control his anger now, and Cassandra hurriedly put the width of the sofa between them. 'As far as Eve is concerned, you're her mother, and that makes any relationship between us taboo.' He scowled. 'But you know what? That's okay. I don't need another woman like you in my life.'

CHAPTER ELEVEN

THE aircraft began its decent into San Felipe in the late afternoon, local time. She had been flying for hours and hours, first in a huge jet and then in this small turboprop, and Eve, who hadn't yet set her watch for San Felipe time, saw it was already after nine o'clock back in England. But she wasn't tired. She was too excited for that. Excited, but apprehensive, too. This was such a big step, and, while her grandmother had urged her to take it, she couldn't help the uneasy thought that Jake wouldn't really be glad to see her.

So much had happened in such a short time, and she was still reeling from her grandmother's decision to sell Watersmeet Hall. But the old lady had decided she was getting too old to stay there with only Mrs Blackwood for company when Eve was at work. And, as it seemed that if Eve wanted to continue teaching she would have to get a job in Newcastle, Ellie had decided to accept Adam's invitation and live with them.

Mrs Blackwood didn't mind. She was elderly herself, and had been thinking of retiring for some time. Only Eve presented a problem, and, although Adam had offered her a home too, Eve had decided to get a place of her own.

And that was when the letter from the school authorities in San Felipe had arrived. Apparently, there was a small school on the island, and they needed a teacher. They'd be happy to offer the position to Eve, they'd said, with a two-months probationary period on both sides. If it didn't work out, Eve would be given a return ticket to England.

She'd known at once that Jake had to be behind the offer. What she couldn't understand was why he would feel the need to do such a thing. She'd been left in no doubt about his reaction when he'd discovered Cassie was her mother, and she hadn't been surprised that she hadn't heard from him since.

Her grandmother hadn't hesitated in urging her to take the job, however, at least for the probationary period. 'What have you got to lose?' she'd demanded, when Eve had expressed her doubts to her. 'Just because he was foolish enough to get involved with Cassie doesn't make him a bad person. He obviously liked you, and when I told him you were losing your job at Easter he must have wondered if you'd like a change of scene.'

'When did you tell him I was losing my job at Easter?' Eve had asked warily, but for once her grandmother had been unusually vague.

'Does it matter?' she'd protested. 'This is a wonderful opportunity, Eve. You deserve it. And if you don't like living in the West Indies you can always come home.'

Which was true, Eve thought now, as the misgivings she'd had ever since she'd written and accepted the offer asserted themselves again. She was afraid what she was really doing was just building up more misery for herself in the months to come.

Naturally, Cassie hadn't approved of the idea. When Ellie had rung her daughter to tell her where Eve was going she had been at pains to remind Eve—via her grandmother—that Jake couldn't be trusted. He'd apparently visited Cassie again, before he left for San Felipe, and Eve got the impression that their affair was by no means over.

Of course she'd told no one what had happened in the stables the evening Jake had arrived to see her grandmother. Indeed, there'd been times since then when she'd wondered if she'd just imagined the whole thing. But then she'd wake in the morning with her pillow clasped in her arms and drenched with tears, and she'd know that no fantasy could have created such physical despair.

She wondered if Ellie would have been so keen to send her off to San Felipe if she'd known what had happened. If she'd known how Eve really felt about Jake. Eve doubted it. As far as the old lady was concerned this was an unexpected solution to all their problems, and Eve hadn't had the heart to tell her how she really felt.

Yet how *did* she really feel? Eve wondered now, as the shape of San Felipe solidified below them. Wasn't she secretly looking forward to seeing Jake again, whatever happened? You couldn't care about someone and not care if you never saw them again. However impossible any relationship between them might be, she still wanted to see him, to show him, if nothing else, that she was nothing like her mother.

The plane flew in over white roofs and rich green vegetation, with the white sandy beaches and deep blue waters of the Caribbean framing the exotic picture. There was no airport as such, just a cluster of colour-washed buildings surrounded by a metal fence, with what might have been a barn—or a hangar—at the end of the short runway.

'This is it, folks.'

The flight attendant, a young man dressed in an open-necked white shirt and black pants, got up from his seat before the plane had taxied to a halt and began dragging hand luggage from a locker set at the front of the plane. Apart from himself and the pilot there were no other attendants, but that was okay. There were only a dozen passengers on the flight.

The plane stopped, the door was opened, and Eve joined her fellow passengers as they got up to disembark. A flight of steps had been pushed up against the door, and although she'd earlier experienced the intense heat of the islands in Grand Cayman, it hit her again as she stepped down onto the hot tarmac.

'Have a good holiday,' said the grinning attendant, and Eve didn't bother to correct him.

'Thanks,' she said, her eyes already searching the group of people waiting at the gate. But there was no one there she knew, and she looped her haversack over her shoulder and pushed through into the excuse for a customs hall.

Seconds later she'd had her passport checked, and was waiting to collect her luggage when a hand touched her bare arm. 'You must be Miss Robertson,' said a soft, attractive voice, and she turned to find a slim, dark-skinned young woman standing beside her.

'I—yes,' she said, dropping the heavy haversack on to the floor with some relief. 'Hello.'

'Hello,' responded the woman, her smile warm and friendly. 'Jake asked me to meet you. I'm Isabel Rodrigues.'

'Miss Rodrigues!' Eve was taken aback. She knew from the letter she'd had from the education authorities in San Felipe that the head teacher at the school was called Rodrigues. But she'd never expected anyone like this— as young as this. A vision of Mrs Portman intruded— middle-aged and portly, with greying hair and horn-rimmed spectacles. Isabel Rodrigues was beautiful, and Eve couldn't help wondering exactly how well she knew Jake Romero. 'Um—it was good of you to come and meet me.'

'No problem.' Isabel's voice had a musical quality to it. 'Did you have a good journey?'

'A long journey,' said Eve wryly. 'But, yes, it was good. Interesting. I've never made such a long journey before.'

'So you've never been to the islands before?'

'No.' Eve refrained from saying that most teachers didn't have the funds to holiday in the West Indies. 'I've never been that fortunate.'

'Hmm.' Isabel nodded. 'Well, I'm sure you won't find it difficult to get used to. The heat may be a problem to begin with, but we start school fairly early in the morning and finish at lunchtime, so you won't be required to work at the hottest time of the day.'

'That's good.' Eve fanned herself with a nervous hand. 'It is rather enervating, isn't it?'

'Not to me,' Isabel assured her, as a trolley containing the luggage from the small plane was wheeled into the area. 'How many cases do you have?'

'Oh—only one,' said Eve ruefully, guessing that Isabel Rodrigues would never dream of travelling with only one suitcase. Her slim-fitting slip dress was simple enough, but made of silk, its colours a vibrant blend of orange and yellow that complemented her dark colouring.

Eve, herself, felt out of place in her jeans and tee shirt, despite the fact that she'd shed the leather jacket her grandmother had given her as a going-away present in Grand Cayman. But it had still been a cool March when she'd left London, and nothing could have prepared her for this heat. Even her hair felt like a heavy weight, weighing her head down, and for the first time in years she toyed with the idea of having it cut to a more manageable length.

A few minutes later, with a porter towing Eve's suitcase, her haversack draped about his neck, they emerged into the sunlight. A handful of taxis waited outside the building, but Isabel led the way to where an open-topped Mazda was waiting for them.

'This is it,' she said, with obvious pride, and although Eve had hoped for a saloon, she duly admired the sleek red convertible.

With the luggage stowed in the back, Isabel directed Eve to get into the car. Luckily, she'd spread a light rug over the seats, so that the leather didn't burn their legs. Then, after sliding behind the wheel, she took off.

Eve realised at once that the car being open to the air was no problem. Isabel drove fast, and the breeze off the ocean was cool and delicious in her face. It enabled her to enjoy the fantastic views of deserted beaches lapped by pale green waters edged with foam. Inland, forested gullies rose towards the centre of the island, the thick vegetation liberally interspersed with blooms of dazzling colour. It was all so different, so exotic, and Eve forgot her apprehension in the sheer delight of being here.

'The island's not very big,' Isabel confided as they passed through a small fishing village, nestled above a glassy cove. 'Just twenty miles long and eight miles wide. But we like it. And the Romeros haven't allowed it to become too commercialised.'

The Romeros. Eve wondered if there was any part of the island that didn't depend on the Romeros' approbation to survive. She doubted it. What was it Cassie had said? Jake's family owned the island? Yes, that was it. She wondered again if she wasn't being all kinds of a fool in coming here.

'I understand the school where you used to work has closed?' Isabel said suddenly, making Eve wonder what else might have been said about her.

'It closes in about a week's time,' she agreed, feeling a momentary twinge of homesickness for her grandmother and Watersmeet, and all the people she'd known there. 'Do—er—do you have many pupils at your school, Miss Rodrigues?'

'*My* school?' Isabel laughed. 'It's not my school, Miss Robertson. My mother's the academic, not me.'

'Oh.' Eve was embarrassed. 'I'm sorry. I didn't—'

'You thought because I'm called Rodrigues, I must be *the* Rodrigues,' Isabel said, with an amused sideways glance. 'No. My mother's the head teacher of San Felipe Primary. And, please, call me Isabel. Miss Rodrigues is so formal—Miss Robertson.'

'Eve,' said Eve at once. 'So you don't teach—um—Isabel?'

'Heavens, no.' Isabel grimaced. 'I work for Jake. At the boat yard. I handle all the bookings, the correspondence. I suppose you could say I'm his personal assistant.'

Eve nodded, unable to think of anything positive to say to that news. She should have known a man like Jake Romero would surround himself with beautiful people, beautiful women. Like her mother...

They were approaching the suburbs of what appeared to be a small town, and Isabel slowed accordingly. 'This is San Felipe,' she said, gesturing towards the rows of houses, the small shopping centre that developed as they approached the centre of town. 'This is where most people live, but the school is about half a mile beyond the town, nearer the tourist part of the island.'

'Are there hotels?' asked Eve, surprised to find the place so sophisticated.

'Small hotels,' agreed Isabel, swerving to avoid a bus that was lumbering towards them on the wrong side of the road. 'But the people who come here are mostly deep-sea fishermen, divers—people like that.'

'I see.'

Eve tugged her braid over one shoulder to cool her nape, and hoped it wasn't much further. Tiredness was catching up with her. Long journeys did that to her, and she hadn't really slept well since she'd accepted the job.

Beyond the outskirts of the small town, Isabel turned onto a narrow track that led down towards the sea. A coast road hugged the rim of dunes that were dotted here and there with wildflowers, and further on a clutch of white-roofed houses were clustered beside a wooden jetty. The bleached stumps of a groyne jutted out into the shallow waters, and on the beach below the village several fishing boats had been drawn up onto the sand.

'We're here,' said Isabel, waving at a handful of children who stopped playing to watch them go by. 'The school's just along here, and your house is just a little further on.'

'My house!' Eve was startled. 'I have a house?'

'Jake thought you'd prefer it,' Isabel said carelessly, but Eve sensed there was an edge of resentment in her voice now. 'The previous schoolteacher lodged with us. My Mom and me, that is.'

'I see.' Eve didn't know what to say. 'It sounds—wonderful. I've never had a home of my own before.'

'No?' Isabel sounded a little less disapproving as she glanced her way. 'Well, it's very small. Just a through living room and kitchen, with a bedroom and bathroom across a hallway. Typical San Felipe design. Simple and practical.'

'Just what I need,' said Eve, wondering if Jake hadn't been a little ambitious on her behalf. What did she really know about looking after herself? And how on earth was she supposed to get supplies?

An hour later most of her questions had been answered. Isabel had taken her first to meet her mother, the headmistress of the school. School being out for the day, Mrs Rodrigues was at home, and Eve soon realised that compared to what Isabel had described the Rodrigueses' home was considerably more spacious.

Isabel's mother, reassuringly, was not unlike Mrs Portman, and she was obviously eager to make her new employee feel at home. She suggested Eve should take a couple of days to acclimatise herself to the island, and invited her to have dinner with herself and Isabel the following evening.

'You'll find your fridge stocked, and drinking water in the taps,' she went on. 'We're lucky here on San Felipe. We have plenty of water, and it's perfectly safe to drink.'

Eve also discovered she had an open-topped buggy for her use, sitting to one side of her cottage. 'There are buses,' said Isabel, who had driven the few yards from her home with Eve's luggage, 'but they're not very reliable. Besides, you'll want to see something of the island while you're here.'

It was those last three words that occupied Eve's thoughts as she unpacked her belongings. What did they mean? Was it just Isabel's way of being friendly? Or was she implying that Eve wouldn't stay too long? And, if so, why? Did Jake have anything to do with it? To do with Isabel?

But that idea was not conducive to a relaxed first evening in her new home. And, after taking a deliciously cool shower to refresh herself, Eve checked the fridge.

She wasn't particularly hungry. Bearing in mind it was already late in the evening in Falconbridge, she just wanted something to tide her over until the morning. But she also knew that if she went to bed too early she'd be awake again before it was light.

She prepared herself an avocado salad from the makings she'd found in the fridge, and ate it at the Formica-topped kitchen table. Then she poured herself a glass of diet cola and carried it out onto the veranda at the back of the house. A pair of battered canvas chairs were set in the shade of a striped awning, and Eve sank into one, grateful for the comparative coolness of the night air.

It was almost completely dark now, and although she could still hear the sound of the ocean she could no longer see the water creaming into the cove just a few yards away. But in the morning the view would be waiting for her, she thought, hardly able to believe she was really here. She would have to phone her grandmother in the morning, too, but for tonight she was content just to let the peace and tranquillity of her surroundings drift over her.

She thought she might have fallen asleep for a few minutes, because the unusual sound of a car's engine gave her quite a start. She wasn't alarmed. Although there had been a little traffic past the cottage since her arrival, there were a few dwellings beyond her own.

But then she realised the car had stopped, and presently she heard the sound of boot heels on the flagged path that ran along the side of the house. She blinked. What time was it, for goodness sake? *Eleven!* She should have been in bed hours ago.

Her heart quickened instinctively. She had the feeling she knew exactly who her visitor was, but that didn't stop the panicky wave of excitement that swept over her at the thought of seeing him again. But she would have preferred not see him tonight—not now, when she was feeling so vulnerable. She wished she'd had the sense to turn the lights out before venturing onto the veranda. If there'd been no lights, he wouldn't have stopped. As it was, with the blinds undrawn, illuminating the area like a beacon, she had no choice but to admit to being awake.

Getting up from her chair, she moved to the veranda rail, deliberately putting herself in shadow. He might have the advantage of surprise, but she'd see his expression before he saw hers.

However, when Jake turned the corner, where a flight of shallow wooden steps led up to where she was standing, her heart almost stopped beating altogether. In a sleeveless cotton tee shirt, with baggy khaki shorts brushing his knees, he was just as disturbing as ever, and she realised that, whatever the circumstances, she had no advantage at all when it came to this man.

'Hi,' he said, placing one hand on the stair-rail. 'Can I come up?'

Eve made a careless movement with her shoulders. 'It's your house,' she said, which wasn't exactly an invitation, and, moving back to her chair, she sank down again onto her seat.

Jake took a deep breath and climbed the stairs, even though every nerve in his body was telling him he shouldn't do this. He hadn't intended to come here. When he'd left his house he'd only intended to drive past the cottage, just to assure himself that all was well. That was his excuse, anyway. But then he'd seen the light, and he hadn't been able to resist it. He hadn't realised how much he'd needed to see her again until he'd stopped the car.

'You're up late,' he said, pausing at the top of the steps and resting his back against the post. He wished there was more light, so that he could see her clearly, but what he could see tightened his stomach and quickened his pulse. 'I thought you'd be asleep by now.'

Eve glanced his way. 'Is that why you waited until now to come by? Because you thought I'd be asleep?'

'No.' Jake shoved his hands into the pockets of his shorts, so she wouldn't see the way they'd convulsed at her words. 'I was out for a drive and I saw the light.'

'Isn't it a little late to be out for a drive?' She was sardonic.

Jake shrugged. 'By your standards, maybe. Me—I don't sleep that well.'

Which was nothing but the truth. Since he'd got back from England he hadn't had above half a dozen decent nights' sleep.

Eve looked up at him now. He thought she looked a little concerned, but he couldn't honestly tell in the half-light that illuminated her face.

'Perhaps if you went to bed earlier?' she murmured, raising the glass in her hand to her lips. Then, seeing him watching her, 'I suppose I should offer you some refreshment, shouldn't I?'

Jake's conscience advised him to say no. He had no sense, being here, and he wasn't going to do himself any favours if he let her offer him a drink, if he went into the house.

But the temptation to see her properly overcame everything else. 'That would be nice,' he said, straightening away from the stair-post. 'Do you have a beer?'

Eve got up from her seat. 'Don't you know?' she threw over her shoulder as she opened the door. A huge moth tried to get in and she batted it away before adding tersely, 'Come and see.'

It was years since Jake had been inside one of these cottages, and he was immediately struck by how shabby they had become. He made a brief mental note to have a decorator check them out and update where necessary— which looked about everywhere—but his thoughts were summarily put on hold when he looked at Eve again.

She was wearing a short pink skirt that exposed her long legs, and he thought what a waste it had been to hide them with trousers. She had on a matching top, also different for her, with the kind of spaghetti straps he longed to undo. Was she wearing a bra? he wondered. He didn't think so. She hadn't been expecting visitors, after all. But that didn't stop the sudden rush of blood to his groin.

If Eve was aware of his intent regard, she ignored it, reaching into the fridge and extracting an icy-cold can of lager from the rack in the door. 'Will this do?'

'Thanks.'

Jake took the can from her, flipped the tab, and drank half its contents in one gulp. God, he'd needed that, he thought. He hadn't failed to notice how she'd avoided touching him when she handed him the beer. And, despite her latent hospitality, he was fairly sure she couldn't wait for him to leave.

'So,' he said, watching her as she crossed her arms over her midriff and turned to rest her back against the fridge door, 'you had a good journey?'

A strange look crossed her face at this question, and he wasn't really surprised when her response was equally oblique. 'Haven't you spoken to your spy?'

'My spy?' Jake did a double-take. 'I don't have a spy.'

'But you did send Miss Rodrigues to meet me, didn't you?' she queried, tucking her fingertips beneath her arms. The action caused her folded arms to press hard against her breasts, and Jake was momentarily diverted by an urgent desire to take their place.

Which he *so* mustn't do.

Forcing himself to meet her eyes, he said, 'I sent Isabel to meet you, yeah. I was pretty sure you wouldn't want to see my ugly mug the minute you got off the plane.'

'Oh, please. Only someone who didn't have an ''ugly

mug'', as you put it, would say something like that!' she exclaimed, and he arched a mocking brow.

'Is that a compliment?'

'It was an observation,' she told him flatly. 'I'm tired, Jake. Why have you really come here?'

Because I couldn't keep away?

No, that wouldn't work. 'I thought I told you,' he began earnestly. 'I was—'

'—passing and you saw the light,' she finished cynically. 'Yes, I heard what you said.' She waited a beat. 'Do you expect me to thank you for offering me this job?'

Jake expelled a shocked breath. 'That was a low blow, even for you.'

'Why even for me?' Eve's lips pursed. 'Because I'm Cassie's daughter?' She took a steadying breath. 'I am nothing like my mother.'

'D'you think I don't know that?' Jake stifled an oath at the realisation they'd got off on the wrong foot again. 'After what I've learned about your mother, I wouldn't insult you by even implying you were.'

Eve's brows drew together. 'After what you've learned about my mother?' she echoed. 'What do you mean by that? What has she told you?'

'The truth?' he suggested drily. 'As your grandmother set the ball rolling, there wasn't much else she could do.'

Eve felt sick. 'So you know about—about the Fultons and—and Andy Johnson?'

'I know you've had a pretty tough time,' he said harshly, disliking the humiliated look she gave him. 'Eve, this isn't about the past, or about your mother. Offering you this job—I just wanted to help you, that's all.' He shook his head. 'There are no strings attached.'

Eve's smoky gaze slid over his for a moment, then dropped to the floor. For the first time he noticed she was barefoot, and for some reason that was as sexy as hell. But what she was saying sobered him, and forced him to meet her wary gaze. 'You—you went to see Cassie before you left London?'

Jake was taken aback. He wouldn't have thought her mother would have advertised that interview. 'Yes,' he said evenly. 'Yes, I did. Does it matter?'

'Why did you go to see her?'

'You know why.' He lifted a hand to massage the sudden ache he'd developed in the back of his neck. 'You can't drop a pebble into a still pool without expecting the ripples to spread.'

A tremor ran over her as he spoke. 'It was nothing to do with you.'

'Like hell it wasn't.' He was trying to keep his temper, but she could hear the anger underlying his harsh words. 'I wanted to know why she'd abandoned her daughter. Your grandmother had only given me the bare bones of the story. I wanted to hear it from her own lips.'

'Why? Why should it matter to you?'

'Just accept that it does, right?' he said shortly. He thrust the empty can onto the drainer and pushed his balled fist into his palm. 'Look, it was obviously a mistake to come here tonight—'

'You couldn't keep away from her, could you?'

'What?'

'Cassie. You slept with her again, didn't you?' She shivered suddenly, as if she was cold. 'When Ellie phoned to tell her I was taking this job, she asked her to warn me not trust you. I didn't understand what she meant then, but now I do.' She shook her head. 'Not that I needed the warning. You—'

She didn't get to finish what she was saying. He covered the space between them in one stride, grasping her shoulders and hauling her up so that only the tips of her toes touched the floor. Then his mouth was on hers, hard and bruising, plundering her lips with all the power and expertise of which she already knew he was capable.

And despite everything she melted.

Her breath escaped against his lips as they parted, and then his tongue was in her mouth and she was having difficulty hanging onto her sanity, let alone her balance.

'You knew I'd come, didn't you?' he muttered, his mouth hot and demanding, but sensually appealing. 'You can accuse me of that, yet you knew I'd come.' His hand slid into the coils of the braid that she'd loosened earlier, his thumb abrading the fine cords in her throat that were drawn as taut as violin strings. He swore again. 'I am so predictable.'

She was breathing too quickly, her heart thundering in her ears. She could feel herself getting dizzy, but it didn't matter because this was where she wanted to be and she couldn't pull away.

'You're not predictable at all,' she mumbled, but she doubted he could hear her. Besides, the heat of his body, the hard pressure of his shaft throbbing against her hip, had a hypnotic quality. She felt as if she was floating several inches above the ground.

His hands stroked the sensitive curve of her spine and she couldn't help arching against him, inviting God knew what. 'I couldn't keep away,' he said, almost savagely, cupping her bottom and urging her into even closer contact with his aroused body. 'I had to see you. Pathetic, huh? Particularly as you're prepared to believe the worst of me whatever I do.'

'No.' Eve's head was swimming and she was hardly aware of what she was saying. She didn't want to talk; she didn't even want to think. She just wanted him to go on kissing her and kissing her, drugging her with his mouth and his tongue until her brain joined her senses in a total meltdown. 'Jake, it doesn't matter—'

'It does to me.'

As suddenly as he'd taken hold of her, he uttered an oath and she was free. She stood swaying in front of him, trying to comprehend why he was looking at her with such contempt now when only moments before he had been seducing her with his lips and his hands, but her mind simply couldn't handle it.

'Jake—'

'I did not sleep with Cassandra,' he informed her harshly. 'And if you think I did then I'm just wasting my time.'

'I—I didn't say that—'

'Forget it.' Jake made for the door. 'I already have.'

CHAPTER TWELVE

JAKE was going over the navigation charts with one of his skippers in the cabin of his latest acquisition when he heard the sound of high-heeled footsteps on the deck above.

For a moment he entertained the crazy notion of how he'd feel if it was Eve invading his space. But he knew that wasn't going to happen. Although she was still on the island, working at the school and proving popular with staff and parents by all accounts, she was unlikely to want to see him.

In fact, he hadn't spoken to her since the night she'd arrived, almost five weeks ago. Granted, he'd been away for part of that time, attending boat shows in Japan and South America, but he was fairly sure she was doing her best to avoid him.

Which wasn't easy on an island as small as San Felipe. Jake had actually seen her several times, but always from a distance. He didn't want to admit it, but even after all that had happened she was seldom out of his thoughts, and seeing her, even from fifty yards away, was becoming as necessary to him as breathing.

That was why he'd prevailed upon the good-natured head teacher of the school to offer her the job in the first place. In actual fact there'd been no job as such, although according to Mrs Rodrigues Eve was proving a definite asset. Her arrival had enabled class sizes to be reduced, and, having worked in an English school, she was able to offer the most up-to-date methods of teaching.

'Jake! Are you there?'

His mother's voice called from above, and after bestowing an apologetic look in Dan Cassidy's direction, Jake moved to the foot of the stairs.

'Yeah, I'm here,' he said, and, realising she wouldn't be happy conducting a conversation from this distance, he gripped the rail and started up. 'Is everything okay?'

'Yes. Why wouldn't it be?' To his relief, she'd taken off her shoes in deference to the white-painted deck and was presently seated in the pilothouse, her legs raised to rest comfortably on the dark blue leather seats. 'So this is the new addition to the fleet?'

'It is.' Jake reached the open doorway, propped a shoulder against the frame and folded his arms. 'Do you like it?'

His mother shrugged her shoulders in a careless gesture. Despite being brought up in Massachusetts, where sailing was practically a way of life, she'd never been interested in boats. Her trim five-feet-two-inch frame was more at home on the golf course, or at the wheel of her Mercedes coupé, which was why Jake was surprised to see her here, apparently showing some interest in his job.

'It's very nice,' she said, and Jake pulled a wry face at the unenthusiastic description.

'Damned with faint praise,' he said drily. 'Okay. So that's not why you're here.'

'Well, no.' Lucy Romero swung her legs to the floor and smoothed the skirt of her cream silk suit over her knees. Then she smiled up at him. 'We haven't seen you for some time. I was wondering if you were all right, actually.'

Jake managed a forced laugh. 'You're kidding, right? I see Dad practically every day.'

'At the office or here,' she said dismissively. 'You haven't been over for dinner in weeks.'

Jake shrugged. 'I've been busy.'

'Doing what, exactly? Your father tells me you spend most of your evenings on your own. When was the last time you accepted an invitation to a party? How long is it since you've seen your brother and his wife? I'll tell you—months!'

'I didn't realise you were keeping tabs on my movements,' said Jake a little tersely, straightening from his lounging position and walking towards the bank of instruments at the front of the cabin. 'I'm not twenty-one any more, Mom.'

'What's that supposed to mean?'

'Think about it. The last time you got involved in my affairs I ended up married to Holly Bernstein.' He glanced at her over his shoulder. 'Enough said?'

'Holly was a lovely girl.'

'But not for me,' said Jake flatly. 'No matter how much you and her mother tried to keep us together. Holly was an airhead, Mom. I've got no time for women like that.'

'Haven't you?' His mother sounded snappish now. 'Well, perhaps not recently, no. But from what I hear they used to be the only women you did have time for.'

Jake sighed. 'Perhaps that's because they don't expect more than I'm prepared to give them?' He shook his head. 'Leave it, Mom. I'm happy the way I am.'

'Are you?' She looked doubtful. Then, her eyes dropping the length of his lean frame, she added, 'You've lost weight.'

Jake groaned. 'Mom!'

'Well, all your father and I want is for you to be happy.'

'Then leave me alone.'

'I can't do that.' She caught her lower lip between her

teeth. 'Come for dinner tomorrow evening. Please, Jake. I'll get Rosa to make your favourite meringue dessert.'

He turned to rest against the chart desk. 'You don't give up, do you?'

'Would you want me to?'

Jake gave her a wry smile. 'I guess not.'

'So you'll come?'

'Do I have a choice?'

'Oh, good.' His mother got up from the banquette and came to give him a hug. 'Shall we say—seven o'clock?'

Jake frowned. 'That rounds awfully formal. This isn't a dinner party, is it?'

'Just one or two friends,' said Lucy innocently. 'Now, you can't back out, Jake. You've said you'll come and I'm holding you to it.'

Eve heaved a deep breath and surveyed her appearance in the bathroom mirror without enthusiasm. The little black dress that her grandmother had bought her, which had looked so good back in England, had looked totally out of place here. Which was why she'd been obliged to splash out on an alternative. But now that she had no choice except to wear what she'd bought, she was definitely having misgivings. What did one wear to a dinner party in San Felipe? Particularly one where Jake Romero might be present?

She shivered. She'd gone with the simple ivory silk jersey that the salesgirl in town had assured her was perfect for the occasion, but now she wasn't so sure. It seemed too low cut, it showed too much of her arms, of her body, and it was definitely too short. The only thing she liked was the gold chain-link belt that circled her hips. It might divert attention from the rounded curve of her bottom, but she doubted it. She should have stuck with the long-sleeved grey sheath she'd chosen to begin with.

She sighed. She wasn't sure about her hairstyle either. Despite Isabel's assurances that long hair simply wasn't practical in this climate, having it cut at all had been a stretch. It was still long enough to put in a ponytail for school, but tonight she'd left it loose, and it was odd having its heavy weight swinging against her cheeks.

Still, Isabel had been enthusiastic, and as she and Mrs Rodrigues' daughter had become friends in recent weeks Eve hadn't liked to disappoint her by voicing her doubts. And there was no question that it was cooler this way. She just wished she'd never been offered an invitation to the Romeros' villa in the first place.

It wasn't as if Jake had anything to do with it. She hadn't laid eyes on him since the evening she'd arrived on the island, and from gossip she'd heard around school he'd been keeping a very low profile in recent weeks.

She knew he'd been away for part of the time. She'd heard that from one of the workmen who'd arrived to paint and decorate the cottage. On his orders, apparently. Evidently he hadn't liked it the way it was.

No, the reason she was attending this dinner party was because of Mrs Rodrigues. The head teacher and her daughter had both been invited, but Mrs Rodrigues had developed a severe cold the day before, and she had prevailed upon Eve to accompany Isabel in her place.

'I've spoken to Lucy Romero—that's Jake's mother, you know—and she's quite happy for you to join them,' Mrs Rodrigues had explained comfortably. 'Besides, you'll enjoy it far more than I would.'

Eve had wanted to say that she wouldn't enjoy it at all, but she couldn't do that. It simply wouldn't be true. She told herself it was because she didn't want to disappoint

Mrs Rodrigues or Isabel, but if she was totally honest with herself she'd admit that she was aching to see Jake again. Which was ridiculous, of course, but it did account for all the soul-searching she was suffering now.

A perfunctory knock, followed by Isabel calling her name, heralded her friend's arrival. Eve cast one last look at herself before going out to meet her, determined to find some excuse not to go if Isabel showed any doubts about her appearance.

But in fact Isabel looked stunned when she saw her. Her dark eyes widened with amazement as she took in Eve's appearance, and her, 'Oh—you look nice,' was said in the most half-hearted of tones.

Eve blew out a breath. 'Do you think so?' she asked anxiously, suddenly realising that, despite what the other girl had said, Isabel's hair was fairly long. She usually wore it coiled in a chignon at her nape, so Eve hadn't realised how long it actually was. But this evening it was loose, an ebony cape over one shoulder, threaded with silver beads to match her long gown.

'Well, you certainly look different,' Isabel declared now, and Eve wondered if she was only imagining the tartness in her voice. 'You're a dark horse, Eve. I'd never have recognised you. Compared to the way you dress for school…'

'It's not suitable?' Despite a sudden wariness about Isabel's attitude, Eve didn't have the confidence to trust her own judgement.

'I didn't say that.' There was no mistaking the terseness now. Isabel glanced at the jewelled watch on her wrist and clicked her tongue. 'In any case, we've got to go. I don't want to be late.'

It wasn't the most auspicious way to start the evening, and Eve fretted about what she was doing all the way to the Romero house. Fortunately Isabel had agreed to drive them in her sports car—with the hood up this time, to protect them from the breeze—which meant she had to concentrate on the road instead of her companion. Which suited Eve very well.

Although Eve had never been to Jake's parents' house, of course, she knew roughly where it was. It occupied a beautiful peninsula of land a couple of miles south of San Felipe. It was set back from the road, behind a hedge of flowering hibiscus, and according to one of the other teachers it was quite a showplace.

The marina, where the Romeros' charter company had its headquarters, was in town, and Eve had wandered along the quay there, admiring the many beautiful yachts at their moorings. She'd worn dark glasses, of course, just in case she'd seen Jake, but she'd never glimpsed anyone who remotely resembled him.

'Here we are.'

Isabel was braking hard now, throwing Eve forward as they swept between open wrought-iron gates. A short drive along an avenue of palm trees strung with lights brought them to a forecourt, with an illuminated fountain. One or two cars were already parked to one side of the forecourt, in front of a row of garages, and Isabel parked beside them and pulled her keys out of the ignition.

In other circumstances Eve might have been intimidated, but she was so busy admiring the sprawling two-storey villa that she forgot to be alarmed. A wraparound balcony on the first floor would give a wonderful view of the sea that lapped at both sides of the peninsula, she thought, and the warm sandstone walls were liberally covered with bougainvillaea and other climbing tropical plants.

'Impressive, isn't it?' Although Isabel had barely spoken on the journey, she now seemed to remember her manners. 'Jake's grandfather built this place just after the first World War.'

'It's beautiful,' said Eve, getting out of the car and looking about her. Apprehension was gripping her, however. 'Um—I suppose you know the Romeros very well?'

'I've known them all my life,' said Isabel, which wasn't quite an answer. But then a white-jacketed steward appeared and she grasped Eve's arm. 'Come along. We're expected.'

As they climbed shallow stone steps to the entry, Eve wondered if that was true. Isabel was expected, certainly, but who had Mrs Rodrigues said she was sending in her place?

Whatever, she had no time to worry about that now. Even as her eyes were drawn to a lamplit terrace, where a handful of scarlet-cushioned lounge chairs were set amongst a forest of greenery, a dainty blonde-haired woman came out of the double doors to greet them.

'Isabel!' she exclaimed, reaching for the young woman's hands and drawing her in for an air-kiss beside each cheek. 'How lovely to see you again. What a pity your mother couldn't join us, too. I hope she'll feel better soon.'

'I'm sure she will, Mrs Romero.' Isabel was warmly affable now, no trace of her earlier irritation in her beaming face. 'Oh, and let me introduce you to one of my mother's teachers, Eve Robertson. She came out from England just a few weeks ago.'

'Ah, yes. I believe I've heard of Miss Robertson.' Eve was taken aback when Jake's mother took her hand and gazed up at her with shrewd, assessing eyes. 'I think my son was instrumental in your being offered the post, Miss

Robertson.' She paused. 'Am I right in thinking you got to know one another while he was in London?'

'I—that's right.' Eve decided there was no point in complicating matters by describing how they'd really met. 'It was kind of you to invite me, Mrs Romero.' She moistened her dry lips. 'You have a beautiful home.'

'Thank you. We like it.' Jake mother seemed genuinely pleased with the compliment. 'Well, come and meet the rest of the family. Jake's not here yet, but I'm expecting him to join us very shortly.'

Grateful for small mercies, Eve followed Isabel and their hostess into a large reception hall that was lit by a huge crystal chandelier. Perhaps a dozen other people were standing about in groups, enjoying the Romeros' hospitality. There was music and laughter, and a buzz of small talk that died down significantly when Jake's mother appeared with the two young women.

A grey-haired man, who had to be Jake's father, joined them, and it was he who introduced Eve to Jake's brother, Michael, and his wife, Julie. Julie was heavily pregnant, but she still looked elegant in a form-fitting satin sheath that skimmed her knees. To Eve's relief, she saw most of the women were wearing short dresses, the men less formal in casual shirts and trousers.

Julie seemed to take an instant liking to Eve, and when her father-in-law would have moved on, she said, 'I suppose you find island life a little confining, Miss Robertson?' She tucked a strand of dark red hair behind her ear as she spoke. 'I know I did when I first came here.'

'It's—different,' began Eve, but before she could continue Isabel intervened.

'That's because you're not an islander,' she said dispassionately. 'And if you don't like it you can always go back to England.'

Was that a suggestion or a warning? Eve wondered, as Julie rolled her eyes behind the other woman's back. 'We all know you love San Felipe, Isabel,' she remarked, taking a sip of the mineral water she was drinking. 'But, you know, you're the one who should consider spreading her wings.'

Isabel's lips tightened, but Jake's brother chose to lighten the mood. 'Do you find teaching a rewarding occupation, Miss Robertson?' he enquired easily. 'I can't imagine having the patience to handle one infant, let alone a handful.'

'You'd better get used to it,' declared his wife at once, and everyone laughed.

'Please, call me Eve.' Eve could feel herself relaxing. Michael was like his brother in so many ways, but without the sexual edge.

And then, as Jake's father was handing her the cocktail she'd chosen, she was suddenly aware that someone else had entered the room. She had no reason for the feeling. It wasn't as if someone had announced his arrival. But long before she heard Michael greeting his brother she knew that Jake was there.

She couldn't resist looking over her shoulder at him. It seemed a lifetime since she'd seen him, and knowing he was just across the room brought back all the feelings she'd tried to convince herself she could control.

She knew at once that she'd been wasting her time. She wasn't going to get Jake Romero out of her system by ignoring him, or by pretending that what had been between them meant nothing to her. She was very much afraid it had gone beyond a mere attraction; she was falling in love with him. Even the thought of sharing him with another woman was more bearable than never seeing him, never touching him again.

She caught her breath when their eyes met, and she saw the shock of recognition in his gaze. Obviously his mother hadn't shared her guest list with him, and she wondered if he resented the fact that she was here, in his parents' home.

She closed her eyes for a moment, taking a deep breath, praying for her palpitating heart to subside. It felt as if a whole river of perspiration was flowing down between her breasts, and her dress was clinging wetly to her spine.

Which was ridiculous, considering the room was air-conditioned, but her body seemed to be reacting independently of her brain. Even behind her lids she could see him, so lean and dark and attractive. And so incredibly male.

She was jolted out of her introspection by hard fingers closing about her upper arm. Opening her eyes, she was hardly surprised to find he'd come to stand beside her, or that his eyes were cool and guarded as they thoroughly appraised her appearance.

'I suppose this is where I'm supposed to say, What are you doing here?' he said roughly. 'Believe it or not, I didn't know you'd been invited. If I had I'd have made some excuse and stayed away.'

Eve wondered how she was supposed to answer that. It would be easy enough to counter his claim with a similar one of her own. But she couldn't do it. 'I didn't know if you'd be here either,' she ventured in a low voice, aware that their conversation was being monitored by other members of the party. 'I—I actually hoped you might be. Do you mind?'

Jake's fingers dug into her arm for a moment, and when she ventured a look at his face she saw his eyes were glittering with anger. Taking her glass from her unresisting fingers, he dumped it on a table. Then, after offering an apologetic word to those around them, he hustled Eve towards the sliding glass doors that led outside.

She didn't know what he intended to do. Perhaps this was his way of forcibly ejecting her, she thought, wondering what his parents must be thinking of his behaviour. Certainly there was aggression in the way he slammed open the door and pushed her unceremoniously out onto the patio at the back of the house. Then, with the door closed securely behind them, he virtually frogmarched her towards an unlit portion of the garden.

Eve was wearing high heels, and her ankles were aching when he finally called a halt. With a trellis of night-flowering honeysuckle between them and any prying eyes that might be watching them from the salon, and only the moon for illumination, he swung her round to face him and said savagely, 'Do you enjoy making a fool of me?'

CHAPTER THIRTEEN

'I WASN'T. I didn't.' Eve blinked. His face was in shadow, but she could feel the anger emanating from him. 'I don't know what you're talking about.'

'Like hell you don't. The last time we were together—'

'You walked out on me,' she broke in defensively, and she heard his snort of frustration. 'Well, you did.'

'And you know why,' Jake retorted, and when he lifted his hand to rake back his hair, which had grown longer over the past few weeks, she saw the faint tremor that shook his arm. 'You accused me of sleeping with your mother. Again.' He swore. 'I've never slept with your mother, *ever*. What do you take me for?'

Eve quivered now. 'That—that's what she said.'

'And since when do you believe anything that woman tells you?' he demanded, resisting the urge to shake her.

'You went away,' Eve said helplessly. 'Wh—what was I supposed to think?'

Jake grabbed her arm, as if he needed to hold onto her for support. Then he said hoarsely, 'You wanted me to go away. You told me there could never be anything between us because—because of your mother.'

'I know.' She took a trembling breath. 'But—you didn't argue, did you?'

'Oh, right.' Jake's fingers dug into her wrist. 'You just deliver the biggest bombshell of my life and I'm not supposed to show any reaction? Get real, Eve. I was mad. Mad as hell. With Cassandra, with you, but most especially with myself.'

'Because—because you thought I'd made a fool of you?'

'Do you blame me?' His thumb caressed the fine network of veins he'd found on the inner side of her arm, the roughness in his voice scraping across her nerves like raw silk. 'You should have told me who you were,' he said harshly. 'How you came to be living with your grandmother. That night in the library, for example. Then I might have understood why you'd gone to pieces because another man had forced his attentions on you.'

'It was only a kiss,' said Eve, with a shudder.

'But it meant more than that to you?'

'Yes.' Eve glanced up at him. And then, because she wanted him to understand, she went on, 'It reminded me of all the nights I'd spent sleeping in the bathroom when I lived with the Fultons.' Her lips twisted. 'It was the only room in the house that had a lock on the door.'

Jake groaned. 'Didn't you tell anyone?'

'Yes, I told Emily. This was his wife. But she didn't believe me.' She shrugged. 'Or perhaps she didn't want to know. Anyway, that's why I ran away.'

Jake swore. 'I'm so sorry, baby.' He bent his head and rested his forehead against hers. 'God, Cassandra has a lot to answer for.'

Eve's knees felt weak. 'To—to be fair, she knew nothing about it,' she ventured huskily, lifting one hand to cup his cheek, and he turned his mouth against her palm.

'Do you think that excuses her?' he exclaimed unsteadily. 'No wonder you wanted nothing to do with me.'

'That's not true.' Eve couldn't let him think that. 'You—you confused me. Until then I'd never been attracted to any man. I firmly believed I never would be. I thought I was quite happy, living with Ellie and doing my job. I—I didn't want anything else.'

'And?'

'And so when you came along I resented you. Resented how you made me feel.'

Jake's eyes darkened. 'How did I make you feel?'

'You know,' she protested.

'Perhaps I do.' He paused. 'Perhaps I just want to hear it from your lips.'

Eve shook her head. 'I just knew it was wrong, that's all. I thought you were with Cassie and I had no right feeling anything where you were concerned.'

'But you did?'

'You know I did,' she said shyly. 'Even that night in the library, I— Well, I knew then that you weren't like anyone else I'd ever known.'

Jake covered her hand with one of his. 'I wish you'd told me.'

'How could I?'

'Oh, baby.' He allowed a long sigh to escape him. 'Cassandra and I were never an item. I think that was why she invited me to Watersmeet.'

'So why did you come?'

'Believe it or not, I was asking myself that question from the moment we left London.' His tongue brushed her palm for a moment, but then he controlled himself again and continued, 'I've got no excuse. I was bored, I guess, and I thought it might be interesting to see another part of the country. It wasn't until I met you that I realised that fate must have had a hand in it.'

Eve gazed up at him. 'You don't really mean that?'

'Don't I?' He tucked a strand of silky hair behind her ear. 'I thought I did. If you're talking about what happened after I kissed you in the stables, then I have to admit I don't take rejection very well.'

Eve could hardly breathe. 'You know why I said what I did.'

'I know.' Jake regarded her intently. 'So what's changed?'

'Everything. Nothing.' Eve lifted her shoulders in a gesture of defeat. 'Why are we having this conversation? You offered me a job. Was it, as you said, just because you wanted to help me? Or—or something else?'

Jake's hands slid along her forearms to her elbows. 'What else could it be?' he asked slyly, and her heart did a somersault in her chest.

'I don't know.' She'd go so far, but no further. 'Are you still angry with me? Is that what you're saying? Because if you are—'

But Jake couldn't let her continue. 'I was teasing,' he said roughly, drawing her up on her toes and bending his head to bestow a long, lingering kiss on her soft mouth. 'For pity's sake, Eve, you surely knew how I felt the night you arrived, when I came to the cottage.' His lips brushed her ear. 'God knows, I couldn't keep away.'

Eve trembled. 'You mean that, don't you?'

'I've never meant anything more in my life.'

'Oh, Jake!' She wound her arms around his neck and gazed into his eyes disbelievingly. 'I'm so afraid this is all a dream, and any minute I'm going to open my eyes and wake up.'

'I've had dreams like that, too,' said Jake fervently. 'Particularly when I thought you were going to let Cassandra ruin the rest of your life.'

Eve caught her breath. 'Did you think I would?'

Jake's eyes darkened. 'What was I supposed to think?'

She sighed. 'I suppose. Oh, Jake, weeks ago I realised I didn't care any more. About you and her, I mean. I just didn't know how I was going to tell you. Or—or if you'd care.'

'I care,' he said roughly, but before he could do more than cradle her head in his hands, and study her expectant face, they heard someone calling his name.

'Jake! Jake! Where are you? We're waiting to have dinner.'

'My mother,' said Jake drily, although he could see that Eve had already recognised her voice. He hesitated a moment. 'Are you very hungry?'

Eve gave a soft laugh. 'I'm not hungry at all.'

'I am,' Jake told her fiercely. 'But not for food.' He bent and gave her a swift kiss. 'Wait here.'

He was back a couple of minutes later, and Eve gave him an anxious look. 'Is she very angry?'

'My mother?' Jake laughed. 'Hell, no. Why should she be? She organised this dinner party to try and take me out of myself. She'll be delighted she's succeeded.'

'Oh, but—' Eve faltered. 'She doesn't know me.'

'She will soon.' Jake took her hand, leading the way through tall waving grasses to where low dunes edged a moonlit beach. 'I think Isabel was her original objective, but if she'd asked me I'd have told her she was wasting her time.' He glanced down. 'You might want to take off your shoes. The sand is damp.'

Eve did as he suggested, looking about her in wonder. 'It's so beautiful,' she said, as he took her shoes from her and dangled them from his free hand by their straps. Then, as he helped her down onto the beach, 'Are we going for a walk?'

'Initially,' he said enigmatically, starting along she shore. 'And before that agile mind of yours starts wondering about my association with Isabel, I should tell you that we've never been more than friends.'

Eve glanced up at him. 'I believe you.'

'You'd better.' He raised her hand to his lips and pressed a moist kiss to her palm. 'The truth is, my mother's known something was wrong ever since I got back from England. You won't have noticed, in my haste to get you alone, but I've lost weight, I don't sleep, and God knows I didn't know what the hell I was going to do next.'

Eve wrapped herself around his arm as they walked. 'You could have told me.'

'Yeah. Well, believe it or not, I was considering doing just that. Then I walked into the house tonight and there you were.' He pressed her close to his side. 'Can you wonder I reacted as I did?'

Eve leant her head on his shoulder. 'So what did your mother say when you spoke to her just now? Is she expecting us back?'

'Not any time soon,' said Jake drily. He paused, then said huskily, 'She just said, "Is she the one?" And I said yes.'

Eve could hardly breathe. She was filled with an excitement that was so intense she was amazed she could keep putting one foot in front of the other. She wanted to stop right then, and ask him to say what he'd said all over again. But although he looked down at her for a moment, before stealing another heartstopping kiss, he didn't slow his pace.

With dazed eyes, she forced herself to look where they were going. The shore was totally deserted, a pearl-white stretch of coral sand that gleamed in the moonlight. There were boulders here and there, rockpools that in daylight would reveal the tiny starfish and sand crabs that made the beach their home. And, although Jake's arm was reassuringly warm against her breasts, and his hip brushed hers as they walked, Eve still had the feeling that this was some incredible fantasy conjured up by her vivid imagination.

Then, when it looked as if they could go no further without scaling the cliffs that guarded the other end of the cove, Jake pointed to a villa that was set back behind the dunes. Low and sprawling, its creamy walls blended into its surroundings, and only the light spilling out from its windows advertised its existence.

'Come on,' he said. 'I want to show you where I live.'

Eve's lips parted. 'This is your house?'

'Mmm.' Jake slipped his arm around her. 'Come and see.'

Fifteen minutes later they were installed in Jake's living room. A long, open—plan area, with a huge stone fireplace he promised her he did use from time to time, it was modern without being ultra-trendy. The floors were polished teak, the trio of sofas were a blend of suede and leather, and the low table in front of the fireplace rested on a thick Chinese rug.

'It's beautiful,' said Eve, unable to think of any other adjective to use. 'Do you live here alone?'

'Apart from Luigi, yeah.' He had introduced her to his elderly Italian houseman when they arrived. 'Why? Did you think I kept a mess of women here for my own amusement?'

Eve, who was kneeling on an ivory leather sofa, watching him as he moved somewhat restlessly about the room, heaved a sigh. 'No,' she admitted honestly. 'But you did say you'd been married before.'

'Oh, yeah. For about six months.' Jake grimaced. 'And, for your information, we didn't live here. I had a condominium in San Felipe in those days.'

'I'm glad.' Eve bit her lip. 'Are you going to come and sit down?'

Jake glanced at the small bar set into the wall. 'Wouldn't you like a drink?'

'Would you?'

'No, but as I deprived you of the one my father made for you…'

'I don't want a drink.' Eve took a deep breath. 'I just want you to kiss me.'

Jake pulled a wry face. 'That's what I want, too.'

'So?'

'So that's not all I want,' he said, moving to the back of the sofa and looking down at her with dark intense eyes. 'And I don't know if I've got the will-power—or the strength—to limit myself to just kissing you.'

'Did I say I wanted you to?'

'Eve—' His hands covered hers where they rested on the soft leather, and she shivered a little in anticipation. 'We have to talk.'

'We'll talk later,' she promised him, capturing his hands in hers and drawing him around to the front of the sofa. Then she patted the seat beside her. 'Sit down.'

Jake did so, his weight depressing the cushions beside her so that even if she hadn't planned it that way she slid towards him. She grabbed him, to save herself, her hand slipping intimately over his thigh, and with a muffled oath he turned towards her, covering her startled lips with his.

His tongue invaded her mouth, hot and demanding, reminding her of his taste and his scent. She desperately wanted this, wanted to prove to him that she wasn't afraid of anything when she was with him, that he and he alone could erase all the pain and heartache of the past.

When he lifted his head and looked down at her she was devastated by his intensity. His lean face was taut with emotion, with feelings he was trying desperately hard to control. When he bent to her again there was a dangerous hunger in his invasion, a mind-numbing ardour that enveloped her in its thrall.

'You have no idea how much I've wanted to do this,' he groaned, tipping the straps of her dress aside and laving her shoulder with his tongue. 'I just don't want to hurt you.'

'You're not hurting me,' she protested, parting the neckline of his shirt and pressing her face against his hot skin. There was a film of moisture on his chest and she allowed herself to taste it, loving the way his flesh tensed at the intimate brush of her tongue. 'I couldn't stand it if you changed your mind now.'

'Dear God,' Jake muttered, as her dress slipped away to reveal the skimpy bra she was wearing beneath it. Two half-cups of cream lace barely contained the rounded breasts that were spilling out from them, dusky nipples hinting at the exotic cast of her colouring. 'I couldn't stand it either.'

She was all ebony and ivory, he thought, her skin pale, her hair so thick and dark against her cheeks. When he bent his head, to capture her mouth again, her hair swung against him and he felt its silken strands caress his face.

'Jake…'

His name was a heady sound on her lips. Hearing her use it in that seductive way was like drowning in sensation. His body stiffened automatically, and he thought she had no idea what she was doing to him. The swollen muscle between his legs was becoming a constant ache.

He found the fastener that secured the flimsy bra and dealt with it. Then, urging her back against the cushions, he positioned himself beside her. He didn't lie over her, although he wanted to. There was no way he could hide his arousal if he gave in to temptation.

Even so, he couldn't prevent himself from caressing her breasts, from lowering his head and taking one sensitive nipple into his mouth. She moaned softly, her pulse palpitating beneath his fingers, her hands reaching for him in mute acceptance of her own needs.

Her hands probed inside his collar, twining in the hair that grew longer at the nape of his neck. She was eager, too, he realised, wondering how long it was since she'd allowed any man to touch her. The boy she'd run away with—Andy Johnson?—had he been intimate with her? Jake thought he could gladly kill any man who'd touched her against her will.

She moved against him and he was sure she must feel his taut maleness against her hip. Her response, her willingness, was making him want to move faster than he'd intended, and when her legs parted he couldn't prevent his thigh from pushing urgently between hers.

'Ah, Eve,' he groaned, one hand sliding down to cup her bottom, moving beneath the short hem of her dress to find the soft skin at the top of her legs. She arched against his hand, and that almost drove him crazy. He so much wanted to be inside her, to feel her taut muscles urging him on.

Eve's head was spinning. There was increasing moisture between her legs, which she was sure he must have felt when he touched her there. She almost stopped breathing altogether when his fingers slid partway into her.

Acting purely on impulse, she trailed her hand down his chest to the waistband of his trousers. His shirt was half open anyway, and she completed the task. The buckle on his belt presented the next obstacle, but when she would have loosened it his hand stopped her

'Wait.' Jake's voice was hoarse, and she realised he was no more immune to her explorations than she was to his. 'I don't think you know what you're doing to me. I'm not made of stone, you know.'

'Nor am I,' she murmured, kissing his chest, loving the feel of his springing hair against her face. 'I want you, Jake. I want to make love with you. I don't want to be an oddball any more.'

'An oddball?' Jake gazed down at her with puzzled eyes. 'You're not an oddball.'

'Yes, I am.' Eve took a deep breath and continued, 'I've never let any man get close to me before.'

Jake shook his head. Cassandra really did have a lot to answer for, he thought again. 'Come,' he said softly, once again stopping her when she would have opened his zip to stroke his throbbing erection. 'I want to show you my bedroom. Besides, we don't want to risk being interrupted by Luigi asking if we want more ice.'

'Ice?' Eve felt a sob of laughter rising in her throat as Jake lifted her up into his arms and strode purposefully across the room.

'Not such a bad idea, in the circumstances,' agreed Jake huskily. 'Maybe some ice is exactly what we need.'

A flight of open-tread stairs gave access to the upper floor of the villa. Double doors stood wide into a huge master bedroom, with long oriel windows giving a magnificent view of the bay.

Jake laid Eve on the wide damask-covered bed. Only one lamp was burning, but beyond the windows the moon could be seen throwing a silver pathway over the sea. Its pale light added to the magical beauty of their surroundings, and when Jake lay down beside her she turned eagerly towards him.

Jake was gentle with her now, even though she sensed the urgency underlying his touch. Her dress had pooled about her waist, and she thought her bra must be somewhere between the bed and the sofa downstairs. But such insignificant considerations went out of her head when he bent to nibble at the creamy fullness of her breasts.

She wasn't able to stop herself from trembling, and he lifted his head again, to give her a searching look. 'Don't be alarmed,' he said. 'I like it that you're not so sophisticated. And that you don't honestly realise how sexy you are.'

Eve sucked in her breath. 'No one's ever called me that before.'

'Then they must have been blind,' said Jake thickly, feeling an increasing sense of euphoria at the knowledge that in many ways he was going to be first with her. In every way that mattered at least.

It was a simple matter to slide her dress down her hips, and, releasing one plump nipple, he allowed his tongue to trail a sensuous path from her breast to her navel. She quivered again, as he used his teeth to pull her lacy scrap of underwear away, and fairly bucked against him when he replaced his probing fingers with his tongue.

'You can't— You mustn't—' she began, but as he caressed her he saw the way her eyes grew dark with desire, and her breathing quickened in concert with her body's response.

She climaxed moments later, and he stifled her cry of wonder beneath the hungry pressure of his mouth. It pleased him enormously that she was so responsive, and this time when she reached for his buckle he didn't attempt to stop her.

Even so, it took all his self-control not to lose it completely when she took his thick shaft into her hands. But he wanted to be inside her when he found his own release, and, although she protested, he drew away to tear off his shirt and push his trousers down his legs.

Then he was beside her again, satisfying her impatience and his own by positioning himself above her. Eve knew a moment's panic when she saw how big he really was, but her legs parted willingly when he straddled her.

'Did I tell you that you're beautiful?' he breathed, and she felt the heat of his erection nudging her wet core.

He entered her in one almost smooth thrust, only briefly balked by the unmistakable barrier he encountered. Eve, who hadn't been prepared for the pain after the gentleness of his mouth, tried to stifle her moan of anguish against his throat, but it escaped anyway. She hadn't realised how much her body would rebel at this unfamiliar invasion; hadn't anticipated that it would hurt so much.

Nevertheless, when he withdrew again she was no less distressed. 'No,' she protested, but Jake was staring down at her in stunned disbelief.

'You were a virgin,' he said in a strangled voice. 'My God, why didn't you tell me?'

CHAPTER FOURTEEN

'I told you I was an oddball,' Eve whispered, trying to make light of it, but Jake wouldn't let her go on.

'You're not an oddball,' he exclaimed harshly, but once again Eve intervened.

'What would you call a twenty-five-year-old virgin?' she asked mockingly, but he laid a hard palm across her lips.

'Innocent,' he said tersely. 'God, I'm such an idiot. I thought—after what you'd been through—'

'Because of Graham Fulton?' Eve's lips twisted. 'I told you. I spent all my nights in the bathroom.' She pushed her lips against his palm for a moment, before drawing his hand away. 'And Andy Johnson knew how I felt, and he looked out for me.' She smiled. 'Until I met you, I couldn't bear a man to touch me, you see,' she confessed huskily. 'Ever since—ever since that man came to my room, I've always kept the opposite sex at arm's length.'

Jake groaned. 'Oh, baby, I've been such a fool.'

'It doesn't matter,' she protested, bringing his hand to her face and pressing it against her cheek. 'Not to me.' She waited a beat and then asked tremulously, 'You do still want me?'

Jake groaned again. 'Of course I want you. Now more than ever. But—'

'No buts,' said Eve firmly, levering herself up on her elbows and drawing his hands to her breasts. 'I've wanted you for so long. I couldn't bear it if you didn't feel the same.'

'Dear God!' Jake couldn't prevent himself from crushing her against the soft pillows of his bed. 'I think I've been waiting for you all my life,' he added shakily. His mouth possessed hers with the utmost tenderness. 'I just don't want to hurt you again.'

'You won't,' said Eve, not knowing how she knew this, but she did. 'Please.' Her fingers stroked his swollen erection. 'You can't stop now.'

Which was nothing less than the truth, thought Jake ruefully. But he wanted her to share his delight in their joining, and, although he still blamed himself for acting so recklessly, he ached to be inside her again.

Gently, he spread her legs and eased into her, using his lips and his tongue to relieve any anxiety she might feel. But, amazingly, she received him easily, her body slick and damp from her exertions.

And Jake was blown away again by her sweetness. She was everything he'd ever wanted in a woman, and the muscles in his gut tightened when they felt her willing response.

For Eve, it was equally as moving. Now that she knew what to expect, she welcomed his heat and the fullness his body created. But she was still unprepared for the feelings that surfaced when he withdrew partway before pushing into her again. They were like the feelings she'd had before, only deeper, stronger, causing a wave of expectation to sweep through her abdomen and up her spine until it felt as if she was tingling all over.

Almost instinctively, it seemed, she lifted her legs and wound them about his hips, holding him inside her. Jake took a steadying breath, trying to control the urge to quicken his pace, but it wasn't easy when he could feel the rippling wave of her orgasm tightening her muscles around him.

His body throbbed with the need for his own release, but once again he realised he was in danger of making another stupid mistake. The condom he should be using was still lying in the drawer of the table beside his bed. In his eagerness to make love with Eve he'd forgotten all about it, and he still had the sense to know that she wouldn't have done anything to protect herself.

Dammit, he thought, he couldn't do this to her. But when he attempted to withdraw she only tightened her long legs about him.

'Don't,' she whispered huskily, her breathing hot and unsteady against his throat, and Jake groaned.

'You don't understand—' he choked, but she only covered his mouth with hers.

'I do,' she breathed against his lips, and although he knew what he ought to do, the temptation to let her have her way was irresistible.

Besides, she was making frantic little sounds now that were totally driving him crazy. He was drenched with her scent, with her essence, and, giving in to a force that was stronger than he was, Jake spilled himself inside her.

His orgasm seemed to go and on, and when the shuddering pleasure had ceased he felt absolutely drained. But absolutely replete, too, which was something he'd never experienced before.

He realised suddenly that he was slumped on top of Eve, but when he would have rolled away she stopped him again. 'I've got to be crushing the breath out of you,' he protested, but she only wound her arms around his neck and gazed up at him with wide, adoring eyes.

'I don't care,' she said huskily. 'And before you say anything I don't care if I'm pregnant either.'

'Eve—'

'No, I mean it, Jake. And I don't want you to think it's

your responsibility. You're an honourable man, I know that, but this was my decision—'

'Stop! Stop right there!' Jake silenced her with a hard kiss, and before she could start again he exclaimed, 'For God's sake, I love you! I think I've loved you since the first moment I saw you. And if you think I'm going to let you go now, without a fight, you're very much mistaken.'

Eve's lips had parted for his kiss, but now, when he lifted his head, she found she needed to suck some much-needed air into her lungs. 'I—I don't know what to say.'

'Well, you could say you liked me just a little bit, too,' said Jake, trying to make light of his passionate declaration. Taking her arms from around his neck, he rolled onto his back beside her, staring up at the shadows that hid the ceiling. 'Unless I've jumped the gun again—'

'No!' Eve scrambled up now, to look down at him with anxious eyes. 'It's not that.' She made a helpless gesture. 'I just—well, it's like you said: you've taken my breath away.'

Jake lifted his hand to touch her cheek. 'But you knew I cared about you.'

Eve shook her head. 'My grandmother *cares* about me,' she said fiercely. 'You—you said you loved me.'

'I do.'

'But how can you?'

'How can I not?' he retorted, a little thickly. 'You're everything I've ever wanted, all rolled up in one delectable package.'

She quivered. 'I'm not delectable.'

'Oh, you are.' His fingers slipped beneath the soft weight of her hair. 'Delectable, and sweet, and very, very desirable.' He pulled her mouth down to his, unable to resist the urge to taste her lips again. 'So what are you going to do about it?'

'What am I going to do about it?' she echoed.

'Yeah.' He released her lips and transferred his attentions to the luscious breast that was suspended only inches above his mouth. 'You could start by telling me how you feel about me.'

'Oh, God!' Eve bent over him, cradling his face between her palms. 'You know I love you,' she exclaimed fervently. 'But even now I can't believe that you want me.'

'Believe it,' said Jake huskily, reversing their positions so he could bury his face between her breasts. 'Ever since you came to the island you've been driving me crazy. I knew I had to give you time, but, like I said before, I couldn't eat, I couldn't sleep, I couldn't think about anything but us being together.'

Eve was dazed by his urgency, and not a little shocked by the growing hardness against her hip. 'You—you want me again?' she breathed, the exhilaration of knowing she could do this to him sweeping over her.

'Constantly,' he said, his hand slipping between them to caress her. 'Oh, baby, you have no idea how much...'

Hours later, they had a midnight feast of strawberries and champagne. It was only right and proper that they should celebrate their unofficial engagement in such a way, Jake said, climbing back onto the bed with the bottle of champagne and two crystal glasses in his hands, and Eve stared at him in disbelief.

'Our unofficial *engagement*?' she said, blinking, and Jake grinned back at her.

'Well, you are going to marry me, aren't you?' he asked, and for a long while after that the champagne was forgotten.

But eventually Eve wriggled into a cross-legged position beside him. There were things she wanted to tell him, things she had to tell him, before their engagement became official and Jake couldn't back out.

'I need to tell you about my father,' she said, accepting a champagne-dipped strawberry from him and resting it against her lower lip.

'Your father?' Jake frowned, fascinated by her unknowing sensuality. 'I thought your mother didn't know who your father was?'

'Oh, she knew. My grandmother forced her to tell the truth when she was searching for me.' Eve bent her head. 'He was Cuban, you see, and Cassie hadn't wanted to tell the Fultons that in case they changed their minds.'

Jake gave a low whistle. 'No kidding. So—did you get to know him? Afterwards, I mean?'

'No. Ellie found out he'd been killed in a plane crash in Cuba just weeks after I was conceived. Cassie wasn't lying about that, at least. He didn't want to know that he'd fathered a child.'

'Oh, sweetheart.' Jake pulled her close and pressed a warm kiss to the top of her head. 'You certainly had a raw deal.'

Eve glanced up at him. 'You don't mind?'

'Why should I mind?'

'Oh, I don't know.' Eve hesitated. 'Harry seemed to think it was important that I was half Cuban.'

'Who? That idiot priest back at Falconbridge?' And, at her nod, 'Was that what upset you so much that night?'

'It was the way he said it. And the fact that he thought I was only putting him off because I was attracted to you,' said Eve honestly.

'Hey, the guy had a brain after all.'

Eve cuddled close. 'I do love you, you know.'

'I know,' said Jake smugly. 'That's why you're going to marry me and not him.'

Six months later, Eve sat with Julie Romero on the terrace at the back of the villa. It was early evening, and Julie was nursing her four-month-old daughter at her breast. Watching her, Eve wondered what it would be like to feed a baby. Well, she'd know soon enough, when their baby was born.

Not that that was going to happen any time soon. In fact, apart from Jake's immediate family—and her grandmother—they'd kept the fact that Eve was expecting a baby to themselves. At present it was barely noticeable, although Eve knew her waistline was thickening by the day.

Julie finished feeding the baby and, after adjusting the bodice of her dress, shifted the baby to her shoulder. 'Thank goodness that's over,' she said, with feeling. 'I didn't realise a baby's jaws could be so strong.'

Eve smiled. 'Here,' she said. 'Give her to me.'

'She's heavy.'

'Not that heavy,' said Eve firmly. Then, after settling the baby over her own shoulder, she said, 'What time is Mike getting back?'

'Pretty soon, I hope,' said Julie fervently. And then, realising how that might sound, she added, 'Not that I haven't appreciated you and Jake letting me stay here while he's been away. But I've missed him, you know. Even three days can seem like for ever when you're apart.'

'I know.' Eve was sympathetic, but she was also grateful that Jake had unloaded a lot of the overseas travelling onto his younger brother's shoulders. It meant they spent a lot more time together, and whenever he did travel Eve went with him.

And, as if thinking about him had attracted his attention, Jake chose that moment to come out of the house. 'Mike's just rung,' he said, his eyes going to his wife and the baby. 'He landed a few minutes ago. He's coming straight here.'

'Oh, marvellous!' Julie beamed, and Jake patted her on the shoulder before going to join his wife and baby Rachel on the glider. Julie got up. 'I'll just go and smarten myself up.'

Jake smiled at his sister-in-law as she went into the house, and then at the baby, trailing a caressing finger down Eve's bare arm. 'You know, having visitors can be rather limiting,' he murmured. 'I haven't made love with you anywhere except in our bedroom for almost a week.'

Eve dimpled. 'Is that a problem?'

'What do you think?' His lips caressed her shoulder. 'I prefer having you all to myself.'

'Well, when our baby's born—'

'—he won't care what his mother and father get up to,' said Jake firmly. 'Not for years and years.'

'And it is six months away,' agreed Eve consideringly. 'You might have got tired of making love to me by then.'

'I'll never get tired of making love to you,' asserted Jake fiercely. 'I feel as though I've been sleepwalking for most of my life. Only since I met you have I realised exactly what I was missing. We fit together. Without you I was never totally complete.'

Eve tipped her head onto his shoulder. 'That's a nice thing to say.'

'It's the truth.'

'And I'm the luckiest woman in the world.' She smiled.

'I'm so glad Ellie phoned you and told you what was going on.'

'So am I,' said Jake fervently. 'Although I didn't know if you'd agree to take the job at the school. If you hadn't, I guess I'd have had to find another reason to visit Falconbridge. Though I'd have been devastated if I'd found that your grandmother had sold the house and you weren't there any more.'

'Someone would have directed you to Adam's farm,' said Eve at once. 'But I'm glad it didn't come to that. Ellie so much enjoyed coming here for the wedding. And Adam and his family... I bet they're still talking about travelling in a private plane.'

Jake looked sheepish. 'Yeah, I guess Adam and I got off on the wrong foot, didn't we?'

'Well, neither of you was exactly friendly towards the other.'

'You know why?' Jake grimaced. 'I thought he was another friend of yours. And poor old Adam thought I was another of Cassie's hangers-on.'

Eve pulled a face now. 'She won't like it when she hears she's going to be a grandmother.'

'Like I care what that woman thinks.'

'Well, she did make an effort and send us a wedding present,' said Eve charitably. 'And I'm so happy, Jake. I can't forget that without her we'd never have met.'

Jake sighed. 'Okay. But I can't forget the way she treated you when you were a baby. You can ask me to forgive her, but I'll never forget.'

Nor would she, thought Eve, as Jake put his arm about her. She probed the small mound at her waist with a gentle hand. Her baby would be loved, not just by her and Jake, but by all his family. The way a baby should be, she thought, burying her face in the warm hollow of Jake's neck.

THE INNOCENT VIRGIN

Carole Mortimer

Carole Mortimer was born in England, the youngest of three children. She began writing in 1978 and has now written over one hundred and forty books for Mills & Boon. Carole has four sons – Matthew, Joshua, Timothy and Peter – and a bearded collie called Merlyn.

Don't miss Carol Mortimer's brand-new story *The Master's Mistress*, **available from Mills & Boon® Modern™ in March 2010**

CHAPTER ONE

ABBY stepped into the hot scented bathwater, sat down, and let her shoulders sink beneath the luxurious bubbles, ebony hair secured loosely on top of her head, a glass of champagne in one hand, her mobile phone in the other.

She took a large sip from the former before gently dropping the latter into the water beside her, smiling at the satisfying 'glug' it gave before sinking to the bottom without trace. The four-inch layer of bubbles simply closed back over the temporary dent the mobile had made in their formation.

The landline was unplugged, the speaker system from her doorbell in the street downstairs switched off. Nothing and no one was going to disturb this hour of decadence.

She took another sip of the champagne and gazed from the free-standing claw-footed bath at her surroundings. Twelve scented candles were her only illumination and a dreamy smile touched her lips as she looked at her frankly opulent surroundings. The floors and walls were of peach-coloured marble, the glass-sided shower unit that stood at one end of the large room had all its fittings gold-plated; the towels on the racks were a sumptuous peach of the exact shade as the walls and floor. Monty was sitting on the laundry basket, all her bottles of perfume were neatly lined up on the glass shelf beneath the tinted mirror, the bucket of ice containing the bottle of champagne was right beside her, and—

Monty was sitting on the laundry basket!

Her gaze swivelled sharply back to look at him. No, it wasn't the champagne she had already imbibed; Monty really was sitting on top of the laundry basket, unmoving, those green cat-like eyes unblinking.

Well, of course his eyes were cat-like—he was a cat, after all. A huge white, long-haired Persian, to be exact.

Not that Monty was aware of this himself. Somewhere in his youth someone had forgotten to mention this little fact to him, and now he chose to ignore any reference to his species.

Abby wasn't to blame for this oversight; Monty had already been a year old when she'd chosen him over the other cats at the animal rescue centre. At least, she had *thought* she had chosen him; within a very few days of arriving home with him it had become more than obvious that Monty had done the choosing. Someone soft and malleable, he must have decided. Someone still young enough to be moulded into the indulgent, pandering human he needed to make his life completely comfortable. Enter Abby.

'Well, of course that's going to change now, Monty, old chap.' She waved her champagne glass with bravado. 'No more boiled chicken and salmon for you, I'm afraid,' she warned him ruefully. 'From now on you'll be lucky if I can afford to buy you that tinned food you consider so much beneath your notice!'

Cats, she was sure, weren't supposed to be able to

look at you with scepticism and disdain, and yet that was exactly what Monty was doing at this moment. He had several easily readable expressions, from 'You've got to be kidding!' to the smug 'Aren't I lucky to own an accommodating human like Abby?'. At the moment it was definitely the former.

'It isn't my fault,' Abby assured him with another wave of her champagne glass—which definitely needed replenishing, she decided, and did exactly that. 'It's that man's fault.' She took a huge swallow of her champagne. 'I mean, whoever thought he would do such a thing?'

She wouldn't cry. She wouldn't cry!

But of course she did, her tears accompanied by huge, heaving sobs.

How could he have done that to her? And on public television, live, in front of millions of viewers.

Oh, God…!

Every time she even thought of that she felt her humiliation all over again.

'Weeks and weeks—several weeks, anyway,' she amended tearfully. 'Well, okay, seven.' She sniffed inelegantly. 'All that time I've been gently trying to persuade that man to come on my show. Yes, I know you liked him, Monty.' Her voice rose with indignation on her blandfaced pet's behalf. 'So did I,' she admitted heavily. 'But if you only knew—if you had only heard—I had no idea, Monty.' She shuddered. 'Absolutely none!' If she had she would never have got out of bed this morning!

In fact, it was worse than that. If she had guessed in any way just how deep her annihilation was going to be this evening she would have taken a one-way trip to Bolivia earlier today and spared herself all the pain.

She had always liked the sound of that name. Bolivia. It sounded so romantic, so mysterious, so different. But, knowing her luck, it was probably nothing like that at all. She had always liked the sound of the so-called Bermuda Triangle too, but no doubt that was just another myth…

She had probably had too much champagne.

'Okay, okay, so my thoughts are wandering,' she acknowledged, as Monty seemed to look at her with derision. 'But if you only knew, Monty.' She began to cry again, the tears hot on her cheeks. 'If you had only heard what that man said to me! You would have been shocked, Monty. Shocked!'

Abby had actually passed being shocked where this evening was concerned. She had reached surreal now, able to envisage that whole humiliating experience as if in slow motion—like a reel of film going round and round in the projector.

'Oh, God, Monty!' she sobbed. 'I can't ever leave this apartment again! I'll have to barricade the door, put bars on the windows. I daren't ever go out in public again!' She took another slurp of her champagne, the salt of her tears mixing with the bubbly wine. 'Once our supplies run out, we'll both simply starve to death!' she added shakily.

Four months ago it had all looked so promising. As the weather girl for a breakfast television show—an interesting career move, considering she couldn't tell a cold front from an isobar!—she had been asked to stand in for the female half of the presentation team while the other woman went on maternity leave for several months. She had made a impact, and a well-known producer had approached her with an offer to do six half-hour chat shows, to be shown live the following spring.

The next three months had been a dream come true for Abby—choosing the guests for each week, researching, negotiating the appearance of those guests—and everything had gone well until it had come to the guest she had chosen for her final show.

Max Harding.

Her intention had been to finish the series on a high note. Once the presenter of his own current affairs programme, Max Harding had returned to reporting foreign news and hadn't appeared in a British studio in two years. Not since he had walked away from his own programme, and the lucrative contract that went with it, after one of his political guests had tried to commit suicide on the live Sunday evening show.

Max Harding's personal elusiveness since that time, his flat refusal even to discuss the subject, would make him a prime finale, Abby had thought, for her own series of shows.

But she should have known, Abby berated herself now. Should have guessed what his intentions were when he had finally—surprisingly—agreed to be her guest.

'He meant to hurt and humiliate me, Monty.' Her voice hardened angrily at the memory. 'All the time you liked him so much—that I—that we— How could he do that to me, Monty? How could he?' Her ready tears began to fall again. 'But I showed him, Monty. In fact, I showed everyone watching as well,' she remembered with a pained groan. 'Millions and millions of people sat in their homes and watched as I hit him. Yes, you did hear me correctly; I hit Max Harding—on live television!'

Abby closed her eyes as the memory overwhelmed her. She wasn't a violent person—had never hit anyone in her life before, never wanted to hit anyone before. But she had certainly hit Max Harding this evening.

'Actually, it was worse than that, Monty.' She choked, not at all concerned with the fact that a lot of people might think it strange that she was having this conversation with her cat. Temporary insanity was certainly a plea she could make for her actions tonight, but at the moment it was the least of her problems. 'It wasn't just a gentle slap on the cheek.' She groaned. 'He annoyed me so much, hurt me so much, that I swung my arm back and belted him with all the force that I could. It was perfect, Monty. Right on his arrogant chin.' She smiled through her tears with remembered pleasure. 'You should have seen the stunned look on his face. Then his chair toppled backwards, taking him with it, and he was knocked unconscious as he hit the floor!'

And Monty should have seen her own face as her anger had left her and she'd realised exactly what she had done...

The studio had grown so hushed you could literally have heard a pin drop. The small studio audience deathly quiet, no one even seeming to breathe; the camera crew no longer looking into their cameras but staring straight at her in open-mouthed disbelief.

Her director in the control room had been the first to recover, screaming in her earpiece, 'Abby—what the hell are you doing? Say something,' he yelled, when she could only stand there in mute silence, staring down at the slumped form of Max Harding. 'Abby, do something!' Gary had instructed harshly as she still didn't move. 'This is live television, remember?'

She had remembered then, turning to look at the surrounding cameras, realising they were still transmitting.

In her panic there had been only one thing she could do—no other choice left open to her. With a startled cry, she'd stepped over Max Harding's prostrate body before running out of the studio as if pursued.

No one had spoken to her as she'd run. No one had even attempted to stop her.

And why would they? She had totally blown it—had broken the cardinal rule of not losing your cool on public television, of always remaining calm and in control, no matter what the provocation. *No matter what the provocation!*

Her career was in ruins. She would never appear on television ever again.

Which was why she was now locked in her apartment, with the telephone disconnected, the intercom to the doorbell downstairs switched off, and her mobile lying waterlogged in the bottom of the bath.

'Okay, that last gesture may have been a little drastic,' Abby allowed, as Monty looked at her with disapproval. 'Especially as I'm now effectively unemployed—unemployable!—and will never be able to afford to buy a new one. But do you know the worst of it, Monty? The absolute worst of it?' Her voice shook with emotion now, tears once again falling hotly down her cheeks. 'I know you liked him, but I actually thought I was in love with him!' she burst out shakily. 'I was in love with Max Harding!' She whipped herself with the lash again. 'Now I wish I had never even set eyes on him!'

Until seven weeks ago she hadn't even met him.

Seven weeks ago she had been riding on the crest of a wave, euphoric at her success in landing her own half-hour show, full of enthusiasm as she researched and then met her guests, overjoyed at her apparent overnight success at only twenty-seven.

But seven weeks ago Max Harding had still been just a name to her—a reputation, several dozen photographs. She hadn't met the flesh-and-blood man then.

Hadn't fallen in love with him...

CHAPTER TWO

'YES?'

Abby could only stare at the man standing in the open doorway of the apartment; she hadn't seen this much naked male flesh since she'd sat on a beach in Majorca last year.

And very male flesh it was too. But the towel wrapped around the man's slim waist and the dampness of his dark hair told her exactly why it had taken four knocks on the apartment door for him to answer—he had obviously been taking a shower when she arrived.

Alone? Or with someone? Whatever; this man's semi-nakedness took her breath—and her voice—away.

Not that she wasn't familiar with Max Harding's looks. She had seen him dozens of times on the news over the last couple of years, reporting from one war-torn country or another, and had also watched hours of footage of the political forum programme he'd hosted until two years ago.

But in the first case he was usually wearing some sort of combat gear and a flak jacket, shouting his report over the whine of bullets as they whistled past his ears. And in the second instance he had always been sitting down in one of those high-back leather chairs, wearing a dark formal suit with a shirt and tie.

In both cases he had been on the small screen, minimised before being transmitted into people's homes.

He was huge, was Abby's first thought. It wasn't just his height, of about six feet two inches, he also had incredibly wide and muscled shoulders, his skin was darkly tanned, the ebony hair on that powerful chest tapered down to—

'Seen enough?'

Not nearly enough, was her second, slightly fevered thought. *Oh, dear!* was her wincing next one, as she slowly raised her gaze back to his face, her cheeks awash with embarrassed colour.

Really, it might be some time since she had seen a man naked—or in this case semi-naked—but she *had* seen one or two!

But looking at Max Harding's face wasn't reassuring. She had hoped the severity of his expression on television was due to the seriousness of his subject matter, but even one glance at his rock-hewn features was enough to tell her that those weren't laughter lines beside the intense grey eyes, the arrogant slash of a nose and sculptured unsmiling mouth. This man looked as if he rarely smiled, let alone laughed!

Abby straightened her shoulders, deliberately arranging her features into 'serious but pleasant'. 'I don't know if you've heard of me, Mr Harding, but I'm Abby Freeman—'

She didn't get any further than that. The door firmly slammed in her face.

He had heard of her, she thought ruefully. His reaction was a bit drastic, though! Especially as he must have received at least two letters concerning appearing on her show—one from her researchers, and one from her personally. Neither of which he had answered. But he might at least have—

Her eyes widened as the door suddenly swung open again. A hand reached out to grasp the collar of her jacket, and she was unceremoniously pulled inside the apartment, her boot-clad feet barely touching the luxurious carpet.

'Mr Harding—'

'How the hell did you get up here?' He glowered down at her, somehow still managing to look imposing despite his lack of clothing and the wild disorder of his overlong dark hair.

Abby blinked, totally stunned at finding herself inside the apartment instead of outside it.

She delayed answering as she pulled her white T-shirt back into place beneath her black jacket, her ebony hair loose onto her shoulders, blue eyes wide as she fought her inner feelings of indignation.

'I said—'

'The man downstairs let me in,' she cut in.

'After you told him what?' Max Harding bit out contemptuously, hands on narrow hips.

Bare hips, Abby noted somewhat awkwardly. The towel was starting to slip down those long, muscular, hair-covered legs.

'I'm waiting for an explanation, Miss Freeman,' he reminded her harshly, those grey eyes glacial now.

Abby bristled; he sounded like a schoolteacher talking to a disobedient schoolgirl!

'Maybe you should go and put some clothes on?' she suggested with forced pleasantness. 'I'm sure you—' and she! '—would be more comfortable if you did.'

'I'm not uncomfortable, Miss Freeman,' he assured her derisively, enjoying the fact that she obviously was. His mouth hardened before he spoke again. 'Exactly what story did you spin Henry in order to get him to let you up here without first ringing me?'

That cold silver gaze was very forceful, Abby decided with discomfort. The sort of gaze that would compel you to confess to whatever it was this man *wanted* you to confess to, whether you were guilty or not.

She grimaced. 'I told him I was your younger sister, that it's your birthday today, and that I wanted to surprise you,' she answered truthfully.

That sculptured mouth twisted wryly. 'Not bad for a beginner,' he drawled.

Her cheeks flushed. 'Now, look—'

'On your way out,' Max Harding continued, as if she hadn't spoken, 'you can tell him you succeeded.' He opened the door pointedly. 'I'll tell him what I think later!' he added grimly.

Abby didn't move towards the door. Having got this far, she had no intention of leaving just yet. 'I hope not with any idea of reprimand in mind? I can be very persuasive when I try.' She gave him an encouraging smile.

A smile he made no effort to return, and that steely, unamused grey gaze quickly made the smile falter and then fade.

Back to business, she decided hastily. 'I've written to you several times, Mr Harding—'

'Twice, to be exact,' he interrupted, his terse tone telling her that he liked to be that, at least. 'Two letters, both of which I read before duly consigning them to the bin!'

He had enjoyed telling her that, Abby realised with an annoyance she tried hard not to show—one of them being antagonistic was quite enough! Besides, she couldn't afford to be. She had assured the sarcastic and sceptical Gary Holmes, director of *The Abby Freeman Show*, that she would get Max Harding to appear on her final show. A very ambitious claim, she had come to re-alise over the last few weeks, but she needed some-thing—someone!—really impressive to finish the series if she were to stand any chance of being offered another contract.

Though she did wish she had approached Max Harding before making that ambitious claim to Gary…!

She gave Max Harding a bright, unruffled smile. 'Then you will be aware that the whole of the half-hour show will be dedicated to you—'

'No.'

'Oh, but I'm sure I made that clear in my letter.' Abby frowned. 'I would hardly offer less to a man of your professional stature—'

'Cut the bull, Miss Freeman,' he bit out harshly. 'In this case flattery, professional or otherwise, will get you precisely nowhere! I have no intention, now or ever, of appearing on *The Abby Freeman Show*.' He made the programme title sound like something obscene.

Nevertheless, Abby persevered; this was too impor-tant to allow obvious insults to upset her. 'But you're such an interesting man, Mr Harding,' she said lightly. 'You've seen so much, done so much, and I'm sure the general public would be fascinated to hear about—'

'The general public have absolutely no more inter-est than you do in hearing about any of the things I've seen and done,' he rasped coldly. 'All anyone wants to hear about from me is the night Rory Mayhew tried to commit suicide on my television programme.' His eyes glittered icily. 'It also happens to be the one thing I will never discuss in public. Is that clear enough for you, Miss Freeman?'

Crystal-clear. And he was partly right about the Rory Mayhew 'incident'; obviously it was such a big thing that she could hardly *not* ask about it. But it certainly wasn't the only thing she wanted him to talk about. They could hardly discuss an attempted suicide for the whole of a thirty-minute interview, for goodness' sake.

'I thought about mentioning that initially, obviously,' she conceded. 'But then I thought we could move on to other things. Your last two years as a foreign correspondent have made fascinating listening, and—'

'I said no, Miss Freeman.'

'Oh, please do call me Abby,' she invited, with a warmth she was far from feeling. In fact, the coldness emanating from this man was enough to make her give an involuntary shiver.

'You can call me Mr Harding,' he bit out. 'But first—' he moved to close the door again, its soft click much more ominous than the loud slam of a few minutes ago '—I have one or two questions I would like to put to you.'

The sudden smoothness of his tone was more menacing than his previous sarcasm and coldness, making Abby very aware that she was completely alone in this penthouse apartment with a powerful-looking man. A very angry, half-naked, powerful-looking man!

She gave him another of her bright, confident smiles—although inside she was neither of those things. This meeting with Max Harding wasn't turning out at all as she had hoped. 'Fire away, Mr Harding,' she invited lightly. 'I'm happy to answer any questions you have concerning the programme. In fact, I look on it as a very positive—'

'My questions have absolutely nothing to do with your programme, Miss Freeman,' he assured her scornfully, 'and everything to do with how you obtained my personal address in the first place.' His voice had hardened over this last, his expression grim.

Not much of a chance of him offering her a coffee, then! Or inviting her to sit down in the comfortable lounge she could see through the open doorway behind her.

Not much chance of this turning into a successful meeting, either, if the conversation so far was anything to go by.

'And don't say the local telephone book,' he warned. 'Because I'm ex-directory.'

Her palms were starting to feel slightly damp, and she was sure there was an unbecoming sheen materialising on her top lip.

Nevertheless, she forced another carefree smile to her face. 'The *how* isn't really important—'

'It is to me.' He stood firmly in front of the door now—her only means of escape!—powerfully muscled arms folded in front of that bare chest.

In the same circumstances, wrapped only in a towel, Abby knew that she would feel at a distinct disadvantage talking to anyone. And yet this man gave no such impression—in fact, the opposite. He seemed to know exactly how his near-nakedness was making her feel— and he was enjoying watching her squirm.

Because squirming she undoubtably was. This man, Max Harding, she was becoming increasingly aware, exuded a sexual magnetism that had very little to do with whether or not he was wearing any clothes! There was a toughness to him, a self-containment, that at thirty-nine had been hard earned.

He made a sudden movement, quickly followed by the first sign of amusement, albeit mocking, she had seen on his harsh features. Abby instinctively took a step backwards. 'I don't usually eat little girls like you until after breakfast,' he drawled, grey eyes mocking as he looked her over with slow deliberation. 'You're one of those "bright young things" the powers-that-be in public television have decided the masses want piped into their homes every minute of the day and night, aren't you?'

'I—'

'What did you do before being given *The Abby Freeman Show*?' he continued, unabated. 'Present one of those kids programmes where you have to constantly look like a teenager—even though you're not—and rush around risking life and limb climbing mountains and jumping out of aeroplanes? I'm sorry, what did you say?' he prompted scornfully as Abby muttered something inaudible.

Her chin rose defensively, twin circles of colour in her cheeks. 'I said I was the weather presenter on a breakfast show, and then the stand-in presenter,' she repeated tautly. Withstanding Max Harding's obvious derision certainly hadn't been in her plans for today!

He continued to look at her, his expression blank now, as if he wasn't quite sure he had heard her correctly. And then his mouth twitched and he began to laugh, a harsh, humourless sound that echoed the scorn in his eyes. 'A weather girl?' he finally sobered enough to say disbelievingly.

Her cheeks felt on fire now. 'You don't have a lot of respect for your fellow presenters, do you?'

'On the contrary, Abby, I have *immense* respect for my fellow presenters—you just don't happen to be one!'

This was important to her—very important if she was to prove to Gary Holmes she wasn't the lightweight he insisted on treating her as. But right now, with Max Harding's derision directly in her face, she wanted to turn on her heel and run. Unfortunately, Max Harding still stood between her and the door!

Attack, she was sure, was still the best form of defence. 'I never had you figured for a misogynist, Mr Harding!'

He didn't even grimace at the insult. 'Oh, but I'm not, Abby,' he told her, silkily soft, his grey eyes hooded as he looked her over with slow deliberation from her toes to the top of her ebony head. The arrogantly mocking gaze finally returned to her flushed face and he gave a derisive shake of his head. 'You just aren't my type,' he drawled, with deliberate rudeness.

She should never have come here, Abby realised belatedly. She had thought she was being so clever, fooling Henry downstairs, and had been quietly patting herself on the back at her success all the way up here in the lift. But all she had really succeeded in doing was totally annoying this man. And even on this short an acquaintance she knew he would be dangerous when he was annoyed!

Come to that, he was dangerous when he *wasn't* annoyed. She couldn't imagine what she had been thinking of!

She hadn't really been thinking at all, she finally realized. Had been too stung by Gary Holmes's scornful scepticism that she would ever persuade Max Harding to appear on her show to plan this meeting today any further than actually meeting the man face to face.

'You and my director should meet,' she snapped irritably. 'The two of you have so much in common!'

'Doesn't he like working with amateurs either?' Max Harding taunted.

That was it.

She had had enough.

More than enough!

She had already spent weeks at the sharp end of Gary Holmes's sarcastic tongue; she had no intention of taking it from this man too! Besides, he wasn't going to appear on her show anyway, so she really had nothing to lose!

She drew herself up angrily. 'I have no idea why I ever thought anyone would be interested in hearing anything you have to say.' And she didn't—not anymore. 'You're rude. You're arrogant. You're mocking, and thoroughly unpleasant. And I don't like you!' Her hands were clenched into fists at her sides.

Max Harding continued to look at her for several long seconds, and then he gave a decisive nod. 'That, my dear Abby, is the most honest thing you've said all morning! Come on.' He stepped past her into the lounge. 'I'll put some coffee on to brew while I'm dressing.'

Abby stood open-mouthed, watching him as he strolled across the sitting room and into what she assumed must be the kitchen.

She had been as rude and brutally frank as he was himself, and now he was offering to make her coffee!

She gave a slightly befuddled shake of her head before following him. She would have given up all pretence of politeness long before now if she had known this would be the result.

The sitting room, as she had already observed from the hallway, was spacious and well-furnished, decorated in warm, sunny golds and creams, with a wonderful view over London from the huge picture window. It also looked totally unlived-in—like a hotel suite, or as if the interior designer had only finished his work yesterday and everything was new and unused.

The kitchen was almost as big, with walnut cupboards and gold-coloured fittings. But apart from the coffee percolator, which had already started its aromatic drip into the pot, the work surfaces were bare—as if this room were rarely used either.

'Take a seat,' Max Harding invited, without turning round as he got coffee mugs from a cupboard.

Abby made herself comfortable on one of the stools at the breakfast bar—well, as comfortable as someone of five foot four could be on one of the high stools!—still not quite sure how she had managed to get herself invited in for coffee. But she wasn't complaining. The less inclined Max Harding was to throw her out, the more chance she had of persuading him to change his mind about appearing on her programme.

'Right.' He turned from what he was doing. 'I'll go and throw on some clothes while the coffee's filtering. Oh, and Abby?' He paused in the kitchen doorway, his expression once again derisive. 'Stay exactly where you are!'

She looked at him blankly for several seconds, frowning, her cheeks becoming hot as she realised what he meant. 'I'm not a snoop, Mr Harding,' she protested waspishly.

His mouth twisted. 'That's why you'll never make an investigative reporter!' he retorted, before leaving the room.

Abby put her elbows on the breakfast bar and leant forward to rub her throbbing temples with her thumbs, wondering if all these insults really were worth it. Even if she succeeded if getting him to appear on the show—

which was doubtful!—there was no way, him being the man that he was, that she was going to be able to control the interview. And that wasn't going to help her get that second contract she wanted. Maybe…

'I didn't mean it quite that literally,' Max remarked scathingly as he came back into the room. 'You could have helped yourself to coffee.'

In truth, she had been so lost in her own thoughts she hadn't really been aware that the coffee had stopped filtering into the pot. And, as she looked up at him now, her mind once again went completely blank.

'I'll go and throw on some clothes' was what he had said, and, looking at him, that was pretty much what he had done. His damp hair looked as if he had just run a hand through it, he was wearing a clean, but very creased white T-shirt, and a pair of ragged denims, also clean, but worn and faded, the bottoms frayed. And that was all he was wearing from what Abby could tell. His feet were bare on the coolness of the tiled floor.

He looked sexy as hell!

This side of Max Harding hadn't really been apparent in the tapes of his shows she had watched from the archives, but she had certainly been made aware of it when he'd opened the door earlier, wearing only a towel. And—strangely—she was even more aware of him now, because the clothes hinted at the powerful body beneath.

She straightened, shaking her head. 'Sorry. It didn't occur to me.'

He placed a steaming mug of black, unsweetened coffee in front of her. 'There isn't any milk,' he announced off-handedly as he passed her the sugar bowl. 'I only got back late last night, and I haven't had time to shop yet.'

'Black is fine,' she assured him, though she usually took both cream and sugar in her beverages. Somehow, from the look of the unused kitchen, she doubted he had time to go to the shops very often!

'So.' He sat down opposite her at the breakfast bar, his gaze piercing. 'You have yet to answer my question.'

She could always try acting dumb and ask which question he was referring to— but as he already thought she was dumb that probably wasn't the approach to take!

She shrugged. 'I obtained your address from a friend of a friend,' she said dismissively, wishing she felt more self-confident and less physically aware of this man...

His gaze narrowed. 'Which friend of what friend?'

'Is that grammatically correct?' She attempted to tease, deciding that probably wasn't a good idea either as his scowl deepened. 'You aren't seriously expecting me to answer that?'

He didn't return her cajoling smile. 'I rarely joke about an invasion of my privacy,' he grated.

She raised ebony brows. 'Aren't you overreacting just a little? After all, I only rang the doorbell. You were the one who invited me in!'

'I can just as easily throw you out again!' he rasped. 'And I "invited" you in as you put it, for the sole purpose of ascertaining how you obtained my address.'

'Knowing full well that I couldn't possibly reveal my source,' Abby came back sharply. Challengingly. It was the first rule of being that investigative reporter he had told her she would never be; a source's identity was as sacrosanct to a reporter as the information a client gave to a lawyer.

Max sat back slightly, his expression—as usual!— unreadable. 'Tell me, Abby,' he said softly, 'just what made you think you would succeed where so many others have failed?'

She blinked, not sure she quite understood the question. Surely he didn't think that she trying to attract—?

'Not that, Abby.' He sighed. 'I was actually referring to other requests for me to appear on TV programmes or give personal interviews to newspapers over the last two years. Haven't I already assured you that you aren't my type?' His mouth twisted scathingly as his gaze raked over her ebony hair, deep blue eyes, creamy complexion and full, pouting lips.

Exactly what was 'his type'? Abby felt like asking, but didn't. As far as her research was concerned, he didn't appear to have a type. He had been married once, in his twenties, and amicably divorced only three years later, and the assortment of women he had been involved with over the years since that marriage didn't seem to fit into any type either, having ranged from hard-hitting businesswomen to a pampered Californian divorcee. The only thing those women seemed to have in common was independence. And possibly an aversion to marriage…?

'Well, that's something positive, at least,' Abby came back dismissively. 'Because you aren't my type either!'

Grudging amusement slightly lightened his expression. 'No,' he murmured thoughtfully. 'I should imagine a nice, safe executive of some kind, preferably in television, would be more your cup of tea.'

This man managed to make everything he said sound insulting!

And in this case he was wrong; she had been briefly engaged to a 'nice, safe executive of some kind'—and been totally bored by Andrew's complete lack of imagination. Besides, Monty hadn't liked him…

'Really?' she said wearily. 'How interesting.'

Max continued to look at her for several seconds, and then gave an appreciative grin. 'You sound like my mother when confronted by one of my father's more boring business associates!'

His father, Abby knew, was James Harding, the owner of Harding Industries. His charming and beautiful wife Amy was a banking heiress, and Max's mother. Obviously Max hadn't inherited that first trait of hers!

'Really?' Abby repeated unhelpfully, slightly disturbed by the attraction of that grin—and desperate not to show it.

'*Really?*' he mimicked dryly. 'Am I boring you, Abby?'

So far she hadn't been able to relax enough in this man's company to feel bored! But if he wanted to think that—fine; she needed every advantage she could get with this thoroughly disconcerting man. 'Not specifically,' she drawled, sounding uninterested.

His mouth quirked humorously. 'How about unspecifically?'

She pretended to give the idea some thought. In fact, she very much doubted too many people found this man boring; the level of mental alertness necessary just to have a conversation with him wouldn't allow for that. Besides, the man was playing with her, and, despite what he might think to the contrary, she really wasn't one of those vacuous 'young things' he had initially accused her of being. At least, she hoped she wasn't!

She had left school with straight As and gone on to graduate from university three years later with a degree in politics. But two years of working as a very junior underling to a politician who just wasn't going to make it, despite putting in sixteen-hour days, had very soon quashed her own ambitions in that direction, and she had done a complete about-face, becoming interested in a career in television instead.

Being the smiling face of a lowbrow programme's weather segment hadn't exactly stretched her mentally, but everyone had to start somewhere. Besides, being offered her own six-week series of interviews now was worth the year she had spent getting up at four-thirty in the morning just so that she could be at the studio bright and early to give her first weather report of the day when the programme began at six-thirty.

And even Max Harding, despite his privileged background and a father who had probably been able to pull a few strings for him, had to have started somewhere—

'Sorry?' She shook her head as she realised Max had just spoken to her.

'I asked whether your meteoric rise to fame has had something to do with the way you look rather than any real qualifications to do the job?' He looked at her challengingly.

He had obviously decided to make sure there was no possible chance of her being bored by him any longer!

But if his intention was to anger her by the obvious insult, then he hadn't succeeded in doing that either. She had heard every insult there was these last two months, from other women as well as men, and especially from Gary Holmes, and she was no longer shocked or bothered by them. Well…not much, anyway.

She gave him a pitying glance. 'Which one do you think I slept with? The producer or the director?'

Grudging respect darkened his eyes. 'Either. Or possibly both.' He shrugged.

Now he wasn't *trying* to be insulting—he was succeeding! 'Pat Connelly is a grandmother several times over, I believe, and seriously not my type!' Abby told him derisively. 'And Gary Holmes is just an obnoxious little creep!' she added with feeling.

A veteran director of fifteen years plus, Gary was one of the most handsome men Abby had ever met—but he had the infuriating habit of treating her like an idiot. He obviously disliked her—possibly because he also thought she was a pretty airhead—but as the dislike was wholly reciprocated Abby wasn't particularly bothered by his attitude. Except on a professional level. And he had hardly given her time to prove—

She suddenly realised that Max had gone strangely quiet, and looked across at him curiously, but she was able to learn nothing from his closed expression. 'What is it?' she prompted with a frown.

He seemed to snap himself out of that scowling silence with effort. 'Nothing,' he said abruptly. 'And if it's taken you this long to think about my previous question, perhaps you would be wiser not to answer at all!' he drawled, with some of his earlier mockery. 'Who's scheduled to appear on your first programme?'

She was a little stunned by this abrupt *volte face*, and would have liked to pursue the reason for his sudden silence, but the coldness in his gaze was enough to warn her that she would get precisely nowhere if she did.

'Natalie West and Brad Hammond,' she answered instead, with not a little pride.

The famous couple, both having appeared on prime-time television, but in different series, had been involved in the very noisy and very public break-up of their marriage six months ago, culminating with Natalie announcing it would give her great pleasure to see Brad run over with a steamroller, and Brad retaliating with the claim that he would gladly step in the path of the steamroller if it meant he didn't have to set eyes on Natalie ever again!

It had taken weeks of persuasion and negotiation on Abby's part, but she had finally got them both to agree—separately—to appear together on her opening programme. It promised to be an explosive debut for *The Abby Freeman Show*!

Max whistled softly through his teeth. 'Are you going to supply the steamroller?'

He did have a sense of humour after all! He also, despite his many career-related trips out of the country, obviously kept up with the less serious side of current affairs.

Abby shook her head, her hair silky against her cheeks, blue eyes gleaming with laughter. 'I already checked—even if Natalie felt so inclined, a steamroller wouldn't fit through the studio door!'

Max gave an appreciative chuckle. 'Perhaps you aren't such a lightweight after all!'

It was far from an apology for his earlier rudeness— in fact it was still a remark tinged with condescension— but it was certainly an improvement on his initial antagonism. 'Does that mean you'll reconsider appearing on my programme?' God, how it still gave her a thrill of pleasure to say 'my programme'!

She had earned a certain amount of recognition from her appearances on breakfast television, with members of the public coming up to her in supermarkets and restaurants to say hello, but she was really hoping that having her own programme was going to take her one step further than that, and earn her the professional respect of people like Max Harding. If she ever got the chance, that was!

'Not in the least.' He instantly shot her down, his tone bored and noncommittal. And totally uncompromising. 'And, as you aren't going to tell me who this "friend of a friend" is…' He raised dark brows.

'I told you I can't do that,' she confirmed, her disappointment acute at his continued refusal.

Max shrugged. 'Then it would appear we have nothing else to say to each other.' He stood up, removing his own empty coffee mug and Abby's full one and placing them on the worktop before turning to look at her pointedly.

He was obviously waiting for her to leave.

She had lied her way up here in the first place, and been taken in to this man's inner sanctum, yet still she had failed in her objective. But other than continuing to pressure him—something guaranteed to annoy him even further—she didn't have any choice but to comply with his less than subtle hint.

'You won't be too hard on Henry?' she asked as she followed Max back through the sitting room to the door. She hadn't realised earlier just how strongly Max felt about any invasion of his privacy, and Henry was a man of advanced years, who would have great difficulty finding another job if he was sacked from this one.

Max glanced back at her. 'Calm down, Abby,' he taunted. 'Having witnessed your persuasive powers firsthand—no, I won't be hard on Henry at all.' He opened the door as he spoke.

Her 'persuasive powers'? Did she have some of those? And if she did, why hadn't Max Harding been persuaded?

He shook his head, smiling slightly. 'Don't beat yourself up trying to work out what they are, Abby; all that matters is that they didn't work on me!'

Obviously not—but she would still have liked to know what they were. If she did, she might be able to use them again—to better effect!

But she could see by the derisive expression on Max's face as he stood there waiting for her to leave that he certainly wasn't going to enlighten her. Pity.

'I'll make a point of watching your first programme,' he told Abby softly as she stepped out into the hallway.

She stared up at him suspiciously, uncertain of exactly what he had meant by that, and unable to read any of his thoughts from his blandly mocking expression.

But he had just succeeded in increasing her own first-night nerves by one hundred per cent!

CHAPTER THREE

'WELL, well, if it isn't little Abby Freeman!'

Abby groaned as she sank further down into her armchair, having instantly recognised Max Harding's mocking voice.

Holed up in a corner of the Dillmans' crowded drawing room, having already drunk three-quarters of the bottle of champagne sitting in the ice bucket on the low table beside her, she was in no mood for company. Something everyone else in the room, including her hosts Dorothy and Paul, seemed to know instinctively and act upon—and of which Max Harding had taken no notice whatsoever!

'Go away,' she muttered, without so much as glancing in his direction. She could see the long length of his legs from the corner of her eye, though, and observed that he didn't move by so much as an inch.

'I didn't have you figured as a woman who likes to drink alone.' He sounded amused now.

Abby raised dark lashes in order to glare at him, her gaze belligerent. 'I don't usually drink—alone or otherwise,' she snapped impatiently. 'But I'm sure that you and probably everyone else in this room are aware of the reason I've made tonight the exception.' And several million other people, she thought with another inner groan at the remembered humiliation.

How could she have known? How could she have guessed? Why hadn't someone told her?

'Hey, Abby, it really wasn't that bad.' Max came down on his haunches beside her chair now, the amusement having disappeared from his voice as he looked at her with something like concern. 'In fact, I thought you recovered very well.'

She hadn't 'recovered' well at all, and she was sure that everyone watching the airing of her first show earlier this evening had known it, too.

As previously agreed, she had interviewed Brad Hammond first for ten minutes, chatting warmly about his earlier career and his success now in a popular television series. Then Brad had gone off the set and Natalie had come on for her allotted ten minutes, discussing her own success.

But all the time those interviews were taking place a buzz had been felt in the studio. Both crew and audience obviously waiting expectantly for the time the estranged pair would come on together, with the promise of emotional fireworks in the air.

Except it had turned out Brad and Natalie were no longer estranged!

Abby had announced the two of them coming on together, feeling the tension rising in the studio as she did so, and could have collapsed in a heap when, instead of showing antagonism, Brad and Natalie had smiled warmly at each other before kissing and sitting down close together, their hands entwined, as Brad announced that the two of them had been reconciled for three days.

Abby had been rendered speechless by the announcement. All her carefully prepared questions had become null and void—questions she had spent hours labouring over in an effort to ensure she wouldn't become the cause of further antagonism between the separated couple, intending to leave it to the two of them to set their own scene with as little prompting from her as possible. Brad's announcement had made a complete nonsense of them.

She'd done her best to rally round at this sudden change of circumstances, congratulating them on their reconciliation, asking what their plans were for the future. A *baby*, for goodness' sake; after all the public insults they had hurled at each other over the last six months!

Yes, Abby had done her best to keep the show alive and buzzing, but she had been aware that it had definitely lacked the sparkle and interest she had been hoping for when she'd invited the pair on her show.

And Gary Holmes's snort of derision when she'd finally walked off the set had been enough to send her hurtling for the champagne bottle the moment she'd reached Dorothy and Paul's house half an hour ago.

'Go away,' she told Max Harding a second time, turning away to lift up the champagne bottle, having no intention of crossing swords with him this evening.

Instead of complying with her request, she felt him take the champagne bottle from her hand. Her grip tightened but was no match for Max's superior strength. The fluted champagne glass in her other hand was the next to go, before Max took her by one of her now empty hands and pulled her effortlessly to her feet.

'You need food,' he told her firmly as she began to

protest. 'Otherwise the headlines on tomorrow's tabloids will read "Abby Freeman plastered", accompanied by a photograph of you being carried out of here!' He didn't wait for any more arguments as he tucked her hand into the crook of his arm and guided her into the adjoining room, where a table was set with a sumptuous buffet supper.

Not that Abby had been about to argue with him; the way she'd swayed unsteadily as she got to her feet, with the room tilting dizzily, was enough to tell her that food was exactly what she needed. Even if it was the last thing she *wanted!*

'There you go.' Max placed a heavily laden plate in her unresisting hand before turning to choose some food for himself.

Abby's vision blurred as she looked down at the food. 'Why are you being so nice to me?' She sniffed, not sure she was going to be able to hold back the tears for much longer, despite blinking them away desperately.

He glanced at her, very tall and handsome in a black evening suit and snowy white shirt, although the dark hair was even longer than it had been when they'd met three weeks ago, and the grey eyes were still as mockingly amused.

'I figured someone ought to be,' he drawled dismissively. 'You presented rather a lonely figure sitting in there.' He nodded in the direction of the drawing room.

Pity. He felt sorry for her. And only hours ago she had hoped to finish this evening on a note of triumph. Euphoria, even.

'Keep your damned pity!' she snapped as she slammed the untouched plate of food back down on the table, her eyes sparkling deeply blue, twin spots of

angry colour in her cheeks. 'You've heard of the phoe-
nix rising from the ashes? Well, watch the show next
week and see what a good job I make of doing exactly
that!' She turned on her heel and walked—steadily,
thank goodness!—out of the room, unknowingly beautiful in her midnight-blue knee-length dress, dark hair
loose about her shoulders. She made her way over to
where she could see Dorothy, chatting with a well-
known newspaper reporter.

Dorothy's parties were always like this—attended
by the rich and the famous—although Dorothy herself
was one of the least glamorous people Abby knew. Her
plain black evening gown was an old favourite with her,
her face was homely rather than beautiful, and her figure tended towards comfortable plumpness now that
she was approaching her sixtieth year.

But Abby had known the other woman all her life—
knew that it was Dorothy's genuine warmth and kind-
ness that attracted people to her like a magnet. Her
handsome husband of the last thirty-five years absolutely adored her.

'You can't leave just yet, Abby!' Dorothy responded
with genuine regret at Abby's excuse of tiredness. 'I
haven't had a chance to introduce you to anyone,' she
protested. 'Jenny and I were just commenting on what
an absolute triumph your programme was this evening.
Natalie and Brad have made complete idiots of themselves these last few months, and I don't think there was
a dry eye in the house—well, certainly not in this one!'
she admitted unabashedly '—when they announced that
they're back together and trying for a baby.'

Abby's smile was fixed on her face with sickening
determination. She knew Dorothy was only trying to be

kind by talking like that about her show—the older woman didn't know how to be anything else!—but Abby really wished she didn't have to stand here and listen to this. The whole show had been a disaster as far as she was concerned—and as far as Gary Holmes was, too, if his scornful remarks as she'd left the studio were anything to go by.

'Yes.' Jenny Jones took over the conversation, her manner slightly gushing. 'The Natalie and Brad reconciliation was an absolute coup for your first programme!'

Was it? Or was the other woman just veiling her sarcasm for Dorothy's benefit?

No, Abby realized, slightly dazedly, Jenny Jones looked genuinely disappointed that *she* hadn't been the one to scoop the exclusive.

Abby brightened. Maybe it hadn't been such a disaster, after all? Meaning that perhaps Max's earlier comments hadn't been out of the pity that she had thought they were either?

No—there was no need to go that far! If her show *hadn't* been the complete failure she had initially thought it was, then she still knew she had only scraped through by the skin of her teeth, and someone as acutely intelligent as Max would be aware of that fact, too. And she would rather listen to Dorothy and Jenny's misplaced praise, than Max's mocking condescension.

'My editor is running the story on the front page tomorrow,' Jenny confided. '"Abby Shock: Brad No Longer a Free Man!"'

Abby gave a pained wince at the awful play on her surname. Although she couldn't really have expected much else from the dreadful rag Jenny worked for. But she didn't think Natalie would care for the headline too much, either!

'How clever,' Dorothy put in lightly at the lengthening silence. 'I do so wish I could think of things like that.'

'It comes with experience,' Jenny consoled her slightly pityingly as she laid a sympathetic hand on the other woman's arm. 'I— Oh, look, there's Max Harding.' Her green eyes were bright with the fervour of the predator as she spotted Max entering the room. 'I've been wanting to speak to him for absolutely ages. If you ladies would excuse me…?' she added distractedly, not waiting for either of them to reply before striding purposefully across the room in Max Harding's direction.

'Gladly!' Dorothy muttered with feeling. 'That woman is such a pompous bore!' she added with disdain.

'Dorothy…?' Abby looked at the older woman incredulously. 'I've never heard you say an unkind word about anyone before,' she explained at Dorothy's questioning look.

'No? Well, put it down to my age.' Dorothy chuckled, easily shrugging off her brief bad humour. 'My only consolation is that I know Max will quickly send her away with a flea in her ear! There.' She nodded with satisfaction as she glanced across the room. 'That has to be something of a record—even for Max.' She sounded impressed.

Abby turned just in time to see Jenny Jones beating a hasty retreat from the glacially angry Max. There were twin spots of humiliated colour in the tabloid reporter's cheeks. Having received what Abby was sure was a similar put-down herself only three weeks ago, she couldn't help but feel a certain fleeting sympathy for the other woman.

'Why does he do that?' she mused, shaking her head as she turned back to look at Dorothy. 'And get away with it, too!' she added wryly, absolutely positive that not a single word of Max's rude put-down of the other woman would ever reach the pages of even the tacky tabloid Jenny worked for.

'Because he's absolutely brilliant at what he does, of course,' Dorothy answered. 'And gorgeous as hell, too,' she added with relish.

Abby watched as Max fell into easy conversation with Dorothy's husband Paul. The two men were of similar height and build. Paul's blond hair was sprinkled liberally with grey, but otherwise, to Abby's eyes, he looked every bit as fit and handsome as the younger man.

'I would rather have Paul any day,' she announced firmly.

'Well, of course, having been married to the darling man for thirty-five years, so would I,' Dorothy agreed laughingly. 'But that doesn't mean I'm blind to the way other men look—and Max has to be the epitome of "tall, dark and handsome". And all that brooding aloofness has to be a direct challenge to any normal red-blooded woman!'

Then Abby had to be an *abnormal* red-blooded woman—because she had been daunted by Max rather than attracted to him.

Well…she had been attracted to him too—but the daunting had definitely outweighed that attraction!

'If you like that sort of thing,' she dismissed, with an audible sniff of uninterest.

Dorothy gave her a searching look, warm blue eyes probing now. 'You never did tell me how your meeting with him went three weeks ago…?'

Abby withstood that searching gaze for several long seconds before looking away. 'I told you—he said no to coming on the show,' she said with a casual shrug.

'Yes, but—'

'Dorothy, I really don't want to talk about Max Harding.'

'I'm glad to hear it,' he drawled mockingly from directly behind her, making Abby start guiltily. His grey eyes were openly laughing as she turned sharply to face him. 'I find the subject of me boring, too,' he acknowledged, with a derisive inclination of his dark head.

'Then at least we're agreed on something, Mr Harding!' she came back waspishly, completely disconcerted at having him appear behind her in this way; the last time she had looked he had been deep in conversation with Paul.

'Well, well.' Dorothy chuckled with delight. 'What do you have to say to that, Max?' she teased, obviously deeply amused by the turn in conversation.

Max gave the older woman an affectionate smile. 'That Abby obviously has exceptional taste,' he drawled unconcernedly. 'Here.' He handed Abby one of the two champagne flutes he held in his hands. 'I thought you might be in need of it after talking to Jenny Jones!' He grimaced.

'What a perfectly dreadful woman,' Dorothy agreed as Abby rather dazedly took the glass of bubbly wine from Max. 'I really will have to have a chat with Paul about the sort of people he's inviting into our home. In fact, if the two of you will excuse me, I think I'll just go and have a word with him now.' She gave them a bright smile before moving to join her husband.

Leaving Abby completely alone with Max Harding. Again. And, despite the champagne she had consumed earlier, she now felt completely sober. Stone-cold sober.

'How is it that you know the Dillmans so well?' Max asked lightly.

'As until quite recently I was only a lowly weather girl, you mean?' she came back tartly.

He took a leisurely sip of his champagne, that grey gaze unwavering as it met Abby's seething eyes. 'I didn't say that,' he finally drawled.

'You didn't need to. But it just so happens that I've known the Dillmans all my life,' she told him with satisfaction.

'Really?' Max murmured, his gaze speculative as he glanced across to where Dorothy was now in laughing conversation with her husband. '"A friend of a friend", I believe you said...?' That grey gaze was once again fixed piercingly on Abby.

Damn it! She was sure Max had just set a trap for her—and she had just walked straight into it. Like an innocent mouse into the lion's den. But unfortunately she seemed to have taken Dorothy in with her, and the other woman deserved better than that.

'That description hardly fits Dorothy,' Abby told him. 'She happens to be my godmother.' Dorothy *was* actually the 'friend of a friend' who had told her Max's home address, but Abby had no intention of betraying her godmother's confidence by admitting that.

'Your godmother?' Max repeated evenly, seeming to be having trouble digesting this piece of information.

'Yes—godmother,' Abby confirmed, wondering what he found so strange about that. 'She and my mother were at school together, and they have remained friends ever since,' she added defensively, wondering just what his problem was with that. Although, whatever it was, it had at least succeeded in diverting his attention away from that 'friend of a friend' she had unwisely admitted three weeks ago to have been the source of his address.

She wasn't quite prepared for what he did next. She was sure her comment hadn't warranted derisive laughter!

But laughter was a definite improvement on his usual mocking expression. Laughter lines appeared beside his eyes and mouth, his teeth were very white and even, and he had a slight dimple in the groove of one cheek.

But none of that detracted from the fact she had no idea what she had said that was so amusing.

'So you were telling the truth after all about your producer and director?' he finally taunted, once his laughter had faded. 'It was relatives in high places instead,' he added appreciatively. 'Oh, don't worry, Abby, I'm not knocking it,' he went on, at her startled and indignant expression. 'We all have to start somewhere, and why not use the advantages—the less obvious ones—' he gave her slender attractiveness in the midnight-blue dress an appreciative glance '—that you have at your disposal.'

It didn't matter that Abby had no idea what he was talking about. His mocking tone and derisive expression were enough to tell her it was nothing pleasant. But then 'pleasant' hardly described this man, did it?

She gave a shake of her head, her raggedly layered hair dark and shining as it moved on her shoulders. 'I'm not sure which of us has imbibed the most champagne this evening, Max, but I do know I have no idea what you're talking about. So either you're talking gibberish, or I'm just too befuddled to understand you. Either way, I think it best if we terminate this conversation right now,' she added firmly, more than ever determined to follow through on her earlier decision to make her excuses and leave.

'This is my first drink of the evening.' Max held up his barely touched glass of champagne.

Implying she *was* the one who was 'too befuddled' to understand him. Well, he might just be right about that. It had been a long day—and an even longer evening.

She straightened determinedly. 'I wish I could say it's been a pleasure meeting you again, Mr Harding—'

'Oh, I think we're well enough acquainted now for you to call me Max,' he drawled mockingly. 'As you did a few minutes ago.'

They weren't acquainted at all—in fact, she knew less about this man than she had thought she did the first time she'd met him. 'If you say so.' She gave him an insincere smile, hoping they wouldn't meet again, so she wouldn't need to call him anything. 'I really do have to go now, Max,' she continued brightly. 'So, if you'll excuse me—? What are you doing?' she demanded indignantly as he reached out and grasped her arm when she would have turned and walked away.

It wasn't just that the physical contact was so unexpected—though it was!—but also that Max Harding didn't give the impression he was the touchy-feely type of man that always made her cringe. In fact, to date he had given the clear impression that his ice might be in danger of melting if he actually touched someone, and so he chose not to do it.

'Would you like me to give you a lift home?' came his also completely unexpected reply.

Abby frowned up at him, searching that enigmatic face for any hidden meaning behind his offer. But years of presenting an inscrutable expression to the world in general made that impossible.

'Why on earth would you want to do that?' Abby

couldn't keep the astonishment out of her voice. The last time the two of them had met he hadn't been able to get rid of her fast enough.

And yet he had been the one to approach her this evening—not once but twice, so perhaps...

'I haven't changed my mind about your show, Abby,' he assured her mockingly.

Which was exactly what she had been wondering! Were her thoughts so obvious to everyone? Or was it only this man who seemed to know what she was thinking?

That definitely wasn't a good idea, considering some of the thoughts she had been having about him. They swung erratically between being left breathless by his animal magnetism to actually wanting to hit him!

He was grinning when she glanced back at him—as if he had definitely been aware of *that* thought.

'You can't blame me for trying.' She shrugged dismissively, avoiding that knowing gaze.

'I never blame anyone for trying, Abby,' he retorted. 'But, to answer your earlier question, considering you know exactly where my apartment is, I thought it only fair that I should know where you live, too!'

'Fair' had nothing to do with it. Where this particular man was concerned she was a lot more comfortable with him *not* knowing where she lived!

'It's not far from here, actually,' she said evasively. 'In fact, I walked over this evening.'

He nodded. 'It's a pleasant spring evening. A walk sounds an excellent idea.'

Not with this man it didn't. And why was he being so persistent? He obviously thought her a lightweight in the world of television, and had made no effort to disguise the fact that he wasn't particularly enamoured of her as a woman, either—those remarks about her not being his type had stung! So why was he deliberately seeking out her company now?

His face, unfortunately, revealed none of his inner thoughts or emotions.

'There's really no need for you to accompany me,' she assured him lightly. 'This is one of the safer areas of London.'

'One of the more expensive ones, you mean,' Max drawled. 'I guess having your own show pays a lot more than being a weather girl?'

'I guess it does!' she snapped, blue eyes glittering angrily. He was so insulting!

In fact, she had been quite surprised at just how *much* more her change in status paid. Moving to a new apartment two months ago was only one of the changes it had made in her life. She had a sporty Jaguar in the underground car park of the apartment building, and the wardrobe allowance for her new show was almost more than she had earned in a year at her previous job.

Still, it was really none of his business.

'Do you ever say anything nice?'

'Sometimes—when I forget myself,' he said unrepentantly. 'Do you have somewhere else you have to go?'

'No—'

'Then let's go for that walk, shall we?' he announced briskly, giving her no further time to protest as he took a firm hold of her arm, quickly made their excuses to Dorothy, and pulled her along at his side as he made his way with assurance towards the door.

It had still been light outside when Abby had arrived a short time ago, but it was completely dark now. The high heels of her shoes echoed in the silence of this residential area of the city. In fact, it was almost as if they were the only two people around, with only the distant roar of the Friday evening traffic to confirm that they weren't.

Which wasn't nearly enough, as far as Abby was concerned. Max maintained his light but unshakeable hold on her arm as they walked along together, making her skin tingle with awareness. Maybe she was a 'normal red-blooded woman' after all!

Because awareness seemed to be coursing through her whole body. She was beginning to feel warm all over, her breathing shallow as she shot him a glance from beneath lowered dark lashes.

Dorothy was right. He really was gorgeous as hell. That overlong dark hair was crying out to have fingers running through it caressingly, and those sculptured lips, the bottom one fuller than the top, invited kisses. And as for the obvious power of the body beneath that formal evening suit—! Abby knew exactly how wide and muscled those shoulders were, clearly remembering the silky short hair on that powerful chest, the flatness of his tapered stomach, the force of his—

'You're very quiet— Careful!' Max steadied her as she stumbled slightly. 'Those strappy black sandals look great with your wonderful long legs,' he drawled, 'but they aren't very practical for walking anywhere!'

Max thought she had 'wonderful long legs'! It was amazing how the compliment gave her an inner glow.

Especially as until this moment she hadn't even thought he had noticed she *had* legs. The last—first— time they had met, she had been wearing denims. As for his remark about her being quiet—the more aware she became of him the more tongue-tied she felt. But she couldn't tell him that!

Instead she managed a casual shrug. 'You didn't give me the impression that you wanted to talk.'

'No?' He stood facing her now, his expression unreadable in the dim glow given off by the streetlights overhead. 'What did I give you the impression that I wanted to do instead?' His voice was huskily soft.

Abby swallowed hard, totally aware of how close he was standing, mere inches away from her—so close that the warmth of his breath stirred the feathery tendrils of hair on her forehead. She had no idea what Max wanted to do, while at the same time knowing exactly what she wanted him to do!

She wanted to have his lips against hers, to feel the lean strength of his arms about her as he moulded her body against his, to know the caress of his hands down her spine and against her sensitised breasts. And she wanted the same freedom to touch him intimately.

'Abby...?' he prompted softly at her continued silence. Breaking—thank goodness!—the emotional spell she had rapidly been falling under.

She gave herself a mental shake. This was Max Harding, for goodness' sake. A man who on first acquaintance she had decided was rude, arrogant and mocking—not to mention dangerous. She didn't even like him!

She still thought he was all of those things, but further acquaintance on her part had shown her he was also irresistibly attractive, sensually magnetic—and most definitely gorgeous. So much so that if he *had* kissed her a few moments ago, as she had so wanted him to, she knew she would have just melted into his arms, that the word 'no' would no longer have been part of her vocabulary.

But even acknowledging that to herself was enough to bring her to her senses with the suddenness of a bucket of water being thrown over her. This was Max Harding: cold, aloof and totally unobtainable!

She straightened, determinedly pulling her gaze away from the sensual kissability of those lips. 'Just walk me home and get this over with,' she instructed coolly, inwardly pleased at the normality of her tone—she had expected to sound like Minnie Mouse!

Max continued to look at her for several long seconds and then gave a curt nod of his head—whether of agreement to her statement or dismissal of it, Abby wasn't sure. 'Fine,' he rasped, no longer touching her as he strode forcefully ahead.

Leaving Abby to click-clack along behind him, in shoes that definitely weren't designed for it, in order to keep up with him. But she wasn't about to voice any complaint at the pace he had set. She just wanted to disappear into the privacy of her apartment now. Besides, she wouldn't give him the satisfaction!

Five minutes and probably a ruined pair of expensive shoes later, they reached the building that housed her apartment. 'Thank you for escorting me home,' she said with firm dismissal, and stood as if guarding the entrance to the building, having no intention of letting him get anywhere near her actual apartment.

'Very politely said!' Max's mouth twisted mockingly. 'Your mother and Dorothy obviously attended a good school.'

Abby gave him an impatient look, at the same time aware that there was something at the back of her mind that Max had said earlier, and it had been bothering her. 'What did you mean when you said I had relatives in high places?' She had thought it a strange remark at the time, but she had been slightly side-tracked after it and forgotten to pursue the subject.

Max tilted his head slightly as he looked down at her quizzically. 'You aren't trying to tell me that you don't know?' He sounded sceptical.

Her frown deepened. 'Don't know what?'

'About Paul Dillman's connection to Ajax Television—and consequently Dorothy's?' he drawled.

The obvious response to that was, What connection? But as she really didn't want to let this man know that she didn't have any idea what he was talking about, it was a question she had no intention of asking.

At least, not of Max.

CHAPTER FOUR

'PAUL recently became a major shareholder in Ajax Television,' Dorothy told her as she moved about her conservatory, watering her plants, glancing over only when Abby's silence lengthened. 'I thought I'd mentioned it to you?' the older woman prompted softly.

No, of course Dorothy hadn't mentioned it to her! If she had Abby might have questioned her sudden rise to fame a little more deeply. But she had genuinely thought it had happened as Pat Connelly had claimed—that Abby had done so well during her months of co-hosting the breakfast show that she was now being offered a show of her own.

Despite being awake most of the night thinking about this, she had waited until ten before calling to see Dorothy, aware that the party the evening before probably wouldn't have ended until late, and giving the other woman time to have a lie-in.

Abby hadn't been as lucky—unable to sleep at all after making her hurried goodbyes to Max and retreating to her apartment. Instead, she had paced up and down most of the night, wondering if what Max had claimed could possibly be true.

It obviously was!

Dorothy gave her a searching look. 'Abby? What difference does it make?'

'It makes a *lot* of difference,' Abby said sharply, feeling as if her whole world—well, her professional one, at least—was crashing down around her ears. First last night's disaster, and now this!

Dorothy put down her watering can, giving Abby her total attention now. 'I don't see why. Pat Connelly was the one to approach Ajax with the idea for the show. As I understood it, she had seen you on early-morning television and thought you had something more to give. Paul did become a shareholder a few months ago, Abby, but he's had very little to do with programme selection,' she added, when Abby still looked doubtful.

'Even if that's true—'

'It is,' the other woman assured her, with her customary briskness. 'Obviously when Paul was told of the idea of giving you your own chat show he was absolutely thrilled for you. But that's as far as his involvement went.' Dorothy's gaze sharpened suspiciously. 'Who has implied otherwise?'

Abby avoided meeting the older woman's gaze. 'It doesn't matter,' she said, deciding that perhaps it had been a mistake to question Dorothy about this—even if it had seemed the quickest way of getting an answer. 'I guess I'll just have to work twice as hard in an effort to prove those accusations of nepotism wrong, won't I?' she added with forced lightness.

'Who is "everyone"?' Dorothy looked most displeased. 'It isn't that awful Gary Holmes, is it?' she added disgustedly.

Abby's eyes widened. 'I didn't realise that you thought he was awful, too.'

Dorothy wrinkled her nose with distaste. 'I know he's wonderfully good-looking, darling, and that most women find him irresistible, but I'm well past the age where looks alone impress me. He made a pass at me once—which I thought totally out of line and Paul found highly amusing!' she added.

Abby gave a rueful smile at the image this evoked. 'No, for once this has nothing to do with Gary Holmes.'

'Who then? Not Max?' the older woman protested indignantly. 'Surely not…?' She seemed to be speaking to herself now rather than Abby. 'Despite what you said about him earlier in the evening, I noticed that the two of you seemed to be getting on well together last night. I was absolutely thrilled when you left together a short time later.'

'I can't imagine why,' Abby muttered with a dismissive shake of her head, glancing at her wristwatch. 'Is that really the time?' She feigned haste, although it was actually still only ten-thirty, and since it was a Saturday she had very little else to do but catch up on her laundry. But Max Harding, and yesterday evening were the last things she wanted to discuss right now—with Dorothy or anyone else.

'But we haven't even had coffee yet,' Dorothy protested. 'I was going to ring and have Dora make some.'

'I'll have to take a raincheck.' Abby smiled reassuringly—even though it was the last thing she felt like doing. 'I have to be somewhere else at eleven o'clock.' At home. With the door firmly locked. And the answering machine switched on to take any telephone calls.

Because at the moment she felt as if she needed a little time and space away from the rest of the world in order to lick her wounds in private.

Despite what Dorothy claimed to the contrary, she wasn't one hundred per cent convinced of Paul's non-involvement in choosing her to present Ajax Television's new Friday evening chat show.

'Just ignore it, Monty,' she advised her pet firmly as the doorbell rang for a second time in thirty seconds. 'Mum would have telephoned before coming, and I don't want to see anyone else.' She just wanted to continue sprawling on the sofa, Monty curled up on her chest, loudly purring his approval of this inactivity. 'You know, Monty, all I ever wanted—' She broke off as the doorbell rang a third time.

And kept ringing. And ringing. And ringing. Whoever her visitor was, he was keeping a finger continuously on the doorbell now.

Driving Abby insane!

'That's it!' She finally snapped after a good thirty seconds or so of the incessant nerve-jangling noise. She placed Monty gently on the cushioned sofa—attempting to do it any other way would probably have resulted in claw-flexing disapproval!—before standing up and pressing the intercom impatiently.

'Yes?' she snapped aggressively into the speaker, scowling. 'What is your problem?' She sounded as irritable as she felt, and was not in any sort of mood for visitors. Especially such a persistent one!

'Open the door, Abby,' a familiar voice drawled derisively.

Abby snatched her finger off the intercom as if it had burnt her. Max! What on earth was he doing here? Why—?

The doorbell began to ring again.

She pressed the intercom again. 'Will you stop doing that?'

'As soon as you open the door and let me in—yes,' he replied evenly.

She didn't want to open the door. Didn't want to see Max. Didn't want to speak to him. But the alternative, she realised as the bell began to ring again, was to be driven noisily insane by the sound of her own doorbell.

She pressed the door-release button, moving to shove open her apartment door too, before stomping back into the sitting room to throw herself back down onto the sofa—receiving a hiss and a scratch from Monty as she inadvertently sat down on him.

She picked up one of the cushions and hugged it to her defensively as she heard Max outside in the hallway, followed by the soft click of her apartment door closing as he let himself inside and came to stand in the lounge doorway. The still ruffled Monty refused to acknowledge her visitor by so much as a twitch of an eyebrow.

'Very nice,' Max murmured appreciatively as he moved forward into the room.

Abby was well aware that he couldn't be referring to her— the last time she had checked in the mirror she had looked less than her best. Her hair was in wild disorder from the light breeze blowing outside, and she'd made no effort to renew her lipgloss since her return from Dorothy's. He had to be commenting on her apartment.

It *was* very nice—the rooms spacious and grand, with a fantastic view over the Thames. But she was sure Max hadn't come here to discuss the comforts of her apartment. She didn't know what he *had* come here to discuss, but she was pretty sure it wasn't that!

'Max, what do you want?' she demanded rudely, keeping her gaze cool as she took in his appearance in those ragged denims and a black T-shirt.

God, he really was gorgeous, she acknowledged to herself. Her heart was beating erratically just at the sight of him.

'Coffee,' he replied briskly. 'Black. One sugar.' He dropped down into one of the comfortable armchairs.

Abby blinked dazedly. How did 'What do you want?' equate with 'Coffee. Black. One sugar'? And Monty was no help as a watch-cat either; he had beaten a hasty retreat into her bedroom at the first sound of Max's voice!

She frowned. 'I wasn't offering you anything to drink,' she told him impatiently.

'No?' He raised dark brows, his grey gaze moving slowly over her face before moving down to her slender curves in denims and a blue T-shirt. 'What were you offering me, then?'

Abby felt a betraying tingling down her spine as his husky, seductive tone washed over her, and knew that heat had coloured her cheeks.

Damn it, this man only had to look at her in a certain way, only had to talk to her in a certain way, and all she could think of was the nakedness of his body at that first meeting, her fingers aching to touch the silky dark hair on his chest.

She stood up restlessly, returning the cushion to the sofa. 'I was asking why you're here,' she explained succinctly.

Max looked up at her, gaze narrowed. 'You're looking tired today—didn't you sleep well?'

Abby glared at him. 'No, I didn't sleep well!' How

could she, after what he had told her about Paul's connection to Ajax Television?

He shrugged. 'The reviews were good in this morning's newspapers.'

Surprisingly, they had been—not all as sensationally headlined as Jenny Jones's rag, but very positive nonetheless. One more reputable newspaper had even commented that if the rest of *The Abby Freeman Show* proved to be as entertaining then she was a very welcome addition to the genre.

High praise indeed, but in Abby's mind none of that altered the fact that it hadn't been the show she had planned—or what she now knew of Paul's involvement with Ajax Television. If the formidable English press ever got hold of the fact that she had a personal connection to Dorothy Dillman then they would have a field-day!

'Or does your lack of sleep have anything to do with the fact that Dorothy telephoned me a short time ago and told me I have a big mouth?' Max added softly.

Abby's gaze swung instinctively to look at the mentioned feature. It was such a decisive-looking mouth— a mouth that in spite of herself she longed to kiss! Although at the moment it was set in a determined line as he waited for her answer.

'Did she?' Abby moistened her own lips with the tip of her tongue, her gaze not quite meeting his now.

'She did,' he confirmed with a pointed sigh. 'Something, as Dorothy happens to be one of my favourite people, I wasn't too pleased about. Even if—as I pointed out to her—I was just returning the compliment.' The steadiness of his gaze told her he was referring to the source who'd given her his address.

It was impossible to mistake his displeasure for anything else. The grey eyes were glittering, his earlier mocking humour gone without trace, his restless anger tangible in spite of the fact he still lounged back in the armchair.

'Dorothy is one of my favourite people, too,' she assured him quietly.

'I don't doubt it,' he rasped. 'But she hasn't just told *you* that you have a big mouth!'

No, and she couldn't imagine Dorothy having said that to Max, either. 'Dorothy is far too sweet to talk to anyone like that,' she argued.

Max shrugged. 'Ordinarily I would have said so too, but she told me to put it down to her age.'

Abby remembered that as the phrase her godmother had used the evening before, when discussing Jenny Jones, so perhaps Dorothy had said it after all. Abby's mother, Dorothy's best friend, had gone through the menopause several years ago, and she seemed to remember there had been something of a personality shift then, so maybe that was what Dorothy was referring to when she talked of her age being responsible for her uncharacteristic outspokenness.

'Well, I'm sorry if it was anything I said that caused Dorothy to talk to you in that way.' Abby sighed. 'But, after what you said last night, I needed some answers to some questions, and in the circumstances Dorothy seemed the obvious choice to give them to me.' Even if, as far as Abby was concerned, those answers had been less than satisfactory.

'How about I take you out and we discuss this further over lunch?'

Abby stared at Max now, too stunned by the suggestion to hide her surprise. 'You're inviting me out to lunch?' She looked at him suspiciously.

His mouth twitched as he easily read her disbelief. 'That would seem to be what I just did, yes,' he confirmed mockingly.

Her stare turned to a frown. Why on earth would Max Harding, of all people, be inviting her out to lunch? It was—

'You think too much, Abby,' he told her irritably, and he stood up. 'Grab a jacket and let's go.'

Did she want to go out to lunch with Max Harding? The answer to that was a definite yes!

And it had absolutely nothing to do with continuing her efforts to persuade him to appear on her show, on the basis that any dialogue between them was better than none, and everything to do with the fluttering sensation in her chest and her complete physical awareness of him.

He took some car keys out of the pocket of his ragged denims. 'Yes or no, Abby?'

A part of her so badly wanted to say no—if only to see the look on his face when she did. But the rest of her wanted to say yes—even if she did know it was a mistake to be attracted to this man.

'I'll take your silence as a no,' he rasped impatiently as he turned to leave.

'Yes!' Abby burst out forcefully.

Max came to a halt, slowly turning to face her, his expression unreadable. 'Yes, I can take that as a no? Or, yes, you'll have lunch with me?' His offhand tone implied he was no longer bothered either way.

Which he probably wasn't, Abby accepted ruefully. He had made the gesture—for whatever reason—and the rest was up to her. It was a sure fact that if she said no now he would never repeat the invitation.

'Yes, I'll come to lunch.' She plucked her jacket from the back of the chair, where she had thrown it earlier, deftly slipping her arms into the sleeves. 'After all, a free lunch is a free lunch!' she added with casual dismissal. No need to look too eager!

Max eyed her mockingly. 'Didn't you know, Abby? There's no such thing as a free lunch.'

Maybe there wasn't, but she couldn't for the life of her imagine what price he might consider extracting for buying her lunch; after all, he had told her on several occasions that she wasn't his type. And even if she was, that price might be a little high!

He sighed, indicating his impatience with her delay. 'Would you just get your act in gear? I get tetchy when I'm hungry,' he added ruefully.

Abby slung the strap of her bag over her shoulder. 'How can you tell?' she taunted as she passed him on her way to the door.

'Oh, ha-ha,' he muttered. 'You'll see—I'll be a veritable pussycat once I've eaten.'

A lion or a tiger, maybe. Or at least one of the man—woman?—eating kind!

But, talking of cats…

'Just a minute.' She beat a hasty retreat back into the apartment, going through to the kitchen to check that Monty had enough water while she was out.

When she returned to the lounge she discovered that Monty had left his hiding place and was now graciously allowing Max to get down on his haunches and stroke his silky white fur.

'My cat Monty.' She introduced him wryly. Her *trai-*

torous cat Monty. Really, couldn't Monty recognise an enemy when he saw one?

Max looked up at her. 'This isn't just a cat, Abby, he's a Persian. Rather a magnificent example of his breed, too,' he added admiringly.

'Oh, don't you start!' She raised her eyes heavenwards. 'Monty already has an elevated enough opinion of himself as it is.'

'Quite right too,' Max straightened. 'Are you finally ready to go?'

'Well, I could always do a little dusting, and the bedroom probably needs tidying... Yes, I'm ready to go now!' she taunted lightly, and he shot her a scathing look.

She was even more pleased she had accepted his invitation when she realised he was driving to her favourite restaurant. She loved Italian food, and Luigi's served some of the finest in London. The busy restaurant also had the advantage of being close to the studio where she now worked. Not that it mattered today; she wasn't going back in to work until Monday.

'I asked Dorothy where you like to eat,' Max told her as he saw her pleased expression. Which meant he had intended inviting her out to lunch all the time...

Interesting.

Although the fact that Dorothy knew Max meant to invite her out to lunch probably meant that her mother now knew about it too.

The two women—Dorothy and Abby's mother Elizabeth—spoke on the telephone at least a couple of times a week, and Abby was sure that Dorothy would consider Abby being invited out to lunch by Max Harding as more than enough reason for one of those lengthy calls. Max probably had no idea, but, knowing the two women as well as she did, Abby had no doubt that by the time the telephone conversation came to an end Dorothy and Elizabeth would have chosen the colour of the bridesmaids' dresses and decided on names for their children.

'What's so funny?' Max prompted after parking the silver Mercedes and coming round to open her door for her.

She gave a dismissive shake of her head. 'You had to be there!'

His mouth twisted derisively. 'Maybe I would have been if I'd known it was going to be so much fun!'

No, he wouldn't. One thing she could say with absolute certainty about Max Harding—without any fear of contradiction on his part—was that he certainly wasn't the type of man you took home to meet your mother!

As far as Abby was aware, apart from that very early marriage, at thirty-nine years old he had never been involved in a relationship that even approached that level of seriousness.

She wondered why that was. There was no doubting his good looks, or his sensual attraction, and he was certainly wealthy enough, so Abby was sure that his reluctance about commitment couldn't have come from the females he'd dated. Maybe—

'What are you thinking about now?' Max enquired, his hand lightly on her elbow as they crossed the car park to the restaurant.

Abby gave him a look from beneath lowered lashes. 'The truth?'

'I find that preferable.'

She drew in a deep breath. 'I was wondering if perhaps you had homosexual tendencies.'

'You were wondering—!' Max broke off incredulously. 'By all means be blunt, why don't you?' He gave a dazed shake of his head.

'Well, you did ask.'

'I know I did. And the answer is no. A definite no,' he added impatiently.

Abby gave an unconcerned shrug. 'It was just a thought.'

Max swung open the restaurant door for her to enter. 'Well, in future I suggest you keep those sort of thoughts to yourself!'

'You asked,' she protested. 'Besides, you said I wasn't your type, so I—'

'Jumped to a conclusion a dozen steps ahead rather than one!' He shook his head. 'And I wasn't referring to the whole of the female sex, anyway.'

'Just me?'

He gave her a considering look, that sweeping gaze taking in the whole of her appearance from her silky dark hair to her booted feet. 'I think it might be best if I were to reserve judgement on my previous statement,' he finally answered huskily.

'You sound like a lawyer,' Abby mocked.

'I shall be "taking the fifth" in a moment,' he assured her sardonically.

She shook her head. 'I don't think that applies over here.'

'Then maybe it should,' Max said with feeling.

Exactly what had he meant by that remark? Abby wondered with a fluttering sensation in her chest. Could he—?

'Abby!' Luigi himself was acting as *maître d'* today, smiling his pleasure as he moved to kiss her on both cheeks. 'Such an honour to have you with us today,' he beamed. 'For obvious reasons I couldn't see your show myself last night.' He looked pointedly around the crowded restaurant, which was even more frenetic in the evenings. 'But my wife tells me it was very romantic.' He raised his eyebrows suggestively.

Abby laughed, making no comment on the show herself; as far as she was concerned the jury was still out on whether or not it had actually been a success. 'Luigi, this is Max Harding.' She changed the subject by introducing the two men.

'But of course.' Luigi clearly recognized him. 'It is a pleasure to meet you, Mr Harding.'

'Max, please,' he responded smoothly. 'I telephoned earlier and booked a table,' he told the corpulent Italian.

'I had no idea Abby was to be your dining companion.' The restaurant owner smiled, removing a 'Reserved' sign from a table in the middle of the room and taking them to a window table instead.

'You eat here quite often, I gather?' Max murmured dryly, obviously having noticed the move.

'Often enough,' she agreed, nodding to several people in the restaurant whom she knew—quite a lot of them from the studio down the street.

Max had been so sure that he could persuade her to have lunch with him today that he had booked a table? That sort of confidence, and the fact that she was here and proving it justified, made her feel more than a little annoyed. Was she that easy to read? Or just that easy?

'Dorothy warned me I'd need to book a table if we weren't to be disappointed when we got here,' Max put in quietly, perhaps noticing her rapidly rising indignation.

Seated opposite him, totally aware of him and anticipating one of Luigi's delicious pasta dishes for lunch rather than the crackers and cheese she had intended having at home, Abby decided she couldn't be bothered to argue.

'A glass of your house red, please,' she told Luigi in answer to his question concerning drinks. 'It's very good,' she assured Max as he looked at her enquiringly.

'Make that two glasses of house red—thanks,' he told the other man, before turning his attention back to Abby. 'So how does it feel to be a celebrity?'

She grimaced, fiddling with the small vase of fresh flowers in the middle of the table. 'If I ever become one I'll be sure to let you know!'

Max reached out and put one of his much larger hands over both of hers. 'Take a look around you, Abby,' he advised softly.

She did, her eyes widening as she saw that a lot of the other diners were now sending surreptitious glances in their direction. One or two of those people were actually smiling at her approvingly.

She gave a rueful shrug as she turned back to Max. 'They're probably all wondering who the woman is having lunch with Max Harding!'

He gave a shake of his head. 'I'm yesterday's news, Abby. It's you they're looking at,' he assured her.

Another slightly self-conscious look around the room confirmed that he was right—that she *was* the one people were nodding and smiling at.

She had come in for her fair share of recognition from being on breakfast television for over a year, but nothing like this. Then she had usually been recognised and stopped in the supermarket buying her week's supply of chocolate—or, even worse, in the chemist as she was buying essential but embarrassing female toiletries.

But most of that recognition had been from middle-aged or elderly females; the wave of awareness she could feel in the restaurant now was coming from both males and females—of all ages. Recognition and smiling approval, she realized. Most of those friendly gazes seemed to be smiling indulgently at the hold Max still had on her hands.

She hastily removed her hands from his. 'They'll have the two of us married to each other by tomorrow morning!' she explained with fiery red cheeks.

'Possibly,' Max acknowledged lightly, sitting back with apparent unconcern. 'Need any more confirmation that your show was a success?'

'Lots!' She grimaced. 'Especially as the whole thing seems to be a case of "not what I know but who I know" getting me the job in the first place,' she recalled heavily.

It might also help to explain Gary Holmes's obvious contempt for her from the start—he had known of her relationship to Paul Dillman's wife. Although Max certainly hadn't been aware of that connection until she had told him… Oh, well, perhaps Gary Holmes was just rude and cutting to any young upstart he considered had been foisted on him. Whatever—he certainly didn't like her.

'Well, well, well, Abby. Out for a celebration lunch? Or is it one of commiseration?' The last word dripped with scorn.

Perhaps it was thinking about him, or maybe he was just becoming her nemesis, but Abby could only look up in open-mouthed dismay as Gary Holmes himself materialised beside their table. In fact, she was so surprised she couldn't even speak.

In the event, it was Max who answered the other man. 'A celebration, of course, Gary,' he assured him challengingly as he stood up.

To say Gary looked stunned at the identity of her dining companion was putting it mildly. The older man's face was suffused with heated colour. What followed was the draining of all that colour, leaving him white and drawn.

Max, in contrast, looked arrogantly assured at he stared down at the other, shorter and more slenderly built man.

Gary swallowed convulsively as he tried to return that hard gaze. 'Max,' he muttered unnecessarily.

Max gave a humourless smile, his eyes glittering icily. 'At least neither of us is hypocritical enough to say it's good to see you again.'

Because it obviously wasn't, Abby saw.

The one and only time Gary Holmes's name had come up in conversation between herself and Max had been that first day, when Abby had managed to get herself admitted into Max's apartment. She remembered that Max had gone very quiet afterwards, brushing off her question and changing the subject when she had asked him for an explanation. But now, seeing the two men together, she knew her instinct that day had been correct. These two men heartily disliked each other.

She wondered why.

But Gary was recovering rapidly now, his initial shock fading to be replaced by his usual sneering smile as he turned back to look at Abby. 'Can I take it from the two of you being here together that you have succeeded in persuading Max to come on your show after all?' he taunted.

'You can take it any way you like, Gary,' Max answered harshly. 'Now, if you wouldn't mind? You've interrupted our meal for quite long enough.' He gave the other man a pointedly dismissive look.

'Not at all.' Gary was obviously fully recovered now. 'I'll look forward to working with you again,' he added challengingly, before shooting Abby once last dismissive glance and swaggering his way out of the restaurant.

Abby looked curiously up at Max as he still stood beside the table.

Again. Gary had said he looked forward to working with Max *again*.

When had the two men worked together in the past? Whenever it was, it clearly hadn't been a friendly relationship!

She moistened dry lips. 'Max—'

'Don't ask!' he rasped, his expression harsh and remote as he resumed his seat.

But she wanted to know—needed to know before she worked with Gary again. She was sure that the other man wouldn't let this chance meeting pass without further comment. Which, in her ignorance, she would have no chance of combating.

But Max's frostily closed expression certainly didn't invite further questions on the subject!

In fact, Gary's uninvited appearance had put a complete dampener on their meal together. Neither of them—to Luigi's obvious disgust—did more than pick at the homemade pasta, and both of them refused dessert or coffee.

Max asked tersely for the bill before driving her home in stony silence.

All of which brought Abby to the decision that the

first thing she would do on Monday morning was set about finding out the history of the obvious antagonism between Max Harding and Gary Holmes.

She had a feeling it was a history worth knowing.

CHAPTER FIVE

'I'M SORRY.'

Abby, half in the car, half out on the pavement, paused to turn and look at Max. 'Sorry for what?'

After starting out so promisingly, she had just suffered through the most awful lunch of her life; there had better only be one thing he was sorry for!

His expression darkened. 'Damn it!' His hands tightened briefly on the steering wheel before he turned to push the car door open beside him and stepped forcefully onto the road—instantly having to hold up a hand of apology to the driver of an oncoming car, who had to veer further out into the road to avoid hitting him. Max strode round the car to stand on the pavement next to the watching Abby. 'I'm sorry I was such a lousy lunch companion,' he muttered.

Not the most gracious apology she had ever received, but for all that Abby could see that it was sincere. Although his grim expression didn't exactly encourage questions as to *why* he had been so angry and bad-tempered throughout their meal. She knew the who, of course, just not the why...

But now probably wasn't the time to pursue the subject. 'I didn't notice,' she came back lightly, eyes glowing with mischief as she met his gaze.

'Yeah, right,' he drawled self-mockingly, his dark mood seeming to ease somewhat.

'Would you like to come up for the coffee we both refused at Luigi's?'

Max gave her a look. 'The last woman to invite me in for coffee had something else in mind.'

'I'm only offering coffee,' she assured him dryly.

At least, she thought she was...

Because, despite—or because of!—his lack of conversation during lunch, Abby's awareness of him had only grown. To the point where she was acutely aware of every move he made, of the dark hair visible above his T-shirt, of the way that fitted T-shirt emphasised the powerful width of his shoulders and chest, of the hard sensuality of his face, of the way his hair fell endearingly across his forehead...

She hoped she was only inviting him in for coffee...

His sensuality was something she was too aware of. His aura of totally masculine power touched and inflamed something deep inside her—something that had been totally unknown to her until today. Total physical awareness. And it completely took her breath away. Her body felt incredibly warm, her legs and arms lethargic.

She hoped Max wasn't aware of it, too!

He didn't appear to be as he locked the car before taking a light hold on her arm. 'Remind me to have a word with you later about the fragility of a man's ego,' he told her dryly as she let them both into the apartment building.

Some men's egos, perhaps, Abby thought as they went up together in the lift. The research she had already done on *this* man told her that just because he had never remarried it didn't mean there had been a shortage of women in his life—she had been being deliberately provocative earlier, when she'd questioned his sexual preference! And he was usually the one to bring an end—usually an abrupt end—to his relationships.

Which warned her that she would be a fool to follow up her own obvious attraction to him—if she needed any warning…

Research was one thing, but the man himself was a puzzle within an enigma. And Abby had a distinct feeling he preferred it like that. An only child of wealthy parents, who had lived mainly on the island of Majorca for the last ten years, with no other emotional ties, Max was pretty much a law unto himself.

And everything about him shouted that he intended remaining that way.

Not that Abby was interested in a serious relationship with anyone, either. Her last relationship, of six months' duration, had ended several months ago, and she was in no hurry to repeat the experience of someone wanting to know what she was doing and what she was thinking twenty-four hours a day! Besides, Monty hadn't liked Andrew at all—arching his back and hissing whenever he'd seen him.

But he liked Max, a little voice whispered inside her head.

Something that was reaffirmed when Abby came back from the kitchen carrying two mugs of steaming hot coffee and found Monty sitting majestically on Max's knee, his whole body one big purr.

'What can I say? He likes me!' Max laughed huskily as he saw her disgusted look.

Abby put one of the mugs down on the table in

front of him. 'Enough to have restored that fragile male ego?' she taunted as she sat down in the chair opposite.

'Well, I wouldn't go that far.' He shrugged, his expression sobering. 'I really am sorry about lunch. I invited you out, and then behaved like a bad-tempered idiot throughout. Gary Holmes will do that to me every time!' he added harshly.

Abby eyed him over the top of her coffee mug. 'I know why I don't like him, but what did he ever do to you?'

Max's expression was grim, his eyes glacial. 'I took you out to lunch because I thought we needed to talk, not so that I could answer questions—'

'But we didn't talk, Max,' Abby cut in pointedly, deciding to ignore his deliberate challenge, though she was aware that he was reverting back to that coldly arrogant man of their first meeting, those barriers coming down like the steel of prison bars.

'No, we didn't,' he acknowledged harshly, looking at her with piercing grey eyes. 'Because Holmes's remarks made me realise that I had stupidly allowed myself to become sidetracked from the fact that you're still just another reporter looking for an angle. Worse—you're a chat-show host looking for an angle.' He put Monty to one side before standing up.

That last remark hurt—on two fronts. Personally, because she liked this man far more than was good for her. And professionally, because the intensifying attraction she felt towards this man had made her forget all about her job. The truth was, she found Max so physically mesmerising that she hadn't even thought about her show the whole time they had been together—or the fact that she still wanted him as her final guest.

It was this latter realisation that brought her to her feet, too, eyes sparkling with resentment now. 'You are being extremely unfair,' she snapped. 'I never so much as— What do you mean, you "allowed" yourself to become sidetracked?' she demanded with a frown.

Max gave a humourless smile. '*Stupidly* allowed myself to become sidetracked,' he corrected harshly, that icy grey gaze unfathomable as it swept over her with calculation.

Abby withstood his cold look with a challenging lift of her chin, knowing from the contemptuous curl of those sculptured lips that whatever he was looking at certainly wasn't the same reflection *she* saw when she looked in the mirror every morning.

And the tension was unbearable. The very air seemed to crackle between them as their gazes remained locked in silent battle.

Abby was determined—childishly?—not to be the first to break that gaze. No, not childishly; there was nothing in the least child-like about the way she was looking at Max. Or the way he was looking at her. In fact, his gaze had become altogether adult in its appraisal now, those grey eyes seeming to frown disapprovingly even as his gaze shifted to her mouth.

She couldn't help what happened next: it was pure instinct that made her run her tongue self-consciously over the lips he was frowning at so darkly. A move that only seemed to make his expression become grimmer than ever.

She sighed. 'Look, Max, I don't know—'

'Oh, you know, Abby,' he ground out, even as he stepped towards her. 'You really can't be that naïve!' he added scornfully.

But she was! In fact she had no idea what he was talking about—what she had done...

Every coherent thought left her head as Max reached out to grasp her arms and pull her into the hardness of his body, lowering his head as his lips claimed hers.

She did know, after all. *This* was what Max was talking about. *This* was what had sidetracked him earlier— he was as aware of her as she was of him.

It was a punishing kiss. Max completely skipped the tentative, the gentle exploration, going straight to heated passion, his mouth possessing hers with a fierceness Abby more than returned. Her arms slid up his chest as she pushed the jacket from his shoulders and threw it over onto the sofa, and his arms were like steel bands as he moulded her soft curves against the powerful hardness of his, at the same time making her fully aware of his arousal.

She was so hot, so aware, every nerve, every sense heightened as she kissed him back with all the pent-up emotion of the last couple of hours. This was what she wanted, what she had longed for since the moment she had first looked at Max Harding.

He felt so good, his shoulders so wide and muscled. He smelt so good, a light cologne only adding to the musky smell that tantalised her senses as much as the lips exploring hers with such thoroughness. His hands were now seeking the pleasure spots of her body, palms running firmly down her spine before moving forward to cup her breasts, the soft pads of his thumbs moving rhythmically against the hardened tips.

Abby gasped with pleasure, groaning low in her throat as Max's tongue sought and found hers, before exploring the moist hollows of her mouth, touching nerve-endings she hadn't known existed, taking her to heights she had never known. She was aware only of Max, of the touch of his hands, his lips, his tongue. Every particle of her, it seemed, was consumed by a need that was rapidly growing out of control inside her. She—

She suddenly found herself thrust away from him at arm's length, blinking up at him dazedly, knowing by the flush above the hard cheekbones that he had been as aroused as she was, and with no idea what had caused him to bring a halt to their lovemaking. It certainly hadn't been because of a lack of response on her part, she acknowledged with a certain amount of self-derision, her cheeks becoming heated with the awareness of the depths of her arousal.

She shook her head. 'Max, what—?'

'You have a visitor,' he rasped, eyes glittering as his hands briefly tightened on her arms before he released her with a suddenness that made her stumble slightly. At the same time the doorbell buzzed—for the second time?

If someone had buzzed up already then Abby hadn't been aware of it—completely lost in her desire for Max, in the way he had kissed and tantalised her. But Max obviously hadn't been as mindlessly aroused as her.

'Shouldn't you answer that?' he bit out abruptly, thrusting his hands into his pockets, his expression darkly brooding as he looked at her.

Should she? Did she really want to see anyone just now? Besides, who could it be? Her parents lived in the country, she had seen Dorothy only this morning, and at the moment, with the sexual tension still tangible between herself and Max, she didn't want to see anyone else.

She shook her head. 'I'm not expecting anyone.' Her

gaze locked on Max as she searched for signs of his arousal. And found none.

'No?' He quirked dark, sceptical brows as the buzzer sounded—more persistently this time.

Abby gave a pained frown. They needed to talk, not to be interrupted by a third party. Any third party. The kiss just now had proved that Max was as attracted to her as she was to him. That was why he had become 'sidetracked', as he'd put it, and they needed—

'Just now was a mistake, Abby,' Max told her harshly as he seemed to read her thoughts. 'One not to be repeated!'

'But—'

'Get the damned door!' he grated as the buzzer sounded again. 'I'm leaving, anyway,' he added, sounding disgusted, as he shrugged back into his jacket.

She could feel the heat of tears in her eyes at this total rejection of her, of what they had just shared. But she knew she hadn't imagined his response to her; she wasn't *that* inexperienced!

But in the face of his denial, and the return of the iceman from their first meeting, she knew she would be a fool to pursue it, that she would be only leaving herself wide open to further humiliation. Worse, Max was more than capable of verbally annihilating her if she pushed him any further on the subject.

With one last lingering glance at the rigidity of his uncompromising back she walked dejectedly over to the door to press the intercom. 'Yes?' she said dispiritedly, not in the mood to speak to anyone right now. Except Max. And he didn't want to speak to her.

Maybe, if they hadn't been interrupted like this

maybe they would have ended up in bed together! After which Max would still have left…

'Not interrupting anything, am I, Abby?'

She stiffened, her eyes widening incredulously as she recognised Gary Holmes's insolent tone. She turned quickly to look at Max, knowing by the iciness of his gaze, the sudden tension of his body, that he had recognised the other man's voice too.

What was Gary doing here? He had never been to her apartment before—had never been invited! Well, he hadn't been invited this time either, but he was still here. And it couldn't have happened at a worse time!

What was Max thinking about the other man turning up here?

Hard to tell from that arrogantly closed expression. Certainly nothing good, anyway.

'Abby?' Gary Holmes prompted irritably at her continued silence.

Max's mouth twisted contemptuously. 'He seems to be getting impatient. I should let him in if I were you.'

Well, he wasn't her. And as far as she was concerned Gary Holmes had no right being here. She didn't like him, and certainly didn't want to invite him into her home. He might be the director of her show, but that gave him no right to invade her personal life.

She gave Max one last resentful glare before turning away to speak into the intercom. 'What do you want, Gary?'

He gave an audible chuckle. 'Now, that's a leading question!'

Not as far as he was concerned, it wasn't! Not as far as Max was concerned either, if the scornful way he was looking at her was anything to go by.

She gave an impatient sigh. 'I'm not in the mood for your mind games right now, Gary, so just say what you have to say and then go.'

'That isn't very friendly of you, Abby,' Gary drawled unconcernedly. 'I have a few things I need to discuss with you.'

'We'll talk on Monday—'

'I want to talk to you now, not Monday,' he cut in cheerfully. 'Look, why don't I walk up, instead of taking the lift, and give the two of you time to put some clothes on—'

'How dare you?' Abby gasped, shooting Max a panicked glance.

Gary knew that Max was up here with her, knew they had been making love—even if he had got their state of dress slightly wrong. Although if he had arrived ten minutes or so later, he might not have done...

'Oh, for God's sake, stop acting like some outraged virgin and open the door, Abby!' Gary rasped.

She didn't resist as Max appeared at her side, putting her firmly out of the way before pressing the intercom button. 'I have a better idea, Gary,' he bit out coldly. 'Abby will leave the door locked, and you can go and—'

'Really, Max,' Gary interrupted tauntingly. 'I'm sure you shouldn't be using language like that in front of a lady. And Abby is so very *much* a lady, isn't she?' he continued tauntingly. 'Wealthy parents, private schooling, not having to work her way through university, with the sort of looks and body all that money can buy. Class, with a capital C, that's our Abby—'

'I am not your Abby, damn it!' she was stung into shouting.

'No?' Gary came back mildly. 'Okay, if that's the

way you want to play it. I guess I'll speak to you later, after all. Bye, Max,' he added mockingly.

What was Gary doing? What was he implying? There was only the sound of static on the intercom now.

One glance at Max's icily contemptuous expression and she knew exactly what Gary had been trying to do. Surely Max couldn't really think—couldn't honestly believe—?

But as Max turned away, his expression now more coldly remote than ever, Abby could see that was exactly what he believed.

She drew in a shaky breath, realising as she did so that she was actually trembling. Not surprisingly. First that passionate explosion between herself and Max, quickly followed by this totally unwanted visit from Gary Holmes!

The latter she would have to deal with later—and deal with it she would! The former—well, Max already looked in the process of leaving...

'Max, you can't believe—'

'It doesn't matter what I believe, Abby.'

'But it does,' she protested emotionally. 'I have no idea what—what all that was about.' She gestured in the direction of the intercom. 'I'll have to talk to Gary about that on Monday,' she added determinedly. 'But you can't allow Gary Holmes's warped sense of humour to affect us—'

'Us?' Max repeated tauntingly, smiling with grim humour as he shook his head. 'A few kisses and a little light groping do not make an "us", Abby,' he dismissed.

A few kisses and—! Abby felt her cheeks suffuse with humiliated colour. First Gary, and now this—it was just too much!

She drew herself up to her full height of five feet four

inches, her chin raised challengingly. 'I think you had better leave—'

'Before I say something I'll regret?' Max finished scornfully, his hooded gaze unreadable. 'In the circumstances, do you really think that's possible?'

Probably not, she thought, swallowing her inward misery. If he didn't go soon—very soon—she was very much afraid she might just break down and cry—and in the circumstances that was the last thing she wanted to do in front of Max.

She had no idea what game Gary was playing, or why he should have guessed that Max was up here with her. When Gary had seen the two of them together at the bistro they hadn't so much as kissed each other yet, had surely given off no air of intimacy. Maybe his game was really just with Max—there had certainly been enough animosity between the two men earlier. If that were the case, then she didn't care for being caught in the middle of their obviously long-standing dislike of each other.

Besides, Max obviously couldn't wait to get away from here. From her. And she needed him to go, too, if only so that she could think clearly enough to try and make some sense of what had just happened between the two of them. If there was any sense to be made of it...

She gave a confident shake of her head. 'You aren't interested in what I think, Max.'

'You're right,' he shot back sharply. 'I'm not.' His mouth twisted derisively. 'Good luck with the show next week.'

He didn't really mean that either, Abby knew, as he turned abruptly on his heel, her apartment door slamming forcefully behind him seconds later.

Which was the signal for the tears she had so determinedly held in check to fall hotly down her cheeks.

She had never felt so humiliated in all her life—and, added to that, she didn't know which man she was the most angry with. Max or Gary.

Ten minutes later, her tears all cried out, the comforting Monty purring as he lay curled up on her lap, she had decided that on reflection Gary was the one who most deserved her wrath.

And he was going to get it!

'You have to understand, darling,' Dorothy soothed patiently. 'As Paul has just told you, what you've asked for simply can't be done.'

'Why can't it?' Abby snapped, eyes flashing deeply blue. 'I'm the presenter of the show; Gary is the director. And I'm no longer happy for him to direct me across a road!'

The last twenty-four hours had done nothing to lessen Abby's anger. In fact she had barely slept the night before, for thinking about what had happened with Max and Gary. The weekend with her parents had been as lovely as usual, their company calming, but it hadn't deterred her from her purpose in the slightest; she no longer wanted to work with Gary Holmes.

The first thing she had done after travelling back into London was call and see Paul and Dorothy, with the sole intent of asking Paul to support the demand she planned to make on Monday to have Gary removed as her director. A request he had just turned down.

Not that she had told Paul all the personal reasons why she no longer felt she could work with Gary—

only that personal dislike on both sides, meant that even a professional relationship between them couldn't work.

Paul had listened, nodding his head in all the right places, murmuring understandingly about 'professional differences', but finally had informed her, before leaving the two women alone together, that he didn't have the necessary reasons to support removing the highly experienced Gary from his position.

Dorothy smiled at her now. 'He has a binding contract, Abby—'

'So do I.' She paced the room restlessly, having already refused Dorothy's request for her to sit down. 'And nowhere in that contract does it say I have to work with a man so obnoxious you've told me you won't have him in your home!' She was breathing hard in her agitation.

'I somehow doubt there's anything in that contract that says you *don't* have to either,' her godmother said ruefully, at the same time giving her a considering look. 'What's happened since yesterday to make you so vehemently opposed to him? He hasn't been sexually harassing you, too, has he?' Dorothy looked suddenly alarmed. 'Because I'm sure under those circumstances Paul would act.'

Abby gave her a humourless smile. 'Sorry to disappoint you, Aunt Dorothy, but no sexual harassment to report.'

'I'm not in the least disappointed.' The older woman gave her a reproving look. 'Just trying to understand this sudden aversion to the man. I thought you had spent the rest of the weekend with Elizabeth and Jeremy?'

She had, having left for her parents' house almost immediately after Max left—as soon as her tears had dried and she'd realised she couldn't just simply sit around in her apartment all weekend brooding. She'd had to get out of there, away from the memories of being in Max's arms and the awful scene that had followed.

And so she had bundled Monty into his travelling basket—one where he could see and be seen, of course; Monty only tolerated those train journeys to her parents' on the understanding that he would be duly admired by fellow travellers on the journey, with the added knowledge that he would get to roam freely around the big, rambling vicarage that was the family home.

Wouldn't Max have fun with that little piece of information? She was the daughter of a vicar—and an ex-actress...

It had all the makings of one of those awful jokes, but Abby knew that her parents' marriage was far from a joke. The unlikely pair had been happily married for the last thirty years, and as their only child she had always been surrounded by their love and cosseting.

Which was exactly what she had needed these last twenty-four hours, away from London and all its complications.

Thoughts of Max she had put completely from her mind—they were just too complicated for her to deal with!—giving her time and distance to decide what she had to do about Gary Holmes. Unfortunately, Paul didn't seem to be willing to help her with the decision she had made.

'I did,' she answered Dorothy now. 'But Gary Holmes came to my apartment before I left for Hampshire. No, not for anything like that!' she snapped as Dorothy raised interested brows. 'He's so smug. So superior. As if he knows something that I don't. Oh, I'm sure that he knows a lot of things that I don't,' she went on ruefully as the older woman gave her a teasing look, 'and I'm well aware of what an experienced director he is, that he's been in the business almost twenty years— but, Dorothy, don't you find it strange that no men, and only silly women, seem to actually like the man?'

The other woman shrugged. 'I don't suppose it's essential to being brilliant at his job.'

'No, but—Dorothy, he *wanted* my show to be a disaster on Friday night!'

'Now, that *is* silly, darling,' her godmother reasoned. 'As the director, there could be absolutely no personal benefit to him if that had happened.'

Abby knew that—didn't understand the reasoning herself. She only knew that Gary had seemed disappointed the show hadn't failed on Friday night, that he had *wanted* her to fall flat on her face. In fact, she wouldn't be surprised if he hadn't known of the Brad/Natalie reconciliation! His taunt in the bistro yesterday, about her lunch being a celebration or a commiseration, had seemed to confirm his malevolence. Only the fact that Max had jumped to her defence, and Gary had obviously been not at all pleased to see him there, seemed to have stopped Gary from saying something even more scathing.

She had thought all this through over the weekend and knew that she was right—she just had no idea why.

And, without any reason, she realised that her request to Paul must have sounded slightly ridiculous.

'You're right, Dorothy,' she accepted with a sigh. 'No personal benefit at all.'

Except... As a relative newcomer, if her show should fail she would simply fade away into obscurity. As a seasoned director, and a brilliant one at that—Abby would allow him that!—Gary Holmes would simply move on to directing something else, with no detriment to his career at all.

But was that enough reason for what she suspected…?

Dorothy moved with her as Abby walked to the door. 'Don't be angry with Paul, Abby,' she pleaded. 'I'm sure that if you can come up with something concrete against the man, Paul would be only too happy to help. It's just that, as things stand, if he were to do anything now Ajax Television is likely to be slapped with an unfair dismissal charge. I suppose they could always ask him to resign and see what— No, I wouldn't advise that, either.' She winced. 'The man is just horrible enough to enjoy the fact that you obviously don't like working with him.'

Abby knew her godmother was right. She just wished that she wasn't. She also wished she had some answer to the dilemma herself.

But she didn't.

The telephone was ringing as she let herself into her apartment half an hour later, pausing briefly to open Monty's basket and let him out before hurrying to answer it.

The dial tone buzzed in her ear as she held up the receiver. And yet the ringing sound continued.

Because it wasn't *her* telephone ringing, she realised after a couple of confused seconds.

She put the receiver slowly back on its cradle, frowning her confusion as she looked around the sitting room for the source of the ringing. Her search becoming physical as the noise persisted, seeming to become more urgent by the second as she lifted cushions and newspapers in an effort to locate it.

A mobile phone! Lying half under her sofa, its ringing becoming louder as Abby brought it out fully.

Yes, it was a mobile—but whose? Because it certainly wasn't hers. That was switched off, in her shoulder bag. And she had vacuumed the sitting room yesterday morning; she was sure it hadn't been there then. Only Max had been in her apartment since that time…

She stared down at the silver-coloured mobile with rapidly widening eyes. Max's jacket had been thrown over the back of the sofa; it must have fallen out onto the floor then.

But what did she do now? Take the call and utterly confuse the caller when it was a woman rather than a man answering? Or did she just wait for it to stop ringing and hope they didn't call back?

Of course it could be Max himself, ringing in order to tell her he had dropped his mobile phone. In fact, he could have tried to reach her in the same way several times during her absence over the last twenty-four hours.

She didn't really have any choice but to answer the call, did she?

'Yes?' she prompted hesitantly, after pressing the call button.

'Max?' a female voice came back, almost as tentatively.

Well, hardly, Abby thought with a disgusted raising of her dark brows. 'Actually, no,' she answered more assuredly; she was obviously speaking to one of Max's women-friends—possibly the woman-friend of the moment. Of course, it could be his mother—but somehow she doubted that very much!

'Is this Max's phone?'

'Probably,' Abby answered dryly.

'Could I speak to Max, then?' the other woman asked coolly.

Abby drew in a deep breath. This was the tricky bit. The last person she wanted to talk to was the possibly current woman in Max's life, but at the same time she knew that he wouldn't thank her if she said anything to alienate this woman—something like, No, you can't talk to Max because he isn't here. He just happened to drop his mobile phone when he came to my apartment yesterday and made love to me!

No, Max wouldn't like that at all...

'I'm afraid he isn't here to take your call at the moment,' she answered evasively.

'Oh.' The other woman sounded disconcerted.

'But I'll be happy to tell him that you called,' she added untruthfully.

Max shouldn't even have been making love to her yesterday if he was already involved with someone else!

'I see. Right.' The other woman sounded slightly flustered. 'Okay. Perhaps you could just tell him that Kate called?'

'Just Kate?'

'Just Kate,' the other woman confirmed unhelpfully.

'Shall I tell him you'd like him to call you back?' Abby persisted.

'I think he'll know that when you give him my message,' she retorted.

There was nothing worse than someone cleverer than yourself!

Especially a female someone. 'Okay, I'll do that,' Abby managed to assure her through gritted teeth, before the other woman abruptly ended the call.

Kate.

Max was involved with someone called Kate.

She should have known. Should have guessed that a man like Max would already have someone in his life.

But she hadn't. In truth, it wasn't something she had given any thought to.

If she had she might not have allowed herself to become so attracted to him. If it was possible to control something like that, that was…

CHAPTER SIX

'YOU appear to have my mobile phone.'

She had been expecting this call, of course; Max was intelligent enough to realise that the easiest and quickest way to locate his missing mobile was to ring the number and hope someone answered it. In this case, Abby.

Oh, yes, she had been expecting this call the whole time she'd prepared her own and Monty's evening meal—chicken salad for her, chicken with rice for Monty—and as she'd cleared away the dishes and sat down to go through her notes and research on this week's guest. Mostly in the hope it would distract her from just sitting and waiting for the mobile to ring again. It hadn't succeeded, of course, but it really didn't matter; her research on the writer Barnaby Hamilton was complete, with no hidden surprises.

So, yes, she had known that Max would telephone his mobile at some point during the evening—had expected it—but she could tell by Max's derisive tone that he had already worked out that she would be the one who answered it!

'So I do,' she returned with a calm that matched his own, her hand tightly gripping the silver-coloured mobile.

'Can I come over and collect it now, or are you busy?'

She knew exactly what he meant by that last remark; he still thought, despite her denials yesterday, that Gary Holmes might be at her apartment with her this evening!

'No, I'm not busy,' she came back waspishly. 'But wouldn't it just be easier for me to post it back to you tomorrow?'

She had already given this some thought after 'Kate' had called, and, no matter how she might feel towards Max, she had decided she really wasn't up to another series of his cutting remarks. Her newly realised attraction to him, and the knowledge of Kate's presence in his life, had left her rawly exposed—so much so that she wasn't sure she could bear to see him again just yet.

'Easier for you, maybe,' he agreed dryly. 'But not as immediate. I need the mobile now, Abby. Not in two days' time,' he added firmly.

Of course he did. He was probably expecting Kate to call—probably had no idea that she had already done so!

'That sounds reasonable,' Abby returned coolly—it was the way she had decided she had to be with him if she should ever see him again—prior to finding the mobile, of course, and to Kate's call! But in these circumstances that decision applied even more.

'Oh, I'm glad about that.' He made no effort to keep the sarcasm out of his voice. 'I'll be there in half an hour.' He rang off abruptly.

'Damn him, Monty!' Abby's eyes blazed as she threw the mobile down onto her sofa, glaring at it as if it were the man himself. 'First he kisses me, then he insults me, and now he's talking to me as if I'm slightly simple-minded. Which,' she bit out self-disgustedly, 'considering I'm having a one-sided conversation with my cat, I probably am!'

Not surprising either, considering the battering her emotions had taken during the last forty-eight hours. Gary, she just wanted to strangle with her bare hands. Max...she still didn't know whether she wanted to kiss him or hit him—and at the same time knew she would do neither!

'Damn the man,' she muttered again, even as she hurried through to her bedroom to do something about her appearance.

If she had to see Max again so soon—and it appeared that she did!—then she didn't have to do it looking travel-worn and frankly less than her best. Besides, she needed an extra boost to her confidence if she was to get through this meeting with any degree of dignity at all.

She changed into stone-coloured linen trousers and a fitted brown T-shirt, freshening her make-up before brushing her shoulder-length hair until it gleamed like ebony. Slim, elegant, but not overly so, and self-possessed, she decided as she studied her reflection in the full-length mirror in her bedroom. Not bad at all. She nodded her satisfaction.

Now all she had to do was maintain that confidence in the face of Max's sarcasm—

She dropped the hairbrush she had been using on the bedroom carpet as her buzzer rang, announcing his arrival. So much for self-confidence!

She didn't even bother with the intercom, just pressing the button to let him into the building and moving to open the door seconds later as she heard the ascent of the lift.

'So much for security,' he rasped, totally ignoring the

mobile she held out to him as he strode past her into the apartment. 'You could have been letting in a serial rapist for all you knew!' he added harshly.

Abby closed the door gently behind him. 'Or worse—one of those religious fanatics,' she returned, dark brows raised mockingly.

He looked—wonderful, she thought, aching. Black denims, black T-shirt beneath a brown leather jacket, his dark hair windswept.

His expression, as usual, was guarded as his gaze swept over her own appearance with the same nonchalance. 'Or a religious fanatic,' he agreed, some of the tension leaving his shoulders. 'Not that I have anything against religion. I just don't like it appearing uninvited on my doorstep.'

Abby, in the circumstances of her father actually being a vicar, had no intention of commenting on the subject. 'Yours, I believe.' She held out the mobile to him once again.

He took it, his fingers lightly brushing hers, before slipping the mobile into his jacket pocket. 'Where did you find it?'

She shrugged, moving away from the intensity of his gaze. 'It must have fallen out of your jacket pocket yesterday, when you threw it on the sofa.'

'When *I* threw it on the sofa?' Max repeated huskily.

She had been hoping he wouldn't bring up the subject of that time in his arms yesterday—or the fact that *she* had been the one to remove his jacket in order to be closer to the warmth of his chest and arms.

She should have known he wasn't the sort of man to avoid any subject. As long as it wasn't one *he* wanted to avoid, of course!

Her chin rose challengingly as she met his gaze. 'You had a phone call earlier.'

'Yes.' He nodded, unmoving, his gaze as steady and unyielding as hers.

He knew Kate had called!

And the only way he could know that was if the other woman also had the number of his land-line—or had actually gone to his apartment to see him in person. In order to ask him who the woman was who had answered his mobile? *Oh, what a tangled web we weave…*

But that wasn't Abby's problem, was it? Okay, so she had been the one to throw off his jacket, and consequently cause his mobile to fall out of the pocket, but if Max hadn't been kissing her at the time, touching her so that she needed to touch him in return—

'From a woman called Kate,' she went on—she was sure unnecessarily.

Max's mouth tightened grimly, his gaze once again guarded. 'She told me.'

How had she told him? In person? Was the other woman at his apartment even now, waiting for him to come back to her…?

No! She wouldn't do this! She was thinking and acting like a jealous lover where Max was concerned. Something that after only a few kisses she had no right to do. No matter how much she might wish it were otherwise…

Abby thrust her shaking hands into the pockets of her linen trousers. 'Don't let me keep you,' she told him tightly.

He completely ignored her dismissal as he moved to sit in one of the armchairs, looking up at her thoughtfully. 'You seem a little—tense?'

Her frown was pained now. She'd had the impression

this would only be a quick visit on Max's part—to collect his mobile and then leave. But he seemed to be making himself comfortable.

She shrugged. 'We didn't exactly part on a happy
note yesterday,' she reminded him tautly. 'In fact, I had
the distinct impression you hoped never to see me
again!'

'Did you?' His gaze softened, unnerving after his
earlier stiltedness. 'And yet here I am,' he added. 'Hello,
boy,' he greeted Monty ruefully as the cat jumped up
onto his lap and began to purr for attention.

Attention he received. One of Max's sensuously long
hands began to stroke the long silky fur on the cat's
back, causing Monty to arch in pleasure, his expression
ecstatic.

In the same way that she had when Max had caressed her?

God, this was just too embarrassing; every thought
she had seemed to come straight back to Max. It was
devastating to realise she was so attracted to him she
couldn't think of anything else.

Why him? she groaned inwardly. Why was she so
enraptured with this arrogantly aloof man, who pushed
her away one second and pulled her into his arms the
next, and not with some nice, uncomplicated man like
Andrew, who had wanted to marry her and have lots of
children, be the father of the grandchildren her parents
had begun painfully to hint that they would like?

Max Harding wasn't that sort of man, and he never
would be.

She shook her head. 'I really think you should go
now, don't you?'

A smile still curved his lips as he looked up from

stroking a now settled Monty. 'I thought you said you weren't busy this evening?'

'I'm not—but you probably are!' she said forcefully. Exasperatedly. He had his mobile—why didn't he just go?

He shrugged. 'Not particularly.'

She was going to make a complete idiot of herself in a minute and say something embarrassing—for herself, that was. She doubted that there was very much that embarrassed Max.

'I thought perhaps you had to get back to Kate?' She said it anyway, at the same time refusing to drop her gaze from his suddenly narrowed eyes.

'Did you?' he finally said slowly.

'For God's sake, will you stop answering a question with another question?' Abby's control snapped impatiently, her movements agitated.

Max arched dark brows. 'Am I doing that?'

'You just did it again!' she snapped. 'And if you answer a question with another question you give no answer whatsoever. It's an art you've obviously perfected,' she added derisively.

He was frowning darkly now, his movements studied as he placed Monty on one of the cushions of the sofa and stood up before turning to face her. 'Maybe I was a little hard on you before I left here yesterday—'

'You weren't "hard", Max—you were brutally honest!' she corrected tightly, blue eyes glittering with humiliated memory. 'But then,' she added slightly bitterly, 'why should I have expected anything else from the great, the talented, the acerbic Max Harding?'

Was she going too far? Probably. But she was too angry, too hurt, to defensive about her own feelings for him to be anything else.

He sighed his frustration. 'I'm not someone you should become involved with, Abby—'

'I'm not involved with you,' she interrupted, knowing she lied. How she lied!

'—and, no matter how I might wish it were otherwise, you aren't someone I can become involved with, either,' Max finished.

She became very still, frowning across at him, finding that last remark enigmatic in the extreme. What did he mean, she wasn't someone he could become involved with?

In a sense, the two of them were already involved— their lives were entangled even if their emotions— Max's, at least—weren't. They each knew where the other lived, they had lunched together, had a mutual friend in Dorothy. Their lives might never have crossed before, but now that they had it was unlikely they would never do so again. In fact, feeling about him as she did, Abby hoped they would!

She raised dark brows. 'Are we back to your friend Kate again?' It was difficult for her to keep her voice even and unemotional.

Max's breath hissed harshly through his teeth. 'I would like you to forget that you ever took her call—'

'I'll just bet you would!' Abby came back incredulously, shaking her head. 'You keep your relationship with her pretty quiet, don't you, Max?' she challenged. 'No being seen out together. No photographs of the two of you in the newspapers. No—

'My God!' she gasped as a sudden thought occurred to her. 'She's not married, is she?' she asked belatedly, more disappointed than shocked.

She wasn't a prude, despite having a vicar for a fa-

ther, and knew that even if her guess was right, Max
would be far from the first man to have an affair with a
married woman. The difference was, she wasn't attracted to any of those other men!

'So the great, the legendary Max Harding, is having
an affair with a married woman!' she said scathingly.

Max didn't move so much as a muscle, and yet he suddenly seemed bigger, more powerful, more—dangerous!

Yes, that was exactly how he now appeared, Abby realised with a slightly dazed blink. His eyes were glittering furiously, his face grimly challenging, every
muscle in that tightly hewn body tensed as if ready to
spring. At her? Because she had guessed his secret? But
why should it matter so much that he was involved with
a married woman? After all, he wasn't the first, and she
was pretty sure he wouldn't be the last either.

'This,' he finally bit out with cold derision, 'coming
from a woman who hasn't been in her own apartment
for the last twenty-four hours! Oh, yes, Abby, I know
you've been out all night,' he taunted her, as her expression turned to one of astonishment. 'You see, I missed
my mobile some time yesterday evening, so I rang it to
see who answered. No one answered. Not last night. Not
this morning. Not early this afternoon either.' His mouth
twisted. 'Monty wasn't the only one 'out on the tiles'
all night!'

Abby stared at him. The conclusions that Max had
come to concerning her absence were simply incredible. Okay, so she was twenty-seven years old, unat-
tached and not unattractive—but did that really mean
that the only reason she could possibly have been out
all night was because she had spent it with a man?
Obviously to Max it did.

'As this is the middle of London, Monty doesn't actually go out on the tiles,' she began, knowing her pet's reticence had nothing to do with safety and everything to do with the fact that all his creature comforts were right here. 'And, as it happens,' she continued determinedly as Max tried to speak, 'neither do I! In fact,' she added firmly as her resolve deepened, 'I think the implication is just a clever attempt on your part to distract my attention from your relationship with Kate. How frustrating it must be for you that the two of us talked on the telephone earlier—'

'I think you should stop right there, Abby!' Max cut in icily, his expression grimmer than ever—dangerously so.

Abby refused to back down, just as she refused to let her gaze drop from his cold eyes. 'I think you should just take your mobile and leave.'

He gave a frustrated sigh. 'There's just no reasoning with you, is there?'

'Reasoning, yes. Sheer bloody arrogance, no! I get all the arrogance I can take working with the conceited Gary Holmes,' she added challengingly. And after the accusations Max had made yesterday, and his comments now concerning her absence from her apartment last night, he could make what he liked of that remark!

But there was no telling what he *did* think about it. Max's expression became remotely unreadable just at the mention of the other man's name. 'I would rather not talk about Gary Holmes. And I would prefer it if you didn't discuss my private life with him either.'

'I don't know anything *about* your private life!' Except the brief—very brief—part she had played in it. And about Kate, of course…

Abby gave him a searching look. Was she the 'private life' he was referring to? And, if so, what possible interest could this woman Kate be to Gary Holmes?

Unless the other man knew Kate? Who she was? Whose wife she was?

'Don't even go there, Abby,' Max warned darkly, seeming to easily read her thoughts from her expression.

She had never been good at hiding her emotions; it probably came from being the only child of loving parents who had always encouraged her to believe that honesty was the best policy. Because in her parents' world—in her own world until she was twenty-one and left university—it had been. It was only since she had entered the world of politics and television that she had discovered the truth usually had very little to do with anything. Cynical, perhaps, but it was a lesson she had learnt during the last six years—and learnt it well.

She met Max's gaze unflinchingly. 'I have no idea what you're talking about.'

'I'm warning you, Abby—'

'Threats now, Max?' she taunted lightly, shaking her head. 'Not a good way to divert an interviewer's interest away from a possible story!'

'There *is* no story.'

'Isn't there?' Abby returned tightly. 'You're very emotional about something you claim is unimportant—' She broke off as Max stepped forward to grasp her arms and glare down at her fiercely, his face mere inches away from hers, the warmth of his breath stirring the ragged tendrils of hair on her forehead.

Her first wide-eyed thought was that he was going to shake her until her teeth rattled. Her second was that he was going to kiss her insensible.

The second thought was the correct one.

And it didn't take him too long to do it, either.

Mere seconds after Max had taken her into his arms, his mouth taking fierce possession of hers, Abby had totally forgotten everything but that—was aware of nothing but Max and the desire that glared between them unchecked.

It was as if no time had elapsed between yesterday afternoon and tonight. And maybe it hadn't. Their passion seemed to rage to fever-pitch in seconds.

Abby had no idea, no memory, of going into her bedroom—only knew they must have left a trail of clothes on their way there, since both of them were naked by the time they fell on top of the bedclothes, hands seeking, mouths locked hungrily.

Max's body was just as she remembered it from that first day: lean and hard, covered with fine, silky dark hair, thicker on his chest and down his stomach. His back was wide and muscled, tapering to powerful thighs and long, athletic legs—legs that became entangled with hers as she lay back on the bed.

His dark head bent and his lips claimed the pouting arousal of her breasts. Her body arched as she gasped with pleasure. Max's mouth was hotly moist, his tongue caressing, teeth gently biting, sending rivers of molten pleasure coursing deeply between her thighs. One of his hands was caressing her there, seeking and finding the centre of her pleasure, his lightest touch sending her completely over the edge. The pleasure was everywhere now, inside her, hot, wet, totally mind-blowing.

But there was no time to even catch her breath as Max's mouth moved back to claim hers, tongues duelling, hands seeking, finding. Abby felt Max shudder with pleasure as she touched his hardness, hot and throbbing, guiding him now as he sought to join his body with hers.

He filled her totally, possessed her as he moved inside her with long, slow strokes that quickly aroused her already sensitised flesh to a second climax, her body convulsing about his, threatening to take him with her.

He became still above her, delaying the moment, lips and hands once more caressing. Abby's hands moved restlessly across his back, nails raking the skin there, feeling the way he quivered beneath those caresses, knowing his self-control was reaching breaking point.

And she wanted it to—wanted to feel his own shuddering release, to know that she had pleasured him as he had pleasured her.

And then his movements were no longer slow, his hips pulsing against hers, taking her with him. Their moment of release was completely simultaneous, with Abby no longer sure where Max began and she ended, only able to cling to Max in an effort not to be completely swept away by the tidal wave.

'My God…!' Max groaned as he looked down at her with dark, heated eyes before burying his face in her throat.

My God, indeed. Abby had never dreamt, never known… It was true—love did make a difference!

And she loved Max. Deeply, strongly. In fact, nothing else mattered but the deep love she now realised she felt for him.

It was dark when she woke, some time later, briefly disorientated by the knowledge of another presence. Then, as Max sat up and quietly moved to the other side of her bed, it all came back to her in a warm rush of well-being:

their incredible lovemaking, being held in Max's arms afterwards, her head resting on his shoulder as he cradled her against him and they both drifted off to sleep.

Max hadn't commented on it last night—and she hoped he never would—but he had been her first lover.

She wasn't a prude—hadn't lacked opportunities either. And of course there had been Andrew. It was just that she had been brought up to believe that love, not curiosity, was the only reason for making love with someone—that the body as well as the emotions was a precious gift, not to be given lightly.

But until Max she had never been in love...

And, being the newly awoken lover that she was, even in her sleep she'd been completely attuned to Max's slightest movement—knowing the moment his arms left her and the warmth of his body was removed from her side. She turned her head on the pillow now, to look at the broad expanse of his back reflected in the moonlight from the undrawn curtains at the window. But he didn't move, simply sat there, seeming unaware that she was awake.

'What are you doing?' Even her voice sounded different in her knowledge of what it was to make love: softer, more sensual.

Max turned sharply, his face all shadows in the moonlight, his eyes unreadable. 'I didn't mean to wake you.'

Abby shook her head, her hair darkly tangled on the pillow beneath her. From the wild caress of Max's hands, she remembered warmly.

'You didn't.' She smiled, stretching her newly awakened body. Every ache was a pleasurable one. Even the bruises she was sure would be on her shoulders from the pressure of Max's fingers as their desire had spiralled out of control were something to be cherished and held to her. Like battle scars. Except these were love scars... 'What are you doing?' she repeated more urgently as Max stood up and began to pull on the items of clothing—denims, and boxer shorts—that littered the bedroom carpet.

He zipped his jeans over perfect hips before answering her. 'Leaving you to get some more sleep.'

'But—'

'I need to get home to shower and change; I have an early appointment this morning, Abby.' He moved to sit on her side of the bed, reaching down to caress the hair from her face, smoothing the frown from between her eyes with the pad of his thumb. 'I'll call you later, okay?'

No, it was not okay. She didn't want him to leave, didn't want to go back to sleep, wanted the two of them to make love again. And again. And again. She wanted Max to stay!

Her absolute certainty from last night, of loving and being loved, began to fade in the increasing daylight in the bedroom. Max's expression revealed nothing of what he did or didn't feel towards her. Last night had been incredible, a revelation to Abby, but she could see none of that reflected in Max's face. In fact, his expression was once again totally unreadable.

Abby felt like crying.

Max looked at her searchingly for several long seconds, and then he was gone from the side of the bed, standing up forcefully. 'I will call you, Abby.'

'When?' she asked—and despised herself for doing so. She sounded like someone clinging to a man who didn't want to be clung to.

'Later,' he promised harshly, before turning away to

stride into the other room—probably in order to collect the rest of his abandoned clothes.

Abby's instinct was to follow him—an instinct she instantly resisted, instead lying unmoving in the bed, her hearing acutely attuned as she heard Max dressing, talking briefly to Monty, heard her apartment door opening and then closing softly seconds later.

Max had gone.

After sharing with her the most beautiful, memorable experience, he had simply dressed and left.

Because last night hadn't meant the same to him as it had to her?

The tears began to fall then, hot rivers of them, scouring and burning as deeply as the love she now felt for Max.

Love. A word, she realised with painful hindsight, that had never passed Max's lips.

CHAPTER SEVEN

'HAS anyone ever told you you're an extremely difficult woman to find?'

Abby glanced up from the sheets of information strewn across the desk in front of her, no welcome in her expression as she watched Gary Holmes stroll into the room uninvited to perch on the edge of her desk, boyishly handsome.

'Do you mind?' she snapped, looking at him pointedly as he sat on some of the papers she had been reading. Or at least attempting to read.

It was an effort to distract herself from thinking about Max and his abrupt departure this morning. Not that it was working at the moment. For her there was nothing except Max.

Even though it had only been five-thirty when he'd left, she hadn't slept after he had gone. Her year of working on breakfast television had disciplined her into waking early and alert; it was a habit she hadn't yet managed to shake off, and Max's sudden departure had completely robbed her of any desire for further sleep anyway.

So she had got up instead, drinking several cups of coffee as she'd prowled her apartment, no longer sure, as the agonising minutes had passed, what had happened between herself and Max.

The more she'd thought about it the more she had come to realise that although Max might have made love with her, he had certainly never said he was *in* love with her—not even during those most intimate moments.

And the more convinced she had become that he was not going to call her later, either.

She had, in fact, become that well-worn cliché, a one-night stand. Her own feelings of love towards Max had just blinded her to that fact.

Until that moment.

She had left her apartment, the scene of her naïveté, like one pursued, rushing to the office she shared with her researchers, glad no one else was in yet as she tried to bury herself in the extensive notes she needed to go through before her programme on Friday evening.

A wasted effort so far. She had no interest in her guest or in the programme, couldn't concentrate on the words written in front of her as thoughts intruded again and again of what had happened the previous night— seeking a balm, anything to salve her cringing humiliation. And finding none.

Gary Holmes, grinning at her cheerfully as he pushed the papers to one side and sat down again, was the last person she wanted to see just now!

His blue eyes narrowed thoughtfully as he looked down at her, almost as if he sensed there was something different about her…

Was there? she wondered, slightly panicked. Did the sort of mind-blowing, sense-filling lovemaking she and Max had shared the night before leave some sort of physical mark for others to see? She hoped not!

She stood up abruptly, moving restlessly to stand in front of the window, her expression shadowed by the sunlight streaming in behind her. 'What do you want, Gary?' she snapped.

Her annoyance was completely wasted on the thick-skinned Gary, and he returned her hostile gaze unperturbed. 'You aren't exactly being nice, Abby. All I've ever wanted was to be your friend.'

Abby gave a scornful laugh; she must have missed that particular conversation! All Gary had ever done was ridicule and belittle her. 'You haven't succeeded!'

'No?' He raised blond brows, his expression thoughtful for a few seconds before he shrugged. 'Maybe you're right,' he agreed without concern. 'But it isn't too late for us to start again?' he added with throaty flirtation.

'Start again?' she repeated. 'And just what have I done to merit this generous offer on your part?' Her eyes glittered with challenge.

He was openly grinning now. 'I may not have liked you very much to begin with, Abby—'

'What a surprise!' She shook her head. 'The feeling, I can assure you, is still mutual.' She had no intention of even *trying* to be polite to this man after the mischief he had deliberately tried to create for her on Saturday.

Initially she had tried, in the face of great provocation, to maintain a professional respect for this man's obvious brilliance as a director, but over the last few days he had been the one to step over the line of that working relationship and into her private life. There, she owed him no respect whatsoever.

'Just what did you think you were doing, coming to my apartment in that way on Saturday?' she demanded.

He shrugged. 'Believe it or not, trying to save you from yourself.' He looked at her with narrowed eyes. 'But perhaps I'm too late to do that...?' he said slowly.

Something about her *was* different, Abby realized, and embarrassed colour stained her cheeks. She had no idea what it could be, what it was that Gary could see that she couldn't, but he knew. It was written there in his scathingly pitying expression; he *knew* she and Max were lovers.

The scorn she could understand—Gary seemed to feel that way about most emotional relationships—but why the pity?

Her gaze didn't quite meet his now. 'I have no idea what you're talking about.'

'Don't you?' he came back quickly. 'Oh, I think you do, Abby.' The colour drained from her cheeks as quickly as it had stained them, and Gary shook his head. 'You're playing with the big boys now.'

'I'm not playing at all,' she snapped, wondering, after her recent humiliation, just how much more of this she could take.

He nodded. 'And that's going to be your problem.' He made himself more comfortable on the desktop. 'Max is a major league player, and you're nothing but a lightweight. In other words, Abby, he'll crush you like a bug that's unwittingly stepped into his path.'

She gave another shake of her head, trembling slightly now, having already come to the same conclusion herself not so long ago. 'Isn't that my business?'

'Not if it's going to affect the programme, no,' Gary rasped. 'As I said, you're a lightweight who should never have been put in this position, but—'

'That's only *your* opinion,' she cut in forcefully,

stung beyond measure that he was repeating Max's words from their very first meeting.

That seemed so very long ago now. So much had happened—and yet in reality it was only a matter of days.

'My professional as well as my personal opinion,' Gary continued remorselessly, a man confident of his own professional worth. 'So, to recap: you're a lightweight, but unfortunately you happen to be the principal in my latest programme. It's in my interest to see that you don't self-destruct.'

'And you believe my seeing Max Harding is going to result in that?' she said scornfully. 'I'm still trying to persuade him into appearing on the show, Gary. Or had you forgotten that?' She tossed back the darkness of her shoulder-length hair.

He gave her another pitying glance. 'How have you been doing so far?'

Not well, she inwardly acknowledged. In fact, she hadn't even given that aspect of their relationship a thought during the last twenty-four hours!

'An open channel of dialogue is a vast improvement on his total non-compliance of a week ago,' she defended evasively.

'Has he agreed to appear on the programme?'

'I told you, I'm still—'

'Has Max Harding agreed to appear on the programme?' Gary repeated through gritted teeth, all mockery gone now, his eyes glittering intently.

She swallowed hard. 'Not yet. But that doesn't mean—'

'He isn't going to.' Gary ignored her protest. 'Not now. Not ever. But don't take it personally, Abby,' he added with some of his earlier derision. 'Max Harding will never appear unscripted on public television again. He daren't. Because he can't take the risk of being questioned about his private life.'

Abby became very still, her expression guarded now. 'What about his private life?' So far she and the researchers had managed to find out very little about that—just normal background stuff, such as parents, education, television credits. The private side of Max's personal life remained exactly that. Private.

Except, she thought dully, last night probably made *her* a part of that private life…

Gary gave her an exasperated look. 'Did you never wonder why Rory Mayhew chose Max's programme to attempt to commit suicide?'

'The man's life was in tatters,' she came back impatiently. 'His political career was in ruins, totally beyond repair after that property scandal. He had only that day been forced into resigning from his government post. It was also rumoured that his wife was leaving him because of an affair—'

'Yes,' Gary put in softly, the full weight of innuendo behind that one word.

Abby looked at him dazedly. She was tired from lack of sleep, upset beyond measure at Max's casual 'I'll call you later'—how many other women had he said that to before never contacting them again?—and just too emotionally fragile to make any sense of whatever Gary was implying.

She shook her head. 'I don't see how any of that has anything to do with Max.'

'No?' Gary gave her another pitying look. 'That rather depends on which of the Mayhews was having the affair, doesn't it? And who with,' he added softly.

Abby stared at him unblinkingly for several long seconds, and then she finally realised exactly what he was saying.

She didn't believe it!

Rory Mayhew's professional life had been over so far as politics were concerned—absolutely no going back on that. The bribes and deals he had arranged during his brief time in government, and the added rumours of the total collapse of his private life had been enough to drive any man to the point of suicide.

Something he had achieved on his second time of trying…

The shamed politician had been seen by a doctor following his behaviour on the Max Harding show, but must have given quite a convincing performance of sanity, because he had been released from medical supervision only two days later. At which time he had booked into an obscure hotel and downed the contents of a bottle of pills, washing them down with whisky.

There had been no Max Harding on hand to stop him that time.

But now Gary seemed to be implying something else about that whole incident. Something totally unbelievable.

She gave a denying movement of her head. 'Rory Mayhew was the one having an affair—'

'Was he?' Gary's smile was completely confident. 'Or was that just something that gained credence once the man was dead? After all—' his mouth twisted derisively '—his reputation was already beyond repair. And—what's the saying?—you have to protect the living…'

What he was implying, what he was saying, was that it had been Rory Mayhew's *wife* who had been having an affair. And that the man involved was Max.

'You don't have to believe me, Abby.'

'I don't!' she said, with more determination than actual conviction.

Because she didn't know!

The whole incident had taken place two years ago, at a time when she had been trying to pursue her own career. Oh, she had seen the programme, had been as shocked as the rest of the general public and had read all the scandalous details that had followed in the newspapers. But she, like everyone else, had only ever known what the press chose to tell her. She didn't really know what had happened, why it was that Rory Mayhew should have felt desperate enough to attempt suicide on television.

'Don't you, Abby?' Gary taunted as he saw her doubts. 'She was in his life then, and she's still in his life now,' he added softly.

Her lashes fluttered uncertainly. She couldn't meet his gaze. 'Who is?'

'Kate Mayhew, of course.'

'Kate?' Abby echoed sharply, clearly remembering Max's excuses about the woman Kate who had telephoned, and his reaction to her suggestion that the other woman might be married. 'Kate Mayhew?'

Was that the reason Max had made love to her? Because he had hoped to distract her attention from his relationship with the woman she knew only as Kate?

No, she couldn't believe that—wouldn't believe that of Max. Gary was just being his usual vindictive self. If only she didn't feel so vulnerable. If only she felt more sure of her own relationship with Max!

Gary was looking at her speculatively now. 'You've obviously heard the name.' He nodded his satisfaction.

'But not from Max, I'm sure. Max likes to play things close to his chest on that particular subject. He'll do anything he can to hide the fact that he's still involved with Kate Mayhew.'

So the woman who'd called had had the same name—that didn't prove anything. Did it?

'How do you know so much about him?' Abby attacked.

'Didn't he tell you?' Gary smiled, standing up. 'I was the director on *The Max Harding Forum* two years ago. So you see, Abby,' he continued mercilessly at her stunned silence, 'I'm in a position to know *exactly* what happened. In fact, if you decide you want to know any more about it, I suggest you come and ask me.' He swung the door open. 'Max, I'm sure, will never tell you or anyone else the truth about what happened,' he concluded with certainty, closing the door softly behind him as he left.

Abby couldn't move. Couldn't breathe.

Gary had been the director on Max's show two years ago? Was *that* the reason for the antagonism between the two men?

What did it matter what the reason was for their dislike of each other? None of that told her what she really wanted—needed—to know. And that was the truth about the Mayhews. What had really happened two years ago. Whether Kate Mayhew was the Kate from the phone call! Because, if she was, that put a whole different light on Max's continuing friendship with her...

But until she did know—and she was far too familiar with how much Gary enjoyed being malicious!—she was more inclined to believe the man she loved than Gary's vicious lies.

Although that didn't stop her sense of unease every time she thought of the possibility of the woman Kate being Rory Mayhew's widow...

'Dinner tonight, Abby?'

This had not been the best day of her life—in fact, Abby couldn't remember a worse one!

. She had spent most of it, after Gary had left, fluctuating between believing totally in Max and their own relationship, and doubts concerning his evasion where that call from Kate was concerned.

She was still inclined to believe that Gary had it all wrong, and that the woman who had telephoned Max wasn't Kate Mayhew at all—after all, Kate really wasn't an uncommon name—but every time she decided that she remembered Max's behaviour over the call, his refusal to discuss it or the woman called Kate.

She had arrived home ten minutes ago, literally feeling like something Monty had dragged in, and really hadn't been prepared, emotionally or in any other way, for Max's telephone call.

'Abby?' Max prompted now at her continued silence. 'If you would rather not go out I can always come over there, and we can order something in—'

'No!' She felt compelled to reject that idea; she had no idea how this evening was going to turn out, and knew that in spite of herself she was still disturbed by her conversation with Gary earlier. Even if that was probably what he had intended all along. 'Why don't I bring some food over to your apartment and we can cook there?' she went on hastily. 'That way you won't have to get up and leave in the morning.' She couldn't stop herself from adding that. His sudden departure this morning still rankled.

Even if he *had* now called, as he had said he would…

'It's been a while, Abby,' he remarked wryly.

'What has?' she came back warily, desperately wishing she didn't feel so uncertain—of Max, of their own relationship. Because if she hadn't she would have been able to tell Gary to take his accusations and innuendos and—

'Abby?' Max questioned sharply now, obviously sensing that something was wrong.

How she wished she could behave differently. How she *wanted* to behave differently! But the truth was she felt battered and bruised—from Max's sudden departure this morning, from her hateful conversation with Gary Holmes later—and was hating the fact that her uncertainties about her own relationship with Max had succeeded in putting doubts into her mind.

'Abby, have I upset you with the way I left this morning?' Max pursued gruffly. 'I told you, I'm a little rusty at this sort of thing. I didn't mean to upset you by leaving the way I did, but I really did have an early appointment.'

At five-thirty in the morning? Somehow she very much doubted that! Unless it had been with the lovely Kate? And if that Kate *was* Kate Mayhew, then she *was* lovely, Abby knew, having managed to find several photographs on file of the tall, beautiful redhead. Now thirty-five, the mother of two young children, Abby also knew that Kate Mayhew had not remarried…

'I'm not upset, Max,' she told him. 'I've been working all day, I only got in ten minutes ago, and I'm tired—that's all.'

'Sure?' His voice had deepened to husky intimacy, causing a quiver of awareness down Abby's spine as it brought sharply back into focus all the intimacies they had shared the previous night.

'I'm sure,' she told him with brisk determination, shaking off that awareness. For self-preservation's sake, if nothing else! 'Look, just give me an hour to shower and change, and I'll come over with some food.'

'Forget the food. Just bring yourself,' Max told her gruffly. 'If we get hungry for food later we can order something in.'

Later. Implying they would be occupied doing something else when she first arrived. And Abby wasn't naïve enough not to know what that something would be.

But she needed to be a lot more certain of him than she was to withstand a second battering to her emotions...

'I haven't eaten all day, Max.' She had been too busy to even think about food! 'I need feeding before I do anything else.'

There was the briefest of pauses before he replied, 'Okay. I'll uncork some wine and have it waiting for when you get here.'

A whole bottle of it to herself, Abby decided as she rang off and moved lethargically towards the bathroom. Preferably with a straw!

She shouldn't be doing this—shouldn't be going anywhere near Max when she was so filled with questions and doubts about the two of them continuing to see each other.

Oh, stop lying to yourself, Abby, she told herself disgustedly. She wanted to see Max again, *needed* to see him. She loved him, for goodness' sake! And once she was with him all Gary's lies, his insinuations, would evaporate, she was sure.

CHAPTER EIGHT

'I WAS beginning to think you had changed your mind,' Max greeted her huskily an hour and a half later, as he let her into his apartment.

In truth, she had. Several times, in fact. Her emotions had fluctuated between wanting to see Max, to be with him and the other extreme of wondering why he had made love to her last night—whether it was because he loved her as she loved him, or for some other reason.

She needed to see him again tonight if only to try and find the answer to that. All the time hoping it was because he loved her!

'Did you?' She moved on tiptoe to lightly brush her lips against his. 'Dinner.' She held up the bag she carried, looking at him beneath from under lashes.

He looked ruggedly handsome in a black silk shirt and faded black denims, his feet once again bare; obviously it was a trait of his when in the privacy of his apartment. Or else it was his way of having less clothing to remove later...

Oh, God!

Just looking at him made her feel weak at the knees. Not only did she know Max intimately, but he knew her in the same way—much more so than any other man. And without any declaration of love, from either of them, how could she help but feel a certain amount of shyness and uncertainty now that she was with him again?

Gary Holmes and his insinuations could just go to hell—she had enough insecurities of her own concerning this relationship without wondering if there was any truth in what he had said!

It was taking every ounce of self-confidence she had to face Max again this evening. In fact, with Max looking at her so broodingly, she suddenly wished she'd inherited some of her mother's undoubted acting ability; she might at least have been able to pretend a semblance of sophistication then. As it was, she had absolutely no idea how to behave with this man who was her lover!

She smiled at him brightly. 'Shall I take the food through to the kitchen?' She didn't wait for his reply before turning and doing exactly that. 'I brought steak, potatoes, and the makings of a salad,' she continued as she unpacked the food, desperately hoping to hide her increasing tension.

Max's next comment proved she hadn't succeeded. *Sorry, Mum!*

'What's happened, Abby?'

She opened wide cornflower-blue eyes. 'Happened?' she repeated with a puzzled glance.

Max was standing only inches away now, his expression more brooding than ever. 'You seem—different.'

Well, of course she was different! She was no longer a twenty-seven-year-old virgin, but this man's lover. And she had no idea and no experience of how to behave in a situation like this!

'In what way do you feel I'm different this evening?'

she asked casually. 'If you mean I seem a little tense, then you're probably right. Unlike you, Max, I'm not just a little rusty; this is all new to me.'

'Do you think I don't know that?' he murmured huskily, moving forward to take her into his arms, his gaze intent on her face. 'Why me, Abby?'

He had known he was her first lover. That just made it all the more embarrassing. Max was thirty-nine, obviously a man of experience, and probably found it incredible that she had actually been a virgin. And, having no idea how he felt towards her, she could hardly come out with a declaration of love, now, could she?

She smiled, determined to salvage some of her shaky pride; after all, she was in her late twenties, not an immature schoolgirl. 'Why not you?' she came back flippantly. 'I always was a late developer, but every girl has to start somewhere!'

His gaze was searching now. A gaze Abby withstood with effort.

Max shook his head. 'If you had told me I would have been more—gentle.'

He had been 'gentle' enough for her to fall more deeply in love with him than ever!

'Why didn't *you*—' she poked a friendly finger into his chest '—tell me that Gary Holmes was the director on your programme two years ago?' Changing the subject, even to one as unpleasant as Gary Holmes, seemed like a good idea at that moment.

A shutter came down over Max's features, telling her of his sudden tension. 'You've talked to Holmes today?' he said harshly.

'Well, of course I've talked to Gary today; he's the director of my show too, you know,' Abby came back lightly—perhaps she did have some of her mother's acting ability after all?

She certainly didn't want to be having this seemingly playful conversation with Max. What she really wanted to do was scream and shout, to cry, to demand he tell her exactly what was going on, to pummel the hard width of his chest with her fists as she felt he was pummelling her heart.

Max's arm dropped from about her waist and he stepped back, his expression wary now. 'And what else did he have to say?'

She shrugged. 'You know Gary—as acerbic as ever.'

Max's mouth thinned. 'Exactly what did he say to you, Abby?' he rasped harshly.

Her mouth twisted. 'Just his usual bluster, really. Mainly directed at the fact that I'll never persuade you into appearing on my show. But then, I already know that, don't I?' she added with a casualness she was far from feeling. 'Look, could we start cooking dinner now? I really am hungry.' Every mouthful would probably choke her, but she was determined to get through this.

Because, if she were to salvage anything from this relationship at all, it was becoming increasingly obvious that she needed to know what had really happened two years ago. Was still happening?

Max seemed to shake himself out of his sudden tension with effort, taking the steaks from her to begin preparing them for grilling. 'I think I now understand the reason why you aren't in the best of moods this evening,' he remarked lightly. 'Gary Holmes used to have that effect on me too!'

Abby turned away to wash the potatoes. 'You still haven't told me why you didn't mention he had been your director,' she prompted.

Max grimaced. 'Gary Holmes, and working with him, are things I've tried to block out of my mind.'

It wasn't exactly an answer. Any more than Gary's attitude towards Max had been explained by either of them. But it was obvious the two men disliked each other intensely, and it was yet another riddle Abby felt she had to get to the bottom of.

'Here, let's have a glass of wine—' Max poured them both a glass of the red wine he'd uncorked '—and forget all about Gary Holmes.'

She only wished that she could, Abby acknowledged as she obligingly sipped the delicious wine. But no matter how she tried she simply couldn't forget the awful things Gary had said to her.

'How did your meeting go this morning?' she asked, once they were sitting down to eat their meal.

Max had prepared the table in the dining-room before she'd arrived, with silver cutlery and lighted candles. Very romantic. Except Abby didn't feel very romantic. What she really felt was an inexperienced fool. And fools, she knew, made bad company. Hence her less that scintillating conversation.

How much different this could have been, she cried inwardly. If she hadn't already felt upset by Max's sudden departure this morning. If Gary hadn't poured his vitriol into her ears.

She could see by Max's rueful expression that he was less than satisfied with the way the evening was going too.

'Not very well,' he answered her, sipping his wine. 'I spent the best part of two hours over a mediocre breakfast, convincing a man that I'm not interested in having my biography written and that at thirty-nine I'm only halfway through my life, not at the end of it.' He grimaced. 'No doubt he'll go ahead and write an unauthorised version, anyway.'

'A biography?' Abby's interest quickened. 'Now, that *would* be interesting,' she said slowly. Very interesting!

Max gave her a reproachful grin. 'If I'm not interested in appearing on a half-hour chat show, I'm certainly not interested in seeing a book about myself!'

She kept her lashes down in order to hide the sudden flare of hurt in her eyes.

That had been very neatly done. Too neatly. Letting her know that nothing had changed with regard to appearing on her show, but doing it without actually antagonising her. Because he still had the woman Kate to protect! That knowledge had nothing to do with anything Gary Holmes had told her this morning about the other woman's full identity—she still didn't trust him!—and everything to do with Max's own attitude with regard to the other woman.

And that would hurt no matter what Gary had said to her. She and Max were lovers, and yet there was another woman in his life called Kate that he refused to talk about. Not exactly reassuring to any new lover, was it?

How many other women in the last two years had wondered about Max's friendship with the other woman, too? And how many of those relationships had floundered because of it?

More to the point, why was Max so secretive about the relationship?

The answer to that, if the woman really *was* Kate Mayhew, was all too easy to guess, Abby realised painfully; any public relationship between Kate Mayhew and Max Harding after the scandal two years ago would dredge it up all over again—perhaps even lead to speculation concerning exactly what their relationship might have been then.

In the same position, Abby felt she would say to hell with it and let the media do their worst. The fact that Max and Kate hadn't only seemed to confirm that they had something to hide...

'This evening isn't going too well, is it?' Max rasped suddenly, giving up all pretence of eating his own meal and pushing the plate away.

If he hadn't left so abruptly this morning... If Gary hadn't told her the things he had, causing her concerns to become full-blown doubts... Abby knew it would all have been so different then, that instead of being on the defensive, guarded in her words and actions, she would probably have behaved like a simpering lovestruck idiot. In retrospect, perhaps this was better. More painful, maybe, but better.

Her gaze was still guarded as she looked across at him. 'We don't know each other very well, that's all,' she said, with an attempt at unconcern.

He frowned darkly. 'That didn't seem to bother either of us last night.'

Sadly, despite everything, Abby knew it wouldn't bother her if he were to take her in his arms again now either.

'Perhaps that's the problem?' she suggested lightly. 'We jumped ten steps ahead of where we really were.'

'Well, it's too late to go back on that now!' Max flung the contents of his wine glass down his throat before standing up and moving forcefully away from the table.

Abby gave a pained frown, a little surprised at his sudden anger. 'I wasn't suggesting that we should—'

'No?' he challenged, pouring himself another glass of wine. 'What is it you want from me, Abby? What do you want to know about me?' His eyes were glacial. 'Parents? Siblings? An exchange of the names of past lovers?'

The latter might be interesting. And painful. And destructive. She also very much doubted that Kate Mayhew would be included in that exchange!

She gave a half smile. 'I already know about parents and siblings from my research. As for past lovers— wouldn't that be a little boring for you, considering I don't have any?'

He gave her an impatient glare. 'Contrary to what you may think, I don't have that many either!'

Abby shook her head. 'This isn't very helpful, is it? Perhaps I should just leave?'

Max stopped his pacing to stare down at her frustrat-edly. 'Is that what you want to do?'

Yes! No! She didn't know!

If she left she wasn't sure when, or if, she would see Max again.

Max seemed to have the same doubts, taking a step towards her. 'Abby, I don't want to fight with you,' he groaned.

She swallowed hard. 'No…'

She had no defences when he took her in his arms— but then she didn't really want any. Held in Max's arms, being kissed by him, able to feel his response to her, she had no doubts whatsoever…

Doubts came later, much later, when she woke in the darkness of Max's bedroom early the next morning, her body still aching pleasurably from the intensity of their lovemaking.

She had been lost from that first kiss, their responses to each other wild and abandoned.

Too much so?

As if both of them had known they were trying to hold on to something so fragile it might break when exposed to the outside world?

There had certainly been no words of love from either of them. Just those intense hours of lovemaking, and Max cradling her in his arms as they both drifted off to sleep.

Max was still sleeping, she realised as she turned on the pillow to look at him. The early-morning light showed his face looking younger and less strained, with the darkness of his hair falling endearingly over his forehead.

God, how she loved him!

Enough to know that she had to be the one to leave this time. That if she stayed she would only do or say something she might regret—that she *would* regret. If Max wanted to take this slowly, to let time and familiarity decide whether or not they had a future together, then that was what she would have to do.

She slid silently out of bed, gathering up her clothes from where they had been thrown the night before and going into the adjoining bathroom.

Max was still asleep when she came back from taking her shower. She gave him one last wistful look before letting herself out of the apartment.

She was too restless to go back to her own apartment, and went to her office instead. There was something she needed to do before she saw Max again…

If the security man found her early arrival strange, he didn't say so, greeting her cheerfully enough as he let her into the building. One advantage of being on a weekly TV show!

The day before, after Gary Holmes's insinuations, she had impulsively got a copy of Max's show from two years ago from the archives, and then decided she didn't want to look at it.

Because it might confirm what Gary had said?

Maybe, but this morning, since she was alone in the building, apart from security, with no danger of being interrupted—especially by the gloatingly sarcastic Gary!—it seemed like the ideal time for her to sit and watch it.

As she had known it would be, it was distressing viewing. Rory Mayhew's despair was so utter that Abby's heart ached for him.

Those emotions dominated her first two viewings of the recording, but the third time she began to concentrate on other aspects of it—on Max's responses to the other man's rapidly escalating incoherency as Rory Mayhew seemed the worse for drink.

Max had obviously tried to direct the conversation under great provocation, tried to keep things under control. But when Rory Mayhew had produced an old service revolver that looked as if it might have seen use in the Second World War and started waving it about erratically, it had become obvious that the other man was beyond reasoning with.

His voice slurred from the alcohol he had consumed before appearing on the show, Rory Mayhew had begun to rant and rave about the things he was being accused of, the mistakes he had made, how they had cost him his career, the respect of his colleagues and his friends, and how he feared he was about to lose his wife and children too.

But never once during that tirade had Rory Mayhew accused Max of being involved in his downfall.

Gary's insinuations, she was sure, were exactly that—and, moreover, they had been made with the deliberate intent of driving a wedge between herself and Max.

She shouldn't have waited. She should have watched this recording yesterday, she berated herself impatiently. It didn't take away her uncertainties concerning the woman Kate, of course, but it did add to her impression that she and Kate Mayhew were not one and the same woman.

Damn it, she had been unfair to Max last night, and now she had left this morning without any word of farewell. What on earth was he going to think of her?

It was only nine-thirty now, she realized, after a glance at her wristwatch. Other people were starting to arrive in their offices. She could still go back to Max's apartment—maybe with coffee and Danish for their breakfast?

One thing she did know. She couldn't simply leave things like this between them!

The sun was shining as she walked back to Max's apartment. The birds were singing, the coffee and Danish she carried smelled delicious, and the prospect of being with Max again made her smile at the people she passed.

But the colour drained from her face as she turned the corner and saw Max standing outside on the pavement, talking to a woman just about to get into a car parked there. Because the woman, Abby knew without a doubt, was Kate Mayhew!

She easily recognised the other woman from the photographs she had seen of her, and her breath caught in a gasp of protest as she watched the other woman reach up and hug Max before getting into her car and driving away. Max's smile was wistful as he watched her leave.

Abby didn't even hesitate. She dropped the coffee and Danish into a bin before turning and walking hurriedly away, the tears falling hotly down her cheeks. There were no doubts left in her mind now, absolutely none, that the woman Kate was indeed Kate Mayhew. And, from the touching scene she had just witnessed, the other woman was still well and truly in his life.

'Why are you here, Max?' she prompted dully, her emotions still numbed by the scene she had unwittingly witnessed that morning.

After her abrupt departure she had been expecting a telephone call from him all day—had been prepared to deal with that. What she hadn't been prepared for was for him to actually come to her apartment this evening!

But she should have been, she realised heavily; Max had no idea she had seen him and Kate together this morning!

He looked at her frowningly. 'I was a little surprised to wake up this morning and find you gone...'

He would have been even more surprised if she had still been there when the lovely Kate had paid him a visit!

She shrugged, standing across the room from him, her shaking hands thrust into the back pockets of her denims. 'I was under the impression that was the way it was done.'

He gave a pained frown. 'I've apologised for my behaviour yesterday morning—'

'And your apology was accepted.' She nodded abruptly.

'But—' Max broke off whatever he had been about to say as his mobile began to ring, his expression one of irritation as he took it out of his pocket to check the number of the caller. 'If you'll excuse me—I have to take this,' he muttered, before moving into her kitchen.

His behaviour, in light of all Abby's unanswered questions, was like a slap in the face.

The caller was Kate, she thought instantly.

And then as quickly she chastised herself. Max must have dozens of friends and associates, family too, who'd feel comfortable telephoning him at eight-thirty in the evening. The caller didn't have to be Kate Mayhew. She was becoming paranoid, Abby acknowledged heavily. Believing everything Max did or said was somehow connected to the other woman.

She still had no idea what she was going to do about their relationship. Despite what she had learnt earlier today, and judging by his appearance here this evening, Max was obviously quite happy to let it continue. But she knew that she couldn't. Not under these circumstances.

She needed to know why Max had made love to her. Was it because the first time he had wanted to put a halt to their conversation about the woman called Kate who had called him? And the second time because Abby had been asking him questions about Gary Holmes?

Honesty had always been such a big part of her life. It was far too late for her to behave in any other way now. She could try simply asking Max for the truth about Kate Mayhew, telling him what she had seen this morning, but in reality she had already asked him about the other woman—several times—only to be told by Max not to go there.

'I have to go, Abby.' Max strode forcefully back into the room, his expression grim. 'Something's happened.' He ran a hand through the dark thickness of his hair. 'I can't explain right now, but—' He shook his head frustratedly. 'I have to go,' he repeated flatly.

'Okay,' she agreed dully, her gaze studiously avoiding meeting his.

'Abby…?' He grasped her arm as she turned away, one hand moving beneath her chin as he forced her to look up at him.

It didn't help. He looked so good, she loved him so much—and he was probably leaving her to go to another woman!

'It isn't what you think, Abby. Hell, I don't know *what* you think!' he ground out, shaking his head impatiently. 'This is what happens in my life—the way that it is. I receive a call and—'

'And you have to go,' she said evenly.

'Damn it, yes—I have to go!' His hands dropped back to his sides as he moved away from her. 'You've worked in television for a while now, Abby, in the media. You must know how it is—how my life has been for the last two years since I went back out as a political reporter. My stage is now the world stage, and when something of a political nature happens in it I have to go where it's happening. No matter what might be going on in my own life at the time,' he added heavily.

She gave a confused frown. 'You're saying that call was work-related?'

'Well, of course it was work-related. What else—?' Max broke off abruptly, his gaze narrowing on her with slow deliberation. 'You have been different the last couple of days, Abby,' he began slowly, 'and I'm pretty sure, knowing him as well as I do, that this change probably has something to do with Gary Holmes. Unfortunately, it isn't something I have the time to deal with right now.' He glanced down at his wristwatch impatiently. 'I have transport waiting for me, and I really do—'

'—have to go,' she finished for him, unable to hide the pain in her voice.

'Abby, when I get back we need to talk.' Max stood close to her again, cradling either side of her face with warm hands. 'Really talk. All I ask in the meantime is that you shut your ears to anything Gary Holmes might have to say about me.' His mouth tightened. 'I should have dealt with him long ago. I realise that now. This time he may not leave me any choice. Will you trust me on this for a while, Abby?' He looked down at her intently.

How could she trust him when she had actually *seen* him and Kate Mayhew together?

But not trusting him, she realized, now that she was with him again, didn't stop her loving him...

She had never felt so miserable in her life.

'I'll call you as soon as I can,' Max promised huskily, before his head lowered and his lips claimed hers with an aching need, sipping, tasting, as if he were committing the taste and feel of her to memory.

She didn't understand any of this. How could Max kiss her like this, be with her like this, if he really was involved with another woman?

Another woman he was even now leaving her to go to?

She pulled away. 'You have to go, Max,' she reminded him distantly.

He sighed. 'I wish it didn't have to be like this.'

So did she. But in retrospect perhaps this separation from Max was exactly what she needed to get back to her normal confident self; it was a sure fact that this relationship, a triangle she couldn't even begin to comprehend, was doing nothing for her whatsoever!

* * *

As she sat in her office the following day, eating a working lunch, watching the breaking news on television of a terrorist attack on the leader of one of the Middle Eastern countries—he'd been taken hostage—which was threatening to bring down the whole already shaky government, she wished that she and Max hadn't parted quite so distantly.

The voice of Max Harding—live coverage was unavailable at the time, due to the continuing unrest in the country—was informing her that so far there had been no ransom demand made for the kidnapped leader, and that the country was in turmoil as its citizens feared further action, possibly military reprisals, that would lead to all-out war in a country that had already known its fair share of death and destruction.

CHAPTER NINE

'YOU look terrible, darling.' Dorothy voiced her concern as she sat across from Abby in the conservatory of her home.

Abby gave a wan smile; even with the help of blusher on her cheeks, she knew that her godmother only spoke the truth.

But the last week had been the worst she had ever known—continually watching the news just in order to hear the sound of Max's voice.

The news from the war-torn country—the terrorists had executed the leader rather than releasing him, and the military were retaliating with force—was far from encouraging. But she had heard nothing from Max personally, and as each successive day passed her anxiety for him grew. The way they had parted and her unasked questions about his relationship with Kate Mayhew had faded into the background in her single-minded concern for his safe return.

In fact, her godmother's telephone call this morning to ask her to come over to the house had been a happy diversion of those worries. Although, looking at Dorothy's slightly flustered expression, she was beginning to have her doubts, sensing that the other woman wasn't happy with this conversation at all.

'Dorothy, has something happened?'

'Well, yes, darling. I'm afraid it has.' Her aunt sighed her obvious relief that Abby had introduced the subject. 'And Paul thought that the news might be better coming from me—'

'Dorothy, you're starting to frighten me now!' Abby stood up restlessly, her face pale. 'What is it? Has something happened to Max? What—?'

'Abby, calm down.' Her godmother looked deeply concerned at her reaction. 'He isn't dead, if that's what you're worried about.'

Well, of *course* it was what she was worried about. The country he was in was extremely unstable politically, and the fighting between the terrorists and the military had increased over the last two days. Max's reports had ceased altogether. In fact, there was very little news coming out of the country at all at the moment.

'Sit down, Abby—please,' Dorothy instructed briskly. 'Take deep, calming breaths, drink some of this.' She handed Abby the glass of water she had poured. 'And I'll tell you the little that we know.'

'Oh, God…!' Abby groaned weakly, her hand gripping the water glass so tightly she threatened to break it.

'I said he's all right, Abby,' her godmother insisted firmly. 'Max managed to get a message out through the television network there, who then passed it on to the English network, who passed it on to Paul, who passed it on to me, feeling it would be better if I spoke to you.' She drew in a deep breath. 'Apparently Max and his cameraman were caught up in some shooting a couple of days ago—he wasn't injured,' she added quickly, as

Abby paled even more, 'but the terrorists—wishing to play on a world stage, presumably—took the two of them hostage two days ago—'

'Two days ago?' Abby repeated disbelievingly. 'But there's been nothing on the news, nothing in the—'

'There's going to be. Which is why I'm talking to you before that happens,' Dorothy told her gently. 'After shooting the leader of the country, these terrible people obviously realised they had left themselves with no leverage. A foreign news crew must have seemed like a good way to recapture some of that leverage. There's going to be a news bulletin relayed later today, stating their demands,' she concluded heavily.

Abby felt sick. She couldn't believe this was happening. And she knew as well as the rest of the world how these situations usually turned out.

They needed to talk when he got back, Max had said. But what if he didn't get back?

'Drink some of your water, Abby,' Dorothy instructed firmly.

She did so without even knowing she had. 'What do they want?'

'What do they all want?' The other woman sighed. 'Freedom from tyranny in their given country, the release of political prisoners. It's never going to happen, of course. The military will eventually take control again, and put in one of their own as leader, and so it will all start again.'

Abby moistened dry lips, thoughts racing but going nowhere. 'And Max?'

Dorothy sighed. 'As I said, he's one of the people the terrorists are now holding as bargaining power.'

But the western world didn't negotiate with terrorists. Not now, not ever…

She swallowed hard, feeling as if her world had been turned upside down, and inside out; like everyone else, she had watched these situations before. But, although she'd watched them with compassion for the hostages' families, it had been in a detached way, never dreaming it would one day happen to the man she was in love with.

Did anyone ever think something so horrendous could happen to someone they loved?

'Abby, Max wanted you specifically to know that he's okay.' Dorothy came down on her haunches beside where Abby sat, taking one of her hands in both of hers.

She looked dazedly at the other woman. 'He did?'

'He did.' Dorothy squeezed her hand reassuringly.

'I— But— What about Kate?' Even in her complete shock she couldn't help but think of the other woman in Max's life, of what this might mean to her.

'Kate?' Her godmother looked puzzled now. 'I know nothing about anyone called Kate. The message that he's okay was for you and you alone.'

He was okay for the moment. Until the terrorists' demands weren't met. And then, as had happened so many times before, the killing would start.

Oh, God…!

The misunderstandings, the uncertainty between them, now seemed totally unimportant. Only Max and his safety mattered to her now.

And Kate Mayhew.

Because, much as Abby hated the fact, much as she hated the other woman's role in Max's life, she knew that she couldn't let the other woman just hear about this as a news item flashed on the television screen. That would just be too cruel after what the other woman had already gone through.

Someone had to go and tell Kate Mayhew what had happened.

And that someone would have to be Abby.

'I'm terribly sorry.' The other woman smiled at Abby blandly as the two women stood in the golden south-facing drawing room of Kate Mayhew's London home. 'I believe you told my housekeeper that your name is Annie Freeman?'

'Abby,' she corrected automatically, not so sure, now that she was here, that this was a good idea.

It had been instinctive, perhaps—the need to see someone, be with someone, who cared for—loved?— Max as much as she did. But here, in the quiet elegance of Kate Mayhew's home, with family photographs of before and since Rory Mayhew's death adorning every surface, Abby was having serious doubts.

The fact that Kate Mayhew was so startlingly beautiful didn't help.

The tall, slenderly elegant redhead had always looked lovely, of course—a beautiful accessory on her politician husband's arm—but the last two years, away from the public stadium, she had become even more so. The denims and T-shirt and loosely flowing red hair were certainly not anything she would have worn as the wife of a serving minister, and made her appear much younger than the thirty-five Abby knew her to be.

'Abby,' the other woman acknowledged, in the cool, well-modulated voice Abby remembered so well from their brief telephone conversation just over a week ago. 'Won't you sit down?'

'I'm fine, thank you.' Abby shook her head; this wasn't a social call, and—instinct apart—she didn't intend staying long. She would just say what she had to say and then leave. 'I believe we spoke on the telephone last week,' she added softly.

A flicker of recognition showed briefly in the other woman's eyes before it was quickly masked. She was looking at her guardedly now.

She was so beautiful, Abby thought dully. Absolutely stunning. And the thought that Max had been secretly involved with this woman for the last two years was heartbreaking.

She had to get out of here!

'Did we?' Kate Mayhew shook her head. 'I'm sorry. I thought you told my housekeeper that you're here in connection with my son's school…?'

It was the best excuse Abby had been able to think of at the time, knowing the other woman was unlikely to let someone involved with the media past the front door. Any more than she would have agreed to see a woman Max was possibly involved with. Abby wouldn't be here herself if she hadn't felt she owed it to the other woman not to let her just see the shocking news relayed over an impersonal television screen!

'I lied,' she told the other woman briskly, just wanting to get this over with now. 'I'm a friend of Max Harding's—'

'Who?' Kate Mayhew enquired with light confusion.

'Oh, please.' Abby really wasn't in the mood to play games. 'Even supposing the two of you haven't remained friends, you would hardly be likely to forget your husband's appearance on Max's programme shortly before he died—'

'I think you had better leave!' The other woman was breathing hard in her agitation, her face pale now, hands tightly clenched together. 'Abby Freeman,' she repeated. 'I realise who you are now. And, let me assure you, I have no intention of talking to a reporter—'

'I'm *not* a reporter!' Abby was just as angry, her nerves stretched to breaking point, sure now it had been a mistake to come here. 'I just thought—wrongly, it seems—that you'd like to know that, no matter what you might hear on the news later today, Max has got word out that he's okay.' He was still alive, anyway. And, really, that was all that mattered. Whether he came back to her or to this woman wasn't important. Only that he should come back.

The other woman was even paler now, sculptured cheekbones standing out starkly, big eyes a deep brown. 'I have no idea what you're talking about.'

'You will. Later today,' Abby warned her abruptly.

Those brown eyes widened. 'Are you threatening me? You get into my house under false pretences, talk about people I don't even know—'

'Don't be so ridiculous!' Abby was beyond patience with this woman now; Max was in danger, and this woman was continuing to deny she even knew him! 'I came here with the sole intention of reassuring you as to Max's safety. But, as you don't even know him, it doesn't really matter, does it!' Her voice broke emotionally. 'Just as it isn't going to matter to you if in the next couple of days he's shot and killed!' There were two spots of angry colour in her cheeks now. 'I'm so glad I don't have friends like you!' She turned on her heel and walked out of the room, out of the house.

And out of Kate Mayhew's life, she hoped.

'What the hell did you think you were doing?'

Abby blinked up at Max dazedly as he stormed into her apartment, his face furious, eyes glacial as he demanded an answer to his question.

Almost three weeks she had been waiting to see him again. Two of those weeks in absolute terror for his life as she recoiled from the awful photographs being shown of him and the other hostages on public television.

The English government had tried every diplomacy they could to secure their release without actually giving in to the terrorists' demands. And then yesterday, finally, the military had managed to overpower the terrorists—having put in place a leader who realised the benefits of a sympathetic western world—and release all the hostages still alive. Max—thankfully!—still amongst them.

Abby had first cried, and then laughed with absolute relief. And then she had cried some more. Her last twelve days had been an absolute hell of a different kind from Max's.

Something Dorothy had told her she looked like when she had come to Abby's apartment yesterday to tell her the good news.

She certainly wasn't looking her best now, she knew— a fact the make-up lady had fussed about four days ago as she'd gone about the business of repairing as much of the damage as she could. Although there had been little she could to do erase the shadows from beneath Abby's eyes from lack of sleep, or the hollows in her cheeks from lack of appetite. Wardrobe hadn't been too happy about the hasty alterations they'd had to make to her suit either, her figure having become almost wraith-like.

Max didn't look as if he had fared too much better. Very pale, much thinner than he had been, his hair in need of cutting.

He had never looked dearer to Abby!

But, after waiting in a state of increasing agitation for

him to come to her apartment once he was safely back in England—his telephone call from the plane had been necessarily brief—at least, she had thought it was necessary, now she wasn't so sure—she certainly hadn't been expecting his first words to be ones of attack!

She didn't understand. She hadn't been expecting hearts and flowers, declarations of undying love—she didn't believe that was Max's style at all—but neither had she been expecting this explosion of anger the moment he saw her.

'Abby,' he grated, hands clenched at his sides. 'I asked you—'

'I heard you,' she cut in forcefully, the strain she had been under, her lack of sleep, lack of interest in food, all finding an outlet in her own anger. 'I heard you,' she repeated more calmly. 'I just didn't understand you!' Her voice broke emotionally. 'What happened between your reassuring call from the plane, when you told me you couldn't wait to see me again, to what the hell did I think I was doing?' She shook her head, tears in her eyes now. 'You aren't making any se—' She broke off, staring across at him now as the truth hit her with the force of a sledgehammer. 'You've spoken to Kate Mayhew!'

He had arrived back in the country only hours ago, to cameras and reporters waiting to welcome the hostages home, and had endured a press conference since then—and yet somewhere in all that activity, Abby was becoming increasingly sure he had found time to telephone Kate Mayhew.

She sat down abruptly, her emotions in turmoil. She had thought—hoped—that Max's concern for her during the hostage situation meant that he felt something like the love she felt for him towards her. The fact that Max had obviously felt that same concern for Kate Mayhew, that he had actually already spoken to the other woman—been to see her first?—now gave lie to that hope.

'Well, of course I've spoken to Kate,' Max retorted savagely. 'You had no right to do what you did—'

'I had every right, damn you!' She stood up again, glaring at him, her heart breaking at how different this reconciliation was from her imaginings; it couldn't have been more different!

She had food waiting in the kitchen to be cooked, the table laid in the dining room—she had even put clean sheets on her bed! None of which, in the face of Max's hostility, were going to be used!

'You had been taken hostage, and the two of you are obviously…friends. I felt that the least I could do was go to her and try to warn her—try to alleviate some of the shock she would feel when she heard the news that day.' The same shock *she* had felt when she heard the news!

Max's hands were thrust into the pockets of his denims—denims that hung loosely on the accentuated leanness of his hips. The last two weeks had taken their physical toll on him: the dark shadows beneath his eyes, the deep grooves beside nose and mouth told of the emotional strain he had been under, not knowing from one moment to the next whether he was going to live or die.

Just looking at him was enough to make Abby wilt with weakness. She wanted to launch herself into his arms, to feel the living strength of him, just to know that he really was here.

He ran a hand tiredly over his eyes. 'Was that your

only reason, Abby? Or was it that you hoped to catch Kate during a moment of weakness, when she—?'

'Stop right there, Max,' she cut in incredulously. 'Do you have any idea of what it cost me to go and see her?' She breathed deeply. 'The two of us were lovers, and before you left you asked me to trust you; I thought my going to see Kate to reassure her of your safety was part of showing my trust in you. Obviously I was wrong!' She turned away. 'I think you had better leave, Max, don't you?' she said dully.

This was unbearable—unacceptable. She could only imagine what Max had gone through the last twelve days, knew only that *she* had felt as if she were poised on a knife's edge, not knowing if she would see him again, only sure that she loved him, longing to see him once more, if only to tell him that.

Now all she wanted was for him to leave—to go back to Kate Mayhew and whatever strange, unfathomable relationship the two of them shared and just leave her alone. She didn't want to be a part of their sordid triangle.

'Abby—'

'Go to her, Max,' she told him scornfully as she spun round to face him. 'I want no part of your relationship with Kate Mayhew!' She stared at him challengingly.

A nerve pulsed in his tightly clenched jaw. 'Kate and I aren't lovers—'

'No? That explains why you have women like me in your life then, doesn't it?' she retorted scathingly. 'I suggest you talk to *her* about it, Max— because I no longer want to hear anything you have to say!'

Uncertainty flickered in his eyes, his gaze searching now on the pale gauntness of her face. 'You look awful, Abby.'

'What a blessing for world peace that you never thought about joining the diplomatic service!' she said incredulously. 'Of course I look awful! I've been worried out of my mind about you—unable to sleep or eat.' She gave a self-derisive shake of her head. 'What a waste of time that was!'

He frowned. 'I heard that your last two shows have been incredibly successful.'

They had been. The ratings last week were the highest they had ever been. And she knew that for the most part she owed that to her worry over Max. It had brought her a new maturity, a seriousness that had completely obliterated that 'bright young thing' he had spoken of so scathingly at their first meeting, leaving in its place a quietly assured young woman who dealt with her guests with a new, forceful capability.

She was surprised that Max, only back in the country a few hours, would already know about that.

'They have, yes,' she confirmed abruptly.

'No more problems with Gary Holmes?' Max probed, his grey gaze intent on her face.

No more than usual. They obviously still disliked each other intensely, and Abby didn't trust the other man an inch, but Max being taken hostage and consequently being no longer in the picture seemed to have created some sort of hiatus in hostilities. The two of them just stepped warily around each other whenever possible.

'Not really, no,' she dismissed woodenly, wondering when Max would go. She needed to cry, badly, and she wasn't going to do it in front of him.

'That's good.' He nodded distantly. 'I— Hello, boy,'

he greeted Monty warmly as the cat strolled over to twine in between his legs.

Abby watched as Max went down on his haunches to stroke the happily purring feline, despite everything her heart aching at how good it was to see Max here, alive and well.

Their meeting hadn't turned out anything like she had expected—hoped—but the fact that Max had come back unharmed was more than enough. If he had come back to another woman it was something she would just have to accept.

And exactly *when* had she got to be so selfless?

The easy answer to that was—she wasn't! Even now she wanted to launch herself into his arms, to feel the physical strength of him around her, inside her, to reassure herself inch by precious inch that he really was safe, to touch him, to kiss him, to just lose herself in the wonder of having him here.

But she knew she wasn't going to do any of that. She had her pride, if nothing else. God, she really was starting to sound ridiculous now! Where was pride going to get her once Max had gone?

It was *her* Max had got a message out to. It was *her* he had—eventually—come to once he was free to do so.

But only, as far as she could tell, in order to protect another woman...

It was too much on top of everything else she had gone through these last weeks.

She bent down to snatch Monty up into her arms, holding him defensively in front of her as Max slowly straightened, his expression guarded. 'I really do think it's best if you leave, Max,' she told him huskily.

He took a step closer, then went very still—like a

tiger poised to spring. 'Do you?' he finally prompted gruffly.

'Yes!' She forced her gaze to meet his, determined to hold her ground; she wasn't sure she could have moved even if she had wanted to!

He shook his head impatiently. 'Look, Abby, even if I want to I can't explain about Kate. Not without—'

'I don't want you to explain about Kate!' she cut in forcefully. What new, fragile lover wanted to hear about a continuing obsession with another woman?

His mouth tightened. 'You just want me to go?'

Her arms tightened about Monty, a move he showed his disapproval of by squirming in protest. 'Yes.'

He looked at her frustratedly for several long seconds, eyes blazing, before giving an abrupt nod of his head. 'Have it your own way,' he rasped. 'This whole thing was probably a mistake anyway.' He turned on his heel and left.

But it needn't have been a mistake. If Max hadn't persisted in deceiving her about his relationship with Kate Mayhew... If she hadn't seemed to trip over the other woman at every turn... If Max had only loved Abby as she loved him...!

'If the sky were really made of marshmallow,' she told Monty emotionally. The saying was a favourite of her father's from when she was growing up and had wished for the impossible. Having Max fall in love with her was definitely one of those impossibles!

'I think I should tell you from the onset that Max has absolutely no idea that I'm here.'

Abby looked across the table at Kate Mayhew, still stunned at having left the studio on Thursday afternoon to find the other woman waiting outside for her.

It had been a strange couple of days. Only concentration on her work had distracted her from the heartache of having Max return safely only to show he cared more about Kate Mayhew's ruffled feelings at Abby's visit to her than he did the distress she had gone through.

To have Kate Mayhew come to see her, suggesting the two of them go and talk over an afternoon coffee in Luigi's, was the last thing she wanted. Or needed.

'Max who?' she asked the other woman dryly.

Kate Mayhew's mouth twisted. 'I deserved that,' she said huskily. 'I was—less than honest with you two weeks ago.'

Abby had known that then, and didn't need it confirmed now, but other than causing a scene and refusing the other woman's invitation, she felt she'd had no choice but to agree to this cup of coffee. A coffee neither woman had touched, incidentally. Luigi's frown was disapproving as the coffee cooled in the cups.

She shrugged. 'It doesn't matter.'

'It does matter,' Kate Mayhew told her, determined. 'I— At first I thought Max was different because of what had happened to him.' She shuddered. 'It must have been so awful for him, never knowing from one minute to the next whether he was going to get out of there alive!'

And Abby had lived every moment of that uncertainty with him. Only to have him return and berate her for visiting this woman...

'It would take much more than a few unstable terrorists to shake Max Harding.' She gave another derisive shrug.

The other woman looked at her with unflinching brown eyes, more lovely than ever today, her fiery red hair loosely flowing, her tailored black suit and cream blouse extremely elegant while remaining completely feminine, her legs long and shapely in high-heeled black shoes.

Next to her, in denims and a cropped white T-shirt, her hair secured untidily on top of her head, Abby felt distinctly scruffy.

'You're in love with him,' Kate Mayhew murmured huskily.

'I don't think so!' Abby gave a hard laugh, determined not to show how shaken she was by the comment.

'Oh, yes.' The other woman gave an assured nod. 'Is he in love with you too?'

Abby's hands clenched around her cooling coffee cup. She felt as if the breath had suddenly been knocked from her body; scenes like this were way out of her league. 'Doubtful, wouldn't you think?'

Kate smiled slightly. 'One never knows with Max.'

Abby shrugged. 'I'm sorry, but I can't help you there.'

The other woman straightened, eyes a candid brown. 'He won't talk about you, of course—'

'Of course,' Abby echoed dryly; he wouldn't talk to *her* about this woman either! 'Well, the fact that Max and I were once—friends has absolutely nothing to do with anyone but the two of us.' Any more, it seemed, than Kate's relationship with Max was any of *her* business!

'Max has been—different, since he came back.'

'You already said that,' Abby snapped. This really was beyond what any woman in love with a man who was involved with another woman—this woman!— should have to endure! 'But if you and Max are having problems then he's the one you should be talking to about them. Not me.'

'No,' Kate told her firmly. 'Max is very protective towards me. To the point where he wouldn't want to do or say anything that might upset me—'

'How commendable,' Abby bit out tightly; sarcasm wasn't normally a part of her nature, but she really didn't know how else to deal with this. 'Look, Kate,' she began again. 'If you've come here to warn me off Max, then I think I should tell you you're too late; we aren't even talking to each other any more! The truth is that Max and I had a—a mild aberration.' Her mouth twisted self-mockingly. 'But it was a mistake—for both of us,' she continued as the other woman would have spoken. 'An attraction that blazed fiercely and then just as quickly blew itself out. I'm sorry if that hurts you, but I can assure you it *is* over.' If it had ever really begun. Which, on Max's part, Abby was sure it hadn't.

The other woman sighed. 'I didn't come here with the intention of hurting you, Abby—'

'I've told you that it doesn't matter to me what you and Max do. It's none of my business. There's nothing between Max and I!' She was so angry with this woman, and with herself, but most of all with Max, for having put her in this position in the first place.

'Max isn't his usual happy self, Abby—'

'I've never seen Max happy, so I wouldn't know the difference!' She had seen him arrogant, mocking, and angry, but she couldn't say she had *ever* seen him happy!

But she had also seen him relaxed and charming, a little voice inside her head taunted. Over the lunch they had shared. And protective of her where Gary Holmes was concerned, gentle with the demanding Monty— and so sensually ignited the two of them had been in danger of going up in flames...

And none of that mattered a damn in the face of his obsession with Kate Mayhew!

The other woman shook her head, a haunted look in those deep brown eyes. 'I made a mistake two years ago, Abby—'

'I don't want to know!' she cut in forcefully, giving up all pretence of drinking her coffee and turning to unhook her shoulder bag from the back of the chair. 'I have no idea whether or not you intend telling Max about this meeting, but my advice to you would be—don't!' Her mouth twisted. 'He has a way of misinterpreting anything that involves me.' And she was already shaken enough by this meeting without having an enraged Max back on her doorstep!

Kate looked up at her as she stood. 'Of course I'll tell Max the two of us have spoken; we don't keep secrets from each other.'

That hurt more than anything else this woman could have said to her!

'He kept *me* a secret!' It was a cheap shot, completely unworthy of her, but in the last three weeks these two people, Max and Kate, had broken her heart. She didn't have to let them continue to do it.

Kate gave a regretful sigh. 'I really didn't come here today with the intention of hurting you—'

'You haven't,' Abby assured her abruptly. 'Goodbye, Kate. I doubt the two of us will ever meet again.' She turned on her heel and left, two bright spots of angry colour in her cheeks.

She had no idea where she went after that, totally oblivious as she wandered from shop to shop, not buying anything, not seeing anything, completely lost in her own humiliation.

Her only consolation was that this time Max couldn't blame *her* for what had happened. At least, he shouldn't. But that didn't mean he wouldn't. He seemed to hold her responsible for everything else, so why not this too?

Her telephone was ringing when she let herself into her apartment hours later, throwing her bag down in a chair to stare at the noisy instrument as if it were about to bite her. Max. It had to be Max. With the intention of hurling more accusations, no doubt. Well, she couldn't face them right now. She wished she had never set eyes on the man.

This should have been such a happy time in her life— one of those magical overnight success stories, that was really nothing of the kind but gave the appearance of being so. Instead she had met Max, and it had all become something of a nightmare.

She ignored the ringing telephone, walking straight past it to go through to the bathroom and run herself a hot, scented bath—always her point of refuge when she was troubled or in distress.

It didn't work this time. Her emotions were too much in turmoil. Part of her wanted to pick up the telephone and tell Max to get his girlfriend off her back, another part of her wanting to put even more distance between the two of them than there already was.

It didn't help that the telephone rang twice more while she was in the bath, setting her nerves jangling anew.

And then, on the fourth time of ringing, a thought occurred to her: Max didn't know her land-line number! She had never given it to him. It was an unlisted number, and the only time Max had called her in the past had been on either his or her mobile! Of course he could have asked Dorothy for it, but somehow she doubted it…

She left a trail of damp footprints as she jumped out of the bath, wrapping a peach-coloured towel about her nakedness as she hurried through to grab up the receiver. 'Yes?' she prompted breathlessly.

'Where the hell have you been?' Gary Holmes demanded angrily. 'I've been ringing you for hours.'

'What do you want, Gary?' she asked warily as she dropped down into an armchair; she'd thought she had made herself more than plain concerning the privacy of her home.

Although their working relationship had continued to be less than cordial these last two weeks, Abby had really been too numbed to react to any of the cutting remarks Gary had made. And over the last couple of days she had simply tuned the man out when he'd tried to ask her if Max would be appearing on her show now that he was back—as if. She'd been concentrating all her efforts on her work in order not to think about Max.

But Gary, of necessity, did have her home telephone number; it just hadn't occurred to her that he might be the one actually ringing her.

'What I want is for you to get yourself back in here now,' her director rasped impatiently. 'We have a change of guest for tomorrow evening, and a hell of a lot of work to get through before then!'

Abby straightened. 'What do you mean, we have a change of guest? Everything is set for Cameron Harper—'

'He's been bumped to next week,' Gary interrupted. 'It would seem that you've succeeded in working your charm, after all, Abby,' he added scathingly. 'Pat called me a couple of hours ago and told me that Max Harding has agreed to come on your show. Tomorrow night—

not for the last show, as you originally suggested he might.'

Abby's hand tightened so hard about the receiver that her knuckles showed white.

Max was going to appear on tomorrow evening's show?

No, that wasn't the question. The question was, why had Max, after all he had said and done, agreed—no, requested!—to appear on her show after all?

CHAPTER TEN

'I STILL don't understand what this meeting is about.' Abby shook her head slightly dazedly as she sat across the table from Gary in the conference room where they were all to meet.

Gary gave her a sneering smile. 'Sounds pretty simple to me.' He raised a sarcastic eyebrow. 'You practised your seduction on Max Harding. He fell for it. And now we're sitting here, waiting for the great man to arrive so that he can tell us what he's going to say tomorrow night.'

It was the last bit she didn't understand. Well, she didn't understand any of this, actually—least of all Max's *volte face*—but she really had no idea why Max wanted a meeting with Pat, Gary and herself at nine o'clock at night. It was going to be hard enough seeing Max again at all, let alone in Gary's presence.

'Hey, don't blame me.' Gary held up defensive hands. 'The great man dictates and we all jump!'

She didn't jump. Had no intention of jumping again. Ever.

And this was *her* show, and no one had even bothered to consult her on a change of guest for tomorrow

evening. Not a good basis from which she should interview any of her guests.

All thought fled as the door opened suddenly and the
energetic figure of Pat Connelly preceded Max into the
room. The small, rotund woman, in her usual sweatshirt
and joggers, her grey hair short and slightly ruffled, looked
slightly incongruous next to the tall, brooding Max, who
was wearing a dinner suit and snowy white shirt.

Abby's gaze instantly swung back to Pat as she swept
forcefully down the room to sit at the head of the long
table. But that didn't mean she wasn't wholly aware of
Max, as he strolled over at a more leisurely pace to take
a seat beside the older woman.

'Obviously Max needs no introduction,' Pat began
with irony, her homely face and less than sartorial elegance belying the fact that she was one of the most dy-
namic producers in television today.

'Obviously not,' Gary echoed dryly, his gaze, when
Abby glanced across at him, fixed challengingly on the
other man. 'What's this all about? Abby is all set to go
with Cameron Harper tomorrow—'

'I've already spoken to Cameron; he's more than happy
to appear on the next show rather than tomorrow—'

'What's the rush?' Gary interrupted his producer.
'Abby always had Max in mind for the last show anyway, so—'

'Max has offered to appear tomorrow, Gary, not any
other time,' Pat told him harshly. 'And, it may have escaped your notice, but it would be in our interest to pursue this while Max's recent—predicament is still so
fresh in people's minds.'

Abby was deeply aware that she and Max weren't
taking any part in the conversation. Not that it was too

much of a hardship for her; she would rather listen at the moment anyway. But she had never known Max to be less than verbally expansive. Especially when he was the subject under discussion!

She chanced a look down the table to where he sat, feeling a jolt of awareness as she found him staring straight back at her, those grey eyes hooded and unreadable, his expression grimly remote.

And as she continued to look at him—like a rabbit eyeing a fox—he raised one dark brow in silent challenge.

He knew about her meeting earlier today with Kate Mayhew!

Without his having to say a word, Abby knew that the other woman had kept to her intention not to keep any secrets from Max.

Well, that was just fine for the two of them. Abby just hoped that the other woman had also told him that *she'd* had no part in setting up the meeting—also that she had refused to discuss him, or their own brief relationship.

'It's done, Gary,' Pat was telling the director when Abby determinedly turned her attention and her gaze back to the two of them. 'So live with it.'

Gary scowled his resentment. 'I was under the impression this was my show—'

'And everyone else was under the impression that it was Abby's.' Max spoke at last, coldly, abruptly, making no effort to hide his contempt for the other man.

'It is,' Abby answered firmly. 'But I don't understand this any more than Gary does. You told me quite adamantly that you wouldn't appear on the show—'

'And now I've changed my mind,' Max bit out harshly.

Her mouth tightened at his sheer arrogance. 'And

now we're all supposed to get down on our knees and say thanks at the shrine of Max Harding?'

'Abby!' Pat gasped her surprise at the attack.

Abby ignored her, keeping her gaze firmly fixed on Max; there was more going on here than Pat could possibly know, and Abby didn't like the feeling of being simply a pawn in a game. Especially when she didn't know what the game was—only that Max was the one making the rules.

Max was looking at her with rueful respect now. 'It's okay, Pat,' he assured the other woman, without looking at her. 'Are you saying that you don't want me to appear on your show after all, Abby?'

He had her, and he knew it—knew that after what had happened to him in the last two weeks she would be committing professional suicide in not accepting the interview he was offering her. Especially if she wanted her contract renewed for another year. It wasn't *that* she was questioning, only his motives for doing this.

Why had he changed his mind now? The only thing that had happened since the two of them had last spoken on the subject that she could see was her meeting earlier today with Kate Mayhew. The other woman in his life…

A meeting, no matter what Max might think to the contrary, that had not been of her choosing…

Although she had no guarantee that Kate Mayhew had told him that when she'd confided that particular secret to him—any more than she had any idea what the other woman had told him about their meeting. If the coldness of his gaze was anything to go by, then it probably hadn't been anything good…

'…go over the list of questions Max has agreed to answer.'

She tuned back into the conversation as Pat put her briefcase on the tabletop and opened it.

'Now, just a minute!' Abby gasped, standing up. 'The list of questions Max has agreed to answer?' she repeated forcefully. 'Where is *my* involvement in that?' She was no longer looking at Max but concentrating on Pat instead. 'I'll end up as merely a mouthpiece—a bystander on *The Max Harding Show*!'

'Do you have a problem with that?' Max asked quietly, before Pat could speak.

Abby's eyes flashed deeply blue as she glared at him. 'I won't do it!' she said determinedly.

'Even at the risk of losing an exclusive?' he challenged softly.

Goading, baiting her. Which only made her all the more adamant. If Max had known her better—if he had known her at all!—then he would have realised she wouldn't be pushed about and bullied in this way.

'Even at the risk of that—yes,' she bit out tautly, her gaze unwavering on his.

The two of them continued their visual battle for several seconds. Max determined and unreadable, Abby stubbornly unyielding.

'Pat.' He finally spoke softly, his gaze remaining unwaveringly on Abby's. 'Would you and Gary mind leaving Abby and me alone for a few minutes?'

Every particle of Abby inwardly protested at such an idea. She didn't want to be alone with him, had nothing to say to him. But then, that wasn't the idea, was it? Max had something he wanted to say to her! And it wasn't too difficult to guess what that something was.

'Won't you sit down, Abby?' Max invited softly seconds later, when the others had left the room—Pat happily, Gary protestingly.

For once, Abby had found herself agreeing with Gary!

'I won't, thanks,' she refused abruptly, her palms feeling damp, her whole body aching from the tension she felt. 'If this is because of Kate Mayhew—'

'Let's leave Kate out of this.'

'I would be happy to!' Abby assured him heavily. 'But that's actually impossible to do, isn't it, Max?' she went on. 'Because everything you say and do begins and ends with Kate Mayhew! She came to see me today—'

'I know that.' His mouth was tight. 'She said that you refused to discuss our relationship.'

Well, at least Kate had been honest about *that*.

'Because we don't *have* a relationship!' she snapped, moving to the other end of the table, as far away from Max as she could get in the confines of the conference room, too distracted by his proximity to be able to think straight—except to know she couldn't allow the fiasco being suggested for tomorrow night's show to continue. 'Why don't the two of you just go public with your relationship, Max?' She sighed. 'It's been two years. The media can be extremely forgiving, and I'm sure with your way with words—' her mouth twisted scathingly '—you could arrange to bring all of this round to a romantic angle they will totally accept!'

'I'm sure I could,' he drawled. 'Unfortunately, that isn't the way it happened—isn't the way it is.'

'I don't believe you!'

'No, I know you don't.' He sighed too. 'But you're just going to have to trust me on this one, Abby.'

'I trusted you once before—I won't do it again!' Her eyes blazed, her face pale.

'No,' he accepted heavily. 'I can see that. But I *will* be appearing on your show tomorrow evening, Abby. And I *will* be answering the questions that Pat and I have already agreed on.'

'Pat had no more had a say in what those questions are than I did!'

'No,' he acknowledged without apology. 'However, the difference is she's enough of a professional to trust in my judgement.'

'And I'm not?' Abby guessed tartly. 'Fine, Max. Go ahead and arrange this between the two of you.' She snatched up her bag. 'But do it on the understanding that I may or I just may not turn up to ask you those questions on my own show!'

Max moved swiftly, grasping her upper arms, shaking her slightly in obvious frustrated anger. 'You are one of the most stubborn women it has ever been my misfortune to meet!'

She faced him unflinchingly, desperately hanging on to her anger in an effort to fight the weakness she felt just at his touch. A weakness that would leave her totally defenceless if she gave in to it. And at the moment those defences were the only thing keeping her from saying, To hell with all this. She didn't care what role Kate Mayhew had in his life, that she just wanted him. Here. Now.

How sad was that?

She shook back the dark curtain of her hair. 'More stubborn than Kate?'

He drew in a sharp breath. 'I told you—'

'To leave her out of this,' Abby finished derisively. 'Maybe I *will* turn up for the show tomorrow night after all, Max,' she said slowly. 'In fact…after some thought, I wouldn't dream of missing it!'

His mouth tightened. 'Abby—'

'Yes?'

He breathed heavily. 'I'm not your enemy, Abby,' he warned softly.

'No?' She faced him defiantly.

His mouth tightened. 'I'm really not.'

'I don't believe that either,' she challenged.

'We sound like two opponents facing each other in a boxing ring!'

'That's probably because it's exactly what we are.' She smiled humourlessly. 'And I should warn you—it isn't a fight I'm prepared to lose!'

Max looked down at her for several long seconds before releasing her abruptly. 'You're making a terrible mistake, Abby. I'm far from being your enemy, and tomorrow evening I intend proving that to you,' he assured her.

'Let the battle commence!' she scorned, before turning on her heel and walking out of the room. 'He's all yours,' she told Pat as she stalked by.

Because he wasn't hers.

And he never would be...

None of that iron control—thankfully—had faded by the following evening. In fact, it was the only thing that kept her from falling apart completely.

That and the professionalism that wouldn't allow her to become simply Max Harding's mouthpiece.

A fact he was shortly going to find out, she realized, after a quick glance at her wristwatch told her they would be on the air in only ten minutes. But on her terms, not Max's.

As usual she had arrived at the studio two hours ago. As usual she had allowed Make-Up to do their work.

Unusually, she hadn't spent any time talking to her guest, putting him at ease before they appeared live in front of the cameras.

She knew Max was at the studio too—had been informed the moment he arrived, an hour ago—but she had made no effort to go through her normal practice of chatting to her guests beforehand, establishing an ease, a rapport, before the show went on air.

What was the point? There was no ease or rapport between herself and Max. And there never would be.

'All set, Abby?' Gary appeared in the doorway of her room.

As set as she was going to be! 'I'm fine,' she said shortly, not particularly liking the feral grin on Gary's face, but knowing there wasn't a lot she could do about it. He knew she was angry about this interview, and he was loving all the tension in the studio.

'You're looking very—professional this evening.' He nodded his satisfaction with her appearance.

Deliberately so. This wasn't going to be like any of her previous shows. It hadn't been hyped as such by the television station throughout the day when they'd announced the change of guest, and Abby had dressed accordingly. The black tailored suit and white blouse were businesslike, her hair was swept up on top of her head, and her make-up was subdued—no lipgloss, only a peach-coloured lipstick, and blusher adding colour to the white of her cheeks.

'I have to go, Gary,' she told him woodenly as she received the signal for going on the air in five minutes.

'I hope you're going out there to get him, Abby,' he encouraged, blue eyes glittering with malice.

It gave Abby her first feelings of misgiving concerning what she was about to do. Anything that Gary could smile on so approvingly had to be suspect, she realized, with a belated flash of uncertainty.

Was it so obvious what she intended doing? That she had drawn up her own list of questions, and intended replacing Max's with them?

Was she doing the right thing? she wondered as she hurried to take her place in the studio.

Did she have any choice? came the second, heartbreaking question.

No, she didn't, she decided with fresh resolve. Max had his own reasons for agreeing to appear on her show, but they weren't *her* reasons. And her personal life might be in ruins, but that didn't mean her professional one had to be too. Max was playing with her—probably in order to continue protecting Kate Mayhew. He had made love to her for the same reason. And, while she didn't want to hurt the other woman, she didn't feel the same compunction where Max was concerned.

Her resolve was shaken even further when she saw Max waiting for her as she walked on to the set, and the colour—so expertly applied earlier—faded from her cheeks.

Max's eyes were hard, his expression grim. 'What are you up to, Abby?' he ground out suspiciously.

She gave him a startled look. How did he know? *What* did he know?

Her new set of questions had been prepared in absolute secrecy. How could Max possibly—? He couldn't, she decided determinedly. He was just guessing. As Gary had. The fact that both men had guessed correctly was more fluke than certainty. And bad luck for her.

She shook her head. 'I have no idea what you're talking about, Max,' she told him. 'Now, if you'll excuse me, I have to go,' she added firmly, as the theme for her programme began to play.

'Abby!' He reached out and grasped her arm in a vice-like grip, his expression intent. 'Abby, I love you!' he told her forcefully.

'How dare you?' she gasped, sudden tears blinding her.

Did he really think she was so stupid, so naïve, that she would fall for a ploy like—?

'I love you,' he repeated grimly. 'It's because I love you that I've agreed to come on this show at all. But there's much more at stake here than your pride or mine, and if you do this, Abby, then I'll have no choice but to fight back!'

She wrenched out of his grasp, drawing inside herself, her eyes no longer glittering with tears but with a fury she had no control over. 'I'll be waiting for you in the arena, Max.'

Pure professionalism took over as she stepped in front of the cameras, smilingly welcoming her audience before she had to introduce her guest for the evening.

The studio audience was buzzing, seemingly aware that something momentous was about to happen.

Just how momentous neither they nor Abby could possibly have guessed!

The interview began exactly as it should have done: Abby and Max were all smiles as they shook hands before taking their seats, and the first four questions were as originally planned, touching on the events of the last two weeks, with Max's replies relaxed and assured as he talked of the ordeal.

But the underlying tension was there nonetheless. And as Abby reached the fifth question of the evening she could sense a change coming over Max. Her resolve wavered once again as she hesitated about stepping from the script he had dictated for the evening.

Arrogantly. Arbitrarily.

No matter what he had just said, he most certainly didn't love her! He—

'So tell me, Abby,' Max suddenly drawled pleasantly, 'how are you liking presenting your own show?'

She stared at him even as she gave an appropriate reply. *What was he doing?*

'I hear rumours of there being a second series?' he continued lightly. 'You must be pleased by the show's success?'

He was attempting to take over the programme; that was what he was doing!

She straightened in her chair, her hands tightly gripped together, her pulse racing as she made the decision to step into the arena.

'I haven't heard those rumours, Max,' she said. 'But, to get back to you: this is the first interview of this kind you've given in two years. Understandably so. And I'm sure everyone watching this evening is aware of the events that led up to your decision not to appear in public again in this way.'

'Abby!' he warned softly, still seemingly relaxed with only the white knuckles of his hands, as he gripped the arms of the chair, to show that he was far from it.

'But it has been two years,' she continued evenly, knowing she was committed to going ahead with this now. 'And I'm sure we would all like to know—'

'Abby. Darling. I'm sure that you don't want me to tell everyone,' he cut in smoothly, 'that the only reason

I'm here tonight is because I could hardly continue to
say no to coming on the show of the woman I'm going
to bed with!'

CHAPTER ELEVEN

'AND that, my darling Monty, is when I hit him,' she concluded with an emotional sniff. 'And why I can never go out in public again. Never see any of my friends again. Never be able to face my parents again!' She groaned with remembered humiliation. 'They were watching all that, Monty. Oh!' She buried her face in her hands once again.

How could Max have done that to her?

And what had she intended doing to *him*? a little voice inside her head reminded her reasonably.

Yes, but that was different. He had *deserved* what she'd been about to do to him!

Besides, she'd had no intention of asking him anything to do with Kate Mayhew. The angry humiliation she felt at Max's hands—even seconds before they'd gone on air he'd tried to make her believe he was in love with her!—didn't extend to deliberately hurting the other woman or her children. Max had been her only target—and instead he had reversed the roles and made *her* the target instead.

She was finished—both professionally and personally. In fact, she would be surprised if she could find the smallest corner of the world who wouldn't know of her humiliation at Max's hands—and mouth!—by morning. Maybe Bolivia, after all? A loud pounding sounded on her apartment door.

Not happy with telephoning, with ringing her doorbell, now someone had actually managed to get as far as her apartment door!

The pounding continued, despite her efforts to shut it out, and through the width of two doors she could hear the muffled sound of a voice.

Max's voice?

She wasn't sure.

And she didn't want to be sure, reaching up to put her hands over her ears. Whoever it was would tire soon, would realise she either wasn't at home or she simply wasn't about to open the door. To anyone. Even if the building were to catch on fire. Like a captain, she would go down with the ship—

The bathroom door burst open. Abby's hands fell away from her ears as she stared at a wild-eyed, frantic-looking Max where he stood in the doorway.

Relief flooded over his features as he saw her gaping at him. 'Thank you, thank you!' he breathed deeply. 'Abby—'

'Get out of here!' she gasped, sinking beneath the rapidly cooling bubbles, not caring that this man had already seen her completely naked; that had been at a time when she had thought there was a chance the two of them might actually be in love with each other. Now it was just a complete violation.

But instead of leaving he stepped further into the room. 'I need to talk to you, Abby—'

'Well, you aren't talking to me here, damn it!' she

burst out incredulously. 'Besides, I don't need to talk to you. What I need, what I really need, is for you to just turn around and leave!' And never come back!

He paled slightly. 'Abby, please let me—'

'Please!' she repeated incredulously, sitting up slightly, the perfumed bubbles still just enough to cover her nakedness. 'You humiliated me this evening—deliberately, coldly, calculatedly humiliated me—and now you dare to say *please* to me?' She glared furiously at him. 'Get out now, Max, and don't ever come back!'

He shook his head, his expression grim. 'I know it must seem that way to you—but, Abby, I never meant to hurt you—'

'Oh, you didn't?' she challenged with sarcasm. 'Strange, because as I remember it that's exactly what you did!' Tears filled her eyes now. 'My parents were watching that show earlier, Max. My *parents!*' Her voice rose in horror at how they must be feeling after hearing publicly that their daughter had been to bed with this man. 'Don't come any closer, Max,' she warned, as he did exactly that. 'You— What's that?' she questioned sharply as she saw the recording in his hand.

'The rest of the show.'

'I don't need a hard copy of that show, Max—it's indelibly imprinted on my brain!' And on those of millions of others…

'I said it's a copy of the *rest* of the show, Abby,' he told her firmly. 'And you really do need to see it.'

'The rest of the show?' Abby repeated scornfully. 'There was no "rest of the show".' The last thing she had heard, before she'd ripped the earpiece from her ear and thrown it on the ground, had been Gary's instruction to go to a commercial break. Instruction? He had screamed the order!

'Oh, yes, there's a "rest of the show", Abby,' Max assured her determinedly. 'Put something on and I'll get this set up to watch.'

'You'll do no such thing,' she raged, very close now to completely losing it. 'Take your recording, and yourself, and just— How did you get in here, anyway?' she suddenly asked suspiciously. 'I know I locked the door.'

'Well, I didn't bother with the "it's your birthday" ruse.' Max sighed as he reminded her of her own initial method of getting up to *his* apartment seven weeks ago. 'But your doorman recognised me easily enough, and once I explained to him that you weren't answering your telephone or your door buzzer, that I was worried about you, he was only too happy to let me in with his key.'

'Oh, great!' Abby scorned. 'Now everyone thinks I'm a suicide case!'

'Not me,' Max assured her with a rueful smile. 'You're too strong, too courageous—'

'Oh, cut the bull, Max,' she said impatiently. 'After tonight the only way I'm going to be able to go out in public again is if I dye and cut my hair and change my name—and even that probably won't work!'

He gave an appreciative smile. 'The change of name we can discuss in a few minutes. But leave your hair exactly as it is; I happen to like it just that colour and style!' He sobered. 'Come and watch the rest of the show, Abby,' he invited softly. 'If you still want me to leave after that, then I will.'

'You most certainly will!' she assured him with feeling. But at the same time knew she no longer felt quite as desperately unhappy as she had.

She had no idea how, but a part of her—the part of her that was in love with him—somehow knew that Max was going to make all of this turn out fine.

Which was laughable after all that he had done!

She didn't have any clothes in the bathroom with her. Instead she put her robe on over her nakedness, its deep blue colour an exact match for her eyes. It zipped at the front from neck to ankles, meaning she was perfectly decent. Besides, what did it matter? Her inner emotions might have been publicly bared this evening, but Max had seen all of her bared!

He was on the sofa when she joined him in the sitting room, and Abby avoided his gaze as she deliberately sat in one of the armchairs. Monty, the continuing traitor, made no move to leave the comfort of Max's knee.

'I tried earlier to explain the situation to him,' she said dryly. 'But I guess he just didn't understand!'

'Oh, I think Monty understands more than you realise,' Max told her huskily.

Her eyes flashed deeply blue as she glared at him. 'He's a man,' she snapped. 'And men usually stick together, don't they?'

Max gave her a long, lingering look. Abby met his gaze unflinchingly. He gave a sigh. 'Let's watch the recording,' he suggested huskily.

'By all means—let's all watch my annihilation!' she agreed coldly.

Max looked as if he would like to argue that point, but instead he tightened his mouth and switched on the recording.

The first ten minutes of her show were exactly—painfully—as Abby remembered them. She had believed herself cool and in control earlier this evening, but the recording showed her to have been tense and obviously nervous, becoming borderline agitated as Max reversed the roles and began to question her, until, taking control again, she had begun to ask him about the events of two years ago.

She stood up impatiently. 'I've seen enough—'

'No—you haven't,' Max said firmly. 'Nice punch, by the way,' he complimented her dryly, as the screen showed him toppling backwards over his chair to lie unconscious on the ground, with a tearful Abby stepping over him as she marched out of the suddenly hushed studio.

It was almost worse viewing the incident like this, as one of the outsiders looking in. And the sudden appearance of an advertisement for a popular brand of nappies only made the whole thing appear even more ludicrous.

She gave a disgusted shake of her head. 'Couldn't they have found something with a little more—?' She broke off, frowning as the advertisement abruptly went off air and the cameras returned to the studio. 'What—?'

'Watch, Abby,' Max invited softly, his face grimmer than ever as his gaze returned to the screen.

She did watch. And listen. As had millions of others, presumably.

Gary Holmes, having left his control room, believing they were off the air, had confronted a still-miked Max as he slowly began to get up from the floor. The conversation between the two men had been both startling and enlightening!

'Satisfied, Gary?' Max challenged, standing to massage his painful jaw.

'Completely,' the other man returned scornfully. 'I

knew when Abby told me she was going to get you on her show that she was going to be trouble.'

'Is that why you've made her life such a misery these last months?' Max challenged.

'Of course,' Gary taunted. 'I tried to get rid of her completely, but that proved harder to do than I'd realised. Not that it matters now, because tonight she succeeded in totally humiliating both of you; what more could I ask for?'

'Kate Mayhew's continued silence, maybe?' Max suggested softly.

'Well, there is that, of course,' the other man derided confidently.

Max gave a disgusted shake of his head. 'I should have just let Rory Mayhew shoot you two years ago!'

Abby shot Max a startled look at this statement. What on earth did he mean? Rory Mayhew had gone on Max's show intending to ruin the man who was having an affair with his wife by committing suicide on his show. Where did Gary come into this?

'Perhaps you should,' Gary continued mockingly on the screen.

'You blood-sucking parasite,' Max told the other man coldly. 'Kate made the mistake of having an affair with you, and despite all her pleading you used it against her by telling her husband when his career was already falling apart.'

'Why not go for total meltdown?' Gary said, seeming horribly amused.

Max shook his head disgustedly. 'He was foolish. And so was Kate, for ever thinking you had any human decency inside you. But neither of them deserved what you did to them.'

'And exactly *what* did I do?' the other man challenged.

'You blackmailed Kate into continuing to see you by threatening to tell her husband of your relationship. And then, without telling her, you secretly blackmailed her husband with exposure, too. Doesn't directing pay enough? Is that it, Gary?' Max challenged. 'Or could it be that you did it for another reason?'

Gary gave him a scathing glance. 'And what reason would that be?'

'That you're a man who likes to have power over others,' Max said. 'You don't want to just stick the knife in, you like to twist it around too!'

'So I played a little game with the Mayhews that went too far. So what?' Gary challenged.

'It wasn't a game. It was people's lives,' Max returned icily. 'It cost Rory Mayhew his life and Kate Mayhew her husband—her children their father! Doesn't that mean anything to you, you bastard?'

'Not a lot, no.' Gary shrugged. 'Besides, you can't prove any of this, Harding,' he added dismissively.

'Oh, no?' Max challenged softly. 'Try looking at the cameras, Gary. See that green light? My live mike? Yes, I thought they might surprise you,' he said with satisfaction as the other man blanched. 'You see, I don't have to prove a thing, Gary. You've done that yourself—very effectively.'

Gary looked like a man who had been hit between the eyes, beyond pale now, looking almost green.

'I've waited two years for this, Holmes. I was never able to prove any of this before. But with your public—*very* public—confession…' He smiled. 'You're finished, Gary. Absolutely. Completely. In fact, I should think that in future you might have difficulty getting a job sweep-

ing the floor of this studio, let alone directing in it—'
He broke off as the other man, with a low, guttural growl,
launched himself at him, his hands going for Max's
throat, a maniacal light in those pale blue eyes.

'He was arrested seconds later for attempted assault,'
Max said. 'And I will obviously be only too happy to
press charges. The police are also going to look into the
events of two years ago to see if they can find any other
charges against Holmes—blackmail included—that
might stick.'

Abby sat in mute silence, completely stunned by
what had taken place in the studio after she'd left.

And the fact that it had been Gary—not Max—who had
been having an affair with Kate Mayhew two years ago!

And now? What was Max's involvement with the
other woman now?

'I felt responsible, Abby.' Max seemed able to gauge
her thoughts. 'It all came to a head on *my* programme,
culminating in Rory's death two days later.'

'He didn't get drunk and bring that gun on your programme intending to hurt *you* with it, did he?' Abby
asked wonderingly.

Max shook his head. 'Gary was always his target. But
there was nothing that he could do, that any of us could
do, to prove what Gary had done to all of them those
months before Rory's death. Yes, Rory made mistakes,
and, no, he shouldn't have got drunk and come on my
programme with his grandfather's old gun.' He shook
his head sadly. 'By that time Rory was totally irrational.
He had some idea in his head that shooting Gary would
put an end to all his misery. But once Rory sobered up
and realised what he had done, in front of millions of
viewers, I don't think he felt he had any other choice

than to kill himself. After that, all I could do was be Kate's friend and keep Gary Holmes as far away from her—and me—as possible.'

'And two years later I came along,' Abby realised weakly. 'Nosing. Prying. With Gary as my director.'

'And then *you* came along,' Max echoed softly. 'Beautiful. Impulsive. Warm. But with Gary Holmes as your director!' he acknowledged. 'He, as he's just admitted, was far from happy at the thought of my being a guest on your show.'

Hence his constant harassing of her on the subject, his deliberate attempts to drive a wedge between herself and Max—even to the point of implying to Max that the two of *them* had some sort of relationship!

'Your obvious anger towards me this evening suited him perfectly, Abby.' Max grimaced.

She raised heavy lids, her eyes pained. 'He knew all along I was going to switch questions on you.'

He shrugged. 'It wasn't too difficult to guess what you intended doing. Of course I couldn't have known what Gary was going to do after you hit me and walked out, but once he came down onto the studio floor and started talking—' He gave a shake of his head. 'It couldn't have worked out better if I'd planned it that way. Although Pat, bless her, must have thought I was completely insane when I indicated she was to keep the cameras rolling.' He gave a rueful shake of his head. 'I think the only reason she did so was because she was still stunned from seeing Abby Freeman lay Max Harding out cold on the studio floor! Where did you learn to punch like that, by the way?' He rubbed his bruised jaw.

There was laughter in his expression, but not malicious, or even full of the cynicism she was used to. 'My father,' she acknowledged, still slightly numbed by what she had just seen on the screen.

All this time—years—Gary Holmes had been largely responsible for pushing Rory Mayhew to the point of suicide. What sort of man was he? A very sick one, obviously.

But she must have really shaken his complacency—more than shaken it!—when she had announced she was going to have Max as the final guest on her show. The one man who, because of his friendship with Kate Mayhew, knew exactly what had taken place two years ago, but couldn't prove Gary's part in it.

All those times he had tried to keep her and Max apart—his sarcasm, his hints that Max was involved with Kate, in Rory Mayhew's death. No wonder he had looked so shocked that day at Luigi's when he'd seen Abby and Max together!

Until that point he must have been so confident, so sure that Max, with his well-known aversion to appearing on public television again, wouldn't even allow her access into his life, let alone actually be out having lunch with her. Hence his completely unexpected visit to her apartment later that day, and his broad hints that the two of them were involved. He must have realised that day that Abby was getting too close to Max, to the possibility of learning the truth about *him*.

Her gaze flicked sharply back to Max. 'I was never, ever involved with that—that excuse for a human being!' She grimaced her complete disgust just at the thought of it.

Max gave a pained wince. 'I know that better than anyone, Abby,' he reminded her. Bringing the warmth of colour to her cheeks as she acknowledged just how he knew that.

'There are other ways of being involved with some-one other than the physical,' she said tightly.

He gave an acknowledging inclination of his head. 'And you knew Gary in none of them.'

'How can you be so sure?' she challenged. 'You certainly weren't a couple of weeks ago. In fact, as I recall you couldn't wait to get out of my bed and escape!'

'I wasn't escaping, Abby—I was running scared!' he told her firmly.

'Max, I saw you and Kate together outside your apartment that morning before you went away. I was bringing coffee and Danish for breakfast,' she added quickly. 'Not spying on you. And—'

'I never for a moment thought you were,' he assured her softly. 'But if the morning you're referring to is the one I think it is, then Kate had called in to see me on the way back from taking the kids to school. She had some good news to tell me—personal news. Abby, the mistake I made that first morning was in getting up and leaving the way that I did. But the fact is, I was— I've never been in love before!' He gave a shake of his head. 'I'm not, nor have I ever been, nor will I ever be, in-volved with Kate,' he assured her. 'I told you—I felt re-sponsible. At least, that's how I felt initially. Then I got to know Kate—and her children. She's a very lovely person, Abby—'

'I don't think I can bear to hear that right now, Max,' Abby cut in dully. 'I'm pleased for her—for both of you—that Gary Holmes has finally been made account-able for what happened two years ago. As you say, there's no way he will ever recover professionally from this evening. But I really can't bear just now to hear how wonderful Kate is—how—how much you care for her!'

That would just be too much, when her own life, both personal and professional, was in ruins.

'I told you earlier—not once, but twice, and again just now—it's *you* that I love,' Max murmured throatily. 'Abby, why do you think I finally agreed to appear on your show?'

'To try to get to Gary—'

'I told you.' He shook his head. 'I had no idea Gary was going to lose it like that. How could I have known? I came on your show, Abby, because I thought it was a way of showing you that I loved you. That my first public appearance in two years being on your show would convince the powers that be that I, for one, consider you a first-rate interviewer.'

'Is that why you threatened me earlier this evening?' Her voice broke emotionally. 'Because you're in love with me?'

'Weren't you intending to publicly crush me?' he returned challengingly.

'I wasn't going through with it,' Abby told him flatly, knowing that was possibly her worst humiliation.

She had sat there in the studio with him tonight, intending to hurt and humiliate him as he had hurt her, and in the end she had known she couldn't do it—that it would hurt too many other people if she did. So she had decided, in that moment of hesitation, to go back to the original set of questions.

'I wasn't going to do it,' she repeated firmly. 'Even as I started to ask you the question I knew that it wasn't the place or the time to air my private grievances. But, feeling threatened, you didn't feel the same compunction, did you, Max?' Her chin rose dangerously.

Max held her gaze with his for several long seconds

before reaching forward to pick up the remote control, pressing the button to resume playing the recording.

And, like a magnet, Abby found her gaze drawn to the screen. The studio was empty now of everyone but Max—Gary obviously having been taken away by the police. Apart from the bruise on his jaw, Max looked none the worse for the scene that had just taken place, and was every inch the seasoned television presenter that he really was.

And then Abby stopped noticing what he looked like and actually heard what he was saying...

'—to thank Abby Freeman for allowing me to use her show in this way to bring Gary Holmes's crimes, past and present, to light.' He spoke confidently. 'I'm sure you'll all agree with me when I say it's my misfortune that she *didn't* actually seduce me in order to get me on to the show. I should be so lucky!' He smiled ruefully as the audience broke into spontaneous applause. 'But any man can dream, can't he?' He gave a rueful grimace as the audience gave an appreciative laugh.

Abby stared across at him. With a few simple sentences and a certain amount of self-deprecation Max had turned her humiliation into something else entirely, making it sound as if she had been part of the whole thing, while at the same time making himself a figure of fun.

'Seriously.' Max's image on the screen sobered. 'Abby took a risk this evening, knowing she had no certainty of succeeding, and I would personally like to thank her. I'm sure that Kate Mayhew, if she were here, would want to do the same. What happened to her husband two years ago was a tragedy—compounded, as we've proved this evening, by the vindictive nature of one man. We've all made mistakes in our lives, and I'm in no way trying to exonerate any of the people involved, but those human weaknesses didn't have to end in the tragic way that they did. Tonight, I hope, has put an end to two years of personal speculation for Kate Mayhew and her family, and I'm sure that you'll all join me in wishing her and her children well for the future.'

There was another spontaneous round of applause.

'*The Abby Freeman Show* will return at seven-thirty next Friday evening, when her guest will be Cameron Harper. I advise you to watch out for the right hook, Cameron!' he concluded lightly, before the theme music began to play.

Abby stared at the screen as it went blank. Max had completely turned the situation round with a few well-chosen words, making Gary's behaviour two years ago the issue, rather than the fact that she had punched Max live on television.

She slowly moistened dry lips, not quite able to look across and meet his gaze. 'What happens now?'

'Well, as I said, Gary has been taken into custody—'

'Not to Gary!' She looked up protestingly. The other man had got everything he deserved!

'Well, for one thing Pat assures me that the executives are already clamouring to renew your contract.'

She swallowed hard. 'They are?'

'They most certainly are. And deservedly so. You're good, Abby—very good.' Max nodded. 'As for the rest—tomorrow morning's newspapers will carry both this story and the news of Kate's engagement and future marriage to Edward Southern, an Australian businessman.'

Abby's eyes widened. Kate Mayhew was getting married—but not to Max!

'It's what Kate came to tell me that morning you

saw the two of us together.' Max smiled at her stunned expression. 'She and the children will be moving to Australia after the wedding next month.'

And with her husband's death and Gary Holmes' involvement in it safely behind her, Kate was now completely free to move forward with her life...

'But I thought— I know you said— How do you feel about that?' Abby looked at Max uncertainly.

'In a word? Relieved,' he told her ruefully. 'After what happened on my programme I felt a certain responsibility for Kate and the kids. But maybe now, with Gary safely out of the picture for a while, we can all get on with our lives.' He stood up, moving towards her. 'And I would very much like my own future to include you, Abby. Do you think that's possible?' he prompted huskily.

She swallowed hard. Max had told her three times tonight that he loved her. In view of what she had just seen and heard on the television recording, was it possible that he had really meant it...?

There was only one way to find out!

She drew in a deep breath. 'I don't know if you're aware of this, Max, but my father is a vicar—'

'I wasn't, but I probably should have guessed.' He smiled. 'Although the idea of a pugilistic vicar may take some getting used to!'

'Wait until you meet my mother!' she warned, knowing her flamboyant ex-actress mother was the last person he would expect to be married to a parish vicar.

He tilted his head to one side. 'Am I going to?'

'That depends.' She moistened dry lips. 'You see, their dearest wish is to see me married to the man I love.'

Emotion flared in his deep grey eyes. 'Abby, are you asking me to marry you?'

Was she? Yes, she most certainly was! She loved him, he said he loved her, and she could imagine nothing she wanted more in life than to be his wife.

'If you are, then my answer is definitely yes.' Max cut in firmly on her thoughts before she could speak, standing directly in front of her now. 'I haven't mentioned it before now, but since I got back I've been offered my own current affairs programme, to be aired in the autumn, and as a married man I would be much happier being closer to home—and you. I love you so very much, my darling. I want to be with you always. I want to have babies with you,' he added huskily. 'Lots of them!'

She stared at him, hardly daring to believe, after all the trauma of this evening, that this could really be happening.

'Okay, I'll settle for two,' he conceded at her continued silence. 'And a guarantee that if either of them is a girl, your father will teach her to box. There are a lot of bastards out there—I should know—and I don't want our little girl getting involved with any of them—'

'Max!' Abby broke in laughingly, with relief as much as happiness. 'I love you so much. I want to be with you too, and we can have as many babies as you like!' Max's babies, with that thick dark hair and those beautiful grey eyes...

He reached out and took her into his arms. 'You never know—we may already have started on the first one...!'

That thought had already occurred to her too.

Wouldn't that be wonderful?

'I love you so very much, Abby,' Max told her intensely. 'So very much!'

And to have Max love her, to love him in return, was all the happiness she would ever want.

A VIRGIN FOR THE TAKING

Trish Morey

Trish Morey is an Australian who's also spent time living and working in New Zealand and England. Now she's settled with her husband and four young daughters in a special part of South Australia, surrounded by orchards and bushland, and visited by the occasional koala and kangaroo. With a life-long love of reading, she penned her first book at age eleven, after which life, career and a growing family kept her busy, until once again she could indulge her desire to create characters and stories – this time in romance. Having her work published is a dream come true. Visit Trish at her website, www. trishmorey.com

Don't miss Trish Morey's brand-new story,
His Mistress for a Million, **available from Mills & Boon® Modern™ in February 2010**

CHAPTER ONE

ZANE BASTIANI stepped on to the tarmac of Broome International Airport and felt the late wet-season humidity close around him like a vice. He glanced skyward in irritation, to where the source of the melting heat shone so unforgivingly above.

He'd forgotten about the heat. Other things had slipped his mind, too—like the sharp blue of the sky, the clear salt-tinged air and the sheer quality of the light. Nine years of dreary London weather and grey concrete architecture had disarmed him completely. He felt like a foreigner in his home town.

Nine years.

Hard to believe it was so long since he'd left with just his name and the conviction to make it big time on his own. Not that he'd wasted a minute of it. Now, with a terrace house in Chelsea, a chalet in Klosters and the chairmanship of the most aggressive merchant bank in London, he was well on his way.

And for every one of those nine years he'd been waiting for his father to call and admit that he'd been wrong, but when the call had finally come it hadn't been from his father at all.

'Not critical,' the doctor had assured him, 'but Laurence asked to see you.'

He'd asked to see Zane.

It might have taken a heart attack, but after all the bitterness between them, any request had to be worth something.

So Zane had taken the first flight out of London to anywhere that might offer the fastest connection with this remote north-west Australian location. His platinum credit card had taken care of the details.

He shrugged the kinks out of his shoulders as he headed for the terminal, steeling himself for meeting his father once again. When Zane had been just a kid growing up, Laurence Bastiani had always seemed larger than life, always the big man with the big voice and the big ideas who'd never succumbed to as much as the common cold. It made sense that it would take something like a heart attack to stop him in his tracks. Even so, it was impossible to picture him now, lying ill in hospital. His father would hate it. He'd probably have checked himself out of there already.

Inside the arrivals' terminal, ceiling fans spun languidly overhead, stirring up barely more than a breeze as travel-weary passengers began to crowd around the luggage carousel.

His one hastily packed leather bag, its red *Priority* tag swinging, came through first. He reached down, hauling it from the carousel, then headed towards the exit, making for the line of waiting taxis, increasingly aware the fine cotton of his shirt was already heavy with perspiration.

How long would it take to re-acclimatise to Broome's tropical temperatures, given he'd been away so many years? Not that it really mattered, he thought dismissively as he curled himself into a taxi and snapped out a brisk command to the driver. He'd be back in London long before there was any chance of that happening.

CHAPTER TWO

THE CRASH TEAM had departed, the tubes and needles removed, the equipment turned off. Strange—she'd grown to hate that incessant beeping of the monitor over the last couple of days with its constant reminder of Laurence's increasingly frail condition. But right now Ruby Clemenger would give anything to have that noise back—anything to break the deathly quiet of the room—anything at all if it meant that Laurence was still really here.

But Laurence was gone.

Her eyes felt scratchy and swollen, but there were no tears, not yet, because it was just so hard to accept. And so unfair. Fifty-five was way too young to die, especially when you had the vision and energy of Laurence Bastiani, the now late head of the largest cultured South Sea pearl operation in the world.

Even now he looked like he was sleeping, his hand still warm in hers. But there was no tell-tale rise and fall of his chest under the sheet, no flicker of eyelashes as if he was merely dreaming, no answering squeeze of his fingers.

She let her head fall forward on her chest, her eyelids jammed together as she tried to see past the yawning pit of despair inside her. But logic had deserted her tonight just as swiftly as Laurence's unexpected departure. And now all she could think about were his final words to her, half whispered, half choked, his fingers pressing urgently into her flesh as the attack that had finally taken his life overcame him.

'Look after him,' he'd managed to whisper. 'Look after Zane. And tell him—I'm sorry…'

And then the monitor's note had changed into one continual bleep and her thoughts had turned to panic. A heartbeat later the doors to the room had crashed open to a flurry of blue cotton and trolleyed machinery and in one swift blur she'd been expertly manoeuvred outside.

By the time they'd let her back in it was over and she'd never had a chance to ask him what he'd meant and why the son who hadn't bothered to contact his father the best part of a decade should need looking after or why Laurence felt he was the one who should apologise for his son's neglect. And she'd never had a chance to demand to know why the hell Laurence would expect her to be the one to do it.

But she had no time to squander on the prodigal son. After the way he'd neglected his father, Zane was so low on her radar he didn't register. Right now she'd lost her mentor, a father figure and an inspiration. Most of all, she'd lost a dear friend.

'Oh, Laurence,' she whispered, her voice cracking under the strain. 'I'll miss you so much.'

The door swung open behind her. She sniffed and took a calming breath. The staff would be wanting her to leave so they could complete the formalities. She lifted her head to acknowledge their presence.

'I'm almost ready,' she said, only half turning towards the door. 'Just a moment longer, if that's okay.'

There was no immediate response, no drawing back and closing of doors, and a strange feeling of unease crawled its way up her spine. Her back straightened in reaction, her arms prickling into goosebumps as the room chilled to ice-cold.

'I'd prefer to visit with my father alone.'

Her head snapped around to where the stranger with the ice-cold tone filled the doorway. And yet, for the briefest second, her heart skipped with recognition—until harsh reality resurfaced, snuffing out her momentary joy.

Oh, they might have been Laurence's eyes she'd been staring at, with their same dark caramel richness, the same shape and heavy-hooded, almost seductive lids. But whereas the older man's eyes had been filled with a mixture of affection and respect, their corners crinkled with laughter over a shared joke or with natural delight at discovering the perfect pearl, the eyes turned upon her now were cold and imperious.

Zane, she realised, her first-impression sensors screaming a red-light warning. *So what that he was Laurence's son?— clearly that didn't make him her friend.*

His body language made that more than plain. His unyielding stance was imbued with antagonism, from his unshaven jaw and short finger-combed dark hair to his designer black jeans and hand-crafted leather boots, planted on the tiled floor like they owned it. Even the contrasting white shirt failed to soften the impression, instead only emphasising his olive skin and dark features. He wore power like a birthright.

She forced her aching back ramrod straight in her chair as his icy gaze swept over her, noticing when it finally came to a halt where her fingers rested, still curled around his father's hand. Disapproval came off him in waves, but she pointedly maintained her hold. She had a right to be here even if he didn't like it. And he obviously didn't. Too bad.

And yet, whatever his faults, part of her recognized that he had to be hurting, too. Despite the two not speaking for years, his father's death must still have come as a huge shock. Even just one day ago Laurence had been expected to make a complete recovery, so when Zane had boarded that plane from London, the prospect of his father's death would have been a remote and unlikely possibility. He would have to be made of granite not to be affected by what he'd discovered once he'd arrived. Nobody could be that hard. Nobody could that insensitive.

'You must be Zane,' she said, trying to steer some kind of course through the jagged ice floes cluttering the atmosphere between them. 'I'm Ruby Clemenger. I worked with your father.'

'I know who you are,' he snapped.

She blinked and took a steadying breath, instantly rethinking her earlier assumption. Maybe he was that hard and insensitive, after all.

'I am sorry about your father,' she persisted, trying again, if only for Laurence's sake, because even if she didn't give a rat's about Zane, she'd wanted so much for Laurence to have his last wish met. She shook her head. 'He wanted so much to see you. But you're too late.'

His eyes narrowed in on hers, intensifying their laser-like quality.

'Too late?' he repeated. 'Oh, yeah, it sure looks that way from where I'm standing.'

She shivered in the frosty atmosphere. Why did she get the distinct impression he was talking about more than his father's untimely death?

Zane battled to hold his mounting irritation in check. *Trust her to be here.* He hadn't seen a single photograph of his father over the last few years that hadn't also featured this woman clinging to his arm. Ruby Clemenger—his father's constant companion, his father's right-hand woman. His father had always been a leg man, and, judging by the long sweep of golden limbs tucked beneath her on the armchair, nothing much had changed.

But right now all he wanted was for her to use those legs to get out of here. This was his father, his grief, *his anger*. He'd travelled the best part of twenty-four hours, only to be cheated out of seeing his father by one. He didn't want to share this time with anyone, let alone with the likes of her.

At last it seemed she was taking the hint. The spark of fight that had flared in her azure eyes had dimmed as she unwound herself out of the chair, her movements slow and deliberate, like she'd been sitting too long. But still she didn't move away from the bed, her filmy skirt floating just above knee length.

Even in their jet-lagged state his eyes couldn't help but notice—he'd been right about the legs. But now she was standing, it was clear her attributes didn't stop there—they extended much further north, an alluring mix of feminine curves and sun-kissed skin, of blue eyes framed by dark lashes and lips generous enough to be begging to be kissed—just the way he liked them.

Just the way his father liked them.

Bitterness congealed like a lead weight inside him. She had to be at least three decades younger than Laurence's fifty-five years; with a body and a face like hers, his father hadn't stood a chance—she was a heart attack waiting to happen!

As he watched, she lifted the hand she'd been holding and pressed it to her lips before gently replacing it at Laurence's side. Then she leaned over and smoothed a thumb over his brow. He watched her dip her head, the loose tendrils of her whisky-coloured hair falling free of the clasp at the back of her head as she kissed his father on the cheek one final time.

'Goodbye, Laurence,' he heard her whisper. 'I'll always love you.'

The words struck him like a blow deep in a place already overflowing with rancour and tainted by a cynicism borne from working on some of the ugliest corporate take-overs in Europe.

Her performance was no doubt all for his benefit. He knew what people were capable of when there were fortunes at stake.

Ruby Clemenger was merely an employee of the Bastiani Pearl Corporation, although clearly her 'duties' extended way beyond her jewellery design. Of course, she would know the Corporation was worth hundreds of millions of dollars. Would she hope to establish there was more to the extracurricular arrangement she had with his father than mutual-needs fulfilment? Was this her way of staking a claim on the business now that Laurence was gone?

She'd have to try one hell of a lot harder than that if it was.

'How touching,' he said, the bile rising in his throat, his patience at an end. 'Now, if you're quite finished?'

Her back went rigid and she stilled momentarily before reaching out her hand to Laurence's cheek one last time. Then she turned and, with barely a glance at him from her glacial blue eyes, side-stepped around Zane and slipped out of the room.

Her scent lingered in her wake, fresh and light in the clinical hospital atmosphere.

Seductive.

Irritating!

He growled his frustration out loud as he moved closer to the bed where his father lay. He was tired, he was jet-lagged and he was angry. His race halfway around the world had been for nothing; as a man who prided himself on beating every deadline thrown his way, the fact that he'd been cheated out of this one cut bone-deep.

But worse still was the realisation that, even with all that going on around him, still he could be swayed by the lingering scent of the last person he should be thinking about—his father's mistress!

'Can I give you a lift to the house?'

Ruby had been waiting outside Laurence's room the last

twenty minutes for Zane to emerge. And when he finally had, he'd pointedly ignored her and her question and headed directly to the nurses' station to talk to the medical staff.

Personally, she didn't care less where he stayed or how he got there, her only wish being that he'd turn around and disappear under whatever rock he'd been hiding under for the past decade, but Laurence's request kept pulling her back. *'Look after Zane,'* he'd implored her. And if he had been able to think fondly about a son who hadn't bothered to get in touch with him for nigh on a decade, then she could at least be civil—if only for Laurence's sake.

The staff slowly filtered away, one retrieving a bag for him from inside the nurses' station. So, he'd come direct from the airport? He'd need a lift somewhere, then. She pushed herself from the chair and tried to forget how much she disliked this man already.

'I wondered if you'd like a lift to the house?' she repeated.

He turned towards her, his features and his jaw set hard as he swung the bag up over his shoulder. The action exaggerated the broad sweep of his chest, revealing all too clearly the power in his muscled arms. Though his build was similar to his father's, he was taller and more threatening than Laurence had ever been. She felt tiny alongside him.

'I heard you.'

'And?'

'And I can take a cab.'

'That would be pointless, seeing as I'm going there, anyway.'

'Is that right?' One eyebrow arched as his eyes glinted with what looked like victory. 'And why would you be doing that?'

For just a moment she hesitated, the arrangement she'd had with Laurence and accepted as normal suddenly sending alarm bells through her. Things were going to have to change, and soon—it was one thing to share a house with Laurence, who'd been more like a father to her than a colleague; it was another thing entirely to imagine living there with his son, with his overt hostility and his latent danger. She could feel the heat rising in her cheeks as she stumbled over her answer.

'Because…I live there.'

His lip curled. A *live-in* mistress. 'How very convenient,' he said. 'My father must have enjoyed having…' *your services on tap* '…your company.'

She angled her chin higher while her eyes remained glued to his. 'Your father was a remarkable man. We shared a special friendship.'

'I'll bet,' he said dismissively. His father had a habit of forming 'special friendships'. The last one had cost Laurence the respect of his son and the complete breakdown of a father-son relationship. He was determined this one wouldn't cost him a thing.

It was only a short trip from the hospital to the house, but the BMW's air-conditioning made driving the clear winner over walking. Zane spent the brief journey staring out the windows, reacquainting himself with his old neighbourhood and trying to ignore the scent that reminded him exactly whose car and whose company he was in.

But at least she didn't talk. He had too much to assimilate right now to continue their battle of words. Already he could feel a tidal surge of bone-tiredness, the legacy of both his long journey and its unexpected conclusion, creeping up on him, numbing his senses and his mind until there were only two things he could be certain of.

His father was gone.

And life for Zane Bastiani was about to radically change. There was little prospect it would be for the better.

Ruby steered the car into a driveway, pulling up outside the sprawling colonial bungalow that had been Zane's home for the first twenty years of his life. He uncurled himself slowly from the car, feeling a sudden and brief burst of warmth that had nothing to do with the brilliant sunlight as he took in the sight of the building.

London and his former life had never seemed so far away.

Built in the nineteen-twenties when pearl shell was gold and those who owned the pearl-lugger fleets were kings, the house was surrounded by wide verandahs and lattice fences lushly covered with flowering bougainvillea, a colourful invitation to the airy and cool interior.

The empty interior.

Bitterness seeped from a wound barely crusted over despite the passing of time. His mother had loved this house, the rambling, high-ceilinged rooms and timber floors, the large windows designed to let the slightest cooling breeze flow through. And she had loved the tropical gardens, which were always threatening to turn to jungle and overrun the house if left unchecked.

His sense of loss changed state inside him, becoming tangible, a solid thing deep in his gut. He could feel it swelling until it cramped his organs. He could taste its bitter juices in his mouth.

'Welcome home,' he muttered under his breath.

'Are you okay?'

He absorbed her words rather than heard them, just one more element to the mix of sensations and memories that reached out to snare him and drag him back into the past.

'My grandfather bought this house from one of the last of the old Master Pearlers,' he said without shifting his focus, reciting the story he'd heard so often from his mother. 'Laurence was just a kid back then. The pearl-shell industry was slowly dying and Grandfather put everything else he had in the new cultured pearl technology. He had a dream to become the first of the new breed of Master Pearlers.'

'And he made it,' she said. 'Between your grandfather and Laurence, it's quite a legacy they've left. Bastiani Pearls is now worth a fortune.'

Her words knifed through his thoughts, slicing them to ribbons, and he turned the full force of his glare on to her.

What was it with these mistresses? Anneleise could never stop thinking about money, either. Even at their last unexpected meeting, just two days before his desperate and now pointless rush to Australia, she'd staggered him by expecting some sort of compensation from him for finally getting it through her silvery blonde hair that it was over. And when he'd laughed out loud, she'd let go with the tears and lamented the opportunities she'd missed while Zane had held her undivided attention.

Even if that were anywhere near the truth, she had plenty of trinkets from their brief liaison that she could hock to tide her over if it came to that. Not that she'd take long to find another mark, if indeed she hadn't already in the time since they'd parted company. She certainly was stunning enough, with her alabaster skin and a fragile femininity that had made him want to protect her at first—until he'd discovered her fragility extended character deep. But at least now he was free of her and her parasitic tendencies. He'd had enough of grasping women, every last one of them.

'Is something wrong?' she asked, her attitude making it clear that she resented his intense scrutiny.

He turned his gaze away, pulling his bag from the boot and slamming it shut. 'Let's go inside,' he said.

Her skirt flirted around the backs of her knees as she led the way up the short set of stairs to the verandah and once again he found himself caught in the heady trail of her scent, the damnable price of chivalry.

His eyes took a moment to adjust as they entered the elegant bungalow. He looked around. The house might have been built over eighty years ago, but his mother had always seen to it that whatever renovations were made over the years had provided the most up-to-date conveniences while retaining the character of the colonial era. He let go a breath when he realised that Ruby's tenure hadn't impacted upon his mother's vision.

'I asked Kyoto to have your old room prepared in case you stayed,' she said, turning slightly towards him. 'I hope that's okay.'

He paused, not believing what he'd heard. 'Kyoto's still around?' It was inconceivable that he was still alive. The former Japanese pearl diver had worked for his family for years, first as cook and then housekeeper. He'd seemed a gnarled old man when Zane was just a boy. 'Surely he's not still working?'

She nodded, a watery smile temporarily lighting up her features. 'Mostly he supervises now—we have a cook and cleaner to do the heavy work.' He watched the wobbly smile slide away. 'But I said he should go home today. He's devastated by the news.'

She pressed her lips together and spun away, turning her back on him, but not before he'd recognised the crack in her voice, the slight tremulous quality to her movements as she'd uttered that last word that told him she was either trying very hard not to cry or, if Anneleise was any guide, trying her best to make him think she was. Anneleise could have written a thesis on the artful use of tears—although he doubted she'd ever shed a sincere one in her life. Why wouldn't Ruby be armed with the same arsenal? It probably came with the job description.

'Well,' she murmured, her back still to him, her voice low and strained as she rubbed her brow with one hand, 'I'm sure you don't need me to show you where your room is. I'll leave you to settle in.'

He could just walk away, keep walking down the passageway to his old room. He could just ignore her and let her know her ploy had left him completely unmoved. He *should* just walk away.

But the urge to show her that he wouldn't fall for her tricks was too great. She needed to know that he knew all about the games women liked to play when there was money at stake. She needed to know that he wouldn't be falling for any of them.

He reached a hand to her shoulder, ignoring her startled flinch at his grip as he steered her around to face him.

He overcame her resistance, tipping up her stiffly held jaw with one hand until there was no way she could avoid his gaze any longer. Slowly, reluctantly, her eyes slid upwards, until their aqua depths collided with his. In the first instant he took in the moisture, the lashes damp and dark, and he had to acknowledge she was good, very good, if she could bring on the tears that readily.

But then he saw what was inside her eyes and it slashed him to the core.

Pain. Loss. Mind-numbing desolation.

All of those things he recognised. All of those things found an echo in a place deep down inside himself, something that shifted and ached afresh as her liquid eyes seemed to bare her soul to him. It was an awkward feeling, uncomfortable, unwelcome.

He watched as she jammed her lips together as a solitary tear squeezed from the corner of one eye. Momentarily disarmed, acting purely on instinct, he shifted his hand from her chin and gently wiped the tear from her cheek with the pad of one finger. Her eyelids dipped shut, her lips parted as she drew in a sudden breath, and he felt her tremble into his touch.

Gears crunched and ground together inside him. This wasn't going the way he'd expected at all. Because *she* wasn't the way he'd expected.

'You really cared about him?'

The question betrayed his thoughts, clumsy and heavily weighted with disbelief. But there was no time to correct it—the thought that Laurence meant more to her than a mere provider of luxury and cash somehow grated hard on his senses.

She dragged in a breath and pulled away, shrugging off his hand as she backed into a cane lounge. 'Is that so hard to believe? Laurence made it easy to want to care about him.'

Her rapid admission changed everything, transforming his confused thoughts into sizzling hot anger in an instant as the facts slotted back into their rightful place. Laurence had *'made it easy'*. No pretence, no circumspection. She'd admitted how it had been between them with barely a blink! And it was exactly what he'd expected. No wonder she felt so crushed. She'd lost her sugar daddy along with her cash flow.

'Yeah. I'll just *bet* he made it easy.'

She edged closer, her head tilted, as if she couldn't have heard him right. 'I'm not sure I understand you. What exactly do you mean?'

'It's hardly that difficult to work out. A rich old man with a taste for pretty women and who could afford to make having one around worth her while.'

If he hadn't been jet-lagged, if he hadn't been awake throughout too many flights over too many time zones, maybe he would have had a chance of fending off her next attack. As it was, he didn't see it coming.

Her flattened palm cracked against his cheek and jaw like a bullet from a gun.

Instantly she recoiled in horror, her eyes wide open, the offending hand fisted over her mouth. She waited while he drew in a long breath and rubbed the place she'd made contact, the skin under his hand already a slash of colour. But he didn't react, not physically, and she felt the shock ebb away, felt her panicked heart rate calm just enough to match the simmer of anger that still consumed her.

'Well, you sure pack a punch,' he drawled, working his jaw from side to side, his eyes narrow and hard like he was assessing her all over again.

'Nothing more than you deserved.' He'd asked for it all right. Why would he think that about Laurence? Why would he think that about *her*? 'And don't think I'm going to apologise. I don't have to take that kind of garbage from you.'

'Because you can't handle the truth?'

'You're unbelievable! You really believe I'm here for Laurence's money?'

'Most people would be lured by it.'

'Then I'm not "most people". I don't want his money. I never have.'

'Then why else would you have been living with him, a man old enough to have been your father?'

She laughed then, mostly because she knew that if she didn't laugh, she'd probably cry with the injustice of it all. He was so wrong. He didn't know his father. He didn't know her. *He knew nothing.*

'I pity you,' she said, much more calmly than she felt. 'Obviously you're completely unfamiliar with the words "friendship" or "companionship".'

He snorted his disbelief and her anger escalated to dangerous levels again. But this time she was determined to keep control. She had to try to remember what Laurence had asked of her. She dragged in a deep breath, battling to stay rational and calm, in spite of his attack.

'Just because you were incapable of showing your father any respect or affection...' she shook her head '...don't assume everybody else was.'

His eyes narrowed dangerously, the resentment contained within so hard and absolute, it glistened. 'So you looked after him out of the goodness of your heart? You stayed merely to keep him company? Next you'll be expecting me to believe you really loved him.'

'*Somebody* had to! God only knows he got nothing but grief from you.'

She jerked herself away, wanting to get out of there, wanting to get as far away from him as she could, but a steel grip on her arm stopped her dead, preventing her escape. She turned, indignant, but the protest died on her lips the moment she saw his face, his features contorted with fury.

'Don't you try to take the high moral ground with me. You have *no idea* what I felt for my father or why. None at all.'

She fisted her hand and wrenched at her arm unsuccessfully. So instead she leaned closer, so close she could feel the anger coming out of him like heat from an open fire. But his anger was nothing compared to hers—she was angry enough for both of them.

'You're right,' she agreed, feeling her lip curl in contempt. 'I have no idea what you felt or why. But whose fault is that? Mine, for being here when your father needed support, or yours, for not caring enough to be here yourself?'

CHAPTER THREE

HOURS LATER, as the first unlayering of the night sky heralded the coming dawn, Zane had given up on sleep. He lay on his bed in the room that had been his for more than half his life, the accumulated photographs and trophies from his youth still exactly where he'd left them. If he closed his eyes, he could almost imagine he'd never left. But he knew he wouldn't be thinking about how things used to be. Because the last few hours had shown him that all he'd be thinking about was a woman with fire in her eyes and venom on her tongue, a woman built like a goddess and who fought like a she-cat.

Even last night, when she'd lashed out and slapped him, she hadn't backed away. She'd come back for more and she'd given more. And even when she'd agreed with him, in their final exchange, she'd hit back with such a sting in her parting comments that when she'd yanked her arm against his grip once more he'd had no choice but to let her go.

She had some spirit. He wrestled once more with the sheets as he tried to get comfortable. What would she be like in bed? He'd lay odds that she'd show as much life out of her clothes, if not more, than she did in them.

He punched his pillow one final time before giving up, swinging his legs off the bed and making for the *en suite*, dragging his hands over his troubled head. What the hell was wrong with him? It didn't matter what she was like in bed, he was hardly about to pick up where his father left off!

Besides, he had more pressing problems to turn his mind to now. There would be all kinds of things to deal with: a funeral to arrange, the future of the business. Naturally he'd be expected to fill Laurence's shoes for the time being, but plans would have to be made for the longer term. He might as well make a start on it before Ruby could interfere. She might have held a high place in Laurence's 'affections', but, now he was here, things were going to change.

Kyoto was waiting for him in the kitchen when he emerged, finally feeling more human after a long hot shower and fresh clothes.

'Mister Zane!' Kyoto shouted in welcome as he approached, his wrinkled face contorted between half-toothless smile, half anguish. 'It's so good you're home. I make you breakfast, "special".'

Sinewy arms suddenly wrapped tightly around him in a rapid embrace before releasing him just as quickly and returning to the task of scrambling eggs as if they'd never touched him. Zane smiled to himself. Kyoto's broken English was just the same, but he could never remember a time when he'd ever been so physically demonstrative. It was strangely touching.

'It's good to see you again, too,' he said sincerely.

'Your father,' Kyoto said, shaking his head as he heaped a plate full. 'I am so sorry.'

'Thank you,' he said, right now feeling Kyoto's loss more than his own, as hot coffee and a heavily laden breakfast plate with a stack of toast on the side was placed in front of him.

Kyoto disappeared, muttering sadly to himself as Zane made a start on breakfast in the large, airy room. It was hours since his last real meal and Kyoto's cooking had never been a hardship to endure, least of all now. He'd almost made his way through the mountain when Kyoto returned and something else appeared on the table before him. He blinked in cold hard shock as he recognised the small padlocked wooden chest.

The old pearler skipper's box had always sat in pride of place on his father's desk and now it sat in front of him, bold and challenging. *Mocking*.

A relic of a former era, when natural pearls were real treasure and the rare bonus discovered while collecting the mother-of-pearl shell itself, any such pearls were deposited through a small hole in the lid and so kept secure during the lugger's time at sea.

But it was hardly pearls he knew the box contained. More like dynamite.

'Your father said you were to have,' Kyoto said in response to Zane's unspoken question.

Zane set his plate aside and drained the last of his strong coffee, never taking his eyes off the chest. The wood had aged to an even richer golden patina than he remembered, the metal handle and lock scratched and scarred by the passage of time, the tiny key clearly in place. Inviting. Taunting. Because it was hardly the chest his father wanted him to have. It was the contents. And Zane knew exactly what was inside.

Did his father honestly not realise Zane knew, or was he merely trying to press the point home—a bitter reminder of the circumstances of his leaving? No question, Zane decided. Of course he would have known. Clearly his father hadn't asked to see Zane in order to settle their differences. He'd called for him to rub them in!

His mind rankled with the stench of the fetid memories. He'd been just a young boy home on school holidays when he'd sneaked into his father's office under the cool verandah and had been exploring through the desk drawers until he'd come across a small battered key. Instantly he'd thought of the box on top of the desk, the box that had been locked as long as he could remember and which had always intrigued him. So he'd scrabbled up on to his father's wide jarrah desk and tested the lock. It had clicked open on the second scratchy attempt. With a thrill of discovery he'd removed the lock and the metal plate from the catch. He remembered holding his breath as he'd lifted the lid to peer at whatever treasures lay inside.

And he remembered the crush of disappointment when he'd found it only contained a stash of old letters. Barely half-interested by then, he'd picked the first from the top of the pile. He'd opened the folded sheet, only to stare at a letter from his father to his so-called Aunt Bonnie, his mother's best friend. There was a list of numbers and something about a house and a monthly payment that made no sense at all to his young mind. But there'd been no time to linger over it once his nanny had discovered him in the room he'd been forbidden to enter and warned him never to look in places he shouldn't in case he learned something he never wanted or needed to know.

For a while he'd wondered what she'd meant but then he'd found a new game to play and gone back to school and he'd forgotten all about it. Until that day, nine stark years ago, when he'd been reminded of the letter and its contents and suddenly it had all made perfect sense!

He heaved a sigh as he considered the box, the stain of bitterness deep and permanent in his mind. What was his father really playing at, leaving him the box like this? Did he expect him to read the entire contents—no doubt their love letters—making sure Zane knew the whole sordid truth? Was this all Laurence thought Zane deserved after walking out nine years before? Was this to be his inheritance? Zane couldn't help but raise a smile ironically as he contemplated the box. He wouldn't put it past him. His father had never been known for his subtlety.

But he wasn't playing into that game. He'd read enough all those years ago to last him. The box could stay closed.

Kyoto whisked away his plates and swept around the kitchen, cleaning everything he touched until it gleamed.

'More coffee?' he offered, interrupting Zane's thoughts.

Zane responded with a shake of the head, giving the box a final push away as he stood. He didn't need any reminders of the past. He had Ruby to do that.

'Thank you, Kyoto, but no. I need to get started on a few things. Is there a car I can use while I'm here?'

'Yes, yes.' He nodded. 'But you are home to stay now, for good?'

Zane dragged in a breath. His immediate plans for the company included making the long-term arrangements that would ensure his speedy return to London and his businesses there. Of course, there would be ramifications of his father's sudden death to deal with—someone would have to take over the running of the pearl business; he'd source a manager somehow—but staying wasn't an option right now. 'We'll see, Kyoto,' he replied noncommittally. 'First, I just need to make sure the company gets through this difficult stage, without my father's hand to guide it.'

'Not a problem,' Kyoto offered, waving away his concerns with a flick of his tea towel. 'Miss Ruby take care of all that, no worry.'

Zane stilled, a knife-sharp feeling of foreboding slicing through his thoughts. 'What do you mean?'

'Miss Ruby already at the office. She take care of everything.'

* * *

If indigestion came in a colour, it would be red. If it came in the shape of a woman, it would take the form of Ruby Clemenger.

She sat now in his father's office, behind his father's desk, like she owned it, making notes on a laptop computer as she studied an open file on the desk.

'You haven't wasted a minute, I see,' he said, announcing his presence in the same sentence.

She looked up, momentarily startled, before the shutters clamped down on her eyes again, turning them frosty blue. Guarded.

'I expected you'd sleep longer.'

He smiled. 'So you thought you'd get a head start on running the company before I woke up?'

She frowned. 'And why would you possibly think that?'

He gestured around the spacious office. 'Because you're here, barely twenty-four hours after my father's death, in *his* office, occupying *his* desk.'

She put down her pen and leaned back in her chair—*his father's chair*—her eyes narrowing to icy blue channels. 'Is that what you're worried about? That I might want to take your precious birthright away from you? That I might steal your inheritance and whisk Bastiani Pearls away from you while you're not looking?'

'You wouldn't stand a chance!' He squeezed the words through lips dragged tight, his jaw held rigid.

She smiled, a smile that exposed her even white teeth but extended no further. 'Then maybe it's just as well I'm not interested.'

'So how do you explain being here now?' he demanded, moving closer to the broad desk. 'It's Saturday. Not exactly office hours.'

I had to get out of the house, she thought. *I had to get away from you.* But she wouldn't say it. Didn't want to admit the blatant honesty of her thoughts, even to herself. Instead she steeled herself against his approach and said, 'I have work to do. Laurence and I were involved in a project together last week when he took ill. The file was still on his desk. And I really didn't think he'd mind me borrowing his office for a while.'

'What kind of work?' he demanded, shrugging off her sarcasm like he expected it.

She surveyed him as he made his way around the desk to her side, taking in the cool-looking chinos and fine-knit shirt, resenting every lean stride he took closer to her. He was dressed for the heat, so why was it that her temperature was suddenly rising?

Damn the man! She'd told herself all night—she'd *promised* herself—that now they'd got their first meeting out of the way, now that they both knew where they stood with each other, that she'd be immune to his power and his sheer masculine force. And finally she'd convinced herself that that would be the case, that she could wear her anger like steel plating around her. But she'd been kidding herself. Otherwise, why else would she have fled the house at first light? And why else would she be feeling the encroaching heat of this man like the kiss of a blowtorch?

Her anger was still there, and the resentment—with just one comment, he'd managed to resurrect that in spades—but there was no avoiding the Bastiani aura.

Like father, like son.

Laurence's power had made him a powerful colleague to work with, a fascinating and inspiring mentor. Zane, though, seemed to take the family trait to a new level, his proximity grating on her resistance, his raw masculine magnetism and fresh man-scent leaving her feeling strangely vulnerable.

'What are these?' he asked, looking down at the drawings on the desk, breaking her out of her reflections.

'The new range,' she said, feeling a note of pride creep into her voice as he sorted through the designs she'd been working on for over six months. 'We've called them the Passion Collection. The launch is a little over three months away.'

'Here?'

'Like all our collections, we'll launch in Broome first, at the Stairway to the Moon festival, then we'll take the collection nationwide with an event at the Sydney Opera House one week later. We'll follow that up with the dealer visits, where we take selected designs to New York and London. No doubt you'll expect to come along, in Laurence's place.'

She tried to infuse some kind of welcome note to her voice, but if he was impressed by the demanding launch schedule or wanted any part of it, he didn't show it. 'These designs are very ambitious,' he said instead. 'Extraordinarily so.'

'Thank you.'

He looked around sharply. 'These are yours?'

She nodded. *Every last one of them.* 'That is why I was employed here,' she told him, holding his gaze. 'I design settings for the pearls the Bastiani Corporation produces.'

'Then you must realise that wasn't exactly a compliment. These designs will never work.'

She stilled, not believing what she was hearing. 'I beg your pardon?'

'These designs—"The Passion Collection": *A Lovers' Embrace.* It's a fine concept, but don't you think it's too ambitious to achieve with just pearls and gold and gemstones? You'll never pull it off. We can't have an entire collection based around such a crazy idea. It's too much of a risk.'

'It *will* work,' she argued, trying to banish the doubt demons that assailed her creative mind at every opportunity without Zane's input to spur them on. 'Yes, it's ambitious, and, yes, it's a risk, but it's already in production. *And* it's almost complete.'

'But not finished and not proven. So the Bastiani Corporation is pinning its future hopes on a collection that could be a major failure?'

'Laurence was passionate about this collection. He was behind it one hundred percent.'

'Laurence isn't here now.'

'But *I* am. And I've been designing pearl collections for Bastiani ever since I started working here—so far very successfully. There's no reason to think this one won't be as successful.'

He put down the drawing he'd been holding and swivelled, leaning back against the desk, his hands poised either side of his legs. 'You'd hardly claim anything else.'

He was too close. Dealing with him while he'd had his back to her was one thing, having him staring her down while hovering alongside was something else. It made her wish she'd pulled on a whole lot more this morning than a floral wrap skirt and a cool, lemon-coloured singlet top. She pushed herself out of her chair, using the pretext of filling her water glass at the cooler, and only turned when she'd taken three steadying breaths.

'Well, I don't intend to let Laurence or the company down now,' she said, in a bid to regain her composure. 'And while we're on the topic, did you ever bother to read those financial reports I know your father had sent to you regularly?' she asked. 'Did you ever take note of what they told you, and of how the profits of the Bastiani Corporation took off exponentially, when instead of selling cultured pearl stocks and basic design elements, we started selling themed collections twice a year?'

'And you're claiming the credit for that, I presume?' He practically snorted the words out, without bothering to make any attempt to answer her question.

'No,' she said, shaking her head. 'I'm not claiming the credit.

Laurence took me on as a junior designer when I was barely out of design school. He said he wanted someone fresh, with no preconceived or outmoded ideas of how pearl jewellery should look. So together we worked on the idea of a themed collection, an entire range that would display the beauty and mystique of the most magnificent and highly prized pearls in the world. So, it was Laurence who had the vision, who had the dream of expanding his business in a way the company had never done before. But the designs were all mine.'

She stopped, feeling suddenly heady, as if oxygen was in short supply. All through her impassioned speech he'd sat, coolly surveying her from his position against the desk, his eyes hooded, almost slumberous.

If she didn't like his attitude, she resented his silent scrutiny even more. In desperation, she took a sip from the glass, trying to fill the space in the conversation, suddenly glad she'd had the foresight to fill her glass now that her mouth and lips had turned desert dry. Condensation beaded as she tilted the glass, running down the side, making tiny rivulets around her fingers. She gasped as two icy drops splashed on to her singlet, leaching into the light fabric in ever-expanding circles.

His eyes followed the movement. He'd been fascinated watching her retreat, seeing her calm herself before facing him and stating her case. He'd been impressed by her no-nonsense sense of her own worth in the company—in spite of himself.

But right now he was more impressed with the way the droplets of water were soaking tantalisingly into the fabric of her top. He liked what it did to rattle her composure. He liked even better what it did to her breasts. In an instant they'd firmed and peaked and, like an invitation he couldn't refuse, he was drawn closer.

'You're turning out to be a woman of considerable talents,' he murmured, as he bridged the few steps between them. He came to a halt immediately before her. She was tall enough, but still she had to turn her head up to look him in the eye. That was good—that gave him an uninterrupted view of the sweep of her throat and the swell of tanned-to-honey-gold skin that disappeared tantalisingly under her singlet top.

She swallowed as he reached out a hand between them, her eyes wide like a startled doe's, fearful and uncertain. He put his fingers to the pearl choker at her throat, lifting it gently from her satin smooth skin, feeling the pearl's warmth where it had lain against her flesh.

'And is this one of yours, too?'

She couldn't breathe, she couldn't move, as a fear she hadn't felt in a long time resurfaced, threatening to swamp her. *Danger*, she recognised. The man meant danger. He was way too close, way too imposing and when he'd reached out a hand she'd thought— Oh, Lord, just the way he'd been watching her breasts had felt like the graze of a man's hand. And if his gaze could be that powerful… If he'd reached out to touch her there…

But instead he'd picked up her choker, the trace of his fingertips against her throat a tingling trail, searingly heated, shockingly intimate. She shuddered under his touch, a rush of realisation, some sixth sense alerting her that this danger was like nothing she'd known before. This brand of danger was more potent, more powerful and much more magnetic.

'It's beautiful,' he said, his voice husky and low and further tugging on her senses as he examined the piece. 'Just like its wearer.' His eyes lifted till they met hers. 'Did you design it?'

Breath rushed into the vacuum of her lungs. But she couldn't let herself reflect on what he'd just said, even though his rich dark eyes seemed intent on making her forget everything else. She had to concentrate on the necklace—and on what he'd asked.

It shouldn't be so hard, not to talk about one of her favourite pieces. Suspended on a band of nitrite, the single gem was held in place by an intricate coil of gold. The pearl, a magnificent eighteen-millimetre perfect round, had been a gift from Laurence following the success of their first collection. It had seemed appropriate that she should wear it today.

'I made it,' she admitted at last, reaching up to her neck instinctively, only to encounter his hand still cradling the piece. For a second their fingers brushed and lingered—and she saw something fleeting skid across his eyes, a spark, a surge of flame, and a corresponding heat pooled low in her belly.

'That's some pearl,' he murmured without letting go, his eyes now on her lips and not on the pearl at all. But there was no time to consider why that should be so, not with his mouth hovering near, the subtle tugging pressure he was exerting on her choker drawing her closer.

She swallowed, tried to make her mouth work, her senses filled with the scent of him, warm and woody and wanting her.

'Thank you,' she whispered, already imagining the taste of his lips on hers, already liking it. 'Laurence gave it to me.'

He blinked, his eyes changing from caramel warm to granite cold in an instant. Then he dropped the choker and straightened.

'No doubt you made it worth his while.'

The mood shattered, with her thoughts in total disarray. This time when her fingers found her pearl they circled the precious gem like it was a talisman, praying for it to give her strength. But she would need more than a pearl if she intended to keep this man at bay.

So she gathered her thoughts and bit back, 'Oh, yes. I'd certainly like to think so.'

Anger lit the eyes filled so recently with desire. *Anger and disgust.*

'Tell me it's not true,' he demanded. 'Tell me you didn't sleep with my father.'

She stared up at him and allowed herself a half-smile. So he wasn't disgusted with her? He was disgusted with himself, disgusted that he could be attracted to someone his father had slept with. Maybe Laurence's gift would protect her after all, because as long as Zane saw her as the pearl master's mistress, she would be safe from him. And, more importantly, she would be safe from her own quavering resistance.

'I don't have to tell you anything! It's none of your business.' She moved to go around him and return to her desk, but his hands grabbed hold of her shoulders, dragging her in, imprisoning her close to him.

'Did you?'

She looked down at his hands. 'I'm surprised you can even bear to touch me.' Then she focused her gaze until it was needle sharp and hitched one eyebrow provocatively. 'Or are you merely intent on ensuring you inherit *all* your father's assets?'

She didn't wait for his response. She shrugged off his hands and marched to the desk, collecting up her designs and plans. 'Excuse me, I'd love to stay and chat, but I have work to do. And then I'm going home—to pack.'

'Why? Where are you going?'

'I don't know,' she admitted halfway across the room. 'But it's going to be bad enough working with you until the launch. There's just no way I can stomach the thought of living with you, as well.'

'What do you mean,' he called out behind her, '"until the launch"?'

She dragged in a breath and slowly swivelled around, sending up a silent apology to Laurence as she did so. But it wasn't so much that she wouldn't honour his deathbed request, she told herself, she was merely putting a time limit on it.

'I'm giving my notice, Zane. I'll stay until the launch of

the new collection. I'll finish what I have to do. But then you won't have to put up with me any more. I'll be leaving Broome—for good.'

CHAPTER FOUR

LAURENCE HAD CLEARLY had other ideas. A few days later both Ruby and Zane sat dumbfounded in Laurence's former office as his executor explained the terms of his will.

'I don't understand,' Ruby said uncertainly. But it wasn't that she hadn't heard the lawyer the first time; it was just that it made no sense.

Derek Finlayson breathed an apologetic sigh. 'I realise it's a lot to take in right now, but basically what it comes down to is that you and Zane have been bequeathed equal shares in ninety per cent of the Bastiani Pearl Corporation. As of now you each control forty-five per cent of the business.'

'But…' She looked around for help, but Zane wasn't giving any. He sat, rigid and fixed, his face a tight mask. 'But I don't want it.'

Zane swung his head around, the disbelief in his features reading like an accusation.

She shook her head. Nothing made sense. Just last weekend she'd moved her things out of the house and into a cabin at the Cable Beach Resort. It was five-star luxury all the way, but that wasn't the reason she'd chosen it. It was because it was about as far away as she could possibly get from Zane. And she'd figured it would only be for the short term. Already

she had some interviews lined up with jewellery manu-
facturers in Sydney. In the past few years, she'd made herself
a solid reputation with the Bastiani Corporation. The successful launch of the Passion Collection would seal it. If all went
well, she'd be on her way out of Broome in just a matter of
months.

But if she stayed…

She couldn't let herself think about what that would be like.
Right now she knew she'd be gone from Zane and his
poisoned atmosphere in less than three months. She couldn't
bear to think about what it would be like to have to survive
any longer than that.

'I *don't* want it,' she insisted, her throat squeezed tight. 'I
don't understand why Laurence would have done this at all. In
fact, I've already started making arrangements to leave Broome
for good. I have job prospects. I won't even be here—'

The solicitor removed his glasses and rubbed the crinkled
bridge of his nose and looked like he was about to say something, before he stopped suddenly, as if thinking better of it.
Instead, he gave a measured sigh and replaced the glasses,
peering intently through them down the long sweep of his
nose at her. 'Clearly, under the terms of the will,' he started,
his words delivered slowly for more effect, 'Laurence
expected you to remain here in Broome to co-manage the corporation with Zane. Maybe you might want to take a moment
to reconsider your position? The remaining ten per cent of the
business will be apportioned among the employees and house
staff based on length of service to the company. They will
need the business run profitably for their benefit, as well.'

'Let her go,' Zane interrupted. 'She doesn't want to stay!
I'll buy her out.'

Derek Finlayson blinked and directed his grey steely gaze
towards Zane. 'I understand your distress, Mr Bastiani, but

it's your father's wishes that I'm concerned with right now.
Laurence clearly wished for both you and Miss Clemenger to
manage the business for the benefit of *all* the stakeholders.
But, after all, it's been Miss Clemenger who's been working
alongside Laurence for several years now. Right now she
would be more familiar with the actual business. It's crucial
she stays, you must see that.'

'I haven't exactly been sitting on my hands, myself. I have
businesses of my own to take care of in London.'

'Your father provided for that,' said the lawyer, riffling
through his notes, letting the acid in Zane's comment slide by.
'Ah, yes, here it is. You'll have whatever time you need to
return to London and do a handover. I can run you through
the details later.

'Now, Miss Clemenger,' he continued, 'Laurence clearly
knew how you felt about looking after the business and the
employees. And he trusted you to champion those rights and
to carry on his vision—to keep the Bastiani Corporation at the
forefront of the industry in both pearl design and innovation.
He trusted you to look after the company's profitability for
not only your benefit, but for theirs, as well. Is there anything
else I can say that will help convince you?'

'But if she doesn't want to stay—'

'No!' Ruby wheeled her head around, blue eyes clashing
with seething brown. 'Mr Finlayson is right. Laurence wanted
this. He wanted me to stay. I'm not about to walk away from
my responsibility to the business or to the employees. And
there's just no way I'm going to let Laurence down!'

Derek Finlayson's lips pulled into an unfamiliar smile as
he pounded the table with his fist. 'That's the ticket! Laurence
would be proud of you, my dear. As for you, Zane, how long
do you think you'll need to hand over your businesses? That
is…' He regarded him through shrewd eyes, his eyebrows

arched '…if you *do* intend to return to Broome to co-manage the business?'

'Oh, I'll be back,' he said, looking at Ruby, his hostile eyes incinerating the air between them. 'Make no mistake about that.'

'How did you manage that?'

The lawyer had gone, the room was empty of everyone except her and Zane, yet the atmosphere still felt too crowded, too thick with tension, too thunderous with his snapped words.

Her mind a whirl, Ruby barely registered his question over her own panicked second thoughts. *She was trapped.* She'd been so close to walking away, just twelve short weeks away from being free, and now she was locked into the Bastiani Corporation, effectively shackled to a man she despised. *Shackled by pearls.* Had Laurence had any concept of what he'd done to her?

"Look after Zane," his father had begged. She wanted to laugh. From what she'd seen, Zane needed nobody to look after him. But she'd look after the company, she had no problem with that. But as for Zane, Zane could look after himself.

'What an extraordinary coup.'

'What do you mean?' She responded absently as his words finally filtered through, more intrigued right now that he saw things so differently to her. Why on earth would he think this was what she wanted? The concept that she was now suddenly worth a very large fortune, in addition to what her own family connections provided her with, was no compensation for her growing fears.

Laurence had done her no favours.

This was no beneficial bequest.

This was a sentence.

'It's not like you're family. You're merely an employee. So

how did you manage to convince my father to leave you forty-five per cent of the company?'

She dragged her eyes away from the bookshelves she'd been staring through and looked up at him, trying to blink away her confusion.

'I did nothing to "*convince*" him. I had no idea your father decided to frame his will that way. Why would I?'

'No idea?' He snorted his disbelief. 'You lived with him and you make out you didn't know? Surely you can understand that's just a little difficult to believe.'

She shook her head. 'Of course I didn't know! I told you I was resigning. You knew I was leaving. Why would I have made those plans if I'd known anything about Laurence's bequest?'

'Don't play the innocent. You never had any intention of leaving! Not while you had a chance of benefiting in my father's will. Saying you'd stay till the launch safely covered you there.'

She sighed, raising both her hands to the ceiling. What was the point of trying to convince him? What did it matter what he thought? 'It doesn't matter what you believe,' she acceded. 'The fact is, Laurence has given me no choice. I have no option but to stay.'

He laughed, harsh and bitter, seizing on her admission. 'Funny how quickly a few hundred million dollars can make you change your tune. Of course,' he mocked, disbelief dripping from his words, 'we know it's not really the money.'

'I *don't* care about the money! Not for me. But if I leave, what happens to the employees? You'll be gone for how long? Who would manage the company? How is that going to carry on Laurence's vision? I can't do that to people I worked with, that Laurence wanted to be looked after. I can't do that to people like Kyoto, after all his years of service.'

'You'll stay for the sake of the employees? How noble of you.' He leaned up close. 'Pardon me if I don't believe there isn't just a smattering of self-interest involved.'

'No pardon necessary,' she hissed back. 'I wouldn't expect you to believe anything, let alone the truth. You've shown a marked absence of that ability ever since you arrived back in Broome.'

'And you've shown a remarkable *inability* to admit to the truth! Why do you pretend to be something you're not? Why do you pretend not to understand what is so obvious to everyone else?'

She put her hands on her hips. Damn the man for his constant slurs and sordid innuendoes. 'So what is it that's so obvious to everyone else, Zane? What exactly do you mean? Maybe you should get it right off your chest.'

'You need it spelt out? Okay! Why the hell would my father leave you such a huge share of the company? Forty-five per cent! You've already admitted my father was special to you. So why would he leave you a fortune if you weren't something very much more than special?'

A rush of blood surged and crashed in her ears, urging her to fight.

'You're saying your father settled a fortune on me for living with him—for being his mistress. Is that right?'

'Got it in one.'

'Why is it with you that everything has to come down to sex?'

'Doesn't it?'

She wanted to disagree, but then, wasn't this exactly what she wanted him to think? If he hated her for sleeping with his father, then he wouldn't want to touch her, and if he didn't touch her, then she'd have a chance of resisting this bizarre magnetism of his, she'd have a chance of not falling victim to his power.

So instead of giving in to the inciting jungle beat of her heart and lashing back a reply in the negative, she embarked on a different course. Arching one eyebrow provocatively, she pasted on a sultry smile and pushed her chest out conspicuously. He liked her breasts, he'd already made that more than clear. And then, as if on cue, his eyes followed the movements of her bustline, his gaze hot and hungry, and her smile widened. She knew she was baiting him, but it was no more than he deserved. He'd already made his mind up about her and it suited her purposes. Why not go with his prejudices? Why not play them for all they were worth?

'Well, you've sure got me there, Zane,' she said, her voice intentionally husky as she ran one hand slowly down the curve of her hip. 'You *know* damn well I was special to him. Obviously our relationship meant a lot more to him than I realised. I never expected him to be quite so generous in return.'

The scarlet hue to his skin deepened as his throat corded and kicked out a pulse.

'You know,' she said in mock understanding, placing a flirty finger along her cheek as her tactics bore such luscious fruit. 'I know what your problem is. I suspect maybe I was even more special to him than his own son. That's what really gets your back up, isn't it Zane? He loved me, and not you. That's what you can't abide. That's why you hate me so much, isn't it?'

He propelled himself a step closer, his movements charged with super-anger, his features contorted with rage, and Ruby's heart skipped a beat. Why was he so angry when she was merely agreeing with whatever tawdry views of her he already held? His enraged features told her she'd more than made her mark—she'd gone too far!

'Zane…' she uttered, taking an instinctive step backwards as he powered closer. 'I didn't mean—'

The pulse in his brow hammered visibly, his eyes wild with turmoil, and whatever she'd been going to say was forgotten in the broiling atmosphere.

'Of course he loved you more than he loved me. Why wouldn't he want to?' he said, his voice strangely soft, at odds with his entire posture. He reached out a hand and she could see the tension in his corded muscles, his tight skin. She flinched, but his hand moved to one side, to touch her hair, to softly curl a loose strand around his finger, to curve the back of his hand over her cheek as his eyes travelled over her face, burning a trail down to her shoulders, her bustline. Then lower....

She swallowed. 'No,' she whispered, sensing the danger had shifted gears and taken a new direction—a new direction that had her body humming with interest instead of shrinking away in fear. She licked her lips, her breathing suddenly shallow and unreliable as if he'd burned up the oxygen between them. 'I didn't mean that. I was wrong—'

He hushed her mouth with a finger from his other hand, stopping her words and her breath in the same instant. His scent wound its way into her, his taste leached into her recently moistened lips and his touch was so tender. So tender when he should be so angry.

She didn't want him to be tender. She wanted him angry. Angry was consistent. Angry she could deal with. But this sudden tenderness...

Somehow this was infinitely more dangerous.

'You *were* right,' he admitted at last, dropping the hand at her mouth to skim down her throat and over the fullness of her breasts like an electric charge that made her gasp involuntarily as it scorched a trail all the way down. 'You obviously gave him something I never could. But I have to ask myself one question. For a forty-five per cent share in the company, for something like two hundred million dollars—'

He hesitated, his face just a hair's breadth away from her, his pause like a vacuum between them while his heated gaze continued to read her eyes, to caress her lips, as brazen as a torch brand on her flesh while the gentle pressure on her hair kept her close. And then his head tilted as his lips curled up into a thin, contemptible smile.

'Well, it sure begs the question—just how good *are* you in bed?'

CHAPTER FIVE

LIKE A GUNSLINGER'S trigger finger, her hand itched to let fly. His face was temptingly close and already she knew how satisfying it could be to crack her open palm against that arrogant visage. But too often lately with this man she'd let her emotions rule her actions and she'd lashed out either verbally or physically, only to immediately regret her lack of control. She wouldn't let herself give in to that base instinct again, no matter what the provocation.

Instead, she jammed her fingers into a tight knot behind her back and forced out a laugh even while her nails dug sharply into the flesh of her palms.

'I wouldn't give that a second thought,' she said, flicking her head away, yanking the curl of her hair from his reach. 'Because that's the one thing you'll *never* find out.'

Triumph fizzed in her veins as she turned for the door. She'd done it! She'd kept her cool *and* put him well and truly in his place.

He watched her stride away, her chin thrust high as if she'd just won some major battle, even though her movements still looked wobbly, almost as if she was having a hard time making the transformation from warm and soft to cold and aloof. And she had been only too warm and soft and alive a moment ago. He'd felt her sculpted perfection under the glance of his hand. He'd sensed her feminine power. She was magnificent when she was enraged, and yet with a vulnerability that cracked any hard edges right off.

No wonder his father had fallen so hard. He suppressed a growl. He didn't want to think about her with his father! To throw herself away on someone like him—*what a waste*!

But if she'd thought she'd got away with the last word—bad luck.

'My father always was a sucker for a bit on the side,' he reminded her, 'but for all the millions you've been gifted, I sincerely hope he got enough *bang for his buck*.'

Her eyes blazed with fury in a face flushed with rage. '*How dare you!*' she fired, wheeling her body around to confront him, her stance aggressive, ready to fight. 'You can say or think what you like about me—I don't care!—but I will *not* stand by and hear you denigrate your father's memory. What kind of son are you that you can say such things when Laurence is barely cold in his grave? Your father was a man of integrity—not that you'd have any concept what that means!'

His eyebrows rose of their own accord. So she still had fight? He had to hand it to her, she didn't give up easily. But then, given the right financial incentive, she'd soon buckle.

'Trust me,' he assured her, as he leaned back lazily against the desk. 'I know more about my father than you give me credit for.'

She laughed. 'I'd sooner put my trust in a crocodile!'

'Come, now, Ruby,' he soothed, setting his voice to bored reasonableness. 'You know you don't have to defend my father any more. So drop the act. You've got your reward. Why not take it?'

'What? You seriously think I consider Laurence's bizarre bequest as some kind of *reward*? By forcing me to work alongside you? A prison sentence would be more appealing right now.'

He pushed himself away from the desk towards her. 'For once, I couldn't agree more.'

Her eyes narrowed as he moved closer, as if surprised by his ready agreement, her body becoming more erect, more defiant with each step he took.

'Clearly neither of us wants to have anything to do with the other. So I have the perfect solution.' He smiled. 'I'll buy you out. I'll pay for your share of the company with cold hard cash. You can be out of Broome on the first available flight. Out of here and able to take advantage of those job opportunities you've got lined up elsewhere. Not that you'll need a job ever again with what you'll walk away with.'

Oh, yes, the idea definitely held appeal for her, he could tell by the tilt of her head, the hope in her eyes. Was she working out her price? Without a doubt.

'The lawyer said—'

'Whatever the lawyer said is irrelevant,' he argued with a swipe of his hand for emphasis. 'This is between you and me. We're the major shareholders now. What we decide goes.'

'And the launch?'

'Is almost set to go. You'll get credit for the designs, of course' —*and the blame when the collection fails*— 'and you'll be free to set yourself up doing whatever you want. Except this time, you won't have to go looking for pearls. This time the whole world will be your oyster.'

She hesitated, and he could see he almost had her, just as he'd always known he would. *Because he knew her type only too well.*

He pressed home his advantage. 'The chance of a fresh start,' he argued softly. 'With as much money as you'll ever need.'

Suddenly—*unexpectedly*—she shook her head. 'No,' she insisted. 'There's no way I could do that. You're forgetting

Laurence. He wanted me to stay and help manage the company. He didn't want me to take the money and run. He knew the business would need some kind of continuity.'

Zane threw his hands up in the air, as much with frustration at her sudden turn-around as with the slight to his management skills. He might have been away from the business for a few years, but who the hell was *she* to doubt his talents? 'I grew up in this business! I led the most aggressive and successful merchant-banking operation in London. And you think I'm not capable of taking over from my father?'

She surveyed him coolly after his outburst. 'Your father clearly had doubts.'

He clamped his mouth shut over a hissed breath. Oh, for someone who looked like a goddess, her words came with an acid burn. If she was trying to drive his price up, she was doing a damned fine job of it. Yet no price would be too large to have her gone!

'I'll pay you out,' he reiterated, the words squeezed out between his teeth. 'I'll pay a premium of twenty per cent on the shares' worth. You'll walk away with a fortune. You won't get a better deal anywhere.'

Her eyes widened. 'You'd pay me that much?'

More, he knew, if that's what it took. 'Then you'll take it?'

She shook her head and again his hopes dived.

'Keep your precious money, Zane. I'm not in the market for a better deal. Because you've just confirmed what I'd already suspected. I can't sell my shares and leave you to take over completely. Do you really think I could abandon the employees' ten per cent share to your mercy? What chance would they have? You'd probably do your best to steamroller them just as you're trying to steamroller me.'

'I'll take care of them.'

'I don't think so. Because if your management skills mirror

your people skills, then this company is in major trouble. There's no way I'd leave you to run this company on your own.'

He swallowed his pride and asked the one question he thought he'd never hear himself ask. 'So, how much do you want?'

It was a victory of sorts. Even she could see that. No matter that he was no doubt still regarding her as some kind of gold-digger, out to extract whatever she could from his father's business while she had the chance. He'd all but pounced on her earlier hesitation as confirmation of his prejudices. And she *had* hesitated, because for a few moments the prospect of leaving had seemed so attractive—the thought of escaping from this incessant sparring, the thought of never seeing Zane again, was like a siren's song calling out to her in her mind. Especially when the alternative, staying in Broome, was the last thing she wanted to do. She didn't want to work alongside Zane. That future was fraught with turmoil and danger and constant conflict, *but be damned if she'd let him drive her out*.

'You don't get it,' she told him. 'I don't want your money. You can't buy me out of this company.'

'*Everyone* has a price.'

She looked up at him and smiled. 'Then maybe you should just face the fact you can't afford mine!'

'You won't stay,' he warned. 'You won't last ten minutes after I return from London, if you're here that long. And then you'll beg for me to buy you out. Then you'll take the money and run!'

She curled one lip up at him. 'There's no way I'll sell out to you. I'd sooner *die* than leave you in charge!

Damn this weather! Zane pushed back in his leather executive chair and locked his arms together high above his head, stretching shoulders and muscles weary from long days and nights at his desk reorganising his business holdings. Outside his office, small hail crashed horizontally into the windows, leaving icy trails down the glass and rendering his prime city view a blurry mess of grey.

It was supposed to be spring, but for the last few days he'd seen enough sleet to last a lifetime. And for the first time in his life he couldn't wait to get back to Broome. Because right now Zane needed sunshine and heat. He needed colour and contrast that only Broome could provide, from the fertile green mangroves to the azure blue waters of Roebuck Bay; from the red pindar dust of the dirt roads leading out of town to the pristine white sands of Cable Beach.

And he needed to see one particular woman....

He jerked upright in his chair and slammed his fists down hard against the desk.

Damn Ruby Clemenger!

From the moment he'd arrived back in London, instead of concentrating on how he would defray the management of his European interests, his mind had been gate-crashed with non-stop visions of Ruby, sending his mind reeling and his plans into disarray. No wonder it had taken him longer to organise his affairs than he'd expected; it had been impossible to concentrate on affairs of business when he had in mind affairs of a much more carnal nature. The visions had plagued him by day, the dreams had tormented him at night and the hunger gnawed at his insides like a vicious rodent seeking escape.

Visions of her lying naked on his bed, her hair splayed across his pillow, framing her face, her eyes wild with need. Dreams of being tangled together with her, satisfying that need in the best way he knew how. But it was the hunger that was the worst of all. Hunger for a woman's honey-gold limbs wrapped around him, holding him to her, her head thrown back in ecstasy while he took them both over the edge...

He must be going mad! Why should his father's mistress

stir such thoughts in his mind? She might be beautiful, she might feel like honeyed perfection in his hands, but she wasn't for him. She never had been.

His father had seen to that!

He growled as he closed down his notebook computer. It had been a long time since he'd had a woman. Too long. And it was no help at all that the woman he thought most about right now was off-limits, even if she hadn't been half a world away.

He made a few quick calls before shrugging into his coat and heading for the elevator. His work here was mostly done—his second-in-charge could handle any residual matters, it was time he was handed responsibility, anyway.

Because he needed to get back to Broome. And it had nothing to do with the visions, nothing to do with the dreams or the hunger. In fact, it made good business sense. Because the sooner he got back to Broome, the sooner he could fix up whatever mess she'd made in his absence.

This late at night the slick city streets were quiet fodder for the Porsche's throaty appetite. He pulled up in front of his terraced house, the caged street trees dancing erratically in the squalls, the reflections from the street lights making crazy patterns on the wet roads, and a welcoming light glowing in his downstairs reception room.

Three weeks to the day! Ruby dragged in a breath, battling to downplay the shivers zipping along her spine as she forced her eyes from the desk calendar. But of course she was nervous! The Passion Collection launch was barely two short months away and there was still so much to do—it had nothing to do with Zane's imminent return.

Her eyes drifted from the piece of jewellery she was examining one final time and back to the calendar. Who was she trying to kid? Twenty-one days he'd been gone and for each one of those days she'd looked at the calendar and wondered, when would he return?

And was he thinking about her as much as she was thinking about him?

Damn the man! She didn't want to think about him—didn't want to have anything to do with him. So why was it that even while he was away she couldn't get him out of her mind? Why was it that, even when she was asleep, her dreams were filled with visions of Zane—troubling, heated images that left her sheets knotted and her body strangely aching come first light?

It was like slow torture, this incessant wondering. He'd skirted around any mention of his return in the infrequent business phone calls they'd had. He'd avoided any mention in their email communication. And so with every passing day her sense of dread grew. But it had to end soon. He wouldn't leave her here for too long to manage on her own. He wouldn't stay in London a day longer than it took.

He'd be back.

Back to claim his inheritance.

Back to make her life hell!

She shuddered, and the heavy piece in her hand slipped through her fingers and on to the desk, breaking her out of her thoughts.

'Think!' she demanded of herself, as she picked up the magnificent pendant, the centrepiece of the Passion Collection, checking it to ensure her clumsiness hadn't harmed the precious piece, and her favourite from the collection.

Slowly she spun the magnificent item in her fingers, its delicate ribbons of yellow gold and *pavé*-set diamonds interspersed with strategically placed gold South Sea pearls. At first glance it could be taken merely as a beautiful piece, a successful juxtaposition of art, science and the best that Mother

Nature could provide. But at a certain angle, in certain lighting, another image emerged. Two lovers intertwined, their skin tones captured in the warm lustre of the pearls, their bodies entwined by golden limbs, their passion for ever captured in the warm glow of one thousand tiny diamonds.

A thrill of achievement coursed through her veins as she cradled the piece in her palm. She'd done it! It was the most wondrous piece she'd ever created, the illusion a triumph.

So why was it that images from her heated dreams invaded her thoughts right now? Why should her body tingle with that now familiar prickle of need?

Why should the pendant remind her of Zane?

For once the burr of the telephone was a welcome intrusion. She listened to her harried PA for a few moments before responding. 'It's okay, Claudette. Put her through.'

She heard a dull click and then, 'I want to speak to Zane, not another secretary!' The cool Nordic accent was no match for the heat of her delivery.

Ruby took a breath, her interest piqued. 'I'm sorry, but at the moment Zane isn't in the office. I'm Ruby Clemenger, can I help?'

'Oh.' There was a pause at the other end. 'You're Ruby? Zane's told me all about you,' she added, her voice changing tone, softer and less aggressive and so much more sexy that it almost purred with satisfaction. 'Zane tells me you're quite beautiful.'

Ruby was rendered speechless. Zane had been talking about her to this woman? *And he'd said that?* Rallying her fractured thoughts, she managed, 'And you are?'

'Anneleise Christiansen.' There was a pause, and then, 'Surely Zane's told you about me?'

Not even once, thought Ruby, curiosity warring with suspicion—clearly this woman was no mere business associate!

But then they'd never really had time to discuss anything, not when they were always sparring with each other over the business. There'd never been a chance to get beyond Laurence and the Bastiani Corporation. 'Of course he has, Anneleise,' she lied, giving the expected response. 'But I'm sorry, I'm not sure when he'll be back. Did you want to leave a message?'

'Oh…I just wanted to make sure he made it back to Broome safely—it's such a very long journey and he looked so tired when he kissed me goodbye.'

He'd kissed her goodbye? Oh, no, Anneleise was definitely no business associate. The candid reality of the situation washed over her like a cold wave. She scrambled to focus on the caller, attempting to think logically, but still it didn't stop the images invading her mind—images of Zane kissing someone else, *wanting* someone else, having to tear himself away from the woman with the sex-kitten voice to return to Broome, tired from too much kissing, *too much sex*.

Not that it should matter. She didn't care who he slept with, it wasn't as if Zane really meant anything to her—she didn't even like the man!

So why then had she spent so much of the last three weeks thinking about him? What the hell was wrong with her?

She'd *known* what a bastard Zane was from the very beginning, abandoning his father for so many years without a word, talking about him as if he'd somehow ruined Zane's life! She'd known *exactly* what kind of man he was, and yet still she'd dreamt of him at night, thinking forbidden thoughts, feeling secret things, waking up wanting and strangely unquenched.

How could she have let herself fall victim to his power, if only in her dreams, when he'd only ever treated her like some gold-digging mistress from the start?

She'd been crazy to let her mind be used that way. But now

that she knew he had the no doubt lovely Anneleise back in London waiting for him—never again!

'He'll be sorry he missed you,' she offered at last, thrusting her wayward thoughts aside. 'I'll let him know you rang when he gets in.'

'Oh, and in case he comes in too late to call here, please tell him…' The voice at the end of the line faltered and paused. Ruby heard what sounded suspiciously like a sob. 'I'm doing my best, like he said—trying not to think about just how far away he is.'

Ruby put the phone down, a tumble of emotions and thoughts assailing her. She wasn't disappointed he had a girlfriend, she wouldn't let herself be. That kind of man was bound to have a dozen girlfriends or mistresses or both. So that cold wash of sensation she'd felt when she'd realised who Anneleise was must have had more to do with relief than anything.

In fact, she ought to be grateful to Anneleise for calling. All the times Zane had seemed so physically threatening, all the times he'd invaded her space and consumed her oxygen, the time he'd handled the pendant at her throat—the touch of his fingertips like a scorching brand; the time he'd run the back of his hand down her body, so softly and yet with such devastating effect—he'd done all of those things merely to unsettle her, to make her uneasy and uncomfortable and afraid. They were part of his inventory of tactics, designed to improve his chances of making her leave. And hadn't those tactics almost convinced her before!

She wouldn't fall for that again.

At least now when Zane returned she wouldn't embarrass herself edging around him, half anticipating him making a move on her, and overreacting if he did. She could be cool and professional.

She picked up the passion pendant once again, twirling the work of art in her fingers, wondering how she could do some things so well, how she could get others so wrong. The pendant's inner image mocked her. How she'd ever designed it was a mystery to her—what did she know of passion and romance, anyway? Her history proved she was one very sad judge of men.

It was good to be back. Zane closed his eyes and let the streaming water cascade over his head, neck and shoulders, massaging muscles wearied by hours stuck in a plane. But in spite of the long flight he felt extraordinarily alive, as if just walking out of the plane into Broome's tropical air had reinvigorated him.

He snapped off the hot water, giving his body a sudden and very necessary cold burst. The extra few days he'd spent with Anneleise had done little to take the edge off his need.

He dried and dressed quickly, noting the time. It was getting late, but he had no doubt Ruby would still be at the office. Intentionally he'd avoided any word of when he would return. He wanted to surprise her and give her no chance of covering up anything she didn't want him to see. By now she'd no doubt agree she wasn't cut out to run anything, let alone a business as complex as the Bastiani Corporation. By now she might be more than ready to accept his generous offer.

What he hadn't expected was the gut-punch reaction to seeing her again. He found her sitting in the workroom, making notes as she sat at the long central bench, her sun-streaked hair coiled behind her head, the look on her face intense as she concentrated on the items displayed around her. Around her, more work benches lined the walls, the racks of delicate tools neatly stacked, a colourful mural on the end wall making up for the lack of any natural light except from the narrowest of windows set up high in the maximum-security room.

Under the artificial lighting, even surrounded by some of the most precious gems on earth, she was the brightest and most beautiful object here. The crossover dress she was wearing accentuated the generous swell of her breasts and her narrow waist. The stool below hid nothing of the feminine curves of her behind or the long, fine sweep of her legs tucked together underneath. His mouth went dry. No wonder his father had wanted her. No wonder his father had taken her for his own!

His hands clenched into fists as he stood watching her. What was she doing here, anyway, playing with her jewels? Surely there was real work that needed to be done!

'What are you doing?'

She jumped at the sound of his voice, her head snapping around. Her eyes spent but a moment taking him in, clearly surprised at being interrupted, before instantly freezing over. She turned straight back to her work and continued making notes.

'So you're back,' she said dismissively. 'Good trip?'

He registered an uncomfortable rumble of frustration. He'd expected more of a reaction than this bored disinterest. Where was the panic? Where was the rush to cover her tracks? And where was her physical reaction to his return?

'Getting ready for the launch?' he asked, moving from his place near the door, drawn to her in spite of himself, curious after so many weeks to once more breathe in her scent and see if it was just the way he'd remembered.

'Given the launch is only weeks away,' she said without looking up, 'the question might be considered redundant.'

'And, of course, nothing else is happening between now and then with the business.'

She looked up sharply. 'Your point being?'

'As you say, the launch is weeks away. Couldn't what

you're doing wait for a more appropriate time? Aren't there more pressing matters to deal with in the meantime?'

'And you'd be the best judge of what a "more appropriate time" is, I imagine, given you've been away for three weeks.'

'Why are you always so argumentative?'

'You might ask yourself the same question.'

His teeth ground together at her reply. But he was closer now, so close that he had an answer for that first silent question of his. He breathed in her scent, tasting it on his tongue, and he felt a strange, familiar heat move through him. If possible, she smelt even better than he remembered. Fresher. More alive.

More woman.

'I thought you might like to have dinner with me.' He heard himself speak the words and wondered what the hell he was thinking. He'd been planning on coming back, all guns blazing. But now… 'There's a lot that's happened the last few weeks we should catch up on.'

'You think?' she responded absently, studiously ignoring his presence opposite the bench as she reached for a pair of pearl earrings suspended on golden spirals, examining them closely before jotting down a couple more notes.

What the hell was she playing at! Three weeks ago she'd reacted to him like a woman should. She'd been warm and sensual, her body and her femininity responding to him even while her mouth spat fire. And that was just the way he wanted it. Not that he was interested in her for himself, his father had seen to that. He was more interested in the shares his father had bequeathed her, and if he could make her more uncomfortable about staying and holding on to them, then so much the better. So, what had happened in the interim that she could be so cool towards him? Whatever it was, he didn't like it.

'What do you think you're doing?' he demanded.

'The running sheet for the launch. We've got three models flying in from Europe, all with different colouring. I'm working out which model should wear what. Darker hair will suit some designs better than blonde, but they have to co-ordinate with the designer clothes we've arranged for them, as well. It's too important to be left to chance on the night.'

'No!' he insisted. 'Not that.'

'Then what?' she asked innocently enough, but still without returning his gaze.

'Look at me,' he said, sick of talking to the top of her head.

'I'm busy right now, Zane, and it's late. Can this wait until tomorrow?'

'*Look* at me!'

She froze and for a few moments her breathing was her only movement. Then she replaced the earrings, clasped her hands together on the bench and looked up at him, her eyes wide like a schoolgirl brought to task by her teacher.

'Yes?'

Her cool eyes and bland expression fired up his temperature. What was going on? She was no ice-virgin. It was all he could do not to lunge over the bench and take that oh-so-innocent face in his hands and kiss those lips senseless, until she'd shed this ridiculous attitude and was begging him to make love to her.

And he was only too ready to oblige!

She should never have looked up.

Immediately Ruby longed to turn away from those brooding eyes, that demanding expression and the entire domineering package, but she dared not now. She couldn't back down. And she wouldn't have to, not if she remembered what kind of man he was.

He's arrogant, she reminded herself, starting off a checklist of his shortcomings, *he's bitter and resentful at his father's treatment of him, no matter how well deserved*. And, given the fact he'd kept Anneleise a complete secret, not entirely honourable while he'd feigned interest in her. Was he so low as to stoop to two-timing? She couldn't put it past him, not that she'd be giving him the opportunity!

'All right,' she said with new resolve, angling her chin higher in defiance, 'now you have my undivided attention, what's so important?'

'Have you nearly finished what you're doing?'

'Does it matter?'

'The running sheet! Have you nearly finished?'

He stood over her glowering, his hands planted wide on the bench, his body leaning dangerously towards hers. She tried to ignore the width of his shoulders, the power in his muscled arms as they braced tight against the bench. She battled to keep her eyes away from the vee at his open neck, where the olive skin gleamed under its dusting of dark curls.

She swallowed. 'Maybe, for now. But I don't see—'

'Then I'm taking you out.'

She started to shake her head. 'There's no need—'

'It's getting late. You have to eat.' He leaned closer, until he filled her field of vision and his masculine aura filled the air around her, so thick and intense that she could almost taste it. But what was worse—*much worse* for someone who'd decided he wouldn't affect her any more—his presence triggered a hunger inside her that no mere meal would assuage. He was so fresh from his shower that his dark hair still curled damply above his collar, with his scent infused by nothing more than pure unadulterated essence of man. She swallowed. She had to get out of here.

'And,' he pressed, 'we have matters to discuss. I need a full report on this launch of yours,' he continued. 'You're spending one hell of a lot of money shipping in models and celebrity guests.'

'The budget's already been approved—'

'Not by me! I want a full report.'

She pushed herself up straight, fighting off the unwelcome tingling awareness in her flesh that seemed to follow breathing him in. Damn, but how could he still affect her this way after all she knew about him? She must be more tired than she thought. She needed sleep, deep, uninterrupted sleep, for a chance to build her defences, a chance to overcome this annoying vulnerability that accompanied her weariness. So tomorrow they might talk, but tonight she was determined to sleep.

'Can't I deliver you a report tomorrow, Zane?' she suggested, sliding off the stool, needing to put more distance between them. She started collecting up her papers and slotting jewellery back in secure boxes. 'It's getting late and you must be tired after the flight.'

He moved around the bench to her side, short-circuiting her plans for escape. 'Are you pretending that in all the time I was away, nothing happened in a business this size that I should be informed about now?'

'I sent you emails. Didn't you read them?'

'I read what you sent me.'

'Then that's all there is to know.'

'There's nothing more? Nothing else you had any concerns about?'

She looked up at him, resentful of the way his voice dripped with disbelief. So, to add to her sins, now he thought she was incompetent, incapable of looking after the business she'd been helping Laurence with for years.

'Actually, you're right, Zane. Something did happen that I

should have told you about. I'm sorry it didn't occur to me, not that it will take long to fill you in.'

'Well?' he said.

She locked away the last gems, snapped her notes into her portfolio and stood, facing him. 'You had a message from your girlfriend. She was hoping you'd made it back okay seeing how tired you looked when you kissed her goodbye.'

CHAPTER SIX

HE HESITATED BARELY a second. 'Anneleise called here?'

His words shouldn't have made a dent on her victorious exit. It had felt so good taking this man by surprise that she'd been almost gleeful as she'd made her way out of the room. And yet those very same words—'*Anneleise called here?*'—confirmed what she'd suspected, that Zane had a woman waiting for him back in London, and suddenly she knew there'd been no mistake, no misunderstanding. His interest in her had nothing to do with attraction and everything to do with intimidation.

And somehow her victory didn't feel quite so satisfying any more. Somehow it felt flat and empty, and it shouldn't have, because that would mean she cared, and she didn't, not really, and that only made her angrier.

She spun around, sick of the deception, sick of the lies and the pressure-cooker situation she found herself in every time she met up with this man. 'Of course it was Anneleise!' she snapped. 'I don't believe you, Zane. Exactly how many girl-friends do you have?'

'Anneleise is hardly my girlfriend.'

She blinked her surprise, realising he'd moved closer while her back was turned, so much closer that his nearness took her unawares and made her take a step backwards against the bench.

'Your mistress, then.'

'And that would bother you, would it, that I have a mistress?'

'Not at all,' she insisted, looking anywhere but at him. 'Your private life is no concern of mine.'

He said nothing, but when her eyes found him again it was to witness the corners of his mouth slowly turn up. Somewhere his eyes had found a glint that gave them an edge— heat, power, *danger*—setting off a sudden bloom of warm tingles inside. Her breath caught as she battled uselessly to quell the reaction.

'Forget Anneleise,' he said, moving closer. 'She's just an old friend. You don't need to feel jealous of her.'

'Oh, no,' she protested, shaking her head. She wasn't jealous! She didn't care! 'You've got the wrong idea.'

He smiled a wolfish smile of disbelief that made much too rapid a change to another expression—more intent— more urgent.

More ravenous.

'I missed you,' he admitted, his voice low and rough. 'I missed your arguments and your flashing blue eyes and most of all I missed how good it felt to touch you.' He lifted one hand and smoothed a loose tendril of hair behind her ear. She shuddered as his fingers grazed her ear, mesmerised by his words, her pulse hammering so loud in her veins she was sure he would feel its frantic beat.

His head tilted closer, his eyes forcing hers to lock with his and his fingers cupping her chin. 'Did you think about me while I was gone?'

'I…' She blinked, casting her eyes from side to side, working out the quickest route to escape. 'I honestly don't recall. I had a lot to think about.'

This time he laughed, throaty and low in a way that warmed her spine to melting point and made her forget all about running. 'That's a shame, because I did. I thought about you a lot. You cost me a lot of sleep.'

'That's a pity,' she said with a lot more bravado than she felt. 'Maybe you can take something for it.'

'Oh,' he said, his lips just a whisper from her own, his eyes seductive, their holding power like a magnet. 'I intend to....'

Time slowed between them, her world suddenly shrunken to that split-second of understanding, to that hitched breath of anticipation that came in the moments before a kiss. Already she could feel his lips on hers. Already she could taste him. Already she was welcoming him....

Momentarily he noticed her aqua eyes change, swirling with questions and uncertainty, but then his focus moved wholly to the sensation of meeting her lips. He welcomed their tentative warmth, he revelled in their sweetness. With his free arm he circled her waist to prevent any sudden retreat, as the hand cupping her chin swept around her neck, but aside from one initial bolt of shock she made no attempt to escape. Emboldened, he moved deeper into the kiss. She was warm and lush and the way she tasted in his mouth, the way her curves fitted so tantalisingly against his body, only ramped up his desire.

His lips moved over hers, softly, caressing, *coaxing*. Damn, but she was sweet. He'd known she'd taste good, but he'd had no idea just how much. He'd known she felt good, but he'd had no idea how much better she'd feel pressed up close against him.

Her hands appeared at his waist, her fingers settling and curling into his shirt as if unsure, hesitant. He trawled in a breath at the contact. It was a start—she was touching him, and he willed her to explore further. It wasn't enough to feel her hands through his shirt, he wanted to feel her hands tight against his skin, her nails biting into his flesh. He wanted to feel her naked body glide under his.

He wanted her. Now!

He found the slide clamping her hair. A squeeze of the ends reaped immediate benefits as the length spilled free, tumbling down over her shoulders. He let the clasp fall unheeded to the bench behind as he spread his fingers wide through the unravelling coils of her hair, enjoying the play of the silken strands over his hand and directing her head exactly where his mouth wanted her.

He shifted her away from the bench, enjoying the curve of her behind under his hand, using it to press her hungrily into contact with his aching need as he left her lips to trail hot kisses down the line of her throat. A second hand joined the first, lifting her, pulling her against him and higher…

What the hell was she thinking? The clatter of her hair clip broke through the sensual fog he'd spun around her. Her eyes flew open to the harsh light of reality while even now the liquid warmth of his kisses urged her to close her eyes and give herself up to sensation again.

But that was exactly her problem—she hadn't been thinking at all. And look where it had got her—plastered against him, the bold evidence of his arousal between them, shocking yet sensual, firing up her body and turning her mind completely away from logic to matters much more primitive.

The hands now knotted in his shirt fisted in the fabric and pushed, trying to make distance between them even as his lips ascended the line of her throat to her mouth again. She swallowed and turned her head away, her hands pressing hopelessly against his firm torso. So much strength, so much muscled power lay beneath her hands, so much to resist. And her body felt so weak, so languid and liquid, her spine soft and yielding, her breasts hyper-sensitive and welcoming of every tiny graze against his shirt. But she had to resist!

His mouth sought hers, his hand steering her head closer.

'Zane,' she urged, turning her head, resisting the pressure. 'Stop this.'

His mouth worked the line of her jaw while one hand slid up around between them, cupping one breast almost reverentially, squeezing it so tenderly she almost reeled from the simple and yet utterly sensual wave of pleasure that roiled through her.

'You want this,' he whispered huskily against her skin so that even his words were a caress. 'I can feel it.' Then he brushed his thumb over her peaked nipple and she shuddered anew as a battery of sensations assailed her, setting her core ablaze and melting her closer to him, when being closer was the last thing she needed.

In desperation she summoned the most potent weapon she had in her defence.

'And what do you want?' she demanded in a quavering voice she barely recognised as her own. 'To find out how you rate compared to your father?'

He let her go as if she were poison, thrusting her away from him without a word. Shakily, she seemed to come to terms with her sudden release and made her swift withdrawal from his presence, one eye over her shoulder watching him guardedly, waiting for him in case he struck again. But he didn't move. He let her go and only when she had removed herself from the offices completely did he let his fist slam hard into the surface of the bench.

The crunch of bone and flesh against the solid bench top hardly registered. But then, nothing could feel worse than the self-disgust he felt for himself right now. Three weeks had turned him into nothing more than an animal! He would have had her—he could have had her—right here tonight. He was so close to lifting her atop the bench and pushing himself between her thighs and taking her....

He would have taken his father's mistress!

So much for believing himself a notch up on the evolutionary scale. He was no better than his father. No better than the man he held in such low esteem. He made his way out to his car, absently rubbing his fist in his other hand, still burning with need, high on testosterone.

High on self-loathing.

It was bad enough that Ruby had slept with his father. It was bad enough that she'd loved him and had been his mistress.

But his real problem was why, in spite of all that, he still wanted her.

She should never have let him kiss her! How could she pretend that she didn't want his advances, how could she claim she was unaffected by his sheer magnetism when she had all but given him an open invitation?

For two days they'd avoided each other, managing for the most part to stay out of each other's way, barely speaking beyond a grunt when they came across each other, but that wouldn't last, Ruby knew, as she switched on her desktop computer and put her purse in her desk. They couldn't run the company that way. Sooner or later they were going to have to talk. She looked down at her diary notes and swallowed when she saw what her PA had registered alongside nine-thirty.

Meeting with Zane—boardroom.

She knew there were matters to discuss—Zane was still waiting for her report on the launch budget and there was a visit to the opening of the imminent pearl harvest to organise—but knowing there was work to be done wasn't enough to stop the overwhelming sense of dread surrounding her. She didn't want to see Zane; she didn't want to be exposed to him or his powerful magnetism. *Didn't want to be attracted to him!*

"You want this," he'd told her, and he'd been right, and no amount of denying it would make a difference. She'd let him kiss her—it had been her choice. She'd allowed him to caress her, to touch her intimately like he possessed her and she'd enjoyed it and she'd wanted more. She'd wanted to be swept away.

She'd wanted to be possessed.

And she could have been, if she hadn't snapped to her senses. But even then, it hadn't been her determination that had saved her. It had been Laurence. Just as he'd protected her once before when she'd needed help, so he was her shield now.

Just how long would Zane believe they'd been lovers? And what would happen if he discovered the truth? What good would she be to Bastiani Corporation then—unable to leave if she was to carry out Laurence's wishes, unable to live with herself if she succumbed to what her body craved?

It must never happen.

He was waiting for her when she got there, firmly entrenched at the head of the table, his face grim, the tapping pencil in his hand signalling his impatience, although the clock on the wall behind clearly showed she was barely a minute late.

'Nice of you to join me at last,' he snapped.

She smiled as sweetly as she could under the circumstances. 'Oh, I assure you, the pleasure is all mine.'

She could see his jaw grinding in response, his lips itching to let go with another sarcastic jibe and she knew he was still angry with himself for what had almost happened two nights before. And that suited her just fine. The angrier he was, the easier it was to forget how he'd made her feel and the easier it would be to repel him.

He waited while she sat down two places from him,

twisting the pencil between his fingers. No way was she going to sit any closer to his humming tension.

'Right,' he said, 'let's start with that report you promised me on the launch budget.'

Two hours later Ruby felt like she'd been tumble-dried, her mind reeling from the relentless interrogation she'd just been subjected to, but if he was impressed by the way she'd defended and fought for and justified every last dollar to be spent, he didn't show it. Instead, his mood seemed to be getting blacker by the minute.

They ran through the remaining items on the agenda more quickly, working out security arrangements for the launch, sparring over a small change to employee conditions Ruby had proposed and making plans for a visit the next week to one of the pearl farms for the start of the upcoming harvest. Ruby wasn't keen on accompanying Zane, but the pearl-farming business had changed a lot since he was last involved and it was important that she passed on things that she'd learned, now that Laurence wasn't around to teach Zane himself.

That matter finally settled, Ruby started collecting her papers to leave, when he spoke.

'One last thing,' Zane began. 'I think it's time we set down some ground rules for how the business should be managed. Here's how I see things working. Now that I'm back in Broome, I'll take over the day-to-day management of the company and you can go back to design work full time.'

Ruby felt her blood pressure surge as she sank back into her chair. She dredged up a thin smile. 'I appreciate that you're so interested in my input in making these ground rules and in ensuring I have time for my design work, but I actually enjoy the managerial side of the business, Zane, so I'd prefer to keep my hand in if it's all the same to you.'

One glance at his scowling face was more than enough to tell her that it wasn't the same to him.

'That will hardly be necessary,' he countered. 'I'm in charge now. And you'll have a chance to focus on what you're employed here to do.'

'You seem to forget I'm not just "employed" here now. I actually own almost half of the business, a business I was helping to manage in addition to my design work before Laurence died.'

'My father was sick. I won't need your help.'

'Laurence wasn't always sick. *Plus*, I believe my share in the company entitles me to a say in how the business is managed—just as your father obviously intended.'

His nostrils flared and a vein in his temple pulsed dangerously in the silence that followed her comment.

'Don't make the mistake,' he warned softly, the dark storm cells of his eyes never leaving hers, 'of making this more difficult than it has to be.'

His quiet words carried like a threat in the super-charged atmosphere and she only hoped her blue eyes relayed the ice-cold hostility she felt for him right now.

'Or what?' she challenged. 'You'll kiss me again?'

The pencil between Zane's fingers snapped. She held her breath as the pieces tumbled from his fingers and clattered on to the table, a sound that only served to ramp up the tense atmosphere.

Zane didn't care about the pencil. His head was pounding and his eyes were too busy burning up a trail from her eyes to her sweet lips. Oh, yeah, they sure were sweet. Lush and tangy like ripe tropical fruit and only too eager to open under his and be devoured, despite her protestations. And now she was daring him to kiss her?

Not a chance!

He shifted his gaze back to her eyes again and allowed himself a smile, feeling for the first time today that he had the upper hand at last.

'If that's what you're hoping for, then I'm afraid you're in for a big disappointment.'

He left the room before she could protest, satisfied he'd got in the last word and smug in the knowledge that he'd survived the entire meeting, resisting the urge to throw her on to the boardroom table and finish the job he'd started two nights before.

He could resist her, despite her lush curves and her sweet mouth.

He would resist her. And, dammit, he'd show her her rightful place in the process!

CHAPTER SEVEN

TWO HOURS NORTH of Broome, in a pristine and sheltered cove off the Kimberley coast of red cliffs and green mangroves and pure white sand, the boat met up with the operations vessel that would manage the harvest of the first of Bastiani's ten pearl farms. Here the waters were clear and blue, the oysters lying below the surface of the water in panels attached to long lines in order for them to sway back and forth with the flow of the rich tides.

Ruby lifted her face to the sky and breathed in the warm salt-tinged air as the high-speed launch nudged alongside the operations vessel. It was so good to be away from the tension-laden air of the office, not that the source of that tension had remained there.

Today he looked more relaxed than she'd ever seen him, in tailored shorts and polo top, his thick dark hair whipping around his face as the power boat had made its exhilarating trip along the coast, his sunglasses hiding eyes she'd sensed were parked long and intense on her if the prickling sensation in her skin was any indication.

Their meeting a few days ago had precipitated a frosty intolerance between them in the office. Whenever possible, they'd avoided each other. When it was unavoidable that they had to meet, they'd grated on each other like icebergs passing through the same narrow strait. But underneath the chill, Ruby had felt his heat, the seething resentment leaching from him like a life-force, his eyes always tracking her movements like a predator. Watching. Waiting.

Why did he persist? If he'd accepted she was off-limits, why did he still watch her? Why couldn't he just leave her be? Or was he merely determined to get rid of her any way he could and he'd decided that making her uncomfortable, bombarding her constantly with this knife-edge tension, was the way to do it?

Damn him, he wouldn't be rid of her that easily!

She gathered up her few things as the boats bumped together over the light swell, determined not to let him undermine her trip today. There was a real buzz of excitement among everyone to be here at the start of a new harvest and Ruby felt an enormous sense of expectancy. Every pearl was special, but there were some that caught a designer's eye, some that simply begged to be set off in the perfect setting. Right now she couldn't wait to see what new opportunities the harvest turned up.

She turned to the side of the boat to find Zane offering his hand to assist her as she climbed from the fast launch up on to the operations vessel. His eyes were masked by dark glasses, his jaw tight and for a moment she drew back. The last time they'd touched each other... But he was only offering a hand and it would be churlish to refuse, so with a hesitant nod she held out her hand, allowing him to wrap it securely with his larger one, anchoring her to him as she clambered up and over. She jumped to the deck alongside, wanting their contact to be as brief as possible. But he used his leverage to pull her closer before she landed, so that she had to reach out a hand to his chest to stop herself from falling into him.

She looked up into his face, suddenly breathless, her heart racing irrationally and with the innate knowledge that under those dark glasses his eyes burned hot and heavy.

'Thank you,' she managed to say, *I think*, as she stepped back, peeling her hand from his chest before her fingers had the chance to curl and test the firm, muscled flesh just milli-metres below.

The grim set of his mouth curled just enough to hint at a smile before it disappeared behind a sigh. He sucked in a breath and released her, turning away instead to greet the op-erations vessel manager.

Ruby blinked and gathered her thoughts as the manager welcomed them aboard before giving them a brief tour of the vessel, introducing them to the crew as they went. Then they waited while the first panels of oysters were recovered from the sea and watched, fascinated, as the shells were prised open just enough to remove the treasure within.

In awe, they watched silently as the technician used a pair of long tweezers to remove a perfect pearl from the very first oyster before skilfully seeding the shell with another bead, slightly larger this time, and then releasing the clamp from the shell and completing the operation.

Several times they watched this process, marvelling at the treasure revealed after the shells had been submerged for years beneath the sea.

'How long since you've seen this process?' Ruby whis-pered to him as the technicians continued their delicate work.

'Too long to remember,' he admitted honestly, totally fas-cinated by a world that should be all too familiar to him, but which suddenly seemed new and exciting. 'Things have come a long way. I remember they used to bring the shell to shore to perform these operations.'

She nodded, as the technician repeated the process on the

shells from the next panel, discarding the few that hadn't lived up to expectations for shell and pearl meat. 'This way ensures the oysters are disturbed for the shortest time possible. The yields have increased considerably.'

It made good business sense, and not for the first time Zane was bitterly reminded of what he'd missed out on over the last few years. While he'd been carving his own career out in Europe, trying to prove his point, his father had still been innovating, still improving the business. And for many of the years he'd been away, Ruby had been by his father's side.

And she'd learned something in that time, from what he'd seen—certainly more than what he'd first given her credit for. He shifted slightly, not entirely comfortable with the knowledge that there was more to Ruby than a pleasingly arranged set of physical attributes. Mind you, out here, where they were surrounded by a crew of twenty or more, was the perfect place to appreciate them. He could look, he could admire. Where was the harm in that? He could even touch, like he'd done, taking her hand in his as she'd transferred from the launch and pulling her into him. Out here he could risk that—the touch of her skin, the sweet swell of her curves—without the danger of getting carried away. *Like a taste of forbidden fruit.*

He leaned closer to her now, not because he particularly wanted to ask her another question, but because it was an excuse to get nearer and put his mouth close to her ear and once more breathe in her own individual scent.

'How many pearls will they do today?'

She turned slightly to answer and he caught her aqua eyes flicker with confusion. 'We talked about that on the way out. The vessel should manage around five thousand per day. It should take around ten days to get through the harvest at this particular farm.'

They'd talked about it before? That was news to him. But

then, maybe he'd been more focused on the way she looked, in slim-fitting khaki shorts and a cool white shirt over a white crop top. Not that there was anything overtly sexy about it. Maybe it was the combination of the hip-fitting shorts, the honey-skinned legs, and the mere hint of an outline of a light bra under that fine shirt that did it. Perhaps it was the inch of skin that peeked out so invitingly between her shorts and her knotted shirt whenever she moved the right way. Or maybe it was just that it was her, wrapped up inside it all. Whatever it was, he hadn't been tempted to take his eyes from her the entire trip.

And now she was close enough for him to breathe her in, and to deconstruct all the individual scents that made her up: the tropical tang of her shampoo, the kiss of her subtle body wash, a hint of a perfume, soft and light, and the unmistakable essence of her, heightened by her excitement. It curled into his senses and drew him like a magnet, even when he knew it shouldn't.

Reluctantly he turned his attentions back to the operations and both of them watched intently as the process continued, noting the huge differences in the pearls that were retrieved, each pearl an exciting discovery, some perfectly round, some marked by the constrictions of bands of muscles that had grown about them, some imperfectly shaped and some small ones, called keshi pearls, formed unexpectedly, completely by nature. And the colours were something else. The range went from silver-white to pink and gold and every shade in between, their rich nacre a feature of the South Sea pearl that made them so sought after.

He shared the thrill as each new pearl was discovered. He felt the disappointment when the seeding had failed and he realised how much he'd missed this business. Somehow the cut and thrust of corporate takeover life seemed to pale next to this wild and vivid business.

He looked back at Ruby's profile, her lips plump and slightly parted as she watched the harvest in wonder and awe. And she was so much a part of this business, vital and alive and so fresh.

Forbidden fruit, indeed.

And, oh, so damned tempting.

'The pearls will be graded once they're back in Broome,' Ruby told him as the launch powered its way back. 'We'll keep the best of the gems for future collections and the rest will be exported to other markets overseas.'

He nodded. 'It's good I came out today. So much has changed, even in the space of a decade. It seems my father really knew what he was doing.'

She placed a hand on his forearm and smiled widely up at him like he'd finally said something right. 'Thank you,' she said, her eyes reflecting the aqua of the ocean, the loose tendrils of her hair whipping around her face like they'd come alive.

And her smile reached down deep inside him till it gripped tight and damned near pulled him inside out. He'd never seen her smile like that before and certainly never aimed at him. Completely unexpected it was very, very sexy.

He had to fight the sudden urge to pull her face to his mouth and kiss her senseless. He wanted to feel the way those lips curved under his mouth. He wanted to taste that smile.

And then he'd taste every part of her!

'Thank you for what?' he asked, his voice half-choked, because then he'd already forgotten what she was talking about. Instead he was thinking about that night in the workroom when he'd succumbed to temptation and kissed her, her body supple and pliant and her roundness perfectly filling his hands, cradling his heat. He'd been disgusted with himself for weakening and letting that kiss go so far.

But since then there'd been times he'd regretted he hadn't gone further....

'Thank you,' she answered, 'for finally giving your father credit for something.'

He closed his eyes against the sun, shaking his head as his vision ran blood red. Damn whatever it was she was doing to him!

He didn't want to think about his father right now, and what he thought of him and why, not with her hand resting on his arm and the tendrils of her hair forming a sunkissed halo around her face while thoughts of her he had no right having made him hard.

But if he didn't think about his father, he would likely give in to this inexplicable need he felt for her.

His gut twisted into a knot, hungry and aching for something he couldn't have.

Someone he couldn't have!

He let her hand slip away as he raked his fingers through his hair. For she would never be his. He could never take up where his father had left off. How could he sleep with his father's mistress? How could he make love to the woman his father had bedded? But then, how then could he stay in Broome, living with this insane desire, feeling the need consume him every time she was near, burning to possess her and yet knowing that he never could?

He couldn't live that way! So there was only one answer. *He would have to get rid of her, whatever it took.*

Still locked in his own private machinations, Zane steered the car towards Ruby's hotel. If it wasn't bad enough that he'd been foolish to insist that he drive her to and from the boat dock today, he'd arrived back on land to find a message from Anneleise waiting for him, despite him telling her not to contact him here. So much for sorting things out in London. He would have to do something about her, too. It was also bad enough that she'd turned up at his house uninvited and with a copied key, without pursuing him out here.

Lost in thought, he barely registered it would be night soon, the sun dipping lower, sucking the blue from the sky and transforming it with a pale lemon wash. The colour of the sky was the last thing on his mind. First of all he had to deal with Ruby. He'd go and see the lawyer first chance he had. Derek Finlayson would just have to be made to understand that this arrangement wasn't working, no matter what he believed Laurence had wanted. They couldn't run the company together—not with the way things were between them—not with her history. And if Zane increased his offer for her shares, maybe he could get Finlayson to speak to Ruby and convince her to take it. Maybe she would listen to the lawyer.

Alongside him, Ruby shivered and rubbed her arms.

'Cold?' Zane moved automatically to adjust the air conditioning. It was the first they'd spoken since getting into the car. After a few weeks in London the late afternoon air felt warm to him, but he knew that was different for locals. Once acclimatised to the intense, tropical wet season, anything else felt cool by comparison.

'Not really,' she said, rubbing the bridge of her nose. 'I guess I just didn't realise how tired I am. Today was a good change. It's nice to get out of the office.'

An unwelcome twinge of guilt niggled at him. He'd left her to manage the company by herself while he'd taken care of his business back in London with barely a thought to her professional needs. In fact, he'd been waiting for her to fail, *willing her to fail*. She'd had to handle all her normal design work plus the business side of things that Laurence had bequeathed them both. But in spite of everything he'd believed, she hadn't failed. On the contrary, her business emails during his absence had been to the point, their content clear, and he'd had no need to intervene, no need to question anything she'd recommended, the disasters he'd anticipated never arising.

And then he'd returned and things had got a whole lot more complicated.

He snatched another look sideways while waiting to turn off the highway. The stress had obviously cost her. She'd relaxed back into her chair, her eyes closed, and, highlighted in the sun's setting rays, he could see the shadows under her eyes and the tension that lined her jaw. And yet there was still something about her, the shape of her eyes, the line of her cheek, the fullness of her mouth, generous and inviting. And then there was her body…

She opened her eyes and caught him watching her. Hers widened momentarily, but still she didn't look away. Instead her head tilted slightly and she asked, 'Why do you hate your father so much?'

He turned his attention back to the road, making his turn when it was clear. 'Who says I hate him?'

'Only just about everything you say or do. And the fact you left and didn't bother to contact him for nine years. Today was the first time I've ever heard you say a decent thing about him, but when I mentioned it you clammed up, like you'd broken some vow to yourself never to say a kind word about him.'

That wasn't the reason he'd closed the conversation down, but he was hardly going to tell her what he'd really been thinking about. 'I just call it like I see it.'

'What happened all those years ago that you could just take off like you did? What went wrong?'

Everything, he thought, his knuckles turning white on the steering wheel. *I couldn't bear the sight of him.* 'I had my reasons.'

She was quiet for a moment. Then, 'Does it have anything to do with your mother's death?'

His head snapped around. 'What makes you ask that?' he asked gruffly.

'I don't know. It's just you must have left shortly after she died.'

'She didn't die. She was killed.'

The words hung heavy and full-bodied in the air between them. It didn't make sense. 'Laurence mentioned a car crash.'

'And did he tell you who was driving?'

Desperately she tried to recall the story Laurence had shared with her late one evening after a minor attack some years ago, when he was feeling unusually mortal. 'I'm not sure. But I know it wasn't Laurence, if that's what you're suggesting.'

He laughed, short and bitter as he pulled into the car park opposite the hotel looking over Cable Beach, out to where the sun was a blazing orange-rimmed disc dipping lower and lower towards the ocean in a sky that now glowed in a thousand different shades of gold.

'You're so quick to defend my father! No, he wasn't driving. But did he tell you anything about the woman who was driving the car, the woman who hit the embankment that caused the car to roll over, crushing them both and killing my mother?'

She searched her memory, but whatever he was looking for she couldn't find. 'I don't know. You tell me.'

He exhaled on a long breath, his palms damp and his chest tight like it was bound by steel bands. 'Bonnie Carter,' he squeezed out of lungs bereft of air. 'My mother's best friend since school, her bridesmaid on her wedding day and my godmother. She was just about part of the family.'

'I don't see the significance,' Ruby admitted, her head shaking.

'No? Neither did I until the crash,' he went on, his voice as flat and bereft of life as she'd ever heard. 'Then it all made sense.

'Bonnie was so beautiful. Oh, I always thought my mother was, too, but in a different way. My mother was average height and build, but with a smile that made anything else irrelevant. Whereas Bonnie could have been a model, tall and long legged and with a face that turned heads.' He looked pointedly at her. 'A lot like you. It never occurred to me to wonder back then why she hadn't married.' He swivelled his whole body around towards her, his eyes boring into her with such intensity, with such raw pain, that she flinched from the connection.

'And for all of those years she was playing up to my mother, the perfect best friend, the adoring and generous god-mother—for all of that time she was operating behind my mother's back, secretly servicing my father's needs, being paid to act as my father's whore!'

He thrust open his car door and stepped outside, suddenly needing more space and air around him than was provided by the confines of the car. He walked across the strip of lawn to the wooden railing that marked the edge of the dunes leading down to the beach and sucked in great lungfuls of the fresh Indian Ocean air, trying to fill the vacuum left inside him, trying to vanquish the stale memories of the past.

At that very moment the molten sun dipped silently on the horizon, touching the surface of the ocean, flaring briefly as it merged with the sea. Behind him he heard the muted click of the car's passenger door closing.

He didn't turn. He just gazed over the sea and watched as the ocean accepted the burning sun bit by bit into its depths until its light was just a last desperate pinprick and then nothing. Just as his father had extinguished so completely any prospect of a father-son relationship for them.

'Zane,' he heard Ruby say. 'I'm sorry.'

'It's not your fault,' he replied.

She ignored the bite in his words. 'I just can't believe it, though. Laurence would never have done that to your mother. He was a man of honour, of integrity. He loved Maree. I know he did. You must remember that.'

'Then why did he sleep with Bonnie?' He spun away from the sea and the sunset to face her. 'I'd grown up listening to him advocating integrity and ethics and that family comes first for as long as I could remember, but when it came down to it, he was just a man. A weak man, as it turned out. Laurence admitted as much.'

'But... When?'

'After the crash. My father went crazy, consumed by grief. I discovered he was organising a double funeral and that he was planning to bury both of them in the family plot— together! I knew both women were close, but this was crazy. When I challenged him about it he even had the gall to tell me Bonnie had given him something my mother never could.'

'I can't believe he would betray your mother like that.'

Even in the darkening sky his eyes burned with coal-black fury, dark and resentful. 'Why? Did you think you were the only one who took my father's eye! Did you think you were special?'

He turned back to the sea, one hand wringing his neck, the other hanging loosely by his side. 'When I begged him to deny he'd ever slept with Bonnie, he wouldn't. He couldn't! Because he'd kept Bonnie as his paid mistress and he'd betrayed my mother, and so I walked out of Broome the minute my mother was in the ground. And he never once tried to stop me.'

Quite the contrary. He could still hear his father's heated words ringing in his ears—'You'll never make it on your own'; 'You'll come back crawling on your hands and knees.' But he hadn't come crawling back. And he'd well and truly shown his old man that he could make it on his own.

So why did he feel so hollow?

Surely victory should taste sweeter?

But he'd arrived home too late to make his peace with his father. Too late to hear him admit he was wrong. And too late to stop his father from taking another mistress, this time one he wanted for himself!

Around them the night sky descended, shades of purple deepening to ink black.

Ruby hugged her arms to her chest. It couldn't be true. The Laurence she knew wasn't like that. And yet something must have happened. A chill descended her spine. Could that be the key to Laurence's final words to his son? 'Perhaps,' she started, thinking aloud, 'perhaps that's why—'

She broke off, but he rounded on her. 'That's why *what*?'

She blinked up uncertainly at him and hesitated. She'd never told him. The timing had never been right. It had never made any sense. But maybe now…

She swallowed. 'Maybe that's why your father wanted to apologise.'

'What are you talking about?' he demanded, taking a step closer to her. 'When was this?'

'Just before he died. I was holding his hand and he said, "Tell Zane I'm sorry."'

'His parting words,' he accused, 'intended for *me*, and you didn't think to pass them on!'

'I'm so sorry,' she whispered.

'And that's all he said. *Nothing* more?'

She looked away, out to sea, out to anywhere she wouldn't have to meet those eyes, their glare accusatory, their pain hauntingly vivid. But she wouldn't tell him the rest. *'Look after Zane.'* He didn't have to hear that. He wouldn't want to hear it.

'There was no time for more. The machines started beeping and people came from everywhere. It was the last thing he said. Not that it seemed to make any sense.' She looked back at him, her tone shifting to accusatory. 'You were the one who'd left Broome. You were the one who'd walked away from your own father. Why should he have to apologise to you?'

His breath was fast and furious, his chest pumping air.

'So you chose not to tell me.'

'It wasn't like that!'

'Then tell me, what was it like?'

She opened her mouth to defend herself, wanting to tell him that he'd hated her on sight and no more so than when he'd learned his father had left her half of his inheritance; wanting to protest that somehow they'd never really had the opportunity for a heart-to-heart chat; wanting to shout that it was payback for thinking she had been Laurence's mistress. But she knew in her heart that there was no defence for what she'd done. She'd decided he wasn't worthy of Laurence's apology and she'd made no attempt to tell him. She'd kept words meant for Zane to herself because she didn't understand what they could mean and she'd let Laurence down in the process.

'I'm sorry, Zane,' she said instead. 'I should have told you.'

'I'm speaking to the lawyer first chance I get.' He forced the words through gritted teeth. 'I'll work out a settlement, but I want you out of the business and gone from Broome.'

'But the launch—'

'It's your precious collection! You'll stay for the launch and the dealer presentations overseas where you'd better sell the collection well, but then I want you out of here. And I'll make it more than worth your while.'

She hissed in a breath, angling her chin higher. 'I already told you, I don't want your money.'

He stormed to the car, swinging his door wide open. Then he looked back at her standing there, his face a bitter mask.

'If there's one thing I've learned in business, it's that everyone has their price. Whores especially!'

His words ripped into her psyche, slashing her to her core as he reversed the car and accelerated away, leaving her as cold and shocked as if her lifeblood had spilled from the wounds and splashed out on to the ground.

After the story he'd told her tonight he would never believe the truth. It had suited her to never set him straight, but now there was no chance he would ever see her as more than his father's whore.

But he had a right to be angry with her. Wouldn't she feel the same way if someone had kept her a family member's final words from her? She'd failed in her duty to convey a promise. She'd let Laurence down, unable to honour either of his dying wishes. She hadn't passed on his apology. And by not doing so, she hadn't come close to taking care of him like his father had asked.

Two simple requests. She'd blown them both. How, then, could she hope to live up to Laurence's expectations of her in the business? How could she ever hope to work with his son again?

She couldn't.

'You win, Zane,' she whispered as the tail-lights of the departing car swung around a corner and disappeared from view. 'I'm leaving.'

It was like stepping from the wet season into the dry. She was in the office at five the next morning and, as soon as she'd sent the email to Zane confirming that she agreed to leave after her launch commitments had been honoured, it felt like the dark clouds had gone and the intense humidity had blown away. Soon there would be no more storms. And soon the air would be fresh and pure.

An unfamiliar sense of optimism filled her senses as she headed to the workroom to spend the morning making a final check of all the pieces in the collection, ensuring that any last-minute manufacturing changes had been made before signing off on each piece.

Because escape was at hand, escape that she'd hungered for ever since Zane had appeared on the scene, and an interview with the lawyers to put her parting arrangements in place was potentially only hours away. And if Zane wanted to press her with money to make her leave, she'd barely slept last night for working out the best thing to do with it. She didn't want it for herself, but it might as well go somewhere it was needed.

The bulk of it, she'd already decided, should go in trust to the employees. After all, if she was abandoning them then she'd make sure they were taken care of, maybe not quite as Laurence had intended, but in such a way that they would not be left completely to Zane's mercy. She'd get the lawyer to have the money invested with the employees as beneficiaries. Then, whatever Zane did, whatever became of their original ten per cent share, at least they'd have some guarantee of an income in the future.

The balance, the twenty per cent premium he'd offered for the shares, would go to the work her sister Opal was doing in Sydney. Pearl's Place, the women's refuge her sister had established, was expanding, driven by demand for its services. Ruby had always been too far away to help with Opal's work before, but now she would have the funds to help in a significant way. If she could achieve both these things without short-changing the employees, then wasn't her leaving doing good? Surely Laurence wouldn't hold that against her?

She turned the passion pendant in her fingers, feeling the burst of achievement that always accompanied seeing it. But this time there was another emotion mixed in. Sadness. It would be a relief to leave, but there was a sense of loss, too. The years she'd spent with Laurence had been wonderful. He'd taught her so much, he'd given her so much. But at least she could give him the Passion Collection, dedicated to his memory. It would be her final parting gift.

'I'm glad you've seen sense at last.'

She snapped up her head to find Zane filling her vision, his body language wearing his triumph like a prize, his eyes flashing victory. She swallowed back on an erratically beating heart. He wasn't the only one gaining something out of this. She was also a winner. She pushed herself higher on her stool.

'You got my email, then.'

He moved closer without answering and she swallowed, the air in the room noticeably thinner, the temperature suddenly rising.

So much for leaving behind the wet season, she registered as he moved to her side. She'd forgotten just how hot and stifling the dry could be.

'What's that?' he asked, looking down at the object cradled in her hands.

Instinctively her fingers closed protectively around the pendant—would he see what she'd seen inside it?—but then sense prevailed and she opened them, exposing the centre-piece of the Passion Collection to his gaze. 'The passion pendant,' she said. 'It's finished.'

He frowned, not believing what he was seeing. His gaze narrowed as he recognised the piece. 'This is the pendant you created for the collection? The one I saw as just a drawing?'

She nodded as he took the pendant, the heat from his hands brushing her skin like a warm glow. He held it up to the light, moving it around in his fingers, watching the play of light and shade on the surface of the gems, seeing the image within revealed.

The lovers' embrace!

Ruby had turned a concept into a reality, the experience of passion into a work of art. His skin prickled as the illusion winked back at him—the warm glow of flesh in the pearl nacre, the wonder of long golden limbs, entwined around those of her lover. It was passionate and provocative and it made him see all kinds of things—heated, forbidden, dangerous…

Then wonder turned to revulsion as reality interceded. Who was he kidding? The collection was to be dedicated to Laurence. Who had been Ruby's inspiration if not him? It was his father he was seeing, the remnants of their relationship, preserved for posterity, *no one else*!

He thrust the piece back into her hands and stormed to the door, his movements weighed down with need, heavy with self-recrimination. Oh, the collection would be a success, he had no doubt of that now, not if she managed to convey the same sense of passion throughout the entire collection.

But at least afterwards she'd be gone and he wouldn't have to deal with these constant reminders of her unavailability any more.

'Zane?'

He turned at her call. 'What is it?'

She frowned. 'The lawyer—how soon can we see him?'

With a jolt he remembered why he'd come to find her. 'Finlayson has taken leave. I didn't want to deal with his clerk about this.'

'So how long do we have to wait?' She sounded anxious, no doubt desperate to get away. Had she been thinking about the money after all, and about all the things she could do with it? He'd thought as much. How quickly she'd changed her tune.

'Relax,' he said, wishing he could take his own advice. 'He'll be back in a month. I've made an appointment for us both for his first day back on deck—the day after the launch.'

In a way it was easier working with Zane after that. They both knew what had to be done in the business leading up to the launch and they understood what was to come afterwards. Just knowing there was an end date on their working together made everything so much more bearable; almost like releasing the steam from the pressure-cooker situation they'd been trapped in together up until now.

Ruby threw herself into the launch and the plans to take the collection afterwards to Sydney and then on to the New York and London dealers. Zane had already decided not to accompany her on the overseas trip, although he planned to attend the Sydney show, so it was almost as if she would be escaping the business even earlier than she'd expected. She could hardly wait.

And it was wonderful to be able to concentrate her efforts on the design side of things once again and let Zane assume more and more of the management issues. Not that she didn't keep a watchful eye on what he was doing. She was still equal managing partner and there was no way he was going to run the business into the ground. But as the weeks went by she had to admit he had a real flair for the business and their arguments became fewer and farther between.

Preparations for the launch consumed days and weeks in a whoosh. When she wasn't going over the details, checking and rechecking everything to make sure the evening ran to plan, as the days counted down to the launch Ruby kept a nervous eye on the weather forecasts for the evening.

Timed to the minute, with a parade of the most spectacular pieces in the collection, the ceremony was set to conclude a scant five minutes before the rising of the full moon and the famed Stairway to the Moon phenomenon.

It was the one thing she couldn't control and she knew it was a risk. If all went well, the full moon would rise like a giant pearl over Roebuck Bay, its light catching on the damp tidal flats and building the appearance of a staircase rising up from the earth to the moon. Cloud cover would mar the illusion. A clear night would crown the evening's success.

Ten minutes before the first guests were due to arrive it seemed everything was in place. Ruby stood in the ballroom of the Stairway Hotel, looking out the large picture windows, scouring the sky for any trace of cloud and battling to keep her nerves in check. Never had a collection been so spectacular. Never had a collection meant so much. But would the audience see it that way? So much was at stake.

Behind her the staff were putting the finishing touches to the seating, tying colourful satin bows around them and preparing trays of champagne glasses.

'Looks like you got lucky.'

Zane appeared at her elbow holding two flutes of champagne. 'Congratulations,' he said, his voice deep yet strained as he offered her one. 'You've worked flat out on this launch. And you even managed to get the weather to co-operate.'

She looked back over the bay, allowing herself a smile in answer when all she really wanted to do right now was remember how to breathe. Zane was complimenting her? It was true that in the last few weeks since she'd decided to leave they'd formed an unsteady truce, but that rarely went beyond approval of budgets or promotional plans.

But that wasn't all that was threatening her ability to breathe. Some time since she'd last seen him he'd taken advantage of the suite they'd each been offered and changed into a crisp white shirt and a black dinner suit that made him look somehow darker and more dangerous than ever. His hair, freshly showered, clung in damp waves and he smelt good, clean and strong. *Intoxicating.* All of which she could have dealt with if not for the vibe emanating from him, a highly pitched tenseness surrounding him, setting her already strained senses to prickling alertness.

She flicked a glance his way, unsurprised to see him still watching her, only confirming what she'd felt so bone deep.

'I'm not sure if I need champagne right now. I think I need to keep a clear head.' Not that there was any chance of that while this humming tension surrounded her.

He took a sip, but it was the way his eyes drank her in that kick-started the low, fluttering heat deep inside.

'It'll relax you.'

I doubt it, she thought, even as she raised the glass to her lips, her senses heightening by the second as he brushed her arm with his as he raised his in a toast.

'To the launch,' he said, his eyes never leaving hers. She raised her glass in salute and drank again, not sure if it was the champagne already fizzing in her veins or something else.

'I think I'm too nervous right now to relax,' she admitted.

'Don't be,' he said. 'I don't know how you did it, but from the buzz going around it looks like the launch is going to be a huge success.'

If only she'd been talking about the launch. Ruby dragged her eyes from him and gazed out past the mangroves and across the flats. At high tide the sea would rush to fill the bay, transforming it a vivid blue, but for now, at low tide, only a narrow aqua ribbon of creek remained, bisecting the flats, a reminder of the colour to come with the returning tide.

It was almost like the change in Zane. This past few weeks he'd seemed so different; they'd worked together like a real team and, while he was giving her credit for the launch, he'd shouldered much of the load himself and she'd been more than happy to hand over responsibility. He could be such a different person to the man who'd hated her on sight. It was almost as if the tide had swept out on him, leaving a taste of the real Zane exposed beneath.

And tonight he was even more different, the air around him more highly charged, unsettling her, and causing urges to ripple through her that she had no right in feeling. It was easier when he hated her. It was easier, then, to hate him back. But now...

He could sense her tenseness. He could see it in the way she held her shoulders rigid. It emanated from her like a living thing. Tomorrow they'd see Derek Finlayson and sort out the terms of her departure and no doubt her tension would slide away—as it would settle things for them both. But that was tomorrow and right now Derek was no help to either of them and so the urge to reach out and massage her bare shoulders, to massage out the kinks, and soothe her troubled muscles, was almost overwhelming. She'd be gone soon, gone from Broome and gone from his life— What would it hurt to touch her? Just one touch of her honeyed skin, one chance to skim his hands over that satin perfection...

He hauled in a breath and clamped down on the urge, balling his free hand into a tight fist. He mustn't do it. He mustn't touch her. If he put one hand on her skin it would be too difficult to resist sliding the tiny shoestring straps down her arms, to kiss the skin at that place on her throat that betrayed the hitched beat of her heart, to peel away the gown that wrapped its way around her so tantalisingly.

The silvery pink gown hugged her form, her every movement giving light to the tiny sequins scattered between the shell-like shapes worked into the fabric, her hair gathered low at the nape of her neck to accentuate the strand of perfect pearls from which hung a small pendant from the Passion Collection, its design still voluptuous and evocative.

She blinked, the colour rising in her cheeks at his unashamed appraisal.

'You look beautiful,' he couldn't help but tell her. 'Like treasure from the sea.'

Her aqua eyes held with his, just long enough for him to admit the rest with his own— *I want you.*

Like a blow to the gut, that single truth forced the air from his lungs. There was no point denying it any longer. There was no point pretending. He wanted her.

And nothing would stop him having her.

The soundless words echoed in the heightened air between them before her attention was snagged by voices. Her eyes widened as she looked around him.

'It's showtime,' she said on a breath, depositing her near-empty glass on a side table.

Before long the place was humming and the formal part of the evening and the speeches got underway. Zane spoke briefly in his father's place, introducing Ruby and surprising her yet again by crediting her as the genius behind the collection. Then it was Ruby's turn. She took the podium and talked about the magic of working with pearls, in ancient times considered gifts from the gods and even the tears of the moon, and that was why she considered there was no better night than the full moon to celebrate the Passion Collection. Battling the prickle of tears, Ruby finally dedicated the collection to Laurence Bastiani's memory, recognising him as a man who'd pursued a dream and made that dream a reality for everyone to enjoy the most beautiful pearls in the world.

And then it was time for the collection to be unveiled. The

models paraded the catwalk, all of them stunning, all of them dressed to kill. But it was the pearls that the audience had come to see and it was the pearls that held their interest as, for all their beauty, the models were merely the backdrops to display the finest that nature could provide. Necklaces featuring pearls and tourmaline, long ropes of perfect golden pearls, bracelets rich with gold and voluptuous baroque shapes and earrings elegant yet bewitching—the crowd accepted each offering with mounting excitement, only to erupt in triumphant applause when the final piece, the magnificent passion pendant itself, was displayed.

It was too much! Tears, this time of success, filled her eyes. Someone squeezed her hand. *Zane*.

'Congratulations,' he said. Then he lifted her hand to his mouth and kissed her palm, the feel of his lips, the graze of his tongue on her sensitive flesh turning her liquid inside. 'Now go up and take a bow.'

Somehow she managed to negotiate the few short steps to receive a standing ovation from the audience, cameras flashing as the models embraced her.

Only the haunting sounds of a didgeridoo, the signal that the moon would soon be rising, could interrupt the excitement. Doors leading from the ballroom to a large balcony deck had been opened and the audience gathered drinks and filtered outside to the now darkened evening, their chatter still filled with awe at the collection while they kept one eye out on the horizon.

Zane handed her a fresh glass of champagne and steered her to their VIP seating.

The crowd had quietened, as if everyone was holding their breath in anticipation, the timeless music winding a spell around everyone, holding them enthralled as it seemed to beckon for the moon to appear.

And then behind the low hills across the bay emerged a tiny

pinprick of light. The crowd gasped collectively as all eyes focused on that one spot, as slowly the magnificent full moon emerged, bit by bit, bright and beautiful and so, so large.

Gradually, as it crept higher above the horizon like a giant pearl, its lunar glow illuminated the tidal flats with a shaft of golden light that slowly made its way down to the earth, step by golden step, until the stairway was complete. And there it was, a ladder, rising in front of them, so bold and vivid and real, a stairway to the moon.

He watched her profile, saw her expressions change and reflect the awe she was feeling at the spectacle, her lips slightly opened, her eyes bright and luminescent. Reflecting the awe back at him.

So many times he'd witnessed this phenomenon in his youth that he'd taken it for granted. But now, watching Ruby's features filled with wonderment, with the ancient sound of the didgeridoo heralding the occasion, it was like watching it for the first time. It was like suddenly understanding the magic. It was a moon made for lovers. Made for them. And he understood. He had no choice but to want her. Like the moon rising every night, it was inevitable.

In spite of everything he'd believed, in spite of the failure he was sure the collection would be, she'd captured the wonder of the illusion in her designs, she'd captured the beauty of the moon and all of nature with her pearls and he'd like to capture her with them, to wind them around her, to see them warm and lustrous on her flesh, and to tug her close with them.

'It's beautiful,' she said, leaning over towards him, her voice a breathless whisper.

'You are,' he agreed softly against her ear, her scent adding another dimension to the images, the hunger inexorably building inside him, becoming fraught with desperation. 'Very beautiful.'

He felt the tremor move through her, but she didn't pull away. He wrapped an arm around her shoulders to support her and after a second's hesitation felt her relax into him. Her skin felt warm and smooth and the tension she'd worn before the launch had been replaced with a melting languor in her muscles that only made him harder.

The moon climbed higher into the night sky and the staircase steps fractured and drew apart and the illusion slowly began to fade, the stairway transformed to a golden memory. People started talking among themselves and moving around, taking advantage of the finger food that had been laid on while they'd been watching the moon's brilliant display.

She made a move against his arm and sense told him he'd have to let her go. There would be photo calls waiting for her, interviews by the press, a world of people and clients to impress, further frustrating his need to be with her. But before he released his hold completely, he leaned over and nuzzled the warm skin under her ear. 'Later,' he whispered against her answering quake.

It was late. The guests had filtered away, the last of the reporters and photographers had departed and the moon wasn't the only thing that was high. Ruby had never felt more vitally alive, the blood in her veins a highly charged cocktail of success, adrenalin and two glasses of champagne. Nothing stood a chance of wiping the smile from her face tonight.

She turned to farewell the last guest, but it was Zane who folded her hand in his.

'Zane!' she said, practically glowing. 'Isn't it wonderful? The collection is a success.'

'It's a triumph,' he agreed, drawing her closer so she had to look up to him, close enough that his scent was welcomed into her senses like a missing ingredient. 'And you're the star of the collection.'

His words added to the intoxicating mix circulating in her veins. She had done well. But for Zane to acknowledge it…

'I'd also like to add my congratulations on your success tonight.'

'Thank you,' she whispered back, unable to turn her eyes away, even as his face drew slowly nearer. She watched his lips, hypnotised. She waited, feeling his warm breath melding with hers, wrapping around her, set to the music of her heartbeat. And then his lips touched hers, their pressure like a butterfly kiss, the feeling warm and sensual and their gentle movements across hers stirring ragged heat inside her, dissolving her bones, melting her resolve.

He pulled away till their intermingled breath was their only point of contact.

'It's late,' he said, his voice gravelly, his grip on her hands tight and urgent, 'and it would be crazy to drive when we have rooms already booked.'

She didn't want to drive, either. She was way over the limit, drunk on success, drunk on raw need, drunk on the danger she sensed she was in tonight.

All night long she'd found herself replaying the words he'd spoken to her over and over in her mind, lingering over them, tasting them—'*You look beautiful,*' he'd said, '*like treasure from the sea.*' And she'd felt so good, just the way he'd looked at her, and that had been before she'd felt the squeeze of his hand, the rasp of his tongue against her palm. That moment she'd come close to meltdown.

She looked up at him, still heady with accomplishment, reluctant to end the evening when it had gone so very well and when Zane had been so much a part of making it so. Maybe because his dark eyes were warmed to liquid, glossy with heat, like chocolate spiced with chilli, spicing up her own need, setting her thoughts to reckless.

'I don't plan on driving anywhere tonight.'

Sparks flared in his eyes, the tight line of his lips relaxing enough to turn up at the ends. 'Then I'll see you to your room.'

Just to her room? Or beyond? She shuddered at the pictures suddenly crowding her mind's eye, pictures of her with Zane, kissing her, undressing her, making love to her. Her breasts tightened and ached under her fitted bodice. Just the notion of sharing her bed with Zane turned her dizzy, her senses tingling. But this was Zane— What was happening?

She let him take her hand and lead her from the building, out into the gardens and the warm night air. He looped one arm around her shoulders as they strolled past the tumbling waterfall and swimming pool and through the stands of palm bushes, the air sweetly scented with frangipani, their brilliant white petals glowing softly in the moonlight. Halfway to their rooms she convinced herself it was easier to curve her arm around his back than to leave it awkwardly between them, and was immediately rewarded by the flush of contact, her hip brushing against his thigh, her breasts edging on his chest. He felt warm and accommodating yet still so tightly controlled under her hand, and she itched to pull back the layers of his clothes and find the source of that heat, to find the source of that control.

Lost in sensation she stumbled forward, her fine heel trapped between paving stones. He swung himself forward to catch her, his free hand missing her arm, cupping instead one breast as he arrested her fall. Her shoe jerked free behind her and she fell further into his hand, only straightening when she'd regained her footing. His hand gentled its hold and for a moment she thought he might remove it completely. But she was wrong. It lingered there, his touch now more like a soft caress than a life-saver, the subtle movement of his fingers like a call to her need.

She looked up into his face, and against the soft moonlight his features were shadowed but intense. His dark eyes glinted with desire and his breath came like a low growl.

She lifted a hand to cover his—to take it away?—but if she'd ever intended to, then she forgot the moment her skin connected with his. She felt his hand touching her, she wove her fingers between his, she slid her fingers along and circled the band of his wrist as all the while he gently stroked her breast, and then she squeezed his hand—a silent supplication—that told him—*more*.

She didn't have to wait long for his answer. He caught her hand in his, quickly snared the other and wound them behind her, holding her captive, pressing her tight against him as his mouth descended upon hers. This time his kiss was different, deeper, more urgent, more testing. His lips were warm and he tasted of coffee and fine wine, of darkness and moonlight and she wanted to drink him in. His hands slipped down, cupped her behind and pulled her deliciously up against him. She gasped when she felt his power, felt his raw need, and all the while his mouth wove a spell on hers.

He drew his head to the side, raining tiny kisses up the line of her jaw. 'I want you,' he growled, his voice straining and urgent.

'I know,' she answered without hesitation. Because if she hesitated, she'd think, and she didn't want to think. Tomorrow there would be time for thinking, time for planning. Tomorrow there would be lawyer visits and settlements and no doubt a resurgence of the anger and resentment that had marred their first months together. *But this was tonight.* And tonight would be her only chance to live out the one fantasy that had preoccupied her dreams and snuffed out all others. She would have him, just as she'd long dreamed, if only for this one night.

He drew back and looked into her face, as if wanting to

assure himself that she knew what she'd just agreed to. But if he was surprised by her acquiescence, he didn't show it. Instead his eyes just glinted with approval. And without taking his eyes from hers, he swung her into his arms and swept her through the gardens.

He moved darkly through the balmy evening, her weight seemingly no trouble to him even as he climbed the stairs to the exclusive suites, the lines of his face chiselled in the soft moon glow. He could be a pirate, she thought, or a creature of the night spiriting her away. Tonight under the full moon, he could be anything.

And tonight she would be his!

CHAPTER EIGHT

'I MUST HAVE YOU!' he groaned, wheeling her around and pressing her against the closed door, his mouth crashing down on hers once more. Her lips parted under his sensual onslaught, welcoming the interplay of tongue and lips and mouth and skin.

He slid down the thin straps of her gown and swivelled her away from the door just enough to drop his hand behind her so her back arched towards him. He freed her breasts and groaned at their peaked beauty, muting the sound as he filled his mouth with one perfect breast, his tongue circling, tasting, his teeth toying with the hardened bud of her nipple before he set to work on the other peaked perfection.

His mouth was at her neck, back to her mouth, and the blood roared in his veins, pounded in his head, blotting out everything but the need. The need consumed everything. The need was everywhere, in his mouth, his hands, his skin. Then she writhed under him, pressing her belly closer against his erection and he groaned into her mouth. And that need—right there!

He wanted to make love to her. He'd imagined it, he'd pictured it, he'd fantasised about it for as long as he could remember.

But now there was no time to make love.

Right now he had to take her.

Her skirt frothed like sea foam in his hands as he rucked up her hem. Meanwhile her hands were in his shirt, under his shirt, sliding under his waistband, further inciting him. His hands reciprocated, circling her, releasing her from the scrap of lace fabric that was his final barrier. His hand cupped her mound, his fingers separating her, her slick wetness his reward but also his downfall. The urgent drumbeat of blood drove him onwards, prevented him from lingering where he would otherwise take his time, where he would later explore. But for now there was but one thundering imperative, one desperate, crashing need.

She clung to him around his neck, her arms wrapped tightly as he sucked her into his kiss while he freed himself. She tasted of sweetness and pleasure and everything he'd ever lusted for and any second now he'd feel that sweet perfection all around him and that knowledge powered him, urging him on. He lifted her, wrapping her legs around him, opening her up to him, and finding the core of her need and pressing himself, seeking entry to her tight honeyed depths, desperately seeking absolution from this driving need before he exploded outside.

'Please, now,' she cried urgently, her legs tightening around him, urging him home, and he responded, angling her closer and taking advantage of her slickness with one desperate lunge. The angle was better this time, he felt the resistance shift and give way and then he was in paradise—a frantic and frenzied paradise, powerful and passionate. Bliss.

Muscles clamped around him, Ruby's grip constricted around his neck and over his own rush of blood and heat he was certain he heard a scream—not of fulfilment, but of pain—and suddenly her tightness made sense. Horrible, chilling sense.

And paradise turned to hell.

* * *

His chest still heaving, his breath ragged, he withdrew, the need that had consumed him rendered insignificant in the pained knowledge of what he had done. He tugged her arms from around his neck and let her slide to the floor before he adjusted his clothing. Her lips were tightly pressed together, her mascara-smudged eyes clamped shut and aimed floor-wards, moisture welling up from between the lids as she wrenched her dress up over her naked breasts.

'Why didn't you tell me?' Shock turned his heaving words into an accusation.

Her eyes opened and flashed cold fire at him. She swiped at her tears on her cheek with the back of one hand. 'And you would have believed me? I don't think so.'

'You let me believe you were sleeping with my father!'

'You believed what you wanted to believe! You decided it the moment we met and nothing I said or did was going to change that. You as good as labelled me his whore!'

He spun away, his mind in turmoil, hands clutching at the back of his neck. She was right. He'd had her pegged from the very beginning. And he couldn't have been more wrong. She couldn't have been his father's mistress. She was a virgin.

Had been a virgin!

She'd cried out in pain. He'd been so desperate to have her, so rushed he hadn't even waited to get her to the bed. It shouldn't have been like that for her first time.

He turned to see her retrieving her silky underwear from the floor. She'd adjusted her dress, slipped her arms back into the straps and straightened when she saw him watching her, balling the panties between her hands.

'Did I hurt you?'

No more than usual. 'Does it matter?'

'I didn't mean to hurt you. I didn't know…'

'I'm fine,' she said, when it was clear she was feeling anything but.

He took a step closer. 'Ruby—'

'Forget it! It was a mistake,' she said, turning for the door handle. 'I think we both realise that. It's just as well I'm leaving Broome soon.'

He crossed to her, punching the door closed before she could pull it open more than a few inches. All this time he'd assumed she'd been his father's mistress. All this time he'd been wrong! His father had never slept with her at all. And that made no sense, not with what he knew of his father. Not given the fact she'd lived with him!

'Don't go like this. Can't you see? This changes things—' He didn't know how, only that it must.

'This changes *nothing*!' she stated, her voice edging towards hysteria. 'It was a mistake, that's all. Tomorrow I'll meet you at the lawyer's office and we'll settle my departure arrangements, just as we planned, as if tonight had never happened, which I'm sure suits us both. And now—' She looked pointedly at his arm, still holding the door closed '—if you'll excuse me?'

He studied her, a muscle in his jaw popping as his eyes searched her face. She was right. It would be much better for both of them if they pretended this had never happened. He reached for the latch and swung the door open wide.

She must have been crazy to have gone along with him tonight! Safely in her room next door, she pulled off her gown and threw it on the bed before pulling on new underwear and casual linen pants and a top. She yearned for a shower to wash the touch, the memory of him away, but she dared not, here. Just as she dared not cry. The tears had been perilously close in his room, his rapid departure from her like a slap in the face. He didn't want her when she was someone's mistress—he didn't want her when she was a virgin. When would she get it through her head—*he didn't want her*! It was her shares he wanted, shares he believed were rightly his.

Well, as of tomorrow, he'd have his precious shares!

In a rush of frantic activity she collected up her few possessions. There would be time enough for a long bath, time enough for tears later. Tears for all the mistakes she'd made tonight.

She'd believed she'd wanted him so much that it wouldn't hurt and she'd been wrong. Way wrong. Even now she ached, that part of her tender and pulsing.

She'd been wrong again when she'd hoped he wouldn't notice that she was so inexperienced.

But she'd made the biggest mistake of all in letting it happen in the first place.

Only one thing held her together. Tomorrow they'd see the lawyer and have the legalities of Zane's buyout of her shares taken care of. Then it was just a matter of weeks until she concluded her Passion Collection obligations and she'd be gone. She'd be free.

Escape was at hand and it had never felt so sweet!

She caught her reflection in the mirror near the door as she left and it stopped her dead. She had mascara smudged beneath each eye, her lips looked plump and swollen from the Zane's ministrations, and her smile—the smile she'd brandished tonight and believed would last for ever—had disappeared from trace.

For a man who'd just been on an extended holiday, Derek Finlayson looked exceedingly tense. Over his reading glasses he peered with undisguised concern at them both seated ramrod straight at opposite corners of his desk.

'What can I do for you both?' he asked. 'The note in my diary was quite vague.'

Zane looked sideways at Ruby, but she gave him nothing, clutching on to some kind of letter in her hands and looking steadfastly away from him, just like she'd ignored his presence since he'd arrived in Finlayson's office this morning. He'd arrived early, hoping to have the chance for a few minutes' private consultation first, only to find her already waiting. So she couldn't wait to leave Broome? Why didn't that give him the buzz of satisfaction that it should?

Only the shadows under her eyes were some consolation. So she'd lost sleep last night, too? *Good.*

'We'd like you to draw up some paperwork,' he said, turning his attention back to the lawyer. 'Ruby has decided to leave Broome after all. She's agreed to sell her share of the business to me.'

Derek Finlayson blinked slowly twice before looking across at Ruby. 'Is this true, Miss Clemenger?'

She nodded. 'I have the collection tour to finalise, but as soon as I return from New York and London in two weeks' time, I'd like everything to be ready for my departure.' She unfolded and handed over the paper she'd been holding. 'Here are my instructions for the proceeds of the share sale.'

Derek took off his wire-framed glasses and regarded the paper on his desk suspiciously. 'You're both sure about this, then?'

'Absolutely,' replied Zane emphatically.

'Even though we discussed that you both working jointly in the Bastiani Corporation is what your father intended, indeed, wanted?'

'It doesn't matter,' said Zane. 'This arrangement clearly isn't working and we both believe it's time to do something about it. I've offered to buy Ruby's shares at market value.'

Her head snapped around. 'What about the premium?

You mentioned a premium of twenty per cent. What happened to that?'

Air hissed through Zane's teeth as he felt his insides tumble and freeze over. *So it was the money all along!* All that talk about not wanting it. All that bluster and pretence that she didn't want anything. And here she was with a letter all prepared—her instructions for the proceeds!

So what that he'd been wrong about her being his father's mistress? Her gold-digger stripes were still boldly in evidence.

'And here was me thinking you weren't interested in the money. Any increase on twenty per cent? Could I tempt you perhaps with thirty?'

She glared back at him. 'You were the one who offered it. Surely you're not thinking about reneging on your offer, not—now?'

She stumbled over the last word, almost as if she'd been intending to say something different. He knew what it was, his mind had already finished off the sentence for her—*after what happened last night*!

Is that why she'd agreed to go with him—because she'd figured on earning that premium on her back? Anger spiked afresh into his psyche.

'Oh, dear.' Derek Finlayson interceded between the pair. 'This is no doubt a forlorn hope under the circumstances, but I do have to ask you both if there's any chance you might reconsider? Your father was very keen that you manage the business together.'

'I'm sorry,' Ruby said, turning her attentions to Derek, her voice soft but determined. 'We've tried to make this work, we really have. But the Passion Collection is just about completed and it's time for me to move on. And Zane has a good handle on the business now. I'm sure that's what Laurence was really concerned about, so I can't see any problems.'

'Besides,' Zane added, 'it's not like he's in a position to make us do something we don't want to. We control the business now.'

Across the desk the lawyer sighed. 'Well, I'm sorry it's come to this, very sorry indeed. But I'm afraid it's not quite as simple as that.' He opened the file, flipping the pages until he found the one he wanted. 'Ah, here it is. You see, when Laurence made the arrangements for his will, he did ask me to withhold one particular detail from you both.'

'What are you talking about?' demanded Zane.

Ruby frowned. 'Why would he have done that?'

'The settlement upon each of you of forty-five per cent of the shares of Bastiani Corporation, and the remaining ten per cent to the employees and staff, came with one condition.'

'What condition?'

Derek Finlayson peered from one to the other over his glasses. 'That in order for the employees and staff to receive their entitlement in the business, and in order for you to receive your inheritance, the two of you would have to manage the business together first for a period of at least twelve months.'

'Twelve months!' Zane exploded from his chair. 'Are you saying Ruby can't leave now? Even if I buy her out?'

'I do apologise. I know what a shock this must be to you both. I didn't agree with him, but Laurence insisted—he maintained that if you knew about this condition in the first place then you'd fight it from the beginning and it would never work. And I must admit, I was hoping you'd never have to be told. But this is the situation…' He took a deep breath and looked steadily at Zane.

'You aren't in a position to buy Miss Clemenger out because, until that twelve-month period is up, neither of you actually owns the shares to sell.'

'She can't leave?'

'Neither of you can leave the business before that time, not unless you want to forfeit your own and the employees' ten per cent share. So, I'm afraid, if you want to ensure people like Kyoto and others are provided for under the terms of Laurence's will, you're going to have to keep working together for another nine months.'

'It can't be true.' Her voice was barely audible. 'There has to be some way out of this.'

Zane looked across at her, shocked to see her face drained of all colour, her blue eyes large like waterholes in a bleached desert landscape, her anguish plain to see. Guilt twisted his gut and yanked it tight.

Because she was a fighter—he'd seen that time and again over the months they'd been together. She could have taken this in her stride under any other circumstances. She most likely would have relished the challenge.

But not after last night. No longer was she merely anxious to get away with her millions. Now she was desperate to escape from him.

Derek shook his head apologetically. 'I'm sorry, my dear. There's nothing more I can do.'

She shot out of her chair before he'd finished speaking, rushing from the room with a cry like a wounded animal.

'Ruby!'

'Miss Clemenger!' the lawyer said, rising to his feet, her letter held out in his hand.

Zane grabbed his jacket and snatched up the letter on his way out. 'I'll take it to her,' he said.

Ruby stopped running in the park across the road, dragging in oxygen in the shaded gardens in a desperate attempt not to throw up. Escape was such a fragile illusion. One minute

freedom loomed large and promising on the horizon, fresh and
clean and full of promise and so real you could just about reach
out and touch it. The next moment it shattered into dust and
blew away on the wind, leaving you locked in reality.

Locked in hell.

How could Laurence have done this to her? What on earth
had he been thinking? And as for asking her to take care of
Zane, she couldn't even take care of herself. Last night had
proved that. She'd done the one thing she'd sworn she'd never
do. She'd allowed Zane to practically undress her, pushing
down her dress and removing her underwear and she'd
allowed him to press himself into her until he'd broken
through her final barrier.

But worse than that, she'd wanted him to!

She'd behaved like the whore he'd always believed her to be!

Shame turned her stomach again, shame and self-disgust
that she had been a party to the act, and she leaned one shaky
hand against a tree to steady herself, the other hand at her
throat. How could she stay in Broome after what she'd done?
How could she face Zane day after day and calmly talk business
with the knowledge of what they'd done hanging over them like
a dark cloud?

'Ruby!' Zane called from across the road.

She didn't answer, instead moving deeper into the quiet
gardens, still battling to get her churning insides under
control. She didn't want to be reminded of just who she was
locked in hell with.

A few moments later he caught up with her anyway. 'Are
you all right?'

She swung around to face him. 'What do you think? I've
just learned that I'm stuck here with you for another nine
months. Of course I'm not all right!'

'And you think I'm happy about it?'

She turned her back on him. 'I don't care what you think.'

'Don't blame me for what's happened! I haven't done this to you. Blame your beloved Laurence. He's the one who set up this crazy scheme.'

'Only because he didn't trust you! And who the hell could blame him?'

He tugged on her arm, wheeling her around so she could see the colour in his face, the dark fury in his eyes. 'I don't know what his reason was or whether he even had one. I've sure as hell tried to figure it out. But believe me, I'm just as unhappy as you about being stuck in this nightmare.'

'Don't touch me!' she said, yanking her arm free, rubbing her upper arm where he'd held her, her eyes spitting blue fire. Of course he wasn't happy about it. He'd hardly want her under his feet, reminding him of last night's disaster, holding on to shares and control of a company he wanted for his own. Well, she had a solution, at least for the short term. It would give her time on her own, time to think, time to let the humiliating scars of last night's fiasco heal over.

'The Sydney release is less than a week away,' she said, 'but I'm owed some leave. I'm thinking I'll leave a couple of days early. I can catch up with my family before I take the collection to the dealers overseas.'

'All right,' he said cautiously. 'I'll meet you in Sydney before the show.'

'No!' she protested, licking her lips. 'There's really no need for you to come. We've done the major launch here and I'm already doing the tour on my own. I mean, if we're going to be stuck together for months afterwards, maybe it will do us both some good to have some time apart—especially…'

His eyes narrowed as her words trailed off and she was grateful that at least he had the grace to look uncomfortable.

'All right. I'll stay here. But any problems— I want to know about them, immediately.'

Zane checked his messages and slammed the receiver down again, snarling. One message from his London office saying all was well, three messages from Anneleise asking him to please return her calls and not a thing from Sydney. She'd been gone two days already—surely something was happening over there that he should be informed about! He should never have agreed to let her go by herself.

But she couldn't wait to get away from him. She couldn't wait to get her money.

His back teeth ground together.

For a moment there, when he'd first discovered she'd been a virgin, he'd felt things could be different between them. He wasn't sure how—he'd misjudged her, and badly—but suddenly he was aware that the ground rules had changed and maybe, if he could somehow put things to rights, maybe there was a chance to do something more about this desperate need to possess her.

After all, she'd wanted him that night. She'd been like liquid silk in his arms, warm and lush and, oh, so ready. Oh yes, she'd wanted him, the way she'd kissed him, the way she'd opened herself up to him.

He wanted to believe she still wanted him.

Because despite everything, he sure as hell still burned for her!

But cruel reality shook those thoughts right away. It was money she wanted! Despite all her protestations, her panic when she thought she was missing out on the premium for the shares had highlighted her greed more starkly than anything.

Oh, she'd still get her money, she'd just have to wait a bit longer for it. Laurence had seen to that.

The telephone rang and he swooped upon it. *This time!* 'Ruby!' he announced, as if saying it would make it so.

'It's Anneleise,' purred the voice at the other end. 'And I have some wonderful news!'

He'd given up on hearing from Sydney when he finally left the office that evening, slipping on his jacket against the coolish breeze as he headed for his car. An unfamiliar rustle of paper had him reaching into his pocket. One glance at the open sheet was enough—Ruby's typewritten instructions for the lawyer. He'd forgotten to give it to her—not that it was any good to her now. He almost rolled it into a ball to toss away when some of the words he'd glimpsed jagged into his conscience. What was that about a *Bastiani Employees Trust*?

Curiosity got the better of him as he slid behind the steering wheel of his car and fired up the coupé's powerful engine. If it was about the Bastiani Corporation, it was his business, too. He had to check it out. He flipped open the sheet of paper, his eyes widening, taking in the details, working out the sums.

Then, like a poisoned cloud, horror descended upon him, cold, clammy and life-sucking. Horror that he'd misjudged her so badly, horror that he'd got it so wrong yet again.

She was taking none of the proceeds of the shares for herself. *None of it!* Fair value for the shares would be settled on the new trust with any premium paid by Zane for her shares to be donated to some women's refuge called Pearl's Place, in Sydney. No wonder she'd been so worried about the premium! She already had it earmarked for giving away.

He turned off the ignition, but there was no blessed silence, not with the drumbeat of blood in his veins and the blast of recriminations going on inside his head.

How could he have got it so wrong?

CHAPTER NINE

IT SEEMED HALF OF SYDNEY'S glitterati were at the Sydney Opera House to welcome the Passion Collection. It was another fantastic success, all the more special for Ruby by having her sister and mother in the audience, as once again the finale just about brought the house down.

If enthusiasm translated into dollars, this would mean a very good year for the Bastiani Corporation and Ruby could take a good deal of the credit, which was some consolation at least for her forced retention in the company.

But right now, accepting the audience's applause, her heart couldn't help but swell with pride. She'd done what she set out to do so long ago when she'd left Sydney for Broome with just a degree in design and a desire to make the most beautiful jewellery she could. And now she'd become a success in her own right, just as both her sisters, Opal and Sapphy, were successes in theirs. Perhaps one day she'd share her sisters' success in their love lives, too, though there was much less chance of that. So far Ruby had been an unmitigated failure when it came to men.

She bowed one last time, looking out over the crowded auditorium when a movement, unexpectedly threatening and potent, jagged her gaze. Her heart lurched and shuddered. It couldn't be… But a second glance only confirmed the worst.

Zane! Looking dark and dangerous and dressed to kill in one mouth-watering tuxedo. His dark eyes were the only un-civilised thing about him. She swallowed. Their mutual gaze caught and held across the room and electricity powered her senses, setting her flesh to tingling. *With abhorrence*, she insisted, pushing away her body's reaction. Abhorrence laced with irritation. Just what the hell was he doing here, anyway?

She stepped down from the stage as the applause contin-ued, spying Opal and their mother making their way through the crowd towards her. Nervously she looked around, but there was no sign of Zane before she was swallowed into her family's embrace.

'Ruby!' Opal cried as she threw her arms around her sister's neck. 'You're a star!'

Her mother followed suit. 'What a stunning collection. You'll have the whole of Sydney singing your praises.'

'Not only Sydney, all the world.' The rich Italian tones were a welcome sound.

'Domenic!' she shrieked as her handsome Italian brother-in-law picked her up and spun her around in his arms.

'Your designs are so inspired, anyone would think you are *Italiana, tesoro mio.*'

She laughed at his fond endearment—she knew no one but Opal was his treasure—but still she let him kiss her as he set her gently back on to her feet.

'It's so good to see you,' she said, speaking to all of them while she was still looking at Domenic's handsome face, their arms still linked.

She felt a hand on her shoulder, startling her with the posses-sive grip and setting her temperature to overdrive, but she didn't have to see the owner of the hand to know who it belonged to.

'Sorry to break up this happy reunion, but I really need to discuss something urgently with Ruby.'

She looked around at him. He seemed tightly wound, his features rigid and purposeful. 'Zane, what are you doing here? Has something happened back in Broome?'

He wasn't looking at her, he probably hadn't even heard her. Instead, he was staring hard at Domenic, the look on his face dark thunder. And Domenic was giving as good as he got. The two faced each other off like stags about to lock horns.

Opal broke the silence first. 'Domenic, didn't you hear the man? Ruby is needed. Let her go.'

Domenic's eyes didn't leave Zane's. 'Is that right, Ruby?'

'Everyone,' Ruby said, trying to focus while all too aware of the fingers splayed so possessively at her back, the heat stroking her skin, setting it alight under his touch, 'this is Zane Bastiani, my joint managing director from Bastiani Pearls. Zane, this is my family—my mother, Pearl, and my sister, Opal. And this is Domenic Silvagni, my brother-in-law, Opal's husband.'

If he felt like he'd been caught off guard, he didn't show it. Underneath his air of tension he was all charm as he acknowledged the women.

'Domenic,' Zane said as the pair finally shook hands, their eyes less war-like, though still wary, as if still sizing each other up. 'I recognise your name. Hotels, isn't it? I've stayed at Silvers Hotel in Paris—is that one of yours?'

His eyebrows lifted. 'So very far from home, I am indeed surprised. I would have thought you'd be more familiar with the Clemengers Boutique Hotels' connection, given your star designer's heritage.'

Zane shot her a look that would shatter marble, but she ignored him, promising to catch up with her family later on, before letting him steer her towards a quieter space.

'What's happened?' she asked, imagining some major problem back in Broome for him to come personally.

'Why didn't you tell me?'

She had trouble registering his words. Her body felt like one bundle of tingling nerve ends, sparking and shorting every time he touched her with his guiding hand, and keeping them all under control was more than she could handle. Even after what had happened, even after the humiliation and scorn, her body still craved his touch, yearned for it, welcomed it. She clamped down on the sensation. It was a form of madness and she wouldn't give in to it.

Instead she smiled at the guests, accepting their congratulations, as he led her outside the auditorium to somewhere they could talk. 'Tell you what?' she asked, her nerves brittle, anxious to be back in the safety of the reception.

'That you were one of *the* Clemengers.'

'You never asked,' she stated plainly. 'And you were having so much fun painting me that gold-digger shade you keep so handy.'

He grabbed her wrist, swinging her around so she had no choice but to look into his face. 'I didn't know.'

'Obviously. So you made it up!'

'I *assumed*.'

'Same thing!' she hissed. 'You fabricated a story to suit yourself and your own sad prejudices. I told you I didn't need your father's money and you never bothered to find out why. You simply chose to believe I was some gold-digging whore, out for what I could get.'

His eyes flared with anger, then swirled into the muddy depths of contrition.

'That's one of the reasons I came—to apologise….'

She looked pointedly down to where her hand was still held in his iron clasp. 'And this is your idea of an apology? How strange. Most people begin by saying they're sorry.'

'Hell!' He let her go, spinning away and pacing the passageway, his hands sweeping back the sides of his jacket to prop themselves hard against his hips. This wasn't going the way he'd planned, but the bombshell that she belonged to *that* Clemenger family was just more surprise in a long succession of surprises that just proved he'd been wrong-footed from the start. He should have known about her connections and, if he'd done more than just look at the photographs of her on his father's arm, if he'd taken the time to read the articles rather than just toss them into the bin all those years, he might have. At least that would have explained why she didn't need the money. And it might have meant something more than co-incidence that his PA had booked him into a Sydney hotel bearing Ruby's surname.

A group of partygoers swept into the passageway, the air suddenly filled with laughter and gaiety and half a dozen expensive scents.

Once they'd passed he grabbed hold of her hand. 'Come on,' he said. 'We can't talk here.'

'The reception…' she started.

'I won't keep you long.'

He led her by the hand down the steps as she scooped up the hem of her gown in the other. Tonight she looked like a golden memory of the Roman Empire, her hair coiled around her face and collected into a pearl clasp at the back of her head, with matching pearl earrings and bracelet. Her dress was amazing, the amber fabric wrapped skilfully over one shoulder and tightly around her feminine curves to drape gracefully in folds at her feet. He got the impression that if he pulled in the right place, the material would unwind around her, spinning her out like a prize.

'So what did you want to say?' she asked at the foot of the stairs, pointedly removing her hand from his.

He sucked in a breath, gathering his thoughts as they

strolled along the harbour-line. The night was perfect for a winter's evening, balmy and mild and with barely a trace of the humidity he was starting to become accustomed to in Broome. The Harbour Bridge lighting accentuated its elegant span across the harbour and the office-tower lights and houses of the north shore reflected on the dancing surface of the water like glittering gems. And with her large aqua eyes questioning him, the loose coiled tendrils of her hair floating around her face in the light breeze, she made a stunning view infinitely better.

He ached to stop her and pull her into his arms and give life to the dreams that had tortured him since that night in Broome, dreams of completion, dreams of doing it right. But he had less right to do that now than ever. So, instead of telling her how beautiful she was or scooping her up in his arms, he kept right on walking.

'I was wrong,' he began. 'I was wrong about you from the start and everything I've done since then has only made it worse. And I am sorry. So sorry.'

She looked up at him, her brow knotted. 'And that's supposed to make everything all right, is it?'

'Hardly. I just had to tell you. I couldn't wait for you to get back from Europe. It was too important, especially after what happened...'

His words trailed off and they stopped side by side at the edge of the harbour, looking out over the dark water, watching the foaming trail from a ferry cut a swathe across the water.

'I was so very wrong about you,' he admitted. 'I doubted your talent, I doubted your motivation and accused you of everything I hated in a woman, and, to top it all off, then I had to hurt you physically.'

He raised his head to the heavens before continuing. 'You know, I was jealous of my father. So jealous that he had you.

So jealous of your relationship. And it drove me crazy, wanting you when I thought…'

'You thought I'd slept with your father.'

'I'm not proud of it! But is it so hard to understand? You were beautiful, you lived with him and he left you practically half the business— What else was I supposed to think?'

'You might have asked,' she suggested drily, 'instead of accusing.'

'Yes,' he admitted, nodding. 'You're right. But that night at the launch I wanted you so badly that it didn't matter any more, I had to have you before you went away. Just once, to have you. And I was so blindsided by wanting you that I didn't care any more about my father or who you'd made love to in the past— I was past caring. I just had to have you. But the joke was on me. You were a virgin. You'd never been with anyone, let alone my father.'

'I didn't want you to know,' she admitted. 'I was hoping you wouldn't find out.'

He turned towards her. 'But why? I was so fast—too fast. I hurt you.'

'Because I was so close to leaving Broome. It was better the way things were. It was easier to hate you that way.'

'I don't blame you for hating me,' he said. 'I was gutted when I thought you were only interested in the money from the shares. And then I found out why you needed that premium.'

She frowned, her head tilting in question.

'You left your instructions on Derek Finlayson's desk. I was going to return them to you, but I slipped them into a pocket as I raced after you. By the time I found them again you were already in Sydney. And I realised I'd made even more of a mess of it. I couldn't wait until you came back. I had to tell you how wrong I'd been and how sorry I was.'

They stood in silence for a while, each lost in their own

thoughts, the gentle harbour breeze caressing them like a soothing balm.

'I should be getting back to the reception,' she said, 'but thank you.'

He shrugged and nodded. 'There's just one thing I don't understand.'

'What's that?' she said.

'Why did you live in my father's house? I know I was wrong to jump to conclusions, but how did it come about that you shared a house with him?'

She hesitated. 'I guess it would seem odd. But it's a long story. Basically your father saved me.'

'How?'

She took a deep breath and began, speaking softly into the night air. 'I'd come to Broome, fresh out of design college and it was the first time I'd lived away from Sydney. New job, new town, new possibilities. I was so excited. One of my new colleagues lived in a share house with another couple and they were looking for a fourth person to share with. I could have lived alone, but I was keen to make friends.'

She sighed. 'He was always so helpful to me and I was grateful. He drove me to work to save catching the bus and he'd wait to bring me home, even when I was so involved in designing a piece that I'd forget the time. But he never got upset about it. And if I needed anything, any time, he'd offer to take me shopping or whatever.

'It was my other housemates that noticed first,' she continued, 'and they worried enough to mention it to me. At first I thought they were overreacting, maybe even a little jealous. I really believed he was just a nice person, he'd never so much as made a pass at me. But after a while I began to realise they might be right—if I wanted to go anywhere, anywhere at all, even just to the library, he'd be there. If I looked like going out, he'd insist on coming, too. And then someone else asked me out on a date....'

Already Zane felt like growling. Instead he angled his head so he could see her profile as she gazed unseeingly into the distance, and her gown draping softly and swaying seductively with the gentle breeze.

'What happened?'

She looked down at her clasped hands and took a deep breath. 'He went ballistic. He told me that I couldn't go, that he wouldn't let me. Well, I was getting pretty sick of this crazy infatuation of his by then—it was getting to be like living in a prison. I wasn't particularly interested in this other guy, I just wanted a change, to meet a new face—and when I told him to chill out, he told me that I was his and that nobody else would ever have me.' She paused and he saw her tense and shiver as the ghostly reminder of times past moved through her. 'And that's when I got really scared.'

Inside him the anger built. He could detect the fear in her words, even though she was doing her best to keep her voice even, and he had to fight the desire to sweep her into his arms and make it better.

'What about the police?'

'Oh, I'd tried. I'd called them from work and asked if they could help me, but their hands were tied, they said, until he did something concrete they could charge him with.'

His fingernails bit into his flesh. 'What about family? Did you ask them for help?'

She smiled. 'They were all so far away, and can you believe I didn't want to worry them? I know it sounds ridiculous now, but Opal was recently married with a baby coming and the other, Sapphy, was off in Milan setting the fashion world alight. Plus, we'd only just been reunited with our mother, after twenty years—it wasn't like I could really talk to her about anything, let alone something so personal. And both my sisters were so successful, I just couldn't bear the thought of going home a failure. Besides, I loved working with the pearls. I was determined to make this job a success.'

He turned fully towards her, not pretending any longer to be interested in the view. 'You'd never be a failure,' he said, slipping one hand down the curve of her cheek. 'You've proven that in spades.'

She pressed her lips together like she didn't believe it, but then she didn't pull away, either.

'Anyway, to cut a long story short, finally he did something really stupid and the police had something they could act on.'

His gut clenched. 'Did he hurt you?'

She didn't say anything straight away, but he didn't miss her screwed-up face or the sharp intake of air. Then, on a slow exhale, her features gradually relaxed.

'Not physically. But the experience scared me so much—I didn't think I could trust anyone again. He just wanted me for himself. So one day he must have slipped something into my drink, because I woke up in an old fishing hut, somewhere in the scrub outside Broome, that stank of old fishing gear and God knows what else. And it was so hot inside I could barely breathe. My other house-mates raised the alarm and still it took them a day to find me. I was never so pleased to breathe fresh air in my life. I was so scared....'

She took a deep breath.

'Laurence was shocked. He was one of my first visitors in hospital while they checked me out. He hated that one of his employees had done this to another—I think he felt betrayed by this guy—but also he felt responsible that this could have happened in his organisation. My sister and mother came to visit and Laurence put us all up in his house, but after they'd gone home, I didn't want to stay by myself, so when Laurence suggested I stay until I felt more comfortable, I jumped at the chance.' She pushed herself up from the balustrade and swung around to face him. 'It might sound funny, but we'd been working together by then for almost a year and I did trust him. I respected him for his work in the pearl industry and he was teaching me so much. And I knew he valued and respected my work. He was probably the only person in Broome I could trust at that stage. My own father had died a few years before, and Laurence was a better father than he'd ever been.

'So you see…' she looked up at him and smiled '…your father rescued me. He made me feel safe when I was scared. He treated me like a treasured daughter. Can you now understand why I loved and respected him so much?'

Zane shifted uncomfortably in the late-night air. This wasn't the father he'd left, the father he'd damned all these years. She trusted him implicitly, the man he couldn't trust himself. Why was that?

And why was it that his father had been the one to rescue her when all Zane had done was to give her grief?

'You stayed with him all those years. Were you that scared that you wouldn't move out?'

'No. After a few months, once I knew the guy was safely locked up behind bars, I looked for an apartment, but it was right about then that Laurence had his first attack. It was only angina to start, but I couldn't leave him then, not when he needed someone with him. Kyoto was wonderful, but it would have been unfair to rely on him.'

The knot in Zane's stomach twisted tighter. Laurence's heart condition must have gone on for years and his father had never given him so much as an inkling. And Zane had never taken the time to find out how he was—he'd just assumed his bull of a father would last for ever. Grief and remorse swamped him. Why hadn't his father told him?

Why the hell hadn't he bothered to find out himself? How could he have let anger and bitterness so infuse his life that it permeated his every action?

'I'm sorry,' he said. 'I couldn't have been more wrong.'

It wasn't purely his fault, she knew, even though she hated the labels he'd pinned on her. But she'd let him believe what he had, choosing to put up with his antipathy rather than furnish him with the truth because it had suited her. It had been her defence, bolstering her own suspect resistance.

She could tell him that now—or she could leave it. They had months to live with each other after this, after all. It wouldn't make things easier if he had any idea how much she'd been affected by him from the start.

'I really should get back to the reception, now. If there's nothing else?'

He looked at her strangely, his face a complex blend of emotions. 'Actually, there is,' he said at last, as if he'd been weighing up whether or not to tell her. 'For what it's worth, I finally worked out what Laurence was doing when he set up his crazy bequest.'

She angled herself closer, curious. 'Surely he did it to ensure continuity in management and a way to ease you back into the family business?'

'I have no doubt that was part of it. But being Laurence, he had in mind a much grander plan. I think he was hoping we'd end up married.'

CHAPTER TEN

'YOU HAVE TO BE KIDDING!' she cried. 'That's just daft.'

'Is it so crazy?' he contended. 'Or is it just so obvious that neither of us thought of it before?'

'What do you mean?'

'Why else would Laurence leave us both forty-five per cent of the company? He'd never want ownership split that way permanently. But together we own ninety per cent. Don't you see—that must be why he asked Finlayson not to let us know about the twelve months' condition! He didn't want us to fight against his bequest from the start, each resenting the condition. He was hoping our long-term partnership would happen naturally, without being forced.'

'But to marry?' She was shaking her head. It was too fantastic, too far-fetched.

'Why not? What good would it do the business if we both up and left after twelve months? We'd have our share of the business, but who would run it? Or if I took off back to London? I know you could run the business, but when would you have time to work on your designs?

'But if we were married,' he continued, 'he'd have ensured the management base of the company into the future. Not two separate parcels of forty-five per cent, but combined almost a full ownership. So he arranged to put us together for twelve months. He gave us the shares, the conditions, the incentive of looking after the staff so that you wouldn't back out of it before your year was up. The rest he left up to us.'

It was insane. She was still shaking her head, signalling her denial of his crazy claims with every cell in her body.

'Why would Laurence do that?' Although, even as she asked, she was remembering his dying words. '*Look after Zane.*' Could marriage have been what he'd intended all along?

'Laurence was looking to build a dynasty. He'd already built the biggest and most successful pearling operation in the world, but his only heir had walked out on him. There was no way he was leaving its future to chance—he had to get me back and Laurence no doubt thought you'd be a good match for me. He was clearly proud of his protégée designer. Maybe he saw you as someone not only to lead the business into the future, but also to lure the prodigal son home?'

'If he was so into control, why wouldn't he have just made it a condition of the will that we were to marry to inherit, then?'

'Because he knew or suspected that we were both as strong headed as he was and that we'd never have gone along with something so proscribed. In my father's strange way of thinking, this was subtle manipulation.'

She brushed both his suppositions and his arm away with the same irreverent sweep of her hand. 'And now you're giving credence to this bizarre theory of yours? I simply can't believe you'd endorse anything that smacked of having your father's hand in it. In fact, I'd have expected, the way you feel about him, that you'd run a mile from anything you thought he was trying to manipulate you into.'

A muscle in his cheek twitched dangerously. 'We have learnt something about each other while we've been together.

As you say, I had that exact reaction at first. And then I got to thinking… There are worse ways to be manipulated.'

'I can't believe you're serious. Are you so desperate for control of my shares that you'd actually consider marrying me?'

'Why do you think this is about the shares?'

'What else would there be in it for you?'

He smiled uncertainly and came closer, the reflections of the walkway lights adding to the fire in his eyes, his movements measured and predatory, like some dark animal about to pounce.

'*You.*'

Oxygen!

She needed oxygen to get her mind to work, to power her muscles into action—into escape. But there was no oxygen left to power her thoughts or her body, it had all been burned up in the fire storm of his approach.

'I wouldn't blame you if you never wanted to see me again. But all I've dreamed of since you left Broome is to have a second chance with you, to make up for the mess I made of things and to make love to you properly, the way it should have been done. The way you deserve to be made love to.'

She swallowed back on a lurching heart while his eyes drank her in, feasted on her and then suddenly she was in his arms and it was his mouth, his hot mouth, devouring her and she was back in Broome, back in the hotel room, the same sensations, the same passion that had swept her away that same night with no thought to the consequences.

His hands circled her, pressing her tight up against him, reminding her starkly of what they had almost shared. She clung to him, feeling her body mould to his, her muscles strangely weakened and yet her senses empowered at the same time.

Because she wanted him. She wanted to feel him fill her once again. Her body hungered to feel him deep inside her. Her body craved the completion she'd been cheated out of before.

And he wanted her. Now he even talked of marrying her. Could that mean he felt something for her amidst all that?

His hands swept up the curve of her spine, rounded her shoulders and cupped her face as his kisses slowed.

'I want you,' he whispered. 'And I need you, tonight.'

She shuddered into his heated embrace as his words re-iterated his body's communication. 'But...' she said, trying to think when all she could do was want. 'But maybe I should get back to the reception.'

One hand moved, like a heated flow of ecstasy, down her jaw to her chest, cupping one breast in a warm embrace, brushing over her nipple in a way that made her dizzy with need.

'I know. But I need you. Now!'

It was a giddy journey back to the hotel. Giddy and hot and lightheaded. She was aware of his hands on her, holding hers, stroking her back, holding her tight at the waist, and yet, for all the innocence of how this might have looked to the casual passer-by, it felt like something else completely. Because nobody else could see the intent that accompanied his grip, nobody else could feel the electric hum of desire that coursed from him to her and back again.

Clemengers Hotel lobby was always marked by calm ef-ficiency, but at this hour the atmosphere was even more hushed and discreet. Without asking, he led the way to his suite, never taking his eyes off her or letting his hands stray from her, never giving her one opportunity to back out. But she wasn't going anywhere. Not without Zane.

Because she was hungry for him and hungry for more of what he could provide, as if what had happened in Broome had been the entrée, teasing her appetite to critical levels, and tonight would bring the main course. What had she missed out on that night? Whatever it was, she was going to find out and more.

'This time, I'll do it right,' he whispered once they were safely inside the darkened room and something inside her swelled and bloomed. He raised her chin and kissed her lips and this time she sensed something new in his kiss, a tenderness, a taste of something deeper than desire. Commitment? Did it mean he really believed this crazy theory of his?

Then his fingers stroked the fabric covering her breasts and she gasped into his mouth and forgot how to think, giving herself up to the sensation as he trailed tiny kisses down her throat, covering her bare shoulder with his lips, easing his fingertips under the neckline of her gown. Already her prickle of arousal was turning into a rush of need.

'Such a beautiful gown,' he said, letting his fingers explore further, sliding them between the fabric and her skin, capturing one breast, his fingers ministering to it, worshipping it like it was a prize. 'But right now…' he smiled down at her, his eyes warm and filled with longing '…I want you out of it.'

Her breath stopped as he picked her up in his arms and carried her to the large king-sized bed in the bedroom adjacent. Once there, he kissed her again and deposited her gently, almost reverentially, on the soft cover of the bed. He moved to the windows and slid open the heavy curtains, letting the room fill with the soft glow of the harbour at night.

Then he turned back and looked at her and the world stood still.

Seconds were consumed, or it could even have been minutes, in the heated glow from his eyes. Like a flame it lapped at her skin, surrounding her in its warm embrace.

He shrugged off his jacket, threw it over a chair, pulled the end of his tie and tugged it from his collar and let it fall to the floor. Buttons were flicked through, one by one, as slowly, deliberately, he stoked up the fires. She swallowed, her mouth ashen, her body tingling, as she propped herself up against the pillows, flicking off her heels and tucking her legs beneath her.

If that night in Broome had been hurried and over too quickly, then obviously this night was to be slow and languid.

He undid the buttons at his wrists, his eyes never leaving her, and her eyes were drawn to the cleft in his shirt, to the olive skin, and dark curls hinted at below until she ached to reach out and touch him. Then he tugged free his shirt tails and, as if he'd heard her silent pleas, walked to the bed and sat down alongside her, so close that she could feel his desire curling into hers, meshing with her own.

He wound a hand around her neck and drew her face to his mouth and kissed her. Languidly. Deeply. She reached a hand between them, slipped it under his shirt and felt his rushed intake of breath as she explored the sculpted form below, encountering the tight nub of a nipple, running her nails through the spring of chest hair.

Emboldened, hungry for more, her other hand followed suit, drinking him in with her hands, from the tight lean abdomen to his broad shoulders. Impatiently she scooped the shirt over his shoulders, wanting more, and he obliged by wrenching it down his arms and tossing it to the floor. There'd been no time for such exploration before and she revelled in it, luxuriated in the masculine tone of his skin, the coarse hairs over the sculpted muscles.

He pulled back, his breathing rough, his eyes turbulent. 'Like I said—' his voice was gritty and low as he traced his fingers under her shoulder strap '—we need to get this off.'

It seemed such a blur after that. There were so many sensations, so many discoveries, so many rewards. He slid her dress down, she pulled through his belt, he peeled away her stockings and she released him from his silken pouch until finally, gloriously, both were naked.

He pulled the clasp from her hair, letting it float around her shoulders as he lowered her down among the pillows. In the low light her skin shimmered and gleamed, satin smooth and as rich as the nacre of a pearl, and as much as he ached to bury himself inside her, as much as he burned with need, after what had happened before, he knew that this moment was too important to rush.

He touched a hand to her face, stroking it down her neck to where another pendant from the Passion Collection lay against her skin, the design staggering in both its simplicity and its powerful suggestion. 'Beautiful,' he said.

Her hand reached for the heavy pendant and she lifted her head. 'Should I—?'

'Take it off? No,' he said, inspiration hitting him in that instant. 'Wait…'

He swung off the bed and padded across the room, his body magnificent, a study in shadow and light and such raw masculine power that she caught her breath, shuddering with anticipation for what was to come.

He reached into his jacket. *Protection*, she assumed with relief. Thank God one of them was thinking tonight. She'd long ago given up. And then he was back, something small deposited on the bedside table with a rustle and something else in his hands.

'What are you doing—?' she asked.

Cutting off her protest, he drew out a long rope of pearls and lassoed it around her neck, draping it in between her breasts, catching one wrist in a loop that travelled over the feminine curve of her tummy and down lower, much lower, where they kissed the whisky spring of curls.

'I borrowed it from the collection,' he admitted. 'I had this dream about you adorned with pearls. And pearls must be worn or without contact with the skin they fade and lose their lustre.'

She was just about breathless as the pearls went to work, stroking her skin like a thousand fingers, but warm like living things, moving against her skin like nature's caress.

'They were worn just this evening.' Her voice sounded strange to her ears, husky and tight.

'Not like this, they weren't.'

He leaned back and surveyed his work, his eyes glinting and hot with appreciation. 'Perfection,' he said. 'My treasure from the sea.'

And then his mouth was on hers, his body within heated proximity alongside, his hands exploring her feminine form, worshipping her, setting her body alight. And every time she moved her hand, the pearl rope shifted, rolled, tantalised, tugging at her senses, magnifying the experience.

He drew back, taking a loop of the rope and coiling it around her breast and then he dropped his mouth on to her peaking nipple, laving her, suckling her so that her back arched, driving her further into his mouth. First one breast and then the other, driving her wild, separating her from a woman with thoughts and plans and career to simply a woman of need, desperate pulsating need.

Then his mouth dipped lower, following the line of pearls on her flesh, tracing its path down her body. He kissed the tiny swell of her tummy, the scoop of her flesh that fell away from her hip bone and, when he parted her, she knew she was lost. One touch of his fingers, one flick of his tongue and she came apart, her body fracturing around him, absorbing him.

And just when she thought it could get no better, that she was on her way down from the most spectacular high she'd ever had—he entered her, in one long thrust that arrested her fall and took her up again. This time there was no resistance, no pain, only the welcoming build of intensity; with each thrust he took her higher, ever higher, building the pressure all over again, urgent and pressing as her body welcomed him, enclosed him, sought to retain him. And between them the pearls gleamed against her damp skin, moving as part of her, capturing the rhythm only to still at that point of no return, that point that preceded her plunge once more over the abyss.

But this time she wasn't alone.

He unwound himself from her arms and eased away for a minute, his body slick and spent, his breathing ragged, his mind and senses blown away. Never before had he found a woman so responsive. Never before had he come so totally undone. He turned and looked at her, struck by her beauty now more than ever, her hair wild in abandon on the pillow, her lips plump and pink and thoroughly kissed and a mantle of pearls whose beauty didn't come close to matching their wearer's. She could be a painting by Botticelli, a goddess emerged from the sea, a modern-day Venus.

Her eyes fluttered open. 'Zane,' she whispered in a way that made his insides curl.

He loved the way she responded. Already he wanted more, wanted to press himself into her, feel her tightly encased around him. He moved back to the bed, dropping his mouth to her breasts, alternately teasing them with the pearls and then his lips and teeth, loving the feel of her in his mouth, loving the taste of her.

He gasped when he felt her soft fingers brush against him, taking him by surprise. He held his breath, willing her to touch him, to cradle him in her hand, but what she answered with was completely unexpected. He growled with pleasure as coils were wound around him. He responded the only way he could, by hardening even more, filling the pearl coils even tighter, reminding him of another sweet, tight place….

'You're playing with fire,' he warned her.

'I want you again—now.'

He choked back a gasp as she tugged, tightening the noose still further. 'And you think that's the way to get me?'

'I think so,' she said, smiling up at him even as she applied more subtle pressure to her pearl lasso.

'So who said you're the boss?' he jibed, dipping his mouth to her nipple once again and studiously ignoring the urge to fill her right now. 'I thought we were supposed to be partners.'

'I never said you couldn't come, too.' Then she tugged at the pearls in such a way that they uncoiled around him in a whoosh. 'I need you—inside me—now!'

It was all he could do to focus long enough to prepare himself before plunging once again into her welcoming depths.

She was a witch, a sea witch, and right now what he needed was more of her magic.

It was a new day. A brand new day. A fizz of excitement zipped through her as she stood out on the tiny balcony, concentrating the sparks in places and muscles already protesting their overuse. Last night had been fantastic, mind-blowing and a revelation.

As for regrets? How could she have any? Zane was an amazing lover, he'd proved that so many times last night she'd lost count. And he'd made her feel so special, so precious. He'd wanted to do it right for her, and he had.

He'd felt so right.

Across the harbour the colours were changing and the new sun lit up the city coming to life. She sighed. What would Laurence really think? Had this been something he'd wished for all along, that they become a partnership in more than just their shareholding?

She smiled as she watched the pink sky wash away to grey and then blue. There was no guilt. Somehow she knew Laurence would approve. And somehow she suspected

Laurence knew she would fall for him. After all, Zane was his son—how could she not love him, too?

Love him?

She trembled in the early morning cool, pulling her plush hotel robe more tightly around her even as the first warming rays of sunlight washed over her. *She couldn't love him.* Not Zane. Not after everything that had happened between them. And yet…there was something that moved inside her that couldn't be ignored. Something that had his name inscribed on it.

He wasn't the complete villain she'd painted him from the start. Just as he'd assumed the worst of her, she'd misjudged him, too. And at least now she had some inkling of why he'd believed the things he had.

But could she be falling for him? Could she really be falling in love with Zane?

How could that have happened?

He stood silently, watching her standing wreathed in light, a beam of sun catching on the silken highlights in her hair, the sculpted perfection of her features.

Even the sun wanted her. Even the sun marked her as the one.

What was she thinking as she gazed out over the bay? Why had she abandoned his bed? Was she suffering morning-after regrets? He wasn't, that was a certainty.

As if suddenly aware of his presence, she turned her head. Her eyes widened and then she smiled that smile he'd first seen that day on the boat coming back from the pearl farm, that smile he'd wanted to see again, the smile he wanted to see made just for him. And just like that time, it was incredibly sexy. It lit up her face just as it stoked his fires. He knotted the loosening towel at his waist tighter and walked up behind her, wrapping his arms around her and burying his face in her neck.

'You're up early,' he muttered against her throat.

'And you're...*up*,' she acknowledged, wiggling her bottom tantalisingly against him.

He laughed, or rumbled more like it, a sound filled with intent as he pulled her back inside the French doors where the sun could still capture her, but they were safe from other eyes.

He kissed her sensitive mouth as he eased her up on to the marble side table, pushing in between her legs.

'Maybe you could help me with that,' he suggested, sliding her tie undone. She trembled as he drew her robe apart and slid his arms around her waist to catch her behind.

'I'm claiming you,' he said. 'Just like I claimed you in the night, I'm showing the morning that you're mine.'

His towel dropped from his hips and with a thrill of pure pleasure her eyes took in the magnificent fullness of him. She felt him nudge against her until every part of her was waiting, wanting, anticipating, and then he was pushing himself into her, taking her in one long, slow, sensual slide.

Filling her.

Impaling her.

Claiming her.

Instinctively she wrapped her legs around his waist and took him deeper until he pierced her heart. Had he meant what he'd just said? Because the primal rush she'd felt when he'd appeared, naked-chested, with just a white towel lashed around his hips; the primitive urge to mate that she'd felt when he'd pressed into her; even the feel of his body now cocooned in hers—they were nothing compared to the thrill of hearing him say that he wanted her, that he was claiming her for his own.

His words heightened his love-making, turned joyfulness to bliss, and when she came, as he pumped his release into her, there were four words she read clearly written amid the fireworks-lit heavens of the new day.

I love you, Zane.

CHAPTER ELEVEN

ZANE EMERGED FROM THE BATHROOM, already in a suit and tie, shaved and perfectly groomed, ready for his flight back to Broome. The mere sight of him caused her breath to catch, the hint of mischief in his eyes and his turned-up mouth turning her flesh to a slow sizzle. But he'd be out of the suite in less than five minutes, and still they'd not had a chance to talk. What would happen when she returned to Broome?

'We haven't had much of a chance to talk,' she said, nervously sipping on an espresso she was praying would lend her its strength.

His wicked smile turned up another notch, his eyes looked like they were peeling the robe from her. 'Not that we wasted a minute of the time we had.'

She blushed with the intensity of his gaze. 'At least we can forget about all those crazy ideas about marriage now, I guess?'

'Forget about it? Why the hell would we want to do that?'

She blinked, hope meshing with confusion in a tangle of thoughts inside. Why would he still want to go ahead with it? Unless…

Unless he felt something for her, too. Something beyond physical need.

She tried to laugh, to belie the tension she was feeling. 'So why would you seriously consider it? It's not as if you have to go to the trouble of marrying me to get me into your bed.'

'Who says marrying you would be any trouble?' he said, downing his tiny cup of coffee like a shot.

'Zane, be serious!'

'I am serious. I can't see what your problem is. We know we're compatible. We share a business and we've shared a bed, *most* satisfactorily. We've got more going for us than most people. And it appears we have Laurence's blessing. Your mentor. The person you admired and looked up to, more than anyone in the world. It's what *he* would have wanted, after all—to have you as his daughter-in-law, to provide him with more heirs. You don't want to let him down.'

She swallowed, her mouth suddenly dry and scratchy again. Right now this wasn't about what Laurence wanted. 'Well, then, what about love? Shouldn't love have something to do with it?'

His brow drew down a fraction, but then he just sighed and dropped an arm casually around her shoulders. 'It's not compulsory, if that's what you're worried about. I'm sure we'll develop some form of deep-seated affection over time. In fact, that's probably preferable to love.'

She reeled at his words, but at least he'd cleared up one question for her. He didn't love her. He might never. 'How can you say that?'

He shrugged. 'I know that love didn't help my mother. She worshipped my father, for all the good it did her. He betrayed her, just the same. She loved him more than anything and yet still he could abuse that trust and love and take a mistress. So maybe it's better not to love. Maybe it's better to save the emotion for the bedroom.' He planted a kiss to the back of her neck. 'We'll no doubt need it.'

If his last comment was an attempt to warm her after the

rest of his cold words, it failed miserably. She turned away and rose out of her chair, appalled, sickened by his cynical words. So what did that say for her love? What good was that to her if he felt this way? How committed would he be to her if he didn't love her—if he didn't ever expect to? Would he, too, expect to have his interest on the side, like he claimed his father had?

No, she couldn't bear that!

'Your father loved your mother. I know he did. He was devastated by her loss.'

'If he really loved her, he would never have taken a mistress! He would never have elevated her to the position she occupied.'

She shivered and crossed her arms over her chest, the force of his bitter resentment erecting a solid wall between them, reminding her of all the reasons why such a marriage could never work. 'I don't even know why we're talking about this. We don't have to get married. It's not as if it's a condition of the will.'

'Laurence clearly expected it.'

'You don't know that! Not for sure. And, frankly, I think you're wrong to even imagine that a marriage could work when there's no love involved.'

'Why? Can you honestly say that love was instrumental in your own parents' relationship?'

'I know that my father's lack of it was instrumental in their marriage breakdown!'

He hesitated, his head tilted, as if assessing the import of her words. Then he stood and crossed to where she was standing, putting his hands on her arms.

'Okay, maybe I'm rushing it. We have another nine months together before we have to do anything. Meanwhile, you'll be away for a week. Take your time—think about it while you're gone—and when you come back we can talk about it again.'

Then he kissed her one more time and headed for the door. 'Promise me you'll think about it?'

She nodded as he left. She'd think about it, certainly, not that it would do him much good. She could never marry him, not with his prejudice against his father, not with his cynical view of love and marriage. It just wouldn't happen.

'So tell me about Zane?'

Ruby looked over her cup of coffee suspiciously. When Opal had suggested getting together in her apartment for a chat, Ruby had suspected it wouldn't be too long before the fishing expedition got underway. 'Deft change of subject, big sister. I thought we were talking about how the hotel business is going.'

Opal laughed, scooping up her dark-haired, twelve-month-old toddler on to her knee and giving him a sandwich finger to munch on while four-and-a-half-year-old Ellie sat quietly on a rug, flicking quietly through a stack of books. 'Give a girl a break!' Opal pleaded. 'I live in a hotel. I work in one. I go to bed counting hotels instead of sheep. I'd much rather talk about a hot-looking guy any day. And you have to admit, Zane is one hot-looking guy—especially given the way he looks at you!'

Ruby put her cup down. Zane was no doubt already halfway back to Broome by now and tomorrow she'd be flying on to New York. Thinking time, she'd figured, intending to mull it over in her own mind during the long flights, but maybe it would be good to discuss it with her sister, first. Her emotions had been on so much of a rollercoaster ride since Zane had appeared on the scene, she could do with a fresh perspective.

'What exactly did you want to know?'

'You know, all the good stuff. What's he like? Is he a good kisser? And exactly how serious is it between you guys, anyway?'

'Who says I know how he kisses?'

Her sister grinned at her too-fast rebuttal. 'Well, you were missed at the reception last night—until someone spotted you both out on the promenade.'

Ruby felt her colour rise and turned away. 'So, it was just a kiss. That doesn't mean there's anything going on.'

'You have to be kidding! You saw how he acted last night when he showed up, the way he looked like he wanted to tear Domenic limb from limb for just touching you! That guy is seriously hooked.'

Ruby sipped her coffee and thought back to when she'd introduced the two. Is that what had been going on? She'd been so assailed by conflicting emotions and sensations, from the tingling awareness when Zane had arrived, to the shock when he'd taken hold of her shoulder and the huge satisfaction when Zane had realised her connections. There had been so much happening that she hadn't been able to make sense of it all at the time. Could Opal be right though? Had Zane really been jealous?

Mind you, what if he had been? It meant nothing more than that he wanted her in his bed and he was willing to face down the competition. It was pointless reading any more into it than that, no matter what she might have wished for.

'So,' Opal continued, handing little Guglielmo another tiny sandwich, 'how do you feel about him?'

She sighed. 'Confused,' she replied honestly, trying not to think too much about the night she'd just spent in his arms, the joy of being joined with him, the bliss at the way he made her feel and then the hollow emptiness of the uncertainty that followed. The harsh light of day wasn't just a cliché, it had become a reality.

'I really wish I knew. We couldn't stand the sight of each other at first. I hated the way he'd seemingly abandoned his father and he hated the closeness I shared with Laurence. But as for now—sometimes I think he might be the most special man on earth, but at other times…' She hesitated. 'At other times, I'm not so sure. Sometimes he can seem so angry and I don't know how he can ever get over it.'

'Angry with you?'

'No. He's angry at Laurence. He's bitter about his mother's death and it colours his view of so many things. He says his father had a mistress all the time he was married, apparently his wife's closest friend. It seems it was the mistress driving the car in which they were both killed.'

Opal's eyes opened wide. 'My God! And I thought our family had a bizarre history. But you knew Laurence well—what do you think?'

'I can't believe Laurence would betray a trust that way. He was a man of integrity. I'm confident that the Laurence I knew would never do such a thing.'

'Then it's easy,' Opal said, lifting a squirming Guglielmo from her knee and back down on to the floor. 'You just have to convince Zane of that.'

Sure, Ruby thought, *piece of cake*, as she watched Guglielmo toddle happily over to his sister, plonk down beside her and pick up a book, too, upside-down, but not that he cared. She smiled, watching her young niece right it and hand it back before her younger brother could protest too loudly.

Both her sisters really seemed to have it all: the great careers, the drop-dead gorgeous husbands who were also their soul-mates, and, to top it off, now also beautiful families. Only this morning she'd learned the wonderful news that her sister Sapphy was expecting twin boys. By all accounts both she and husband Khaled were over the moon.

'Guglielmo's such a gorgeous baby. And he's going to look just like Domenic when he gets older, a real lady killer. And Ellie is so cute, too. Both your kids are just so beautiful.'

Opal turned her attention from the children and looked Ruby straight in the eye. 'You know, you and Zane would make beautiful babies.'

Ruby looked up sharply. *Babies?*

Then it hit her. *Zane's babies.*

How special would that be—to give him a child, a tiny Zane, maybe to build a family with him, to replace something of what he'd lost?

But it was a fantasy.

She sighed, knowing she should probably say nothing, but needing someone to confide in. 'He has mentioned marriage.'

'Oh, Ruby! That's fantastic!' Opal reached over and hugged her sister. 'Congratulations! When are you going to tell Mum?'

She shook her head. 'I told him I hadn't decided.'

Opal sat down again, stunned. 'But what on earth for? I mean, you love him, don't you?'

Ruby stared at her sister and blinked. 'Is it that obvious?'

'Come on,' her older sister said, 'Zane's not the only one putting out signals. Don't you know the way you look at him? And when you guys are together, you're both so hot it's a wonder you don't start bushfires.'

'Maybe. But that's lust and right now that's the only thing we have between us. Zane doesn't love me. He all but admitted it. He thinks we'll eventually form some kind of affectionate bond. I don't think I can do that. I can't marry a guy I love knowing he doesn't love me in return. I couldn't settle for mere affection. Look what happened to Mum, driven away, driven crazy, because she loved too much.'

Opal picked up Ruby's hand and patted it between hers, a knowing look in her eye. 'Hey, have faith! Zane loves you, I'm sure of it. But sometimes these men take a while to come to terms with being in love—maybe he just doesn't realise it yet.'

Zane tried to catch up on sleep on the flight back to Broome. There hadn't been much of that last night. He growled out a sigh and stretched back in his wide business-class seat. Just thinking about last night made him hard all over again. Ruby was honeyed perfection, inside and out. It was going to be one hell of a long week sleeping alone, waiting for her return. Maybe he should have gone with her after all, and left the pearl business to take care of itself. Maybe then she wouldn't have been so edgy.

What had that been all about?

Couldn't she understand that marriage would make so much sense? Laurence had clearly had such an outcome in mind from the start, as the perfect way to cement his young protégée to the business for ever. And what better way to get his son home and keep him there? Zane allowed himself a smile. The idea of a lifetime of nights spent with Ruby had a lot of appeal. It would never make up for what Laurence had done to his mother, but he sure had to hand it to the old man. It was one hell of a plan.

Now he just had to get Ruby to fall in with it. He closed his eyes and settled the chair to recline, crossing his arms and ankles.

She'd come around.

Could Opal be right? Ruby drove herself crazy with that question over the next few days. When she wasn't meeting with high-powered clients and agent representatives, her mind was churning, tossing around the possibilities. Only two things were certain. First, that she loved Zane, and second, that she'd happily spend the rest of her life with him if only she could be certain her love would be returned and not wasted.

But what if Opal was right and he loved her already? What were the chances? What if he didn't love her and she married him and he was never able to reciprocate that love?

Could she afford to take a risk? Should she?

In the end it was a television hostess in London who answered her question for her. Sonia Clarke was the morning television queen and already a big fan of her designs. Today she was sporting her own signature string of perfect silver-white pearls and matching earrings that she'd ordered especially from Ruby's previous collection. It was the first of a long line-up of appointments she had today before leaving later that night from Heathrow on the long flight home, an entire day earlier than expected due to a flight rescheduling. It had meant some major reorganisation of her own schedule, but she'd managed to fit everything in at a squeeze.

The interview was going well and Ruby appreciated Sonya's extensive knowledge of the industry and her appreciation for the gems. It was a good way to start the day. Then Sonia asked her why she thought her designs were so successful the world over. With barely a thought Ruby proceeded to go through her usual answer—she was fortunate enough to be able to work with the most beautiful pearls in the world and she'd always been given a lot of scope by Laurence to put her heart into her work. It was then that the Sonia said it.

'If you don't mind me saying so, I think your success is also due in a large way because you take such risks with your work. The Passion Collection is a case in point. Who else would imagine that a jewellery design could be so evocative could so resemble a lovers' embrace? But you obviously achieved that because you're a risk-taker. You couldn't have done it, otherwise.'

Ruby stared blankly at Sonia and mumbled something in

response and somehow even managed to make it through the rest of the interview. But she couldn't get the words out of her head. She was a risk-taker. And it was true. She took major risks with her designs every day.

Maybe it was time to take a risk on Zane.

Ruby stepped on to the tarmac of Broome International Airport and felt the familiar heat wrap around her like a warm embrace—*a lover's embrace*. Broome had never felt so good. And she couldn't wait to surprise Zane. It was a Sunday and he'd probably be home. She wasn't even going to wait until she'd gone to her room at the hotel and freshened up. She'd go straight to the house and with any luck she could freshen up with him.

The taxi driver pulled into the driveway and helped her out with her bag. He was just pulling out on to the street when Kyoto came clambering down the stairs urgently, his aging knees angled wide over his slippered feet.

'Miss Ruby! Miss Ruby!'

It was no welcome-home greeting. 'Kyoto, what's wrong?'

Kyoto didn't have time to answer before she appeared on the verandah, all elegance and grace and Nordic swish, one hand resting gracefully on the balustrade, the other propped against an upright beam, looking to all the world like she owned the place.

'So *you're* Ruby. But aren't you home early? Zane told me we had until tomorrow.'

CHAPTER TWELVE

RUBY'S BLOOD TURNED TO ICE, frozen crystals piercing her flesh, tattooing the word '*fool*' in giant letters on her heart. The woman was beautiful, like a tall white lily, her features classical, her clothes couture, and she was so obviously not 'just an old friend' of Zane's.

And if the swell under her liquid silk gown was any indication, she was also pregnant!

Her gut churned. Oh, my God, surely it couldn't be—*Zane's baby*?

No wonder he hadn't given her a hard time over her insisting she do the overseas tour alone. He'd planned to ship his mistress in while she was gone. And after all that talk about marriage!

'You must be Anneleise,' she acknowledged. She looked searchingly over at Kyoto, his face a wrinkled mess of concern. 'Where's Zane?'

'Gone to the office,' Anneleise crooned from the verandah. 'He said he had work to do, but I'm betting he's sorting out some lovely trinkets for me. He's so thoughtful like that. He'll be back later this afternoon. Shall I tell him you dropped by?'

Ruby ignored her, trying even harder to ignore the thought of

Anneleise wearing one of her designs, having it adorn her porcelain skin, having Zane make love to her while she wore it…

'Kyoto?' she said, trying to keep balance, to maintain some kind of hold on reality. 'What's going on?'

'I'm sorry, Miss Ruby. He say she should go before you get back.'

'I'll just bet he did,' she whispered under her breath.

'It's okay, Kyoto,' crooned Anneleise, floating down the stairs like a silken viper, 'it was inevitable that we'd meet up at some stage, what with us both having Zane in common.'

If Ruby thought Anneleise looked stunning standing up on the verandah, it was nothing to how she looked close up. Fine boned and long-limbed, her almost translucent skin and silvery blonde hair gave her a fragile, almost ethereal look.

And after twenty-plus hours travelling, Ruby felt like a damp rag next to the finest silk.

Anneleise looked down at Ruby's luggage and frowned. Were you expecting Zane to give you a lift somewhere?'

Ruby's breath hissed through her teeth. *Not quite*, but there was no way she was staying now. Obviously she was surplus to requirements. 'Yes,' she lied. 'Just to my hotel while we talked over business. But I'll get a taxi.'

Kyoto gave her an apologetic look and bowed slightly. 'I'll call,' he said, before heading back into the house.

Anneleise placed a pale hand against her brow. 'It's so hot in the sun. I feel quite dizzy.'

Her brow pulled into a frown as Anneleise's slim-fitting dress pulled taut over her stomach as she settled herself down in the covered swing, resting one manicured hand on her tummy.

There was Zane's dynasty in waiting! All that talk about what Laurence had wanted had meant nothing. Because he didn't care what Laurence wanted—he never had. All he cared about was his blessed birthright—and he'd do anything to wrest control from her, even if he had to marry her. He'd get his shares and a convenient lay in the process. And in Sydney she'd shown him just how convenient she could be.

What a total fool she'd been!

'I really don't know how you put up with this shocking heat,' complained Anneleise, fanning her face with her hand. 'I thought it would be winter here now.'

'It is winter,' Ruby retorted, finding the day warm but by no means unpleasant. 'But here in the tropics we call it the dry.'

'Then the sooner Zane comes home to London the better. I don't think I could take too much of this. He has such a beautiful home in Chelsea. You must visit us there some time.'

Ruby sucked in a breath. It just got better and better. 'When do you think that might happen?'

'I'm not sure. Once he's sorted out some problem with the shares or something.'

Her ears pricked up. 'What problem?'

She shrugged, and even managed to do that elegantly. 'Something his father made a mess of, apparently. I don't know the details, only that it's keeping him here much longer than he intended.'

Ruby said nothing, while all she wanted to do was scream. And yell. And hit someone.

Mostly Zane.

What was the point of all that rubbish he'd spoken about them managing the business together into the future? What was all that garbage about marriage? Or was there method in his madness—to marry somebody he knew he could trust to look after the company, enabling him to flit off to Europe and his blonde bombshell whenever he felt the urge?

Or was this his way of seeking the ultimate revenge upon his father? Marry the whore and take total control without having to spend a cent.

The bitter sting of tears pricked at her eyes, but she forced them back. Damn the man! But the last thing she would let herself do was to allow herself to cry in front of his paramour.

The taxi was a welcome sight. 'It was lovely to meet you,' she heard Anneleise call from the swing as Ruby hurled both herself and her hand luggage into the car.

'Are you all packed?' Zane hoped she was. He was in no mood to put up with more of Anneleise's delaying tactics. He was in no mood to put up with Anneleise, period. He'd taken himself off to his office for hours today so he didn't have to put up with her attempts at gentle persuasion.

Anneleise pouted and reclined languidly on the swing, setting up a gentle swinging motion. 'Do I really have to go already? It's such a long journey.'

'You should have thought about that before you invited yourself here. You'll be on that plane, today.'

Before Ruby gets back! Two times now he'd thought he'd had her, he'd thought she was his for the taking, and then he'd thrown a spanner in the works and said something stupid and blown it and she'd gone cold and backed right away from him. He wasn't prepared to risk that happening again. And Anneleise made for one mighty big spanner.

'But in my condition…'

'You should have thought about that, too!'

'You were so nice to me in London.' She pouted, sounding confused. 'I thought you cared.'

'You needed help. I got you that help. I would have done the same for a sick dog.' But all the same he wished he hadn't. 'Where are your bags?'

'You had a visitor while you were out.'

'Oh,' he replied, only half-interested, thinking more about how he was going to get around the problem of admitting that

Anneleise had been here at all. Ruby had enough problems trusting him without him adding to his sins by thinking he could keep it a secret. But he'd have to pick the right time. He had too much ground to make up first. He lifted the boot of the car and looked over to the house, half-expecting Kyoto to already have her bags ready and waiting.

'So, I was thinking maybe there's no rush for me to leave after all. I mean, now that we've actually met.'

Cold dread seeped into his spine. He snapped his attention back to Anneleise, who was smiling, her eyes wide with the excitement of someone sharing a secret.

'Met who?'

'Why, your little friend Ruby, of course.'

Agony tore a swathe through him, all but wrenching his guts from his body.

'Ruby was here?'

She laughed and right at that moment he'd never heard such a sick sound or hated anyone half as much. And he'd felt sorry for her in London!

'She's quite pretty.'

He had to get to her! He slammed the boot shut.

'Kyoto!' he yelled, already halfway to the house. 'Kyoto!'

'But she seemed upset about something.'

He spun around, half-needing to know, half-dreading the answer already. 'What did you say to her?'

She eased out of the chair and glided across the lawn towards him. 'Oh, nothing in particular and nothing that you didn't tell me in London. Just how you were planning to return after you'd sorted out this business with the shares.'

My God! He could just imagine how Ruby would take comments like those. He'd still hoped to buy Ruby out back then. 'I said that *if* I returned to London it wouldn't be for some time.'

She shrugged and looked up at him innocently. 'Isn't that almost the same thing?'

Zane ignored her. He was too busy estimating the amount of damage Anneleise had done. He had no doubt her barbs were calculated, but she wouldn't have had any idea of the amount of poison they contained. She would be delighted if she only knew.

'Kyoto!' he yelled again before turning around. 'Kyoto can order you a taxi. But I want you out of here now. And I don't want to find you here when I get back.'

'But you knew I was coming. I called you when I booked!'

'And I told you to cancel!'

'So where are you going?' she demanded, her voice cracking with the inevitable tears. Not that they'd make any difference.

'Where do you think I'm going? To try and repair some of the damage you've done.'

He entered the house's cool interior, dark after the bright sunlight. Where was that man? This was no time to take a nap!

'You love her, don't you?'

Anneleise sounded angry, her attempt at tears obviously already abandoned as useless, and for a moment he was going to snap back that she was wrong, just like she was wrong thinking there was any hope of a relationship between him and her.

And then it hit him. He couldn't say that. Anneleise had for once spoken the truth. She was right.

He was in love with Ruby!

Anguish melded with fury at the revelation. How could he have not seen that until now? How could he have missed so obvious a truth?

He stormed into the kitchen, his mind in turmoil, his heart in shock, his senses blown away.

And that's when he found him.

CHAPTER THIRTEEN

CABLE BEACH SEEMED to stretch forever, disappearing into the distance in both directions, its endless white sands and brilliant turquoise sea all framed by a boundless sky. Ruby got the impression that if she just kept walking she'd disappear too, that she'd fade into the distance like the coast line. And right now the idea held a lot of appeal.

Sand whipped around her ankles and stung against her face, but it didn't matter and unlike the other beach-goers, who'd headed back to the resort when the wind picked up, she didn't try to shelter from the wind. Her eyes were already gritty and swollen, she had nothing to fear from the elements.

It was people who could wreak the most damage. People that you trusted and who let you down. It was people who inflicted the deepest cuts.

She wandered further down the deserted beach, her sandals clutched in one hand, slapping against her legs as she walked, her toes splashing in the shallows of the Indian Ocean. She didn't know how long she'd been walking. She didn't really care. And what else could she do? Sleep had eluded her. An hour of lying on her bed, seeking the bliss that only deep, dreamless sleep could provide, had shown her that.

So she walked, and she kept on walking. And only when

the sun had started to dip towards its inevitable union with the ocean did she turn around and head back to the resort.

There was no missing the flashing message button on her phone. The phone rang again and she let it ring until it rang out. If that was Zane, she didn't want to talk to him. Anybody else she didn't need to talk to right now. So she ignored it, instead stripping off and standing under a hot shower for a long time, letting the water wash away the sand-streaked tracks of her tears, wishing it could so easily wash away the bitter tracks through her heart.

Minutes later, there was a noise, a thumping. Someone was pounding on her door.

She didn't have to open the door to know who it would be. *Zane.*

Maybe if she was quiet, he'd eventually get sick of pounding. Maybe then he'd go away.

Or maybe she should just call security and have him removed. She turned off the taps and reached for a towel.

'Ruby,' she heard him yell. 'Open the door.'

She put her hands over her ears, thinking that she should turn on the taps again. It had been better when she couldn't hear his voice.

'Ruby!'

'Go away. I don't want to talk to you.'

'You have to come. It's Kyoto. He's collapsed.'

'What happened?' she asked as she buckled herself into the seat belt, studiously averting her eyes from anywhere near him. She looked a mess, her eyes puffy and red, her hair still wet from the shower, and still she was the most beautiful thing he'd seen all day. He put an arm around the back of her seat.

'Ruby, we have to talk.'

'No. Only about Kyoto!'

'But—'

She turned then and hit him with the full force of her shattered eyes. 'I thought you said we had to get to the hospital!'

The sight of her eyes, the damage he'd caused so openly displayed in their depths… His lungs felt sick and tight, but still he put the car in gear, pulling out from the car park. He'd known it wasn't going to be easy to make up for what had happened, but how the hell was he going to get her back after this?

'I found him lying in the kitchen.'

'His heart?'

'The doctors are assessing him now. It might be his heart, or it could be anything. He's old. But his condition is critical and I thought you should know.' He looked over at her. 'I was calling for hours. Where were you?'

'I went for a walk,' she said blankly.

'I'm sorry,' he said.

'I don't want to talk about it,' she replied, turning her head away.

It was too soon. Too soon to be returning to this place. Too soon to be holding another dying man's hand. She'd barely seen him over the last few weeks, too wound up about events in her own life to think about him. She should have thought about him. She should have done something! Someone placed a gentle hand on her shoulder.

'You need to leave now.'

She let herself be led from the room, feeling a blessed numbedness descend over her. Maybe that's what happened when you felt too much, she decided. Maybe she'd tripped some kind of sensory overload button and everything had shut down

Then she took one look at Zane waiting for her in the corridor and the pain sliced right through her again.

She breathed in deep. She wouldn't let herself think about Zane. Right now she had to focus on Kyoto, on thinking positive thoughts for him. 'Will he make it?' she whispered.

Zane's expression was bleak, with not a trace of the reassurance she craved. 'They don't know, but he's very old. There may not be a lot they can do.'

Tears welled in her eyes, blurring her vision. 'Then that's Laurence gone and now maybe Kyoto, too.'

She bit down on her lips, looked down at the floor, somehow managed to squeeze out the words, 'Thank you for bringing me.'

'Come on,' he said, not touching her. 'I'll take you home.'

'No!' she said as the car pulled into the all-too-familiar driveway. 'You said you'd take me home. I want *my* home.'

'We need to talk,' he said.

'And I told you I don't want to talk. How could you even bring me here? I won't go in there, not knowing *she's* inside.'

'Anneleise is gone.'

'And that's supposed to make everything all right? The European mistress has been packed away and now it's time for the Broome mistress to take up residence again? I don't want to go inside and I don't want to talk.'

'It's not like it seems.'

'Well, I know that she's certainly not "just some old friend", like you made out.'

'I know.' He took a deep breath. 'I'm sorry. I should have told you before. We did have a brief affair. Very brief. But it was over months ago. It didn't seem important.'

'A baby isn't important?'

'You can't believe it's mine!'

'Why not? I know you spent time with her in London and then you let me take the overseas tour alone so you could sneak some time here with your mistress. Damned inconvenient for you both, with me coming back a day early. She said you'd told her you two had until tomorrow. She must have been gutted to have been shunted off tonight.'

'You think I'd do that if it was my baby? What kind of monster do you think I am?'

'A monster who'll do anything to regain a birthright he believes was stolen from him.'

He sighed, long and hard. 'Ruby, I can straighten all this out. Just give me a chance. But not here. Come inside. We both need a coffee, maybe even something stronger after the few hours. And if the hospital calls—'

'You've got a mobile.'

'That needs charging. I don't want to miss them if they call—do you?'

Inside the house she waited on one of the large living-room sofas. He handed her a coffee, their hands brushed and she shivered.

He peered more closely at her. 'Cold?'

'Yes,' she lied, not wanting him to know how much he still physically affected her, even after all he'd done to betray her trust. 'The coffee will help.'

'It's probably shock,' he offered. 'And the fact you're almost dead on your feet.'

'You were going to straighten everything out,' she said, wanting to deflect the conversation from herself. 'Maybe you ought to get started.'

He looked at her evenly. Then he sighed and sat down opposite, depositing his brandy down on the table between them.

'I met Anneleise at a dinner party. She seemed bright and intelligent and I was attracted to her. We dated a few times and, yes, we had what you'd call an affair. It was entertaining for a while, but I soon learned that there was nothing below the surface, that she was fragile emotionally and she was also very clingy. When I told her we wouldn't be seeing each other again, she refused to accept that it was over. I was hoping that being out here would finally give her the message.'

'But you saw her in London!'

'I didn't intend to. She came to me for help. She'd discovered she was pregnant by her latest lover.'

'So why didn't she go to him for help?'

'He wouldn't help her. By the time she learned I was in London she was desperate, possibly suicidal. So I found her a psychiatrist and a quiet health clinic where she could take her time and think things over. I didn't realise that by helping her I'd make her think I still cared about her. But she kept on phoning and texting. Then she arrived here yesterday. I certainly didn't want her here.'

'You make her sound like some crazy stalker!'

'Exactly.' He tilted his head. 'It seems we have something in common, wouldn't you say?'

She blinked.

'Except,' he continued, 'unlike in your case, she never threatened me physically. She was just more of a nuisance. I never felt scared of her until today, when I found out you'd come home early and you two had met.'

He held her eyes across the table.

'She's a parasite, Ruby. I'm sorry I ever met her. I'm even sorrier that you had to go through what you did. I'm sorry that I hurt you because of her. Is there any chance you can forgive me?'

His eyes were dark and troubled, and he looked more worried than she'd ever seen him, the lines of his face strained and tight. She'd seen that face, eyelids closed next to hers on the pillow, had woken with those eyes staring into hers and a kiss hovering on his lips and she so wished she could smooth those lines away now.

But it was too late.

'It doesn't matter,' she said. 'It's not just Anneleise, though, is it? It could be anyone. And this goes deeper than whether or not you have a mistress. It's what's important to you that bothers me. I just can't trust you—the things she said about you—'

He jumped to his feet. 'She lied!'

'Maybe, but what she said echoed with my own concerns about you. It's the shares you care about. You'll do anything to get hold of them.'

'That's not true!'

He was too big standing over her, too imposing. She stood up and moved away, crossing her arms protectively around her. 'You talked to her about it when you were in London! You told her you planned to return to London when you'd worked out this "problem" with the shares. This to a woman you claim is stalking you! Why would you do that?'

'It wasn't like that!'

'I was the problem with the shares, wasn't I? I have been all along. Me and my forty-five per cent. And you finally worked out what to do with me—marry me and then you could manage them all, and have whomever you wanted on the side! If not Anneleise, then whoever else was flavour of the month.'

'No! Anneleise was trying to upset you. Don't let her poison work. She said those things because she was jealous of you.'

'Why would she be jealous of me? She doesn't even know me.'

'She knew you because I talked about you in London. I spent a few hours sitting next to her bedside while she settled into the psychiatric clinic. I talked to her about Broome and about your designs and how ground-breaking they were. She obviously saw you as a threat. Not that she was ever in the running.

'But that's not the only reason she wanted to hurt you.'

'What else could there be?'

He moved closer, his dark eyes imploring, his hands palm up between them. 'Because she realised something I was too stupid to realise myself. She saw something I was blind to. And that is that I want to spend my life with you, if you'll have me. And that's why I want you to marry me.'

He reached for her hands and took them in his own and squeezed them gently.

'Because I love you.'

CHAPTER FOURTEEN

HE WATCHED THE TANGLE OF EMOTIONS rumble like wet-season storm clouds across her blue eyes. He waited, hoping that at last he'd got it right, that at last he'd done the right thing.

'Oh, no,' she said, finally wrenching her hands out of his.

He blinked. He couldn't have heard right.

'No?'

She was still shaking her head. 'No way!' She swung away. 'What is this? The latest chapter from your corporate takeover manual? "How to Marry a Major Shareholding—101".'

'What are you talking about?

'First you haven't been able to buy my shares and then you can't convince me to marry you, so now you bring out the big guns. That's what I'm talking about.'

'I love you, dammit! It happened.'

'Well, I'm sorry, Zane, but it won't work. I'm sick of the lies. I'm sick of the deception and the betrayals. I'm sick of not being able to trust you. And lying to me about loving me won't help.'

'I'm not lying. Why can't you see that?'

'What I see is that you're suddenly so anxious to marry me you'll try anything. And the only reason I can think of for marrying me is to get closer to my shareholding now that you can't buy me out and so you can control it alongside yours. To give you back the share of the company you no doubt feel you were cheated out of by your father, and because in your deluded mind you probably see it as the ultimate revenge— you were going to live your life the way you always accused your father of doing!'

'I want to marry you because I want to be with you! I want to spend my life with you. So leave my father out of this. It's got nothing to do with him.'

'Your father is the sole reason I'm here! Without him I would be long gone. Because your father was a good man, a very good man. Yes, he was hard at times, but he was a man of integrity. But you can't see that. And it affects your judgement just as it affects the type of person you are. And I have to tell you, you're not a patch on Laurence. You're not half the man he was.'

Blood crashed through his veins, thumping so loudly in his head that it was impossible to see anything but red-hot rage.

He never thought he was perfect! But to be held up next to his father like that—maybe it was time she learned more about his father than what Laurence wanted her to know.

'You think my father was perfect? You think he was beyond reproach?'

She looked at him uncertainly for a moment. Then steel resolve once again filled those blue depths. 'Laurence always acted out of integrity. I could always trust him. Always.'

'Then just take a look at this!' From the mantelpiece behind him he pulled down the chest, the box bequeathed to him, and turned the key in the tiny lock.

'What's this?' she asked suspiciously.

'Look inside,' he said. 'This is something Laurence had Kyoto hand to me especially on my return. I told you what he'd done when my mother was killed. I told you how he'd elevated his mistress to an equivalent position to my mother. And you didn't believe me.' He pulled off the lock and wrenched open the lid from the box, found the letter he wanted and thrust it toward her.

'This is what I learned when I was just a kid—that my father had set my mother's best friend up in a house of her own, conveniently just around the corner, and settled on her a monthly payment for life. And it didn't make sense until she died and I worked out why.

'Zane, I don't think—'

'Read it! You read this letter. Read them all if that's not enough—they're no doubt love letters that support what I'm saying. Read them and you tell me what you think. See how wonderful you think your mentor really was!'

So she read the letter he'd handed her, and it was just as he'd said: in return for 'services rendered', there followed the payment terms, a monthly stipend and a property.

She sat there, shocked, because Zane was right! The thing she had refused to believe—and she was staring at the proof.

'Zane,' she said, looking up to him, shaken to the core.

'Don't stop now. Read those love letters while you're there,' he said. 'Might as well know the whole sordid truth.'

Reluctantly she picked up another letter, turning it over in her hands before looking up at him. 'But it's not a love letter,' she declared once her brain had made sense of the names. 'It's from your mother to Bonnie.'

'Let me see.' Zane joined her on the couch, looked at the envelope and letter she'd handed to him, and frowned. Not love letters? But he'd thought…

He took in the Italian stamps and the faded postmark showing a date almost a year after he was born and smoothed the pages. He frowned after reading the contents, refolding the letter before picking up another, again from his mother to Bonnie, although this one was from New York, postmarked a week later. Once more he scanned the contents; once more he put it down, more confused, more irritated. After a half-dozen letters, all from different locations around the globe, Zane stopped reading.

Every letter followed the same formula, a brief introduction of where they were and her impressions and then what followed was almost a blow-by-blow description of what the young Zane was up to. 'Zane said this', 'Zane did that', 'Zane took his first steps today, I wish you'd been here to see it.'

And as he read, a prickling shiver crawled along his spine.

'They're all about you,' she whispered, 'every one of them. Reports of what you're doing, how you're growing.'

'I know,' he said, the creeping feeling of unease settling in deep between his shoulder blades.

'And did you notice how they were all signed off?'

Zane nodded, his throat suddenly ashen, the bottom in his world fast dropping away. Had she seen it, too?'

'Maree signed each one, *"from your loving friend forever"* and—' He couldn't speak, couldn't finish what he'd been going to say.

So Ruby finished it for him. 'And *"thank you so much for your precious gift"*.' She looked over at him, with pain in her eyes that must be a mere shadow compared to his own. 'I think *you* were that precious gift, Zane. And Maree was thanking Bonnie in every letter. Because Bonnie was your birth mother.'

'No!' The word exploded from him like a blast from a cannon, even though he'd been thinking the very same thing. But hearing it said, having to acknowledge it as the truth when it couldn't be...

'Bonnie was my father's mistress. She *killed* my mother.'

'Zane…' She stood, placed a hand on his arm. 'Why else would the same lines appear in every letter?'

'It's impossible.' He pulled away. 'I have a birth certificate that names Maree as my mother. There's no way Bonnie could have delivered me.'

'Maybe someone at the hospital was in on it?'

'I wasn't born here. My parents were on holiday in Italy. I arrived earlier than expected.'

Her mind ticked over with the possibilities. 'Then maybe if Bonnie was with them…'

'No maybes!' He slammed his hand down on the mantelpiece. 'It's Maree's name on my birth certificate. I don't have to believe anything else.'

She picked up more of the letters from the box and held them out to him. 'Maybe you should read more. Read them all. How many will it take before you believe?'

He blocked her hand, knocking her wrist and causing the letters to tumble, scattering over the floor.

'I don't want to read any more!' he said with his hands on the mantelpiece, his back to her. 'I can't believe it. I won't.'

Because if he did believe it, then he'd know he'd been wrong, desperately wrong about his father, about his mother, about Bonnie!

Ruby crouched down, gathering the letters up again. One on blue notepaper had separated, the pages falling to individual sheets wide apart on the floor. She picked them up, putting them together, when the different handwriting caught her eye. Familiar handwriting!

She shivered, a wave of tiny needle pricks washing over her. The letter was addressed to Zane. With a rush of exhilaration she put the pages back in order.

'Zane,' she said, holding the letter out to him, her heart

beating like a wild thing in her chest. 'I think you'll want to read this one. It's addressed to you. And it's from your father.'

He turned slowly, regarding both her and the letter with suspicion. Would it mean more madness or would his father's words show Ruby's theory to be the crackpot idea it had to be?

Her eyes urged him to take it, her attitude challenging and at the same time tender, as if she understood. *The woman I love*, he thought, knowing once again he'd blown it with her. And nothing, not anything his father might tell him from beyond the grave, could be more devastating than to know that he'd lost her.

He took the pages from her hand, then he looked down and began to read.

Dear Zane, my son,
This is a very hard letter for a father to write. But after so many years apart I know I must write this down, so you might read it together with the letters from Maree to Bonnie and understand once I am gone. And, one day, you might even forgive me.

The truth is, I should have told you many, many years ago. But I waited too long. Liked the way things were. It was easier. Everyone was happy. We knew that one day you would have to find out the truth, but we put that day off.

But then both Maree and Bonnie were killed together and suddenly the time to let you know was past.

Iron manacles clamped down on his gut, squeezing him tight inside, squeezing the air from his lungs. He collapsed down on to the sofa and continued to read.

You see, while your mother, Maree, raised you and

brought you up as her own child, it was Bonnie who gave birth to you. Maree so desperately wanted children and I wanted a son, just one son. Maree endured five miscarriages, the last one causing complications that meant she could never have children. She was devastated. And I was powerless to help her.

It was Bonnie who came up with the plan. Bonnie saw what it was doing to Maree. She saw that it was destroying her. She wanted to do something to help her friend and the only way she could was to offer her a child that she herself had borne.

I was against it. I didn't want anything to come between Maree and me. I loved her so much. I know you doubted that, but she meant more to me than anything.

But Maree embraced the idea. She wanted it to work and believed it would work—even their looks were similar, both with dark hair and eyes—who would ever know? And so the women calculated the best time and I slept with Bonnie. In all my years, it was the hardest thing I have ever done. Until they both died it is the only time I ever cried. But thank God, it worked. She fell pregnant with that first attempt. I was relieved. Maree was overjoyed. It was a miracle, she said, with hope in her eyes for the first time in years.

Zane's eyes lifted from the page. 'You were right,' he said, his voice flat, belying the paradigm shift going on in his mind and soul. 'Bonnie was my mother. My father slept with her but only once. She wasn't his mistress at all. And all those years…'

All those years he'd damned his father. And he'd damned Bonnie, wonderful, warm Bonnie with her wide smile, always ready to give him a hug or soothe him when he fell over or to encourage him at school—he'd loved her all the years of growing up and then he'd damned her all the rest as being Laurence's mistress. He'd never had the chance to tell her how much she meant to him. He hadn't even hung around long enough to see her buried!

And she was his mother!

Anguish tore at him, leaving the tattered shreds of his soul hanging out to dry.

He hadn't known. He'd never suspected. And now it was too late!

He dropped his head into one hand as he read on.

The women went to live in the village I came from for the few weeks before you were born. The local midwife, a cousin of mine, delivered you. It was no hardship to register Maree as the mother.

Any hesitation I had had about the whole plan ended that day. Maree finally had achieved her dream, a baby in her arms. And I had my son!

I bought Bonnie a house close by to ours. She didn't want it, she didn't want any payment, she'd done this for Maree out of love for her, but Maree and I insisted. So you grew up, surrounded by the love of both Bonnie and Maree, both of them loving you, the women now closer than ever. And one day, I told myself, one day I will tell Zane the truth and he will know. But Maree loved so much being your mother that I couldn't do it to her. Not until she was ready for it. She was so proud to call herself your mother, so proud to have you for her son.

And you loved Bonnie so much, anyway, I thought it didn't really matter, that you couldn't love her any more if she were your mother. Except it did matter. And when they died together that day, I knew I'd waited so long that there was no point telling you at all. You would only hate me for not telling you, hate me for the deception, hate me for the chance of not knowing Bonnie as your birth mother and being able to acknowledge that fact.

And you did hate me. I was angry at the time, very angry as you no doubt remember, but in the end it doesn't matter that you were angry at me for the wrong reasons. I deserved your anger. You took yourself away from Broome and I accepted your scorn as my punishment. In a way I think I lost you when I lost both the love of my life and the mother of my child. But I was always, always, so very proud of you.

He read the rest through a film of moisture blurring the words but not the emotion, eventually sighing, putting the letter down, leaning back in his chair, one hand rubbing his brow.

'Zane?'

He opened his eyes and she was there, leaning over him all beautiful and intent like an angel. 'I made you a warm drink. I thought you might need it.'

He hadn't even realised she'd left the room and now she was back, taking care of his needs. He almost told her he loved her again, the words almost leaving his lips. But he couldn't do it. He couldn't risk making her angry again. He had no wish to upset her, not when he already had so much to apologise for; and, after tonight's revelations, well, now there was so much more.

'Thank you,' he said, taking a sip of the brandy-laced coffee. It was good, warming him momentarily in places so recently left cold and bereft.

And then he thought of something else he could say. Something that he'd never believed, but tonight had learned was true, and something that she couldn't object to hearing. 'My father was a good man,' he said. 'I wish I'd realised that earlier.'

'Oh, Zane,' she said, tears springing up in her eyes. 'Yes, he was.'

'I want to read the rest of these letters. Can you wait for me to take you home? And I want you to read Laurence's letter, seeing that you're the one who worked it all out. Maybe you can find anything else I've missed.'

She smiled and curled herself into the sofa opposite. 'Only if you're sure. And, yes, I can wait.' He handed the blue sheets over to her.

'I won't be long,' he told her, pulling the pearler master's box closer to him and gathering the next batch.

Letter after letter followed a similar formula Ruby and he'd both seen used before. Only, now he read them not as a report of what he was doing, but as a relaying of his childhood holidays through the eyes of the woman who was his legal mother to the woman who gave birth to him. And, from reading them, it was obvious Maree and Bonnie shared an incredible bond.

He thought he'd reached the end, the last envelope, but there was something at the bottom of the chest he almost missed until he was placing everything back in again. A postcard. He pulled it out. Looked at the picture, complete with tattered corners and creased edges. Disneyland Los Angeles. He remembered that holiday. He'd been eight years old. What had Maree written about that?

Then he turned it over and with a shock recognised his own early scrawl.

Dear Aunty Bonnie,
Disneyland is great, but I miss you heaps.
I love you lots and lots,
from Zane.

Thank God! Whatever had happened after she'd died, he'd loved Bonnie when he was growing up and he *had* told her. Here was evidence that she knew just how much. At least as an eight-year-old he'd known how to express his feelings successfully.

So just when had he lost that talent?

He put the postcard down and noticed Ruby lying down, her head on a cushion, her face tranquil at last and her hair in wavy abandon around her face. She'd given up on waiting for him and fallen asleep, but that was no surprise after travelling halfway around the world, only to come home to what must have seemed like hell today. His heart both swelled and stung at the same time at the sight of her. He loved her, but she didn't want him. Why couldn't he communicate so succinctly to her as he could in a postcard when he was only a child? Why was it so hard now to say what was in his heart?

He didn't want to disturb her by removing her to a bed. The sofa was wide and comfortable, so he grabbed a light blanket and tucked it lightly over her, taking heart when he lightly kissed her cheek to see her sweet lips dance slightly to the movement even in her sleep.

'Goodnight, Ruby.'

The phone woke her, startling her all the more because she couldn't remember going to bed, because she didn't immediately know where she was.

She sat up on the sofa, pulling with her the blanket Zane must have tucked around her as she padded to the kitchen. He was already there, holding the receiver and listening intently.

Kyoto! It had to be news. She swayed against the granite bench, grateful for its support.

He put the phone down and looked at her. 'That was the hospital,' he said, confirming her fears.

She moved a step closer, her fingers anchoring her to the bench, afraid to let go. 'And?'

He took a breath, his lips curving into a smile of relief. 'His condition has improved. He's off the critical list. They're still not sure what happened, they need to run more tests, but at this stage they're hopeful he'll pull through.'

Thank God! Ruby threw herself against him in relief, wrapping her arms around him. 'Oh, Zane! That's wonderful news.'

His hands circled her, gently squeezing, gently stroking, his head dipping to hers. She felt him kiss her hair, then rest his head on hers, breathing deeply.

He smelt so good, freshly showered. He *felt* so good, and that familiar tension began to build between them, the awareness that a consolatory hug was turning into something else, something more. She drew in a breath, uncertain, unsure of where they were headed, but knowing that this journey was not over yet. Not until the air was cleared between them.

'I'm sorry,' she said, her face buried in his chest, where it was easier to admit she'd been wrong.

His hands stilled at her back. 'What have you got to be sorry for?'

'For comparing you to your father. For not believing he might be capable of deceiving you.'

'I was so wrong, though. It wasn't anything like I thought.'

'But he let you believe it, and that shaped how you acted and how you felt. Believing what you did drove your actions. What he'd done gave you no choice. And I refused to see that. I didn't trust you.'

'And…now?'

She breathed in deep, savouring his scent, letting it feed into her. 'I should have trusted you. I can't believe Laurence let you believe what you did.'

'I can,' he said. 'He'd known that one day I should be told, but he waited too long—he didn't want anything to come between my mother and me. And when they both died together, there was no point telling me. It was too late for me to acknowledge Bonnie as my birth mother and I'd probably only hate him for the deception.'

'But you hated him anyway.'

'I know. I suspect he never forgave himself for sleeping with Bonnie. My leaving was his punishment.'

'Oh, Zane, I'm so sorry.'

'I'm the one who should be sorry,' he said. 'I put you through hell, believing you and my father—'

'Hush,' she whispered. 'I let you believe it. I could have corrected you at any time, but I didn't.'

He pushed her away enough to look into her face. 'But why would you want me to believe that?'

'Because I was scared of you.' She saw the change in his features and shook her head firmly. 'No. Not like my stalker—never like him. You scared me in a different way—because there was something about you from the very beginning that was like a magnet to me. I was drawn to you and I couldn't understand why. I wanted to hate you and yet I couldn't ignore that every time you touched me I craved more. So I let you believe what you wanted to believe. It suited me to have you believe I was off-limits. It protected me. Until the launch, when I thought I'd be leaving and I just wanted one chance—one night with you before I left.'

'Thank you,' he said, through a smile tinged with sadness. 'It doesn't in any way mitigate the wrong I did you, but thank you.'

Then he pulled her close into him and squeezed her tight, lifting her from the floor, his mouth in her hair, his breath warm and welcoming.

'We have unfinished business,' he growled, putting her down again. 'But right now we have something else to take care of.'

'Can we visit Kyoto?' she asked.

'That's where we're going first. Then there's something else I have to do.'

No onshore breezes permeated this far inland today. The air felt scorching, just to breathe it in seemed to burn the lungs and crack the lips, but Zane barely noticed the conditions. He had far more important things on his mind.

In his arms were the flowers he'd picked up in town to supplement the bright cuttings of bougainvillea he'd brought from home. He hadn't been back here since his father's funeral and then he'd never looked in this direction. He'd never seen the stone, he'd never read the words. But today he did.

Today he knelt down at the side of the grave of the woman that had given birth to him. He touched the sun-warmed stone, ran his hands over its smooth surface, the thick roughened edges; he traced the words of her name etched into the marble and the date of her death and he told her he was sorry.

He placed flowers on her grave and then he did the same on the grave alongside, the grave where the woman he'd grown up believing to be his mother lay, saying a few words to her, too.

Ruby watched him from the shade of a tree as he moved to the third, as yet unfinished, grave that she knew to be his father's. She hadn't realised he'd been intending to come here after visiting Kyoto, who was barely conscious but so happy to see them, but typically so apologetic for causing so much trouble.

She'd helped Zane cut the bougainvillea, assuming they were to take to the hospital. She watched with tears in her eyes as he hunkered down and said something she couldn't hear. Then she saw him push something in the ground, something small, before smoothing the surface over again.

Then he stood and turned towards her, and her world stilled. She could see the sheen on his eyes, she could feel his pain and suddenly she knew what Laurence had meant when he'd made that final request.

Look after Zane.

He'd known what learning the truth would do to him. He'd known what the impact would be. And he'd wanted her, *wanted Ruby*, there to pick up the pieces.

He came up to her, his eyes sending signals she couldn't ignore, she couldn't help but reciprocate, the heat she was feeling now less to do with the temperature. She opened her mouth to say something, but he stopped her.

'No,' he said, his voice like a silken thread, tugging at her senses. 'Let's not talk. Not yet.'

He drove them back to the house and this time she didn't protest, didn't make a sound, because she understood what they were doing there.

Without a word, their eyes and bodies doing all the communicating, he took her hand and led her to his room. Then and only then he took her face in his hands, his fingers stroking her neck, and he kissed her. Deeply. Movingly. A kiss that said a thousand words and more. A kiss that moved her world.

Then slowly, languorously, they undressed each other, with the pace of those that know they have for ever. Each garment discarded bringing new discoveries. Each uncovering of flesh a revelation, like it was the first time.

And in a way, it was.

She soothed him, her hands conforming to every dip, every line of his body. She comforted him. The touch of her hands, the heated embrace of her mouth, even the slide of her body against his, all of these were her instruments of healing. Making up for the hurt. Banishing the bitter past.

She took care of him.

And his kisses were so tender, his touch so sweet that it almost brought tears to her eyes. And when he entered her it did. Tears of happiness. Tears of love. Tears that dissolved into stars as he took them both over the brink.

'I love you,' she whispered, as they lay still locked together in the heated aftermath. His ragged breathing stilled, his head lifted.

'What did you say?'

She looked into his face and smiled up at him, smiled at the confusion she'd wreaked there. 'I said, I love you.'

'You do?'

She smiled and nodded back. 'Oh, yes. With all my heart.'

He blinked. 'When did this happen?'

'I realised it the morning after we made love in Sydney. The new day told me I loved you.'

'Why didn't you tell me?'

'I couldn't, not after what you'd said about not needing love. I thought there was no hope for us then.'

'And I didn't tell you until last night, when I'd finally accepted the truth myself.'

She sighed. Was that only last night? It seemed like so much had happened in such a few short hours. 'Sometimes I felt that you felt something for me, but at other times...'

'You didn't trust me.'

'I'm sorry,' she said.

He took her hand in his and kissed her fingertips. 'I didn't merit your trust. Not then. I knew that I wanted you, but I didn't know why. I was caught between you and too many demons from the past.'

'And now?'

'Those demons have well and truly been laid to rest. I've made my peace with my father. I've made my peace with my mother—both of them. And now, now there's only you.' He pressed both her hands together between his own. 'I was desperate yesterday when I thought I'd lost you for ever. Nothing compared to that sense of loss. Nothing could ever be that devastating again.'

'I was upset,' she said. 'I was coming back to tell you I'd decided to give your crazy marriage plan a shot. I was determined I'd make you fall in love with me eventually.'

He dropped his head. 'I'm so sorry. I can't imagine how bad you must have felt walking back and finding—'

'Shh,' she said, hushing him. 'I don't want to talk about that. There's something I don't understand.'

'What is it?'

'At the cemetery, I saw you place something in your father's grave. What was it?'

He made a low rumbling sound as he exhaled. 'It was the lock and key from the pearl chest.'

'The one that held the letters? But…why?'

'It probably seems mad, but I needed to do it. Because the time for locking away the past is over. That only leads to bitterness and deceit. I can't change what's happened, but from now on there'll be no more secrets. Only the truth.'

'Then tell me the truth,' she invited, applauding his words and his actions. 'I want to hear you say it again. This time I intend to believe it.'

His eyes narrowed, glinted.

'I love you, Ruby. With all my heart and all my soul. I love you for ever.'

She breathed in, her heart swelling large and proud. 'And

I do believe you. Because I love you, too. And, yes, I will marry you.'

His head tilted in question.

She pouted playfully. 'You *do* still want to marry me, don't you?'

'Of course I do, but I didn't want to rush you.'

'But I want to rush. I don't want our babies to be born out of wedlock.'

'Babies?' he asked, as she pulled his head closer for a kiss.

'Oh, yes, lots and lots of babies. You're going to sire a great dynasty of Bastianis.'

His face paused just above her own. 'I like the sound of that.'

She smiled under his lips. 'In that case we better get started right away.'

'Oh,' he growled, rolling her underneath him, 'I couldn't agree more.'

EPILOGUE

CHRISTMAS WAS A NOISY AFFAIR, the whole family gathered in one of Clemengers Boutique Hotel's elegant sitting rooms after the ceremony in the Chapel that had seen Ruby and Zane's hasty marriage blessed and that had felt like a second wedding ceremony to them both.

Sapphy had designed Ruby's gown for the occasion, a gloriously rich silver-blue design that accented Ruby's eyes and that had her looking spectacular as she walked down the same aisle her sister Opal had more than five years previously.

It had been so long since all three sisters had been together and now they weren't just three sisters any more. Opal was there with Domenic and their two children, Ellie and Guglielmo; Sapphy and Khaled, who had come over in their private jet from Jebbai together with their brand new twin boys, Amid and Kahlil; and the three sisters' mother, Pearl, was there, lapping up the experience of being a grandmother four times over.

If Kyoto had been up to travelling they would have brought him to Sydney, too, but he was happy to be home, frail but thankfully alive and still insisting on running the household.

Gifts were exchanged, Christmas gifts and belated wedding presents. Ruby had also made special gifts for them all. To Opal she gifted a necklace of golden pearls and dazzling opals; a stunning pair of sapphire-and-pearl earrings went to twin Sapphy, and to her mother she gave a lush necklace, featuring baroque pearls interspersed with the three gemstones for which she'd named her daughters, opal, ruby and sapphire. Cufflinks would grace the mens' shirtsleeves.

Ellie proudly showed her bracelet of small keshi pearls to anyone and everyone and little Guglielmo just ate sandwiches, played with his new toys and wondered what all the fuss was about.

Zane reached for his new wife when she'd finished handing out the gifts, pulling her sideways on to his lap proprietarily and hauling her in close, welcoming the feel of her lush body under his hands, suddenly wishing they were somewhere more private so he could feel more. Just lately it seemed she'd looked more beautiful than ever. 'Well done,' he said, his lips pressed close against her throat. 'Once again your designs prove you're a star. You're not only beautiful, my talented wife, you're brilliant.'

She snuggled against him. 'Then I hope you don't change your mind when you open this one. I made it myself.'

Her eyes twinkled with mischief up at him, the small package held in her hand, a golden ribbon securing it.

He cursed his stupidity. They'd exchanged presents before they'd left Broome: for her a gleaming silver Mercedes, for him a forty-foot yacht called the *Bonnie Maree*, a total surprise and one that had once more brought tears to his eyes. He'd had no idea she was planning on something extra. 'But I don't have anything for you.'

'Yes, you do,' she whispered knowingly. 'You've already given it to me.' She lifted one of his hands from where it rested over her thigh, placing it low over her abdomen. 'In here is your gift. The most precious gift of all. Your gift of love.'

Blood pumped in his veins, singing wildly as it danced a

proud celebratory beat through him. 'A baby,' he said, the awe he was feeling infusing his voice.

'Your baby.'

'*Our* baby,' he growled, pulling her down till she was sitting low in his arms, close to him. 'I love you,' he told her. 'I love you so much.'

'I know,' she replied, trusting his words implicitly because she knew them to be true. 'I love you, too.'

And then he kissed her, a kiss that said I love you and thank you and for ever, over and over again.

Sapphy noticed first. 'Hey, you two, is something going on over there?'

Ruby laughed as reluctantly they broke off the kiss.

'Well?' said Zane, looking questioningly at her. 'Shall we tell them?'

Ruby smiled back at the man she loved. 'No secrets,' she said. 'Not now, not ever.'

He looked at her in respect and wonder and loved her all the more. And then he kissed her once again, just to make sure she knew it, before together they told them their news.

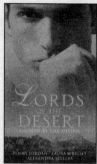 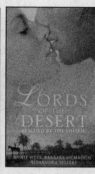 

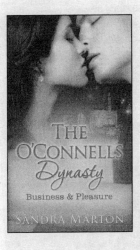
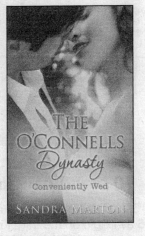

millsandboon.co.uk Community

Join Us!

The Community is the perfect place to meet and chat to kindred spirits who love books and reading as much as you do, but it's also the place to:

- **Get the inside scoop from authors about their latest books**
- **Learn how to write a romance book with advice from our editors**
- **Help us to continue publishing the best in women's fiction**
- **Share your thoughts on the books we publish**
- **Befriend other users**

Forums: Interact with each other as well as authors, editors and a whole host of other users worldwide.

Blogs: Every registered community member has their own blog to tell the world what they're up to and what's on their mind.

Book Challenge: We're aiming to read 5,000 books and have joined forces with The Reading Agency in our inaugural Book Challenge.

Profile Page: Showcase yourself and keep a record of your recent community activity.

Social Networking: We've added buttons at the end of every post to share via digg, Facebook, Google, Yahoo, technorati and de.licio.us.

www.millsandboon.co.uk

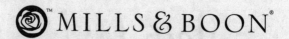